Praise for Ralph Graves and

SHARE OF HONOR

"Ralph Graves has done an extraordinary job of weaving a rich fabric out of fact and fiction. His novel relates one of the most exciting and dramatic periods of American history better than any history book could."

—STANLEY KARNOW

"The savage, heartbreaking, heroic, nearly unbelievable story of the Philippines in World War II will be a vague or 'forgotten' chapter in our American past no more. *Share of Honor* is a rousing book, fiction made especially vivid by Ralph Graves' respect for historical truth, his absolutely sure sense of place."

—DAVID McCULLOUGH

"Rich historical detail and the very best sort of emotional engagement—in a fine treatment of the fate of the Americans, both military and civilian, trapped in the Philippines during WW II . . . . A fascinating story."

—*Kirkus*

"Graves . . . combines the observations of good journalism with the emotional impact of perceptive fiction."

—*Time Magazine*

"Watch out Herman Wouk. Ralph Graves is moving in on your WW II tableaux."

—*Chicago Herald*

RALPH GRAVES

SHARE of HONOR

Harper Paperbacks

Harper & Row, Publishers, New York
Grand Rapids, Philadelphia, St. Louis, San Francisco
London, Singapore, Sydney, Tokyo, Toronto

Harper Paperbacks a division of Harper & Row, Publishers, Inc.
10 East 53rd Street, New York, N.Y. 10022

This Harper Paperbacks edition is published by arrangement with Henry Holt and Company.

Cover photography © 1990 by Herman Estevez
Map design by Jeffrey L. Ward

Grateful acknowledgment is given for permission to use
lyrics from the following: "Goody, Goody," by Matt
Malneck and Johnny Mercer. © 1936 Warner Bros. Inc. (Renewed). All rights reserved. "There's a Great Day Coming
Mañana," by B. Lane and E. Y. Harburg. Copyright 1940
by Chappell & Co., Inc. Copyright renewed. International
copyright secured. All rights reserved. "Deep in the Heart
of Texas," words by June Hershey, music by Don Swan-
der. Copyright 1941 by Melody Lane Publications, Inc.
Copyright renewed. International copyright secured. All
rights reserved. "Beer Barrel Polka," words and music by
Lew Brown, Wladimir A. Timm, Jaromir Vejvoda, and
Vasek Zeman. © 1939 by Shapiro, Bernstein & Co. Inc.
Copyright renewed. All rights reserved.

First Harper Paperbacks printing: January, 1990

Printed in the United States of America

HARPER PAPERBACKS and colophon are trademarks of
Harper & Row, Publishers, Inc.

10 9 8 7 6 5 4 3 2 1

*To the Americans and Filipinos
who endured the years 1941 to 1945
—whether or not they survived*

This is a work of fiction. Every significant character, except MacArthur and Tsuneyoshi and Hayashi, is imaginary. Other historical figures appear only briefly or are mentioned in passing. The town of Carabangay is imaginary.

But all major events—the attack on Clark Field; the defense and fall of Bataan; the Death March; the prison camps of Santo Tomas, O'Donnell, and Cabanatuan; the return to the Philippines; the prison-camp raids—are real. They are based on extensive historical material, including diaries, first-person accounts and interviews.

These things happened to real people.

If we are marked to die, we are enow
to do our country loss; and if to live,
the fewer men, the greater share of honor.

—SHAKESPEARE, *Henry V*

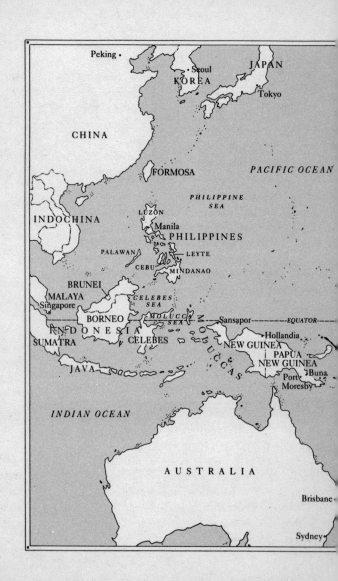

CENTRAL LUZON

0   50   100
Kilometers

0   25   50
Miles

• Baguio

LINGAYEN
GULF

Lingayen

SIERRA MADRE

ZAMBALES MOUNTAINS

LUZON PLAIN

Tarlac
CAMP
O'DONNELL   □ CABANATUAN
• Capas
• Carabangay
• Bamban
• Mabalacat
CLARK
FIELD □   ▲ MT. ARAYAT
• San Fernando

BATAAN
PENINSULA   MANILA
BAY   • Manila

CORREGIDOR ᴖ

LAMON BAY

0   800   1600
Kilometers

0   400   800
Miles

BOOK ONE

DEFEAT

Back to the Palace

Manila, October 1941

Amos Watson was getting ready for what would surely be his most unpleasant visit to Malacañan Palace.

He showered for the second time today, even though October was not the hot season, and shaved himself for the second time. The shaving irritated his valet and chief houseboy, Carlos, whose Filipino sense of pomp dictated that he should be the one to shave Amos before a presidential reception at Malacañan. But Amos Watson was too impatient to be shaved by a perfectionist. He wielded the straight razor himself but made up for it by letting Carlos select his *barong tagalog* and cuff links. He knew that Carlos, after careful thought, would choose one of the three cream-white, hand-embroidered *barongs*. And the gold cuff links with tiny diamonds and sapphires, made for him five years ago at the time of President Quezon's inaugural ball.

These matters meant more to Carlos than to Amos

Watson. Like most of his countrymen, Carlos was so
cheerful and good-hearted that one might think nothing could bother him. His round, wrinkled face smiled
all day long. But he was sensitive and sentimental, his
feelings easily wounded. Filipino hearts were fragile.

"Fix cuff links, sir?"

Amos held out his wrists. Most American businessmen in Manila wore traditional lightweight white
suits with ties, but Amos considered the *barong* the
coolest, most comfortable tropical garment ever invented, even if the delicate piña cloth was not the
most practical. It had to be washed gently by hand
in lukewarm water, then ironed carefully with a cool
iron. A careless *lavandera* could destroy a fine *barong*
in a single washing.

His wife, Marian, used to insert his cuff links when
they dressed for parties, just as he had always hooked
the clasp of her necklace. But she had never loved the
Philippines as he did, in spite of the luxury, the host
of servants, the exotic life. To her it remained a for-
eign country.

Once the last of their three children graduated from
Simpson School in Baguio and went to college in the
States, Marian grew more and more dissatisfied with
Manila life. And when her two sons and then her
beloved daughter elected to stay in California and
raise their own families there, it was finally too much.
Long visits to the States were not enough. Six years
ago Marian had moved back to Palo Alto to be near
them in what she had always considered her true
home.

They never thought of getting divorced. Amos missed her, perhaps chiefly from habit. He still wrote her long letters, and once a year he made the five-day Clipper flight across the Pacific to spend two weeks with her, his children and his almost-unknown grandchildren. But he was always eager to get back to Manila. This was his country.

He lived alone on Dewey Boulevard in the big tropical house built of native Philippine woods, the sides open to any breeze that might occur, the roof steep and the eaves long and overhanging to protect against the torrential rains. Alone, that is, except for his seven Filipino servants and his Chinese cook and his Japanese gardener.

With the cuff links secured, Carlos whisked imaginary specks from Amos's black trousers, then with his handkerchief dabbed a smudge from Amos's highly polished black shoes.

"Okay, sir," Carlos announced with satisfaction. He smiled his big, all-dressed-for-the-palace smile. Then he looked up with sadness at Amos's hair.

"Yes, yes," Amos said. He picked up the silver brushes Marian had given him for a long-ago birthday and delivered several sharp strokes to his bushy white hair, still thick after more than sixty years. Carlos thought his master should use a pomade or hair oil, like any right-thinking Filipino.

"Cadillac is all waiting," Carlos said.

Amos kept a Cadillac and a Buick so that, without inconvenience, he could lend one to a business associate or send a guest to the airport. To Carlos, the

Buick was "the car," while the Cadillac was always, proudly, "Cadillac."

"Good," Amos said. "I'll probably stop in at the Fiesta Pavilion after the reception." That was where Papaya was singing tonight.

"Have good time at the Palace, sir."

Hardly likely. Since last week, Amos Watson's popularity was at its lowest point in all his thirty years in the Philippines. But he owed it to himself to make a public appearance, just to show everyone—including the President, the High Commissioner and General MacArthur—that he was not ashamed to stand where he stood.

The Cadillac waited under the porte cochere. His driver, Donato, stood correctly beside the back door, hands behind his back in relaxed parade-rest position.

"Good evening, sir." Donato smiled and saluted, then opened the door wide.

"Good evening, Donato." Amos was pleased with this young man, an expert driver in Manila's frightful traffic. He drove with verve but, unlike many Manila drivers, he was not reckless, and he did not blow the horn constantly at the horse-drawn *calesas* that clogged the downtown streets. Even inside Intramuros, the ancient Walled City of the Spanish, where the streets were narrowest and the traffic most impenetrable, Donato remained patient and cheerful. Amos respected the necessity of patience in the Philippines, although he thought it a damn poor virtue.

The door closed behind Amos with a solid *chunk*. Donato slid into the driver's seat and asked politely,

"Where to, sir?" even though they both knew that Donato knew where they were going.

"Malacañan."

The name derived from *malakan diyan*, "the place of rich and powerful people." Built right up against the Pasig River, with its big double row of arches facing the water, it had once been the palace of the Spanish rulers and then of every U.S. Governor-General. For the past five years, Malacañan had at last been inhabited by a Filipino. Well, practically a Filipino. Manuel Quezon was actually a half-Spanish mestizo.

At Malacañan, the line of limousines crawled slowly through the imposing gates and up the wide, circular driveway. The lights were on in the lush gardens. Amos could see a few white-jacketed waiters walking along the paths between the flowering shrubs, carrying trays of drinks for the few guests who had come outside to look at the gardens and the river. In the blistering months of March and April, just before the rains, all the guests would have been out there, walking between the big blocks of ice that served as outdoor air conditioning.

When his car reached the head of the line, Amos told Donato to come back in an hour and a half. He climbed out onto the great broad steps. The President's aide stationed here to greet important guests managed, after a quick glance of recognition, to be busy greeting someone else.

After this week's press stories about his war views, Amos was not surprised. He climbed the carpeted stairway to the reception hall.

After all his visits, both business and social, he was still impressed by the glorious room with its vaulted dark wood ceiling, two stories high and intricately carved, its majestic double row of white pillars, its antique chandeliers. It looked its noblest tonight, filled by several hundred people in ceremonial finery and jewels. The American men wore white linen suits or white military uniforms with gold braid. The American women wore pastel evening dresses to create a feminine illusion of coolness. Most of the Filipino men wore *barongs*, and their women were in piña-cloth gowns with graceful *mariposa* sleeves standing up at the shoulders like butterfly wings to frame the face. Only the mosquitoes, impossible to control in this huge old palace, brought matters down to earth. To avoid being bitten, most women wore long sleeves and full-length skirts to Malacañan.

Amos had timed his arrival late enough to avoid the maximum length of the receiving line but not late enough to miss it altogether. He didn't want anyone to think that he had slipped in surreptitiously after the President and Doña Aurora had finished greeting their guests. He was here to be seen, and without apology.

And indeed he was noticed. He could hear whispers about himself as he inched toward the head of the line.

When he got close, he could see that the President, even though smiling and animated, looked tired. Short, slim, handsome, tubercular, Quezon was the most charming politician, Filipino or American, Amos knew. Quezon had all the useful little tricks: a quick smile, bright birdlike eyes, a keen sense of humor, a natural aura of authority despite his frail figure. He was excellent company with men and devastating with women, whom he still pursued with gusto. Impossible not to like him, even though he was ruthless, devious and vain.

An aide stood beside him to announce each guest's name, but Quezon seldom needed any reminder. Amos could see his eyes flick down the line so as to be ready with the right name and the appropriate personal remark. Amos knew that that quick, bright glance had noted him.

"Mr. Amos Watson," the aide said at last.

"Good evening, Mr. President."

Quezon shook hands with far less than customary warmth. In private, after all their years of friendship, Amos called him Manuel. The President always called him Amos, pronouncing it *Ah-mose*, as though the name were Spanish. But not tonight.

Quezon chose not to retreat all the way to "Mr. Watson." But when he said a cold "Good evening, Amos," it was with the American pronunciation of the name. He had to tilt his head back to look up into Amos's eyes. Lack of height never seemed to bother Quezon as it did most short men. Then he said, "Frankly, I did not expect to see you here tonight."

"Frankly, Mr. President, that's just why I'm here."

Quezon frowned, thinking about it, then nodded his quick understanding, though not approval. He turned at once to greet the next guest.

Amos bowed to Doña Aurora, Quezon's pleasant

wife of no distinction, and was free. From a tray he accepted a glass of champagne, a drink he didn't much like but which Quezon, as President of the Commonwealth, was especially pleased to serve.

Usually Amos attended a dinner or reception with at least a few items of business or politics on his agenda. Even though he had officially retired a year ago, in the sense of no longer managing his own cement and pipe businesses, he was still a director of seven Manila-American companies and had investments in many others. He never thought of giving up the intrigues of business life in Manila—the constant attention to detail, the perpetual gathering of useful information about rival maneuvers, deceptions and corruption. His advice and knowledge were much valued—or at least they had been until this week. So far only Boris Cutter of American City Bank had asked him to resign as a director, even though Amos had one of the bank's largest private accounts. But he knew there would be other requests.

Tonight his only agenda item was to be present. Champagne glass in hand, he moved slowly through the hall from group to group, knowing that his tall, white-haired, *barong*-clad figure drew attention. He said good evening to each familiar face and moved on to the next.

His tour was painful, but he kept his face calm— just another social evening at Malacañan. The least difficult were those who were merely embarrassed. They acknowledged his greeting but then escaped as quickly as they could, making no reference to his fall from grace.

The women, both Americans and Filipinas, were easier to handle than the men. They cared less about politics and news, and many of them had complained in recent months about all the endless, tiresome talk of war. To them, Amos's views, though extreme and distasteful, were simply more male war talk.

But not all the women were so indifferent. Old Peggy Ashburn, who had, as usual, exceeded her safe quota of liquor, jumped at him, indignantly twisting her fat strand of pearls. "Oh, Amos," she said, "you have been a *very* naughty boy. You want us all to be scared of the Japs? Those bowlegged, buck-toothed clowns?"

"Well, Peggy, just because they look funny doesn't mean we shouldn't take them seriously. We're not in such great shape out here."

"I never heard such nonsense from a grown man. You must be getting senile."

"Perhaps." He did not intend to run through his arguments with Peggy Ashburn. He smiled, patted her shoulder and kept moving.

Many men were flatly angry. Several turned their backs at his approach. A Philippine Army general whom he had known for six years asked how Amos dared to predict that we were going to lose a war with Japan. "I didn't," Amos said. "I only said we *could*." The general rejected the distinction.

Amos saw a man in a dark blue suit who was mopping his forehead with a handkerchief. Obviously a new arrival who had not yet bought tropical clothes. From yesterday's newspaper picture Amos recognized Smith Swenson, the new Manila manager of the steamship line. Here was at least one neutral party. Amos introduced himself.

"Charlie Ridgway told me to look you up," Swenson said. "He said to give you his best."

Ridgway had run the Manila steamship office in the early thirties and was now back in America, vice president of Pacific operations. "Tell him hello when you write," Amos said. "Did you bring any family with you?"

"My wife and two teenagers," Swenson said. He was flushed and damp. "You have a very warm city, Mr. Watson."

Two teenagers. As chairman of Simpson School's board of trustees, Amos was always on the lookout for new students, especially this year when, as a safety measure, all the army and navy families had been sent home to the States.

"Actually," Amos said, "you've come during the cool season. It gets much worse." He told Swenson the fastest way to get cool clothes made to order. "Where are you sending your children to school?"

"Charlie Ridgway suggested the American School."

Amos shook his head and went into his salesman act. "Charlie's forgotten Manila's awful weather. You really ought to send your children up to Baguio, in the cool mountains. A wonderful school up there, called Simpson. Very high standards. My own three children went there and loved it. I'd be glad to call the headmaster for you. He's a close friend."

"That's very kind of you. Charlie said you were quite an old hand out here."

"Just about the oldest," Amos agreed. After wishing Swenson good luck and putting in one more plug for Simpson School he moved on.

He came to a cluster of white uniforms, heavy with gold braid and ribbons. The MacArthur circle. This was an essential place for him to be seen after the warning he had given the General.

Standing on the rim of the group, Amos saw Colonel Willoughby, MacArthur's big, blustery intelligence chief, and Dick Sutherland, the chief of staff. Sutherland was as disliked as MacArthur's previous chief of staff, Ike Eisenhower, had been popular. Tiny Carlos Romulo, perhaps the most ardent of all MacArthur's Filipino admirers, hovered at the great man's elbow. Among the dozen others paying court, the U.S. Navy was conspicuously absent, for admirals did not choose to hear MacArthur hold forth.

Douglas MacArthur, standing at the center of the group, was indeed holding forth. "The Jap," the ripe, confident voice was saying, "is aggressive—true. He is wily—that is also true. And he is greedy—true, all true. Not content with Manchuria, not content with his thirsty ambitions for China itself, he has thrust his sharp bayonet into the vitals of Indochina. Yes, and make no mistake, he has designs on this country as well. The Philippines, gentlemen, is the key that unlocks the door to the Pacific. I have long thought and often said that he might attack us next April. Now I say perhaps even as early as January. But if he does strike—if he does strike, we shall be ready. He will expect us to withdraw to defensive positions, but that has never been my way. The Jap will be surprised. When and if he comes, we shall meet him at the beaches and fight him on the Plain of Luzon and repel him there. Retreat is defeat."

Although he didn't much care to listen to Mac-Arthur, especially now, Amos grudgingly admired the performance. The general stood straight and tall. He used his hands as eloquently as his resonant voice. His wide, mobile mouth was constantly curving and curling and twisting, as he tasted and savored each of his own words.

Others had noticed Amos Watson's presence. Those nearest him edged away. MacArthur gave no sign, but his next words showed that he, too, had noticed.

"There are those," he said with scorn, "who claim—who have actually said to me in my own office—that we are not equipped or prepared to withstand the Jap's assault. Such—persons—do not comprehend the mettle of the American soldier and his comrade-in-arms, the brave Filipino soldier, whose beloved homeland will be at hazard. We have spent five years building our forces. I say to such—persons—what I say to the Jap himself. I say: *Be-wa-a-r-re*." The final word was an elongated growl.

The hell with you, Amos thought. He deliberately raised his glass to MacArthur, who pretended not to see. Amos moved away.

Although Amos found MacArthur's posturing repugnant, the man was just what the Filipinos needed. They loved his eloquence, his unabashed sense of grandeur. When he promised them that the Philippines not only *can* but *will* be defended, when he told them, "I pledge the blood of my countrymen," when he spoke of "the Holy Grail of righteous victory," when he referred to Corregidor as "the strongest single fortified point in the world," the Filipinos loved it and believed it. He was what they needed, a famous and much-decorated American general who radiated conviction and glamor. But since MacArthur was not getting from either the United States or the Philippines anywhere near the arms and matériel and funds he had requested, conviction and glamor had become the mainstays of Philippine defense.

———

Later, as the crowd began to thin, Amos saw Boris Cutter, who had asked for his resignation from the American City board. "For the good of the bank," Cutter said in his blunt, unpleasant way. Amos had resigned at once, but he was tempted to move his account—all of it, his personal and professional checking, his three substantial savings accounts, all his notes, deposits, bonds, stock certificates, the entire works—away from American City just to see if Cutter would find that equally "good for the bank." Perhaps he would still do it.

American City had always been his bank, long before Cutter's arrival, and he appreciated the treatment he received as a very special customer. Besides, these days Amos wanted to make certain his lifetime assets were completely secured by a bank with headquarters in the States, not a Philippine bank. Amos had worked too many years to let his fortune and his family's inheritance vanish in the smoke of possible war. But there was always Consolidated Commercial, American City's chief rival among the U.S. banks. He would enjoy doing that to Boris Cutter.

He didn't like Cutter, a florid, suspicious man of fifty who took insufficient pains to conceal his contempt for the Filipinos. He demanded tougher terms on their loans because, he said, Filipinos were a higher risk. Amos considered it usury. He was constantly mopping up behind arrogant Americans like Cutter, trying to soothe proud and sensitive Filipino feelings and to make peace. The man was too powerful and important to be ignored. From the day Boris Cutter had arrived from San Francisco, he had worked at becoming a leader of Manila's business community. Not difficult for a man who had high position, plenty of money and a wife who knew how to give elaborate parties.

Boris Cutter was delivering some kind of dictum to Abner Holworthy and Chick Evans, the president and vice president of Charter Transport. Cutter was a talker rather than a listener. He deserved to be interrupted.

"Good evening, gentlemen," Amos said as he joined them. "How's your wife feeling, Chick?"

Chick Evans never got to report on his sick wife's condition.

"Jesus Christ," Boris Cutter said. "What are you doing here?"

"I was invited," Amos said.

"Yes, but that was before—" Cutter stopped in anger rather than confusion. He was a husky man of medium height, much given to tennis, golf, badminton, bowling—all the usual Manila club activities. He had a strong physical presence that he knew how to use. He started again. "If I were you, I'd stay out of sight. Completely out of sight."

"Well, you're not me, Boris. Perhaps that suits both of us. Abner, I've been meaning to tell you—"

Cutter interrupted. "Look, if you don't mind, we were having a private business discussion."

"Go right ahead. I'm a good stockholder with Abner and Chick. And as you know, I'm reasonably familiar with American City. Go right ahead."

Boris Cutter's hard eyes glared. Then he told Abner and Chick, "Call me tomorrow." Abruptly he walked away. Abner and Chick said they guessed it was time for them to be leaving too.

They were more embarrassed than Amos was. He did not consider them friends, although every leader in the American business community knew every other leader. They all belonged to the same clubs. They were all friends in theory, even those who were rivals. But Abner and Chick weren't real friends.

He had not moved a step before he heard a familiar hoarse voice from behind him.

"Something for the column, Mr. Watson?"

Amos completed his sigh before turning around. He never told this newspaperman anything, but it was foolhardy to insult him. "Hello, Sandy. How have you been?"

"No complaints." Santiago Homobono wore a well-tailored dark gray suit. He couldn't wear Manila white, he said, because of the smudge of cigarette ashes. He was smoking now and carrying a glass ash-

tray with two butts in it. He always kept an ashtray
in his jacket pocket. The suit did the best it could to
mitigate Sandy's appearance, which was short and
skimpy. But regardless of his appearance, he was the
most powerful, and most venal, columnist in Manila.
Power and venality went together in this city. He wore
gold-rimmed glasses and a gold wristwatch. "The real
question is, how are *you*?"

"Why, I'm fine, thank you. As you can see."

Sandy squinted through the smoke rising from the
cigarette tucked in the corner of his mouth. He had
shrewd little brown eyes, tough as bullets. "Actually,
Mr. Watson, that's not what I'm seeing here tonight.
I don't think you're doing fine at all."

Homobono had been the first to report on Amos's
affair with the singer Papaya. Far more important,
he had been the first to report, last week, the gist of
Amos's private warnings to Quezon, MacArthur and
U.S. High Commissioner Sayre. Amos knew the news
of his strictly private visits would get out—every office in Manila was a sieve—and it did not surprise
him that Sandy Homobono had it first.

His column, "*Pro Bono*," appeared five times a
week and contained more politics, scandal, gossip and
inside information than one could read anywhere else.
He owed it to two things. Having been a strong, early
supporter of Quezon in the struggle for power, he
was now constantly rewarded for this support. And
he was a hardworking, accurate reporter.

The column had originally been called "*Pro Bono
Publico*" but had been shortened to "*Pro Bono*." The
Manila joke was that it should now be lengthened to

"*Pro Homobono*" because the column so enriched its author. Manila reporters were poorly paid, as Amos thought they should be. He had no use for the press. Sandy got the best newspaperman's salary in Manila, which still wasn't much, but he had other sources of income.

Quezon and his cronies always told Homobono what was about to happen—who was about to make a deal, who was about to get a rich government contract—and this led to what Sandy blandly called his "wise investments." In addition, for between one hundred and five hundred pesos cash, depending on the subject, one could get an item into "*Pro Bono*." Sandy was too proud of his accuracy to report a lie as an actual fact, but for a price he was willing to let someone have his say in a direct quote. Many Manila businessmen availed themselves of this free-market privilege. Americans had to pay more, because Sandy didn't like Americans running his country. He wanted independence for the Philippines. He was constantly digging and jabbing at the American community.

Amos's attitude toward Santiago Homobono was embodied in the rude Filipino injunction *Bawal Umihi Dito*—Don't Piss Here. Whenever one of the long-distance buses that served the Philippines stopped at a gas station or roadside coffee shop or beer joint, the bus driver got out to piss against the handiest wall. Once when Amos was driving to Baguio for a school trustees' meeting, his driver stopped for gas at one of these roadside establishments. The proprietor evidently had delicate sensibilities, because a big sign was painted on the wall behind the gas pumps: BAWAL

UMIHI DITO. But there, directly below the sign, a bus driver was pissing, cheerfully and extravagantly, against the wall. Amos thought the scene epitomized this country: a store owner who chose to put up such a sign, and a driver who chose to ignore it.

Santiago Homobono's scurrilous but accurate column would get no help from Amos Watson. He never told Homobono anything. Don't Piss Here.

"I don't know what you mean," Amos said, knowing perfectly well that his appearance at Quezon's reception was guaranteed a mention in Sandy's column. "I'm just making the usual rounds."

"Well, Mr. Watson, you've never been a good source. But everybody seems interested in you these days." He smiled his little wolf smile and stubbed out his cigarette.

"Yes. Well. Nice to see you, Sandy."

"Nice to see you, Mr. Watson."

Before leaving the reception, Amos was tapped on the shoulder by a man he considered a true friend, Billy Waters, head of Inter-Island Mahogany Company.

"I never thought I'd see you here," Billy said. He had light brown hair and a deep tan. He was a dozen years younger than Amos and had spent only ten years in the islands, but he was as smart a businessman as anyone Amos knew.

"That seems to be the prevailing opinion."

"Why did you do it, Amos?"

"Why did I come tonight? Because everybody expected—"

"No, no. Why did you go around in private to talk

to those three? You're not the only one worried about a war. I could have got a group together, say four or five business leaders, and we could all have stated our case."

"Well, Billy, as you know, I'm not much for groups. Besides, I wanted to talk about the possibility of *losing* a war. Could you have got a group together for that proposition?"

"You're crazy. I'll bet MacArthur really loved that."

"He looked as though he wished I was in uniform so he could have me shot."

"Amos, you've given me a lot of good advice since I came here. Let me give you some. Don't try to do everything by yourself. People don't like it."

"You mean, get on the team."

"Now don't be sarcastic, Amos. It's good advice." He looked at his watch. "Have to collect Dorothy and get going."

"Yes, me too."

Amos had had enough of Malacañan tonight. Things would be more pleasant at the Manila Hotel, where in half an hour Papaya would be appearing. At least it would be dark, and there would be music, and he would not be such a center of attention.

⚌ 2 ⚌

The Fiesta Pavilion

In high school, to her delight and with the help of her own vote, Judy Ferguson was elected Prettiest Girl in both her junior and senior years. At the University of Indiana she was stunned to find she was only the second-prettiest girl in her own sorority, not to mention other girls in other sororities. Now, two years out of college, she was the prettiest American woman in Manila.

And yet all mirrors told her that nothing had changed. Same large gray-green eyes with a high sparkle and long natural lashes—easily her best feature and the one she made sure men noticed first. Same slim, straight nose, a bit short of ideal but not a drawback. Good cheekbones and even better jaw lines, very clean and clear. Okay mouth, perhaps a little wide, but with a nice curve to the lips, especially smiling or laughing. Chin still too long and strong, but this was more apparent in photographs than in life. Good skin, maybe a shade dark but all the better for tanning. Fine figure, tall but not too tall. Legs and hips were best, in her opinion, but no complaints

about breasts and shoulders, from herself or anyone
else.

All very much the same as ever, except for her soft
brown hair, which had been long and wavy in high
school and college but was now cut short because of
Manila's steamy heat. Same Judy, at sixteen or
twenty-four. What had changed was the setting, and
the quality of the competition. Everywhere she went
now—and she went everywhere—she was top of the
line. Her two years in Manila, where single men far
outnumbered single women, had been the best of her
life.

When the car stopped at the Manila Hotel, her
cocktail date, Colonel Kinkaid, wanted to take her
inside "to make sure you're all right," but Judy refused. She was already late for Brad Stone's farewell
party, and walking in with another man, especially a
high-ranking army officer whose wife and children
had been shipped back to the States last spring, would
not help.

Carrying only her tiny rhinestone evening bag, she
walked straight through the big white lobby—white
walls, white columns, graceful white peacock chairs.
Her high heels clicked on the parquet floor. This
grand lobby, all white except for the cool green plant-
ers filled with tropical plants, was the center of Manila
social life, but Judy did not glance around to see who
might be there. Always better to let others look at
her, as they usually did. She wore her knee-length
black chiffon skirt that swirled perfectly as she walked
and her brilliant Chinese-red silk blouse. The blouse
fit particularly well, having been custom-made for her

in Iloilo during her southern-islands cruise with Charlie Adams last year. The old Chinese tailor had indeed known his trade, down to the last quarter-inch of propriety. With the second button open, as it was now, it stopped just short of being indiscreet. She was wearing it tonight especially for Brad Stone, but she wore it as often as she could without being accused of repetition. Manila was a cheap place to live, especially for a pretty woman, but since Judy had little of her own money to spend on clothes or anything else, most of her wardrobe was simple and interchangeable.

Even before she reached the entrance to the Fiesta Pavilion she could hear the music—American dance music, of course, the arrangements copied straight from the latest Artie Shaw and Glenn Miller records. She asked the Filipino maître d' in his white tuxedo jacket for the Cummings table.

"Ah, Miss Ferguson," he said. "They have been asking for you."

Judy had spent so many evenings here that she was not surprised to be recognized, although she could not tell one maître d' from another. She left that to her escorts. A waiter was instantly assigned to lead her around the vast dance floor to the Cummings party.

A few years ago, before Judy's time, this had been merely the hotel dining room, while the roof garden atop the fourth floor was the great evening gathering place. But when an entire fifth-floor penthouse had to be created to accommodate MacArthur's lust for splendor as Quezon's field marshal, the roof garden vanished. To make up for it, the hotel had expanded its dining room far, far out toward Manila Bay, leaving three sides open to the night breeze and the gentle sound of waves against the seawall. The Fiesta dance floor, the size of a small football field, was covered by a domed ceiling and surrounded by high pillars and a ring of many tables.

Brad saw her coming—he'd been looking over his shoulder—and jumped to his feet with the quick balance of a good athlete. He was still in civilian clothes, the inevitable white suit. His red-blond hair had nice waves—she hoped he wouldn't get a crewcut.

"Hey, Judy," he said, "we thought you got lost." His voice sounded relieved but friendly, so she was not in trouble.

"Sorry, heavy traffic," she said. "Hello, Fuzzy. Hello, Anita."

"We just ordered," Fuzzy Cummings said, rising halfway, tall drink in hand. Like many Manila men over thirty, he was getting a little bald and a little portly. He was so rich, or rather his wife, Anita, was so rich, that he didn't have to be very polite, but Judy liked him anyway. Besides, he was treating. Brad Stone, with even less money than Judy, had an innocent talent for attracting well-to-do friends. "We figured a big pork-and-chicken *adobo* was safe all around and might put a little weight on the lieutenant." Fuzzy was back in his chair even before Brad could seat her.

"Fine with me," Judy said. "Is that a new necklace, Anita?"

"Oh no, just one of Mother's."

The soft lighting was flattering to Anita, who could use a little flattery.

"Now that you're here," Brad said, "how about dancing?"

She got up again, refusing Fuzzy's offer of a drink, and let Brad lead her by the hand between the tables to the dance floor. He had the physical assurance she liked in men. The Filipino orchestra was playing "Moonlight Serenade," more or less Glenn Miller—style.

Brad took her in his arms. She let him hold her close and slide one strong thigh between her own. It felt good through the soft chiffon. The strength in his arms felt good, too, and he was just the right height, three or four inches taller than Judy. But he was not one of her favorite dance partners. He thought too much about how and where he was going to move next instead of letting everything flow. For a man who was a natural at all sports, a fine tennis player and an outstanding basketball player and coach at Simpson School, he was strangely cerebral when it came to music, like the history teacher he also was. Had been. He was giving that up to join the army. Stupid, but it was no use trying to argue Brad out of his beliefs.

"You going to come to bed with me tonight?" he whispered into her ear.

Yes indeed, she thought. He was delightful in bed, although they had not had much practice together. She guessed now they never would. "Hmm," she said noncommittally. "Pay attention to the music." She hummed along with the orchestra. Some men didn't like this, but most found it attractive and intimate. She could always tell in a few seconds. Men were what she liked and understood best.

"But I'm going to be one of our soldier boys," he said. "I need comforting."

"If you need comforting, you should have stayed out of the army."

His self-mockery did not fool her. He was very serious about his decision. With his college ROTC training, he thought the country needed him. She was sure the ROTC would never have found him way out here in the Philippines, but he volunteered. Ridiculous—and not even to get ahead! A second lieutenant would be as poor as a schoolteacher. Judy's military taste ran to generals and colonels, admirals and captains, although her true preference was businessmen.

When the band stopped for a break, they returned to their table.

"Just in time," Fuzzy said. This time he didn't rise at all. "*Adobo*'s coming up right now."

The smiling waiter had already set a plate in front of Anita and stood ready to serve Judy. *Adobo* was practically the national dish, if a country of seven thousand separate islands could be said to have a national dish. The pork or chicken or beef was marinated in a spicy mixture of garlic and vinegar, then simmered slowly until the meat was tender and the liquid evaporated. Finally the meat was browned in fat. Tonight's *adobo* came with *pancit*, the spaghetti-like rice noodles. Judy knew Brad would have preferred a steak, which he could never afford to buy for himself.

"Hm," Fuzzy said around a mouthful, "the best in Manila. You won't get *adobo* like this in the army."

"I probably won't get it at all," Brad said. "It's certainly better than the *adobo* at Simpson."

Speaking of his school reminded him of something pleasant. "Judy, you remember my talking about Paradiso? The head houseboy at Simpson? We're going to be in the same outfit. He enlisted a month ahead of me, and they've made him a sergeant. I guess because he's used to bossing a whole staff of houseboys and cooks and gardeners. Or maybe just because he was older than everybody else. I'm going to have to get in the same company with him. Everybody says a lieutenant's best friend is a good sergeant, and Paradiso's one of those men who can do everything."

" 'Paradiso,' " Anita said. "That's one I never heard. After all these years I still love their names. I think my favorite is Ambrosio. Unless it's Potenciano."

Judy thought Filipino names were silly but did not say so. It was just like Brad to get excited about being in the same company with some houseboy. His tan face was flushed. His thin blade of a nose, almost Indian in appearance, seemed even sharper. His eyes, rather small but a startling bright blue, were filled with determination. She knew just by looking at him that he would get his way, that he and the houseboy would wind up in the same company.

It was Brad's determination, even more than his good looks or his physical grace, that Judy found particularly attractive. Compared to most other men she knew, he had an intensity, a fire, that she found hard to resist—especially when it was aimed directly at her, as it was this evening.

The trouble with Brad, unfortunately, was that he wasn't determined about really practical things. Instead of being a teacher or a lieutenant, he could easily have a good business here in Manila. She had suggested several places where she knew there were good openings. Smart, attractive and likeable, he could have made plenty of money—enough to afford paying for his own dates and dinners. Men with far less ability and charm were driving around Manila in Packards. Too bad, she thought for the hundredth time. Everything else about Brad Stone was lovely, but poverty was not Judy's dish.

During dinner, four men she knew came to the table to say hello and to ask her for a dance later. She put them off, but lightly, knowing how to avoid hurt feelings. Not one of them was in Brad's league, except for one thing. All of them had money. Judy enjoyed variety in men, socially if not sexually, and Manila social life constantly provided half a dozen dating occasions every weekend. She missed very few.

After dinner, she and Brad danced again, with Brad pressing his case and Judy pretending not to have made up her mind. Men kept trying to cut in, but Brad explained that this was his last evening before going into the army. Judy backed him up, smiling and saying sorry, maybe tomorrow night.

When the music stopped and the dance floor cleared for the show, Brad pointed to a tall, white-haired figure walking toward a reserved table at the edge of the floor, only a short distance from the band-stand.

"There's Amos Watson," he said. "The one in the *barong*. He's our board chairman at Simpson."

"Yeah, well, he's also in deep shit," Fuzzy said.

"Fuzzy!" Anita objected.

"I mean it. Popping off his mouth about how the Japs could beat us. If the Japs ever show up here, they'll get clobbered."

"That's what the Trojans said," Brad pointed out. "Just the same, he's a great old man. When he comes up to school, he talks to all the students and teachers, and he's *interested*. He even sits on the bench with me during basketball games."

What interested Judy about Amos Watson, whom she had met a few times at the Polo Club, was not his opinions about war. One had to put up with war opinions from virtually every male in Manila. What intrigued Judy was that Watson was said to be one of the three or four wealthiest Americans in the city, an exhilarating statistic, and that he was having a lengthy affair with tonight's singer, a mestiza.

Affairs with mestizas or, for that matter, between Americans were hardly uncommon, but rules about behavior were strict, especially if one was married. Mr. Watson would not be permitted to take his mistress to anyone else's home, even though his wife lived in California. He could not take her to any of the private clubs or install her in his own home. But he could keep a suite at the handsome Bayview Hotel not far from his house on Dewey Boulevard, and he could be seen with her in such public places as the Fiesta Pavilion. He had even given her what was judged to be the third-best ruby necklace in Manila. Considering the jewelry in some of the wealthy old Spanish families like the Zobels and Sorianos, that was quite a gift.

When the floor was empty, a long roll on the snare drum was followed by a couple of bangs on the cymbal. A thin-faced, older Filipino carrying a trumpet joined the orchestra at the front of the bandstand. The lights dimmed over the dance floor, leaving only the bandstand in brilliant light. The Filipino bandleader, dressed like all the others in a white jacket but with a red bow tie instead of a black one, came to the microphone and waited a long minute for silence. Then he waited another moment for suspense. Finally, with a sudden wide smile, he said a single word: "Papaya!"

Through the heavy applause she walked on stage. No, strutted, even though she was quite plump and barely five feet tall. Still in her early twenties, she was the most popular singer in Manila, a city that worshiped its entertainers. Her real name, Judy knew, was Carmen Something, one of those four- or five-syllable Philippine names ending in *ang*. She was half Spanish, which accounted for her pink-orange skin, the exact color of the papaya fruit. She wore a flame-colored silk dress with bare shoulders and, to Judy's delight, the ruby necklace. She had long black hair, with her trademark *waling-waling* orchid tucked above her right ear. Her smile—at the welcoming applause, at the crowd, at the elegant room—was enormous.

And then she began to sing, starting off fast with "Goody Goody." Her clear, strong voice rollicked through the lyric with happy malice over her former lover's misery.

"Goody goody for her"—the trumpet echoed the
    curse—
"Goody goody for me"—another echo—
"And I hope you're satisfied, you rascal you."

Her fist punched the air, and she growled out "rascal" as though it were the dirtiest word in the English language.

The applause was even louder, and Judy watched Papaya milk it, bowing, smiling, waving her plump arms. She wasn't beautiful—her cheeks were too round, her whole face was too round. And her shoulders and breasts were too heavy for her short body. Judy gave her three years before she was too fat to be attractive, but the voice sounded as though it could last forever.

She sang "I'm Stepping Out with a Memory Tonight," her voice now sexy with longing. Brad squeezed Judy's hand, a passionate response that must be taking place at every table in the Fiesta.

Then she did "Amapola" in Spanish and "Stardust," practically the national anthem for anyone under thirty, and "The Ferry-Boat Serenade," mixing the fast and the slow, her personal trumpet player leading each melody. Finally came her signature piece,

"And the Angels Sing." The orchestra faithfully copied the Benny Goodman record as she sang through the lyric, but when they reached the moment for the great Ziggy Ellman solo and the orchestra stopped playing, Papaya's trumpet player looked at her and shrugged, as if to say, That one's too much for me. Everyone knew what was coming.

Papaya also shrugged. Then, without accompaniment, she sang the solo herself, no words, just the bright, powerful voice hitting those rapid notes one after another with amazing speed and clarity.

When she finished, the pavilion erupted. Many of the men stood to applaud and whistle. Papaya took a long time to get offstage. Many bows, many smiles, many blown kisses. Then she stretched out one arm to acknowledge her trumpet player, who pretended to hide his face in shame at his inability to perform the solo. Everyone was laughing and happy, Papaya most of all. Her self-confidence, her joy in life, shone through the room. At last, when nothing more could be wrung from the moment, she stepped down from the stage and walked to the table where Amos Watson stood waiting for her.

Judy asked Brad, "Do you know him well enough to go over and say hello?"

"Sure," Brad said. "I'd like to meet Papaya too."

Judy wasn't especially interested in meeting Papaya, but she did want a closer view of that necklace.

Anita looked as though she would like to join them, but Fuzzy said, "We'll stay here. I'm not about to be seen with Watson."

"That's pretty extreme," Brad said, not really arguing. "We won't be long."

"We'll have some champagne ready for you," Fuzzy said, looking around for their waiter.

Others apparently felt the way Fuzzy did. There was no crowd at Amos Watson's table, in spite of Papaya's triumph.

Brad walked up in his easy, natural way and said, "Mr. Watson? Excuse me, could we just say hello?"

Amos Watson saw Judy and stood up. "Hello, Coach," he said. "You've certainly caused a lot of trouble at school. We'll find somebody to teach history, but who's going to teach basketball?"

"Yes, sir. This is Judy Ferguson."

Watson nodded. "Yes, we've met. Papaya, this is Brad Stone, a good friend from Simpson, and Miss Judy Ferguson."

Papaya shook hands with them both, smiling as though she had just been handed a special treat. She did not seem the least exhausted by her performance. The ruby necklace was indeed sensational, Judy thought. She counted nine stones in crusty gold settings.

"You were wonderful," Brad said with conviction.

Papaya's smile grew even wider. "In that case, won't you have a drink with us? Is that all right?" she asked Watson, who nodded.

Up close, all her flaws were visible, but so were her vitality and good humor. Amos Watson was attractive rather than handsome. His face was lean and craggy, with deep vertical lines and big, bushy white eyebrows. His eyes were direct but held a reserve.

"When do you go in?" Watson asked when they were seated and had their drinks.

"Day after tomorrow," Brad said. "This is sort of my last night out." He glanced at Judy, then at Papaya. "I could hardly have done better."

"He's so nice!" Papaya told Watson, as though she had never received a compliment before.

"I hope they'll let you out for the trustees' dinner," Amos Watson said.

"If they don't, I'll go AWOL. I've asked Miss Ferguson to that, too."

It was another of Brad's free parties, this time at the Polo Club. A lavish banquet and dance for the faculty and juniors and seniors of Simpson, it was billed as the trustees' annual party, but Amos Watson paid for the whole thing, including a special bus to bring everyone down from Baguio. Judy was not wild about the idea of an evening with students, or faculty either, but a private party hosted by the third or fourth richest American in town would be worth that inconvenience. Besides, there would be all the trustees.

"We'll be pleased to have you," Watson said gravely to Judy.

"And also I am singing," Papaya said, as if that surely clinched the importance of the occasion. "And as a special favor to Mr. Watson, no fee!" She laughed happily at her own extravagance.

"I said I'd pay."

She spoke to Judy as though Amos Watson had said nothing. "In this place," she said, waving around at the Fiesta Pavilion, "if they give away a free drink, all they have to do is open another bottle. But if I

give away my songs, soon my bottle will be empty."
She winked and shook an imaginary bottle upside
down over the table.

She clearly didn't think there was any danger her
voice would ever wear out.

"It's better for women not to give anything away,"
Judy said.

Something in her tone made Papaya give her a
quick, shrewd glance. The singer was not the happy
innocent she seemed onstage. "Oh, sometimes," Papaya said. "Sometimes it is all right. Sometimes it is
even good."

And indeed, at the end of the evening, when Judy
and Brad had thanked Fuzzy and Anita for the wonderful farewell party and then taken a taxi to her
small apartment in the San Luis Hotel because Brad
had nowhere else to take her, she carefully unbuttoned the Chinese-red blouse and gave everything
with thorough enjoyment, although it was certainly
as much taking as giving. Judy had gone to bed with
very few men, but she could not remember any time
nicer than this, more consuming than this, even better
than their last time two months ago.

Because she did not have to go to work next day,
they made love yet again in the slow morning sunshine
that poured in through the window. Afterward, while
he was still warm inside her, he spoiled it by asking
her to marry him.

In Manila, she had as many proposals as she was
willing to listen to, and she had every intention of
marrying extremely well someday. But there was no
reason to hurry. She was having too good a time to

marry just now, and besides, this was something she wanted to be sure to do exactly right. He would have to be a very attractive man, obviously, but also one with plenty of money and a position in Manila society. She kept a revolving list of three or four possible men, but Brad Stone had never been on it. Much as she liked and enjoyed him, she could not take him seriously.

God, she thought. If only he had sense and money. Or just money.

= 3 =

Lose Some, Win Some

On his thirty-sixth birthday, the day he had chosen to give up cigarettes, Major Jack Humphrey smoked twenty-seven Camels. Although this was a good half pack less than usual, it wasn't too great a start. There were, however, extenuating circumstances, the foremost being Master Sergeant Maxsie.

Even when he wasn't giving up smoking, Humphrey was always in a bad mood during his morning walk from BOQ to the orderly room. He had to pass his old house, where, until last May, he had lived with Sara, his younger son Jeff and, when he was home from Simpson School in Baguio, his older son Terry. Sara and he agreed that Fort Stotsenburg was their best post ever, better than Fort Benning, better even than Panama. The house was cool, a blessing in the tropics, the Filipino servants took care of everything so that Sara had plenty of time to ride horseback and play bridge with the other wives, and Jack Humphrey had his first battalion command.

It was the Philippine Scouts, not an American battalion, but they were part of the regular U.S. Army and all the officers were American. Besides, the Scouts were elite—damn good soldiers, with pride and discipline. Not like the Philippine Army units, now being put together with haste, paste and confusion. It was a good command and a very good life, if you happened to like the army, as Jack Humphrey did.

But six months ago, all the army families had been sent back to the States. Except for that one time in Panama, when Sara had gone home to have Jeff, they had not been separated since his graduation from West Point fourteen years ago. He missed her terribly. They told each other that it was for the safety of the children, which no doubt it was, but he missed her every day.

With his rank, he might have stayed in their old house, but it reminded him so constantly of Sara that he moved into BOQ for companionship with other men. He played bridge and poker and backgammon every night at the officers' club, drinking a little too much bourbon to take his mind off things, but he still had to walk past their house every morning.

In other ways the walk was pleasant. Stotsenburg was laid out spaciously on flat land, but right behind it stood the tall green Zambales Mountains. In front of it, some dozen miles away across the Luzon Plain, was the beautiful, solitary volcanic peak of Mount Arayat. These days the view and the stillness were continually interrupted by planes landing and taking off at nearby Clark Field, where the Army Air Corps had its growing base, with more and more bombers and fighters. The army was said to have more B-17s at Clark than at any other base in the world. He didn't see much of the Air Corps pilots, whose breast-pocket silver wings always seemed shinier and more prominent than the infantry rifle badge. To Jack Humphrey, an infantryman like his father, the pilots were the Junior Birdmen of America.

By the time he reached the orderly room his khaki shirt was already wet with sweat under his arms and around his waist. In November it wasn't as hot as it would be in a couple of months, but after a few cups of morning coffee his hefty frame always sweated. Whenever they were stationed in warm climates, Sara said, he would just have to look damp and rumpled all the time. When he had been a tackle at the Point, his weight had been a virtue, but not here in the tropics. Of course, today there was more weight and less muscle, and he knew giving up smoking would only make it worse.

As he walked up the board steps to the screen door of the nipa-thatched orderly room, thankful to be getting into the shade and close to his desk fan, he heard his first sergeant call attention. When he came in, the sergeant and the corporal were standing stiff, and the sergeant saluted. Filipinos loved to salute and did it very well.

"Good morning," Humphrey said and nodded at the corporal, who immediately poured a cup of hot coffee into Humphrey's white china mug, added two spoons of sugar and a spoon of powdered milk and handed it to him. This was a moment when he hated not to be smoking.

The sergeant waited until Humphrey had taken

two scalding sips. "Sir, they are coming this morning for Olivo and Dubang."

"No, it's tomorrow."

"Yes, sir, but no, sir, they are coming to get them today. At ten hundred. It is on the telephone."

"Oh, shit," Humphrey said. This would color the whole day, his birthday. A pack of Camels was lying on the first sergeant's desk. He helped himself and lighted up. He knew he was going to lose two of his best sergeants on loan to the misbegotten Philippine Army, but he'd thought he didn't have to face it until tomorrow. "Well, you better tell them."

"Yes, sir, I did. They are standing by."

"Their papers ready?"

"Yes, sir, all ready."

The colonel had given him the bad news last week.

"For Chrissake, Dick," Humphrey had said, "they already have half our officers on loan, and I don't see any of them coming back, either. What do they want from us?"

"They want," Dick Robb said with his dry patience, "two sergeants who speak Tagalog, Visayan and English and who are good riflemen. For training purposes."

"To train what? A bunch of draftees who don't even have rifles? Or any ammunition even if they did have rifles?"

"They're supposed to be getting all that stuff," Robb said. "And thanks for reminding me. Olivo and Dubang are to take their rifles with them."

"Why do both of them have to come out of my

battalion? And besides, Dubang's English isn't that great."

Robb looked at him. He was a thin, quiet man, not easily disturbed. He knew his troops and had picked the right two men. "Because they fit the orders."

"But they're—"

"I know. Just take care of it please, Jack."

Humphrey had told Olivo and Dubang they were being transferred, making sure they both understood it was because they were the very best. He said it was just temporary, not a permanent assignment. Dubang had tears in his eyes.

Then he called Amos Watson in Manila—"Call me any time," Amos had said—not because Amos could do anything about it but just because he was interested in all the troubles Jack Humphrey had been having.

He had given Watson several earfuls during Parents' Weekend last spring at Simpson. Humphrey was off duty then and in civilian clothes, and he felt like letting off steam to Watson, an interested listener and a tough old bird who was said to have a lot of important contacts in Manila. Humphrey thought *somebody* outside the army ought to know how bad things were.

In peacetime, Humphrey said, the army was used to being on short rations, but what was happening now in the P.I. was ridiculous. He was supposed to be putting his Scouts on a readiness footing, and he had nothing to work with. Not enough weapons, not enough ammunition for proper training. Not enough vehicles. Not even enough helmets. And if it was bad in the Scouts, you should see MacArthur's so-called Philippine Army. Training with *sticks* instead of rifles. They don't even have shoes, just sneakers, and even the sneakers are rotten. Pith helmets, sometimes even paper helmets, for God's sake, just so they can get used to the idea of helmets in case the real ones ever get here. The whole thing was a joke—"I can hardly go to sleep at night for laughing."

Filipino privates getting seven bucks a month while Americans got thirty. No wonder they aren't even signing up for conscription. And they have officers and noncoms with no experience and no sense of hurry. Most of them illiterate. All they have is an uncle or father-in-law who wangled them the rank. Who'd want to join that army? There shouldn't be two army commands out here in the first place, theirs and ours. They're all standing around acting as though they had all the time in the world and nothing was going to happen anyway. The only people really busting their ass in this country are all those Japanese "tourists" running around taking pictures of everything, even army bases. You can bet that film isn't going to wind up in family photo albums.

"What would you do about the tourists?" Watson had asked.

"I'd shoot 'em," Humphrey said happily. "If I could spare the ammunition."

Well, at least one thing had finally been fixed: MacArthur had been recalled to active duty last summer and put in charge of the whole show. Of course, what that meant was all this "borrowing" of officers, and now even sergeants, to beef up the Philippine units.

Speaking of borrowing, he took another Camel from his first sergeant's desk and then asked him if he had a pack to spare. The sergeant took one out of the carton in his desk drawer and gave it to him. Maybe Christmas would be a good time to quit smoking. Or New Year's Day.

He could hear the motor and recognize it as a scout car before the vehicle came in sight. The only man in it was the driver. Three chevrons with three rockers, an American master sergeant. Most master sergeants, who were as conscious of privilege as bird colonels, had a PFC or corporal for a driver.

A trim figure in a twin-peaked garrison cap, cocked to the right just so, the master sergeant wore starched, sharply pressed khakis with no sweat streaks. He jumped out of the scout car and walked toward the orderly room as though he were marching: brisk steps, shoulders back, arms swinging in short precise arcs, hands cupped with thumbs against fingertips. The very model of a perfect soldier. Humphrey, a rumpled, sweaty hulk who was about to lose two of his best men, disliked him even before he noticed the ugly birthmark.

The figure pushed through the screen door and took three steps into the room before pausing to salute. As the hand came slowly up to the face and held there, Humphrey saw it. A dark red-purple blotch below the left eye. Irregular in shape, it stood out from the tan skin, running diagonally across the cheek down toward the corner of the mouth. A disfiguring welt.

Humphrey was so taken aback that he was late answering the salute. The sergeant smiled slightly, a crooked twitch of the mouth, as though this had happened before.

"Sir, Sergeant Maxsie. I'm here to collect my two sergeants."

Any sympathy Humphrey might have felt for the birthmark vanished with that arrogant phrase. "They're *my* sergeants," he said. "I'm lending them to you."

"Yes, sir," Maxsie said, with the exquisitely correct indifference of an experienced noncom. "Are they ready to leave?"

"Yes, they are," Humphrey snapped. "Corporal, get Olivo and Dubang over here."

"Permission to smoke?" Maxsie said. This was a deliberately unnecessary question, since both Humphrey and his first sergeant were smoking. "While I'm waiting," Maxsie added.

Humphrey understood the implied criticism. Here was Master Sergeant Maxsie, right on time at ten hundred hours, and where were those two men? Maxsie lighted a cigarette without waiting for an answer.

"Where's your driver?" Humphrey said. "Are you out of drivers the way you're out of sergeants?"

"Major, since I'm the best driver I know, I always drive myself." Having dealt with that subject, he said, "I hear this is a good post."

"Not bad." Humphrey was not about to admit to this man how good it was.

"Better than mine," Maxsie said. "We're over by Cabanatuan, guarding the storehouses."

Cabanatuan was another twenty-five miles beyond Mount Arayat. It had become a huge storage center for food and other supplies so that MacArthur could fight on the central Luzon Plain against any invasion, instead of taking a defensive position on Bataan, as in the original war plan. There was said to be enough rice at Cabanatuan to feed the whole army for several years.

"You need my two best sergeants to watch a pile of rice?" That birthmark was truly ugly. Humphrey wondered how Maxsie could ever have made master sergeant against that handicap.

Maxsie gave him a cool stare. "No, major, I don't. If there's one thing those fuckers know how to do, it's stand around and watch rice. What they need to learn is to soldier." He spoke in a clear, sharp voice, the kind that could rise to parade-ground strength without being misunderstood.

Olivo and Dubang appeared outside, dressed in dark blue fatigues and carrying their barracks bags and Enfield rifles. Humphrey knew the rifles would have been cleaned and oiled this morning, and then would be cleaned and oiled again after the long dusty trip to Cabanatuan. The corporal came behind, carrying the two field packs. They put everything in the back of Maxsie's scout car before entering the orderly room.

Olivo and Dubang saluted. Humphrey returned a

full salute instead of his usual wave. Maxsie signed the transfer papers, tucking his copy in his breast pocket, then buttoning it down and patting it flat. Humphrey wished his men good luck and shook hands with them.

"Remember, sergeant," he said to Maxsie, for Olivo's and Dubang's benefit, "I expect these men back in this battalion as soon as possible. Just as soon as possible."

"Yes, sir," Maxsie said. He actually grinned. "Naturally. If that's everything then, let's go."

Dubang was staring at the blotch on Maxsie's cheek.

"Hop to it, sergeant," Maxsie snarled.

Dubang and Olivo hopped. Maxsie followed them out the screen door. Then at the last moment he turned to Humphrey for a final jab. "Thank you very much, sir." He marched around the car, shoulders braced, got in and drove off for Cabanatuan.

I bet I don't see those two men for a long time, Humphrey thought. Happy birthday, Jack.

———

Sam Phipps was thankful he was the most junior communications officer on MacArthur's staff. This meant he practically never had to see the General, of whom he was terrified. He had never been near the Manila Hotel penthouse, and on the two occasions he had had to deliver important messages to the General's regular office at Number One Calle Victoria, the General had been out. Sam Phipps had, however, peeked into the office on the second floor to see the big clean

mahogany desk backed by the flags of all Mac-
Arthur's earlier commands. There were a lot of them.
In fact, all that gaudy personal history—the flags, the
medals, the triumphs—was part of what made
MacArthur so intimidating. This very office in the
Walled City, as all Manila knew, had been the young
Lieutenant MacArthur's bedroom way back near the
beginning of the century, years before Sam Phipps
was even born. Phipps himself worked in the annex
office, where he was in little danger of encountering
the General.

If he were a West Pointer, like most of the officers
on MacArthur's staff, he might be able to take all this
legend in stride, even to bask in it. The rest of them,
from captain right up to general, talked about "the
Old Man" with self-satisfied pride, as though his legend rubbed off on them. It didn't rub off on Phipps.

Sam Phipps, in his own opinion, didn't even belong
here. He didn't belong in the army, or in the Philippines, and certainly not on MacArthur's staff. The
last thing he had ever wanted to be was a soldier. But
when his draft number came up, he figured that being
a junior Phi Bete at Yale, winning the senior literary
prize for his paper on Keats, and being top of his class
as an English major ought to be worth something—
as indeed it turned out to be. He was checked out by
the FBI for security clearance, commissioned and sent
off to communications school, where he learned
about radio, codes, communications secrecy and the
necessity for meticulous logging in and out of all message traffic. Again, he was top of his class.

When he got his assignment to Manila this summer, along with the unexpected silver bars of a first lieutenant, he assumed he was just a random part of the South Pacific buildup, the same way his draft number had been a random event. Colonel Sampson disabused him the day he reported for duty in Manila.

"Oh, you're not just an accident, lieutenant. The Old Man knows exactly what he's getting, so you better shine." The colonel, seated at his desk before which Phipps was still standing at attention, looked him over. "I'd advise you to start by straightening out that left collar bar before he catches sight of you."

"Yes, sir," Phipps said. He wondered if he was supposed to straighten it right now or wait till he could get to a mirror. The niceties of military obedience still eluded him. He decided he should wait.

The colonel, a ruddy-faced man with straight reddish hair combed across his head from left to right, MacArthur-style, spoke with a measured sarcasm that reminded Phipps of his Chaucer professor. "We decided to take a chance on you, Phipps."

This sounded more like a threat than a compliment. Did "we" mean all of us, or was it the imperial "we" of MacArthur himself?

"The Old Man has great faith in academic accomplishment," Colonel Sampson explained, not necessarily endorsing his chief's conviction but stating it as promulgated law. "He was First Cadet at the Point, you know."

"Yes, sir." Sam Phipps did know because he had read up on MacArthur and been impressed. He hadn't thought of the commanding general as a scholar.

"He also has the highest regard for English liter-

ature and the English language. Not that that will be
any part of your duties."

"No, sir," Phipps said. He was kept at attention
until the interview ended.

Phipps's duties turned out to suit him perfectly.
Every day or every night he reported to the guarded
message center in the annex office, where he read all
the incoming and outgoing message traffic except for
the most top secret stuff. It was flattering to know
practically everything that was going on in Mac-
Arthur's Far East Command, even though he could
not talk about it to friends. As junior officer, he had
to keep the record of all the codebooks and machines
and call signs, and he had to make certain, at the end
of each week, that everything was still there. Whenever a new code or a new monthly set of coding
instructions arrived, he had to sign them in, destroy
the old ones and file a report saying that he had done
so. It was exacting but not onerous work.

While on duty, he was in charge of the enlisted
men who did most of the coding and decoding, but
since they knew what they were doing, it was not a
heavy burden. At least once a shift and often half a
dozen times, the message required an officer's responsibility. Then he had to do the work himself. At
first, the enlisted men watched him, keeping track of
the lieutenant's speed, but when he got the hang of
the various codes, they stopped watching.

He had dreaded night duty because he was afraid
there would be nothing to do except read a book and
drink coffee, but it was often the busiest time. When
Manila went off duty for the evening, Washington

was just coming to work in the morning. Through the middle of the night and the early dawn hours, incoming message traffic was heavy. If a message was labeled URGENT or IMMEDIATE, he had to phone Colonel Sampson and let him decide what to do. Otherwise it could wait until morning.

One Friday night at two o'clock a message came in with no priority label. It approved a recent MacArthur request for three additional PT boats to supplement the half-dozen he now had. Although the approval came through as ROUTINE and estimated that the boats would not arrive until February, Phipps remembered that MacArthur's request had been sent URGENT and had pointed out that his original plan for proper defense of the islands called for fifty PTs. The fact that he was requesting only three right now "does not mitigate my dire need for fifty."

Phipps took his life in his hands and tracked down Colonel Sampson at an all-night poker game celebrating the start of the weekend. The colonel sounded so annoyed that he must be losing. Phipps gulped and read him the message anyway.

There was a long pause. Then Colonel Sampson said, "Well, by God, they finally gave him something. You did right to call. This is worth waking up the Old Man."

Next day the colonel actually complimented Phipps by telling him MacArthur's response: "Never hesitate to wake me with good news."

The boats seemed rather a small matter to Phipps, except for making headquarters a happier place for two days. Also, if he was not mistaken, Colonel Sampson had decided to trust him. He even took to addressing him as Eli, certainly not with affection but perhaps conceding that a Yale background was not necessarily a hopeless flaw.

When he was not on duty, he led a cheerful life in Manila. He shared a small, noise-filled house near the Walled City with three other bachelor officers. The radio or the record player was on all the time, often both at once, and there were no restrictions on women or liquor, both of which were plentiful and cheap.

The other officers introduced him to Saturday nights at the Santa Ana Cabaret out in the suburb of Pasig, "where nobody bothers anybody." The biggest cabaret in the world, Santa Ana had both a large "family room," where parents could dine with their children, and a still larger dance hall and bar, where the atmosphere was not the least bit familial. Santa Ana supplied giant glasses of beer for twenty-five centavos and a horde of *baliarinas*, or dance-hall girls, at one peso an hour for dancing. For another five pesos you could spend the rest of the night at the girl's apartment, breakfast included. Sam Phipps, whose sheltered life at home in Baltimore and at college in New Haven had not prepared him for Manila, would ride back to the city on the streetcar Sunday morning, feeling very tired but very much a gay dog, an accomplished man of the world. He knew he appeared even younger than he was, with his curly brown hair and innocent-looking brown eyes, but on Sunday mornings, he felt extremely grown-up. He still didn't think he belonged here, but he had certainly lucked out. For as long as it lasted, this was the life.

Sam Phipps did not actually see the November 27 cable from Washington. He only heard about it when Colonel Sampson called a meeting of the communications officers.

"This is secret," he said in a severe voice that held none of his customary sarcasm. They were standing in front of his desk. "You will not discuss it outside this room, not even with each other." He put on his reading glasses and picked up a sheet of paper. "I will read the pertinent part: 'HOSTILE ACTION POSSIBLE AT ANY MOMENT. IF HOSTILITIES CANNOT, REPEAT CANNOT, BE AVOIDED THE UNITED STATES DESIRES THAT JAPAN COMMIT THE FIRST OVERT ACT. THIS POLICY SHOULD NOT, REPEAT NOT, BE CONSTRUED AS RESTRICTING YOU TO A COURSE OF ACTION THAT MIGHT JEOPARDIZE YOUR DEFENSE.'

"Does everybody understand that?" He took off his glasses and placed the sheet of paper facedown on his desk.

They all nodded. Phipps was excited to be let in on such important information. He looked around. Yes, the others were excited too. This sounded like the real thing.

"All right, what this means," Sampson said, "is that we are all on red alert. Japan has to act first, that's clear, but we have to know about it—instantly. We don't know what we'll hear or how we'll hear it, but it's bound to come through our message center. Maybe from Washington, but maybe from one of our units out here, or even from the navy. It could come in code, or in the clear, or over the phone, but whoever's on duty, when it comes in, I want to hear about it in fifteen seconds." He looked around from face to face. "If you can't reach me *at once*, don't waste any time. You are to go right up the line. Willoughby, Sutherland, the Old Man himself. That clear?"

"Colonel, when is this expected?"

Phipps was glad he hadn't asked this. He thought it a dumb question, and so did Colonel Sampson.

"If I knew," Sampson said, reverting to his withering tone, "I just might be tempted to pass the word." He paused, apparently thinking whether or not to say something. Then he added, "The General still thinks the Japs won't attack until spring, but this cable is now United States policy and a direct order. This message center will act as though anything could happen at any moment. Any other questions?"

When nobody else asked the obvious one, Phipps finally put up his hand.

"Yes, Eli?"

"Sir, what does it mean when it says, Don't 'jeopardize your defense'?"

"It means that no matter what, General MacArthur is expected to protect this command so it can fight."

≡ 4 ≡

The Last Dance

Three days before the annual trustees' party for the
Simpson students and faculty, Amos Watson learned
that the evening was in jeopardy.

"It is Mr. Homobono calling," his secretary, Miranda, said. "The columnist."

Miranda came all the way into his office at least
a dozen times a day, to bring him mail or iced tea or
papers to sign or to take dictation, but whenever she
announced a phone call, she only stuck her head
around the corner of the door. It was a very pretty
young head, with black hair cut short, and she was
always smiling, even in times of crisis. This was not
a crisis.

"No," Amos Watson said, without putting down
his newspaper. "Tell him I'm busy."

"He say he knows your answer will be no. But he
say this time he wants to tell you something as a favor,
not ask you anything."

Miranda knew perfectly well it should be "he
says," not "he say." But she pronounced "says" like
the plural of "say" instead of *sez*. After he had cor-

rected her many times, she turned stubborn. Now it was always "he say," even though Amos tried to tease her out of it.

The idea of Sandy Homobono doing anybody a favor, other than for money, was intriguing. Amos had learned never to turn down an offer until he heard what the offer was. "What favor he say?"

Miranda's happy smile grew wider. "He not say."

Amos put down his paper and picked up the phone. "Hello, Sandy. Why do you suddenly want to do me a favor?"

"Oh, sir, it is from the goodness of my kind and gentle heart." The hoarse voice mocked the sentimental Filipino style.

Amos laughed. "All right, what's the favor?"

"You have a party coming up."

No harm in admitting that, since it was not a secret. It had been on the Polo Club calendar for months. "Right. At the Polo Club. The Simpson dinner dance. We give it every year."

"Yes." Several long seconds of silence. "Mr. Watson, I think it will be canceled."

"What? By whom?" Amos could hear the sudden anger in his own voice. He had helped build the Polo Club and had served as a director.

"You aren't so popular these days."

"What does that have to do with it?"

"I hear there is a conflict with the Chamber of Commerce reception."

"That's at noon. My party's at night."

"I hear that is changed."

Amos was angry enough to break his rule about

never telling Sandy Homobono anything that wasn't already public knowledge. "Our party has been given every year since my own children were at Simpson. It will take place."

"Thanks very much."

Amos realized after he hung up that he had given Sandy a very usable quote in return for his favor. He told Miranda to get Rory MacMillan on the phone. As soon as he heard the club manager's voice, he knew Homobono's information was, as usual, accurate.

"I was just about to call you, Mr. Watson." The normally pleasant, always efficient voice sounded very nervous. "A problem has come up."

"I know all about it," Amos snapped, and banged down the phone.

During his last term as a Polo Club director, he had helped select Rory for the manager's job, and they had always been on good terms. This could not possibly be Rory's doing. He had simply been handed the nasty job of conveying the directors' ruling. Amos Watson, the notorious defeatist and warmonger, was not to sully the Polo Club's image as Manila's finest private club. Well, my God . . .

Amos went over the list of directors, writing their names down, picking out the best pressure points. He knew he could count on Billy Waters, who must have been away from Manila when the decision was made by the others. But Billy, even back in town, was just one vote. Amos needed more than that. He settled on Boris Cutter at American City Bank and Frank Otis at L.C.L. because they were most subject to leverage. He was glad now that he had not been hasty about moving his accounts out of American City last month. Haste was sometimes essential in business affairs, but never haste motivated by emotion.

But when he gave Miranda the calls to make to Cutter and Otis, she could not complete them. Boris Cutter was "in conference" and didn't know when he could get back. Frank Otis was going to be "tied up in meetings most of the day." Miranda shook her head as she reported these messages. "Both secretaries took too long to give explanations," she said. "They made them up."

Amos had no intention of repeating the calls, only to be turned away again. Besides, there was not that much time left. Instead, he dictated personal Western Union messages.

To Boris Cutter:

CALL ME AT OFFICE BY THREE. IF NOT, AM REMOVING ALL REPEAT ALL MY ACCOUNTS AND ASSETS AT NINE TOMORROW MORNING.

To Frank Otis:

CALL ME AT OFFICE BY THREE. IF NOT, AM SELLING ALL REPEAT ALL SHARES L.C.L. WHEN EXCHANGE OPENS TOMORROW MORNING.

After she had phoned in the telegrams, Miranda told him, "Western Union say guaranteed one-o'clock delivery."

"Good. Then I'll have lunch in, please."

"You think they will call, sir?"

"Oh yes. One peso say Mr. Otis will call first."

Miranda smiled. She never accepted any of the bets

he offered her. She was wise not to take this one. Boris Cutter would wait till the last minute in order to show that he wasn't intimidated.

Otis, the president of Leonard & Clarkson, Ltd., called at one forty-five. He was airy and cheerful. "What's all this, Amos? L.C.L.'s still a damn good stock."

"I don't think so anymore."

"Well, that's your privilege, I guess, but you're making a mistake. Look, if you want to get out, I might buy you out myself, with a little time and a little help from the bank. But you have to give me several days to arrange it, maybe a week. What is it you have, six thousand shares?"

Frank Otis knew perfectly well what Amos's holding was. It was sixty-five hundred, the biggest block held by an outsider.

"No, I'm in a hurry, so I'm selling tomorrow. Just wanted to let you know in advance."

"But Amos, that's far too many shares to offer all at once. Hell, I don't need to tell you. It could knock our stock down a couple of points, maybe more. You won't even get the full price of thirty-four. Actually, thirty-four and a half, as of noon."

"Oh, I'm not hoping for anything so grand. I'm just going to put it all up at a nice even price I feel sure I can get. I'm selling at twenty-five."

There was a long silence. Amos waited. It was quite a wait. Amos had time to unbend two paper clips, a habit that Miranda considered wasteful.

Otis's voice, when it finally came back, was shaken. "You can't do that. That's dumping."

"Right. And I intend to be very open about it, so there won't be any mystery at the exchange. Amos Watson is selling his entire holding at twenty-five."

"You won't even make a profit."

"Actually, I will. I originally bought at twenty-four, so I'll make a few thousand. I'm not greedy."

"Jesus, you'd wreck the L.C.L. market. Everybody's jumpy these days. Everybody will think you know something."

Amos agreed with that. He waited again.

"You can't do this, Amos."

"Sure I can. Unless . . ."

"Unless what?"

"Actually, there is a favor you could do me. I understand there's some confusion at the Polo Club about my Simpson party. I was hoping you could straighten it out."

"Oh. I see. Well, you know, Amos, the directors—"

"You can reach me at home this evening. Or tomorrow morning, before the exchange opens. Got to hang up now. I'm expecting another call."

It was another hour before he heard from Boris Cutter, who was bristling.

"See here, Amos—"

"No, you see here. I want everything ready for withdrawal when the bank opens tomorrow. I will be there with a suitcase for all the paper, and I want certified checks for the complete sum in all five accounts, including interest through this afternoon."

"I don't know what you're sore about, but you

know damn well the bank can't pull such large amounts together on such short notice."

"You'll have to. I intend to deposit everything in Consolidated Commercial before noon."

"Don't tell me I have to," Cutter snapped. "You know it can't be done."

"That's too bad. Then I'll have to tell the press that when American City's largest private customer tried to withdraw his account, the bank couldn't come up with it."

"Nobody would believe you. Besides, you're in no position to go around making accusations these days."

"I'm not so sure of that. Sandy Homobono isn't particularly fond of American business. You think he might be willing to print my charge against the major American bank?"

"What the fuck do you want?"

Amos told him, and gave him the same deadline he had given Frank Otis.

He did not think he would be needing help from Billy Waters, although he should fill Billy in on what was happening. Besides, it would be refreshing to talk to someone on his side. Through Miranda to Billy's secretary, he invited his friend to have a drink with him late this afternoon at the place of his choice— Polo Club, Army-Navy, Elks, wherever.

"She say," Miranda reported, "that Mr. Waters say come to his house."

At five-thirty, Donato deposited Amos at the big modern concrete house on Mabini Avenue, only a

few blocks from Amos's own home. Billy's house—
or, to be more accurate, his wife Dorothy's house—
was too American for Amos's taste, but it was expensive and handsome, befitting the president of the
Inter-Island Mahogany Company. Waters was already an important figure in Manila, a participant in
all the major business groups, and Dorothy Waters
was a lavish, popular hostess. Amos thought they
were going to be the next number-one American couple in town.

Billy greeted him in the living room filled with
bright flower-upholstered furniture, then mercifully
led him into the den, with its dark leather armchairs
and teak desk and cabinets. A lanky, sandy-haired
man in his early fifties, he was almost as tall as Amos.
He had strong green eyes. His thin face was deeply
tanned from many days spent outdoors in the southern islands, buying timberlands and making all the
key decisions about when and where to harvest. He
worked as hard at his business as anyone Amos knew,
always expanding, leasing new timberlands, always
trying new things, some of them adventurous enough
to be classified as risky, but he knew how to bring
them off.

When they were seated with their drinks, Amos
started to report on the Polo Club situation, but Billy
interrupted.

"I know all about it, Amos. Hell of a sorry way to
handle it. All that flimflam about switching the Am-
Cham reception and then making Rory MacMillan
be the one to tell you. Kid stuff. Well, it's done.

But if I'd been here, you'd have had it straight: cancel the party."

Amos was surprised. "But it isn't done. Or rather, I've spent the day undoing it. I'm not canceling the party."

Billy's sandy eyebrows rose. "You think that's wise?"

"It's not a question of 'wise.' The Simpson party has been an annual event since before you came to the Islands. It's my party and it's still on."

Waters shook his head. "I don't see it that way. Look, Amos, you're bad medicine at the moment. I hope it's temporary. The thing for you to do is lie low. This is no time to be throwing a big party. And especially not at the Polo Club, where everybody will hear of it."

"Frankly, I don't care who hears about it."

"Well, I do. It's not good for the club, but more important, it's not good for you. It's not in your own best interest."

"Perhaps not, but I'm old enough to look out for myself. I'm counting on your vote, Billy. You're going to be the next president, and they will listen to you. I believe I've already swung Cutter and Otis."

"Cutter? But I think it was his idea."

"Well," Amos said dryly, "I think I've persuaded him to change his mind. Now when you come along—" He stopped because Billy Waters was shaking his head again.

"Let it go, Amos."

"I don't want to let it go."

"God, you are stubborn. Take the advice of a friend for once. It's really not in your best interest."

"That's the second time you've said that, Billy. Suppose you let me decide my interest."

Waters stared at him for a moment in silence. "I don't blame you for being upset. I would be too. But how many times have you told me not to try to make decisions when you're upset? This time you're wrong. I'm sorry, Amos, but you're not going to have my vote."

If Billy Waters opposed it, that party would not take place. Amos looked at the man who was about to become his former friend. "Do I take that as final?"

"I'm afraid so. You'll thank me later."

Amos sighed. There was no point in arguing with Waters when he had made up his mind. Besides, Amos was no good at pleading. He kept his voice flat and level. "It is in your best interest, Billy, to change your mind. Otherwise it might get out that Inter-Island Mahogany is running two dummy leasing companies for Japanese owners. Contrary to law. Both on Mindanao, one outside Davao, the other north of Cotabato."

Billy Waters didn't move. His hands didn't move, his eyes did not even flicker. He sat still, looking straight at Amos. Finally he asked in a hard, quiet voice, "How the hell do you know that?"

Amos spread his hands. "I keep in touch."

"I suppose it doesn't really matter how you know." He got to his feet. He nodded his head several times to himself, the way he always did when he had reached a conclusion. A decisive man, one of the things Amos had always admired in him. "I don't think we have anything more to discuss."

Amos stood up as well. They did not shake hands when he left, and probably would not shake hands ever again.

A very expensive party.

————

Next afternoon Miranda told him she was going to the Polo Club "to make the preparations." Since this was her fourth year of overseeing the party, he knew everything would be arranged properly. She enjoyed doing it, she was always thorough, and besides, the headmaster, Dr. Clarke, always sent down an advance helper from Simpson.

"Who's helping you this time?"

She consulted the list in her hand, an unnecessary act since Amos knew she would have memorized the name. "It is Felix Logan," she said. "The president of all the seniors," she added approvingly. "He will be the one."

In the Philippines, being "the one" was an important designation, a statement of authority and position. It was also used as a proud declaration of intention. *Who is going to be responsible? Oh, sir, I will be the one.*

"Good," Amos said. "He's very reliable."

"He is nice on the telephone," Miranda said. "He will meet me there."

She smiled her happy smile, displaying the gold canine tooth of which she was so proud. Amos could not remember whether she had smiled as much before he bought her the gold tooth as a Christmas present to fill the dark gap created by a childhood accident. A false white tooth would have been more suitable, Amos thought, but Miranda chose gold. "Gold is more charming," she said. "Benny thinks so too."

Benny was Miranda's fiancé, a nice young man from her hometown of San Fernando. They would have been married long before now, and Amos would have lost a valuable secretary, if Benny had not been conscripted into the Philippine Army. Both families had agreed to wait until Benny completed his service. Amos himself, for a quite selfish reason, had also counseled delay. It enabled him to hang on to Miranda a bit longer. Actually he was very lucky to have kept Miranda as long as he had. It was rare for a pretty Filipina in her early twenties to remain unmarried.

In earlier years of the party a faculty member had been sent down from Baguio to help with arrangements, but Amos had found the teachers unreliable or even indifferent about who should sit next to whom and which students could be counted on to make decent dinner conversation with which trustee's wife. The switch to a student helper had had good results.

Amos remembered Felix Logan. He was the boy with thick glasses who wore a wire-and-sponge-rubber mask during basketball games. He had spent all his sixteen or seventeen years in the Orient, growing up in Japan, then a few years in China, now on the southern island of Cebu, where his father was a railroad manager. Not a particularly good student, Dr.

Clarke said, but popular with both students and faculty and a whiz at getting things done. "The kids call him Felix the Fixer," Dr. Clarke said. "Sometimes I'm not sure whether he runs the school or I do."

It was just like Miranda to say that Felix Logan was "president of all the seniors." It gave him special cachet, made him more worthy to be "the one" to assist her. He was indeed class president, but, thanks to the departure of all the army and navy children, there were only eight seniors at Simpson this year, including Felix himself.

With the party safely rescheduled, and with Miranda and Felix Logan working with Rory MacMillan on the arrangements, Amos assumed no further difficulties could arise. He was caught by surprise when Papaya suggested that perhaps it would be better for her not to sing.

They had finished making love that evening in their suite at the Bayview, and Amos was clad in his white silk dressing gown embroidered with extravagant blue flowers. It was far too gaudy for his taste, but not for Papaya, who had given it to him as "a lover's present." He had no choice but to wear it.

Papaya, to his delight, had no embarrassment about her body and seldom wore anything. Once undressed, she stayed undressed until it was time to leave. She was brushing her long black hair in front of the mirror, obviously pleased with herself and with their lovemaking. With each fierce brush stroke her heavy breasts with the large, very dark nipples lifted and fell. Amos enjoyed watching her, the pale orange skin, the plump shoulders, the fully rounded belly and hips that could not quite yet be called fat, and the good legs that were not fat at all. He also enjoyed looking at the place he had just been, covered with thick black hair that was astonishingly dark against the pale skin.

His contemplation was so pleasant and relaxed that her words intruded abruptly.

"You know, Amos baby, maybe I should not sing at your party." She did not turn from the mirror.

"Of course you should sing. Why not?"

"Well, there is too much fuss about you. I will just add one more fuss."

"Don't be silly. Everybody is expecting you. Anyway, it's a private party."

"Private? With fifty-sixty people at the Polo Club, where all the big bosses are angry at you?" She laughed, but continued brushing. "Besides, you are always telling me, think about my career, don't just sing. Maybe this would not be so good for my career."

Oh, so that was it. "Papaya," he said sternly, "we have a *business* arrangement for this party. I am paying you a fee, and you have promised to sing."

"Maybe I will catch a cold." She put down the brush. "Okay, okay, I will sing." She walked across the room toward him, her breasts swinging with each step, and sat down on the edge of the rumpled bed, facing him.

She looked serious. "Amos baby, this time you listen to me. This time I will be the teacher. You are very smart, smart as anybody I know, but sometimes even smart people need advice. You are very sweet to me, so I give you advice. Good straight advice.

"You should go home. To the States. Not just for a visit but for good. You are always thinking there will be a war, so you will be much better off back there. You are rich, you can live anywhere, maybe build a wonderful new mansion house in California. All your family is there, and you make many new American friends. Rich people make new friends very easy.

"Out here everything has all gone bad. All at once like sour milk. You make too many people too mad all at the same time. Philippine government, American government, all the reporters who don't like you anyway because you don't talk to them. And now you beat up some very important businessmen, just so you can have your party. You think everybody is going to forget all that and pat you on the back like old times? I don't think so. You are a big man here, and when that goes bad, it goes very bad. If you are big, there is no nice little place to step down. You are either top or nothing—zero. Like if I suddenly start to lose my voice, that is it. Finish. You think I can sing at some little cabaret, where everybody says, 'She used to be Papaya'? I think you are finish, Amos baby. But only in the Philippines, not in America.

"You always teach me, be a realist. Be practical. I am going to live to be a very old lady, probably smoking cigars, but I never forget you. Never. A promise, very easy to keep. But it's time, Amos baby. It's time for you to go home. Many good years, all your good memories, including me, now it's time to go home."

She spoke with such sincerity and such obvious

affection that he was very moved. She had, however, missed the most important point.

"But I am home," he said. "I'm already home."

———

Amos Watson arrived early at the Polo Club to see that everything was in order. He liked walking into the main room of the pavilion. He had spent many afternoons and evenings here, along with the club's eleven hundred other members, all Americans and Europeans except for the honorary memberships of Quezon and Vice President Osmeña. Americans hadn't had much practice at colonialism, but they preserved exclusivity just as stupidly and intransigently as the British. How else could you tell you were superior to your subjects? Many of the Americans who came to the Philippines were second-rate people. Genuinely second-rate. They couldn't make it in the States, but out here they belonged to clubs and had servants—a much better life than they could earn for themselves in California or New York. But once here, they all thought they deserved it.

This was the finest grand room in Manila, far superior to the Army-Navy Club or the Elks Club or the Fiesta Pavilion, because it was in native Philippine style. Spacious, with large windows open to the bay, it was all nipa thatch and bamboo and *sawali* partitions woven from sugar cane. From the open rafters, similar to those in Amos's own home, hung luxuriant air plants, trailing and swaying gracefully in the breeze from the bay. The tall pillars supporting the rafters were adorned with ferns, and the bases of the pillars were surrounded by brilliant tropical plants. Two gardeners worked here full-time every day, trimming, pruning, watering, fertilizing, replanting.

Every conceivable social occasion in Manila took place here: teas, cocktail parties, receptions, lunches, dinners, banquets, *despedidas* for departing friends. Old-timers still talked about the 1922 visit of the Prince of Wales, who suffered the most famous head cut in Philippine history while playing polo. More recently, and less bloodily, the welcoming reception for High Commissioner Sayre in 1939 had been so vast that tables set up on the lawn spread all the way to the seawall. Tonight's party would be comparatively modest: fifty or so guests, a cocktail area over by the windows, a buffet table, a small bandstand for Papaya and the orchestra, and a generous dancing area, where the teenagers would have space for their gyrations without knocking over the trustees and their wives.

"Hello, Mr. Watson. Everything's set."

Amos shook hands with Rory MacMillan, who looked the perfect club manager—trim, neat, cheerful. "How are you, Rory?"

"Just fine, sir. And happy to see you here."

"How did the AmCham reception go?"

Rory grinned. "There was a little confusion among some members about just when it was supposed to be, noon or evening, but it went fine. And we had plenty of time to clear away and get ready for you."

"Where's Miranda?"

"She and Felix are out talking to the kitchen. That Felix is quite something. You'd think he was my assistant manager."

"Miranda's counting the lobsters, I expect. She's never forgotten that we ran out one year. Let's get her out, if you don't mind."

When Miranda appeared in her best pink dress, she looked confident, so everything must be under control. She was accompanied by Felix Logan, who also looked confident. He wore the customary white linen suit and a solid maroon tie with block initials embroidered in light red. These days everybody had a collection of solid-color monogrammed ties. He had thick glasses and tousled brown hair, and when he shook hands with Amos, he ran his fingers through his hair, leaving it slightly more tousled. A nervous habit, Amos guessed. He had the light build of a teenage boy who has grown several inches in the last year.

Amos remembered sitting on the bench beside Brad Stone during a basketball game and hearing the coach describe what each of his boys could and could not do. Felix Logan couldn't shoot worth a damn, maybe two or four points a game, but watch the way he guards his man. That guy dribbles like crazy and is one of their best shots, but look how Felix stays on him. That fellow won't score much today. And watch the way Felix passes. He'll wait, no hurry, and then bang, the ball is right there for Chink or John, chest-high, ready for an open shot. And he'll keep that up right through the game, never gets tired.

Amos made the inspection rounds with Miranda, Felix and Rory. He quizzed Felix about the students seated next to trustees and their wives. Yes, Felix had picked boys and girls who would not be tongue-tied or, worse, outrageous. Chink Malone, for example, was stationed at the table with the Ashburns, where he could do no harm because after a few drinks Peggy Ashburn couldn't be outraged by anything.

The presence of trustees and faculty at each table held down the students' drinking. At a party away from school for juniors and seniors, moderate drinking should be permissible. But Rory would keep an eye out as he passed among the tables to make sure no one was getting out of hand.

The bandstand had the right number of places for the small orchestra: piano, drums, saxophone, trumpet, clarinet. "And Felix," Miranda said with awe, "has given the band a list of fifty songs to play. *Fifty*."

"It's just the records that are most popular at the school dances," Felix explained. "I figured three minutes a number, a hundred and fifty minutes, two and a half hours. With breaks, that should be plenty. I also gave them ten spares, in case they didn't know some of the songs."

If there was anything Amos Watson liked, it was organization, which was especially rare among the young. Yet Felix Logan was not boasting, just explaining his thinking.

"He has even talked to Miss Papaya with suggestions," Miranda said.

"I hope that was all right," Felix said. He ran his

fingers through his hair. "I thought she should know which ones were voted Favorite Songs in the yearbook poll, in case she wanted to sing them herself."

"And did she?" Amos asked. Papaya liked to set her own program.

"She's going to do our number-one song, 'There's a Great Day Coming Mañana.' To end with. And then we've worked up a joke song to start out. To make everybody feel good." He grinned. He had a contagious, cheerful grin, revealing that he wore the thick bands and wires of braces.

Amos went on with his inspection. Yes, there would be enough steam tables for the buffet, and the heat under the steaks would be sufficient to keep them warm but not so high as to dry them out. Yes, Miranda promised, we have plenty of lobsters.

Yes, the bartender had been instructed not to make the drinks too strong. Yes, there was definitely enough Coca-Cola to support the expected run on cuba libres.

When he could think of nothing more to ask, Amos complimented them on the arrangements. Since everything seemed to be under perfect control, as usual, he went to take a look at the pool activity.

He strolled through the gardens to the big tiled pool, which, like the dining area, he had reserved for the day. Long before he reached it he could hear the cries and laughter and splashes of teenagers on the loose. He could remember when his own children were making these happy noises at their own Simpson party long years ago. His older son would be forty next month. Time passed.

Amos walked the length of the pool, saying hello

and welcome to everyone, taking care not to slip on the wet tiles. He was glad the weather was so pleasant, bright sunshine with high, distant clouds that held no threat of rain. There should be another of those first-class sunsets across the expanse of Manila Bay.

He came to Brad Stone and Judy Ferguson. Stone's chest was covered with curly red-blond hair, still damp from swimming. Judy Ferguson's fine chest was covered but not concealed by a polka-dot bathing suit.

"Hello, Brad. Don't get up. Hello, Judy."

But Brad was already springing to his feet to shake hands. "Great day for the party, Mr. Watson."

"How's the army treating you?"

Brad Stone winced. "Well, they let me off for this. But I can't spend the night." A quick, regretful side glance at Judy Ferguson said more than he meant it to. "I have to be back by reveille."

"That's too bad." Amos decided to check out some of what he had been hearing from Jack Humphrey. Perhaps things were improving. Brad Stone was in one of the new Philippine units and ought to know. "How's the army itself?"

"It's all right, I guess," Brad said, "as long as we don't have to fight anybody."

"Oh, for God's sake, Brad." Judy spoke for the first time. "Not again."

"No, I'd like to hear."

"It was better in ROTC," Brad said. He was very serious. "At least there everybody had a rifle, and we all spoke the same language. What we have here is what it must have been like in Xerxes' army camp, just before he went after the Greeks. All those folks from different lands, all the different languages and costumes, all of them wondering why they're there."

"Brad, this is supposed to be a *party*."

"I'm sorry," Amos apologized. "Indeed it is. I'll see you both at cocktails. Just about time to get dressed, by the way. The trustees will be here soon."

"Come on, Judy, one more quick swim."

Amos watched them dive into the pool, then walked out alone to the seawall.

The seawall was Manila's barrier against the bay. On the land side it was waist-high, but on the ocean side it dropped down ten or fifteen feet to the level of the water. Often one saw little kids running along the top of it, just to be near the ocean and, in lively weather, to be splashed by the spray of breaking waves. Of course, in a typhoon the seawall gave scant protection. The water simply crashed over it, wrecking lawns and gardens and sometimes homes.

Amos could remember the very year he arrived in the Philippines there had been two terrible typhoons, perhaps the worst in his entire three decades. Luckily, Marian and the children had still been in the States. If she'd been here, she would have packed up and gone home. He was in Baguio when the July typhoon struck—four *feet* of rain in a couple of days. You couldn't even call it rain. It was more like an angry ocean falling out of the sky. Mountain slides destroyed the new Benguet Road and cut off Baguio for days until a pack train with supplies could make it over the mudslides. From that first year, he had never trusted Philippine weather and had never invested in agriculture—not even sugar or rice or coconut oil. A typhoon, which the Filipinos called *bagyo*, or great wind, could scare anybody out of anything.

Today the beautiful bay stretched peaceful and serene in the late afternoon. The orange sun dropped toward the sea, and the water shone. The clouds took on the exotic purple and orange colors that made the sunsets here so famous. The ships, freighters and tankers, a few navy vessels, were mere scattered dots, emphasizing the breadth of this great harbor. Beyond the ships, outlined against the horizon like cardboard cutouts, stood the calm blue shapes of the island of Corregidor and the rugged peninsula of Bataan.

The warmth faded out of the air as the evening breeze came in from the sea. No great wind tonight. It was time to go inside and greet his guests.

All the trustees and wives came—except, of course, Billy Waters. Amos Watson stood near the entrance to the room with Dr. Clarke and his wife, Cynthia, to welcome them. Sam Clarke, like most headmasters, looked less at home in a white suit at the Polo Club than in his tweed jacket at school in Baguio, where his pockets were always filled with notes, schedules, pencils, pipe and tobacco pouch. Amos had urged him to wear a *barong* in Manila, but Dr. Clarke said that was not the proper costume for fund-raising.

The boys and girls emerged from the pool locker room in clusters, now dressed for the party, their wet hair neatly slicked down. The remaining teachers also arrived, and business grew lively at the bar. Brad Stone was in uniform—khakis, not whites. Amos wondered if Brad had not had time to have whites made or just didn't have the money. Judy Ferguson wore a simple white dress, short sleeves and short skirt, with a flame-red scarf as a sash belt. She looked marvelous. He could see she had confidence not only in her good looks but in her popularity. She was very good at being popular.

Finally Rory MacMillan came over. "We're all ready for you, Mr. Watson. Whenever you like."

Amos clapped his hands loudly. "Dinner is served," he announced. "Please help yourselves at the buffet."

He was always amused to watch what happened next. The students, their appetite sharpened by swimming as well as by youth, longed to fall upon all these dishes that far surpassed anything they ate at school. But with adults present, both their teachers and the trustees, they knew they must hold back. Most of them took up hovering positions within sight of the buffet, where they could look at the food without actually standing in line for it.

The teachers, less ravenous than the students but no less impressed by the food, held back for the headmaster and his wife. The trustees, more accustomed to Manila banquets and, because of their age, less ravenous than the teachers, were in no special hurry. They were willing to wait until they finished their drinks.

Amos had confronted this situation so many times that he knew just what to do. With a waiter and tray in tow, he interrupted the Clarkes and the Malcolms. "Why don't you start the line?" he said. "The waiter will take your drinks to your seats."

Soon a full line was moving down the buffet table. Amos knew the students were most interested in the steaks and lobsters and the American-style desserts, but he encouraged everyone to begin with a plate of Philippine hors d'oeuvres, known as *pika-pika*, or pick-pick, because many could be eaten with the fingers. There were *lumpia*, the Philippine version of Chinese egg rolls, and *empanaditas*, meat pastries, and *dilis*, fried anchovies dipped in garlic vinegar, and finger-size bananas. Amos especially urged everyone to try his own favorite, the *bagoong*, a salty, spicy paste of tiny shrimp served with green mango slices.

Amos dined at the head table with the Clarkes, Mike and Betty Malcolm, Felix Logan and bouncy Jane Barker, "the president of all the juniors," as Miranda would have described her. Mike Malcolm was the newest member of the board, with two children in the lower grades. He ought to be a good contributor, Amos had told Dr. Clarke, but don't try to tell him tonight what you need. Tell him how good the school is, and the money can come later.

The best salesmen for Simpson turned out to be Felix and Jane. Both were enthusiastic about the school, and both had nice things to say about the Malcolm children, much to the delight of Betty Malcolm. The parents didn't have to know that Jane and Felix liked everybody. Every once in a while Amos threw in a question to keep things rolling.

Conversation went so easily that Amos was free to keep an eye on the other seven tables. All seemed well. He could detect no pockets of disorder or of sullen silence. A steady stream of students returned to the buffet for second helpings of *ulang*, the small Philippine lobster.

After dinner, while the orchestra was setting up at the small bandstand, Amos stood to make a brief speech of welcome and allowed Sam Clarke to say a few words of thanks to all the trustees, even though the bill was on Amos. Amos believed that speeches should never interfere with pleasure. He then turned the evening over to dancing.

———

It was a nice band, Felix Logan thought, a pretty good small band, and it was playing the right music, all the easy-dancing songs he had requested. "All or Nothing at All," "Song of India," "Little Brown Jug," "With the Wind and the Rain in Your Hair," "Blueberry Hill," "Tuxedo Junction," "I'll Never Smile Again," "In the Mood," "The Breeze and I," "Two Dreams Met." Since he ran the victrola and picked the records for the Friday-night school dances, he knew what everybody liked. Tonight, sprung from victrola duties, he danced with all the girls, even the dogs.

He liked old Mr. Watson. During dinner he had asked some interesting questions about Simpson, not the dreary questions parents asked. You could tell he was not just making talk. He told a few funny stories about the primitive days at Simpson when his own kids went there.

Felix knew from Mr. Watson's secretary, Miranda, that the old man was in some kind of bad trouble over politics. It was also said that he was having an affair with Papaya. Felix would never have guessed that a man as old and distinguished as Mr. Watson could be having an affair with anybody, least of all a hotshot young singing star like Papaya. When she and Felix had cooked up a couple of songs for tonight, he found her nice, funny and very sexy. He knew about rich old guys and sexy young women, of course, but Mr. Watson didn't seem like that. Still, if she was singing for his party, it must be true. Felix, who had never come close to an affair with anybody, wondered if he would ever have an affair with a popular singer. He hoped so, and if he did, he hoped he wouldn't have to wait till he was as old as Mr. Watson, although he wouldn't mind being as rich.

You couldn't tell from tonight that Mr. Watson had any troubles. He was supposed to be very rich. He had to be to throw this kind of party, which Miranda said he was paying for all by himself. Just the steaks alone for all these people . . . and really good steaks, too, not the carabao meat they got at school.

It was great to see Coach Stone again, although bizarre to see him in an army uniform. That was a pretty nifty date he'd brought with him. Felix could see that all the old-goat trustees were trying to get a dance with her.

———

When Amos had dutifully danced with Mrs. Clarke and some of the trustees' wives, he took Judy Ferguson onto the floor. She danced well, light on her feet and with a good sense of rhythm. She felt just right in his arms, not snuggling but not distant, either. Just close enough for occasional awareness of her very fine body, but not close enough to keep them from talking.

"What brought you out here?" he asked.

"To the Philippines? Adventure. I'd spent my whole life in Indiana—home, high school, college."

She made it sound like forever, but she could only be in her twenties.

"And did you find your adventure?"

"Oh, yes!" She smiled up at him.

Enormous gray-green eyes and a wonderfully bright smile, perhaps only slightly artificial. And perhaps only a man of his age would have noticed. No wonder Brad Stone—and every other man at the party—was captivated.

"It must be quite something to be a single pretty girl in Manila these days."

"You bet," she said. This time the smile was completely natural.

"When I came out here, in the early dark ages, thirty years ago, there were no single American women at all. They all had to be imported."

"Well, I'm really imported, too. The school employment office had this letter—it probably went to every school in the Big Ten—saying that Dawson Import-Export was looking for a 'very presentable female college graduate' for their Manila office. In my class, there weren't that many exciting offers for women."

"And you won the job."

"Maybe I was the only one who applied," she said with a little laugh.

Amos admired the answer. It proffered modesty, surely false modesty in her case, but held out the possibility that there had been raging competition for the position. "And that's how you met Brad Stone," he said.

"That's how I met *everybody* out here." Her expression darkened. "Brad *volunteered* for the army, you know." She shrugged, as if to say that was that.

"Thank you for the dance," she said when the music stopped. She gave him a dazzling blast from those big eyes.

Oh, young Judy, he thought with amusement, you are a handful.

"Hey, Amos," Charlie Ashburn said, "this is my dance."

————

Brad Stone had to sit out another dance while Judy was being nice to Mr. Ashburn, one of the trustees. But at least that was the last of them. Judy had promised that after one dance with each trustee, she would stick with him. The evening was slipping by. He wondered again if he should have been so quick to join the army, although he still felt it was the right thing to do. Of course, if he had kept on teaching at Simpson, he would be in Baguio, even farther away from Judy, but at least he could have spent this whole night with her and gone back to school tomorrow on the bus with everybody else.

Mr. Watson loomed beside him. "You're looking kind of forlorn, Coach."

"I didn't mean to. It's a wonderful party." He glanced again at Judy in the arms of Mr. Ashburn. The band was playing "Song of India," and Mr. Ashburn was making the most of the slow, dreamy music. Judy was smiling up at him.

"You're pretty serious about her, aren't you?"

Brad Stone nodded. "Yes, Mr. Watson, I am."

"Brad, since I'm only thirty-five years older than you, why don't you call me Amos."

"Well—thank you, sir."

"Is she serious about you?"

Brad shook his head. "I wish I knew. We have great times together, but of course, Judy has a pretty good time everywhere. It's hard to pin her down."

"When do you have to leave tonight?"

Brad checked his watch. "I have to catch the last train to San Fernando. About an hour."

"But you don't have to be back till morning? What time is morning in the army?"

"Six-o'clock reveille." The band swung into a repeat chorus, giving Mr. Ashburn a few more of Brad's precious minutes.

"That's silly. Why don't you take my car? You won't have to leave Manila till five A.M."

Brad Stone gave Amos Watson his full attention. "You mean it? That would be all right? It wouldn't inconvenience you?"

Mr. Watson was amused. "Why would a man my age need a car at five in the morning? Take it."

Brad could spend practically the whole night with

Judy. Six extra hours. Now he didn't even care if the
band gave Mr. Ashburn still another chorus. "Well—
well, if you're sure. Thank you very much—Amos.
Uh, where should I—?"

"Just tell my driver where to pick you up," Amos
said.

The music stopped at last. "Excuse me, I'd better
tell Judy I can stay."

Amos Watson watched Brad charge across the
dance floor like a man on a mission. He hoped that
Judy Ferguson, knowing Brad had to catch his train,
hadn't made an after-the-dance date with someone
else.

It was nearly time for Papaya. Everything still
seemed to be going well. All the kids were dancing
tirelessly, as were a few of the younger teachers. Most
teachers and trustees had settled down at the tables
to talk and drink. Nobody seemed drunk, as far as
he could see, except Peggy Ashburn, of course. Fortunately she had sprained her ankle this afternoon
playing badminton, which prevented her from falling
down on the dance floor while trying to keep up with
some teenage athlete. In many ways he admired the
old girl. She was old Manila, like himself. Sure, she
was a certified lush, but the blue-rinsed white hair
always stayed in place, and at age sixty she was spry
enough to take up both badminton and swing dancing. She was still a terror at the mah-jongg table. She
always said just what she thought, even though the
words might be slurred.

Rory MacMillan approached him. "Mr. Watson,
that reporter Homobono's at the front door asking

to see you. I told him this was strictly private, but he insisted I give you his card."

Amos took it. On the front were the words *Pro Bono*, printed diagonally in bright blue script, and underneath, in block letters, "Santiago Homobono" and two phone numbers. Amos wasn't sure whether Sandy had been christened, as he claimed, after Fort Santiago, the old Spanish bastion guarding the corner of the Walled City, or whether he had merely appropriated the name as suitable for a defender of the public good. Amos turned the card over. A handwritten message scrawled in ink: "Can I crash your party?"

Amos shook his head. There was no limit to Sandy's gall. But Amos would not mind some recognition for this extremely successful party. A nice story would be refreshing, as well as a deserved slap in the face for the directors who had tried to interfere. "Let him in, Rory."

Sandy Homobono, in a wrinkled black suit with a cigarette dangling from the corner of his mouth, was the least prepossessing figure at the party. As he walked up to Amos, unsure whether to shake hands, he said, "Thanks for letting me in, Mr. Watson."

"Hello, Sandy. I'm sorry you can stay for only a few minutes."

Homobono gave a thin smile. "Is that my quote for the evening?"

Amos couldn't help laughing.

Sandy looked around the room, the shrewd little eyes checking out the dance floor and then passing to each table in turn. "So they let you have your party after all."

"They didn't 'let' me. I insisted."

"Yeah, I heard that. I wonder why they changed their minds."

"I can't imagine. Excuse me, there's Papaya. Get yourself a drink, Sandy."

Rory MacMillan was escorting Papaya into the pavilion. Amos watched her walk just far enough into the room to be clearly visible before she stopped, apparently to look around. Amos had to smile. She had sung here before and had no need to inspect the room. She was only staging her entrance.

The crowd quickly noticed her and began applauding. Papaya flashed her dazzling "Yes, it's really me!" smile and bowed her head in acknowledgment. She wore her pale green evening dress with narrow string straps and completely bare shoulders. A pale orchid was tucked in her black hair above her right ear. Behind her at a suitably reverent distance was her saturnine old trumpet player, Tomaso, carrying his black instrument case. Amos didn't like Tomaso, but Papaya always said he had two redeeming qualities: he was loyal to her, and he was the best trumpet in Manila.

She walked straight to Amos. "I look okay?"

"Yes, extremely okay."

"Good. Then I better sing."

He walked with her to the bandstand and introduced her. Tomaso unpacked his trumpet and got settled in his chair at the front of the orchestra.

Papaya shook her plump shoulders, the way she always did to loosen up. Then she turned to her audience, many of them now gathered directly in front of the bandstand.

"First," Papaya said, "we all sing the Simpson School song together."

This brought stunned silence—and then groans. Amos looked quickly at Felix Logan, standing solemn-faced in the front row. This must be the joke Felix said he had worked up with Papaya, but Amos failed to see the humor. The school song had been written by a former headmaster's wife to the tune of "Rock of Ages." It began "Hail to thee, dear Simpson School, Keeper of the Golden Rule," and then deteriorated inexorably through three verses. The school had to sing it once a year at graduation, but surely not twice!

"I say something wrong?" Papaya asked innocently. "Just the same . . ."

She nodded to Tomaso, who tootled a series of quick notes that definitely weren't an introduction to "Rock of Ages." Papaya raised her arms, sticking out and wiggling the first two fingers of each hand, as though making quotation marks. Then she sang:

"Chitchirichit, alibangbang—"

A roar of laughter and approval from students and teachers interrupted her. Not "Rock of Ages" but the merry Filipino folksong that the basketball team had adopted as its "fight song." Describing a woman all dressed up like a butterfly or a golden beetle strutting down the street, the song had nothing to do with basketball. Amos saw that Felix was hugging his arms with pleasure and nodding up at Papaya.

Papaya laughed too, enjoying the joke on them. "Okay, we start over. Everybody together."

This time they all joined her:

> *"Chitchirichit, alibangbang,*
> *Salginto't salagubang,*
> *Ang babae sa langsangan*
> *Kung gumiri parong tandang."*

She was already a success as she switched to familiar American songs, belting them out in her bright, strong voice. Amos listened to her with pride. She looked and sounded wonderful, and he could feel, as he knew she did, that the whole crowd was with her, even the older people sitting at their tables. Even Sandy Homobono, who was still present and wasn't even smoking. She always looked at the faces of her audience, not to gauge their reactions but, as she explained, to touch each of them with her eyes as well as her voice.

"Thank you, thank you, *salamat*," Papaya said through the long applause after her sixth song. "Okay, we take a few minutes' rest. Don't go away." She had an earnest talk with Tomaso, making sure of something, and then she gave some directions to the rest of the band.

"A nice party, Mr. Watson. Thanks for letting me stay."

"What are you going to write?"

"Oh, don't worry. I'll think of something nice. I

won't mention who got smashed, like Mrs. Ashburn, for instance."

"Mrs. Ashburn had a bad ankle sprain. She is in considerable pain."

Homobono uttered the short barking laugh that had earned him his nickname. He was called Sandy not because it was short for Santiago and certainly not because of his appearance, but because of his laugh, which had reminded somebody of Little Orphan Annie's dog Sandy, who always said "Arf!" in the comic strip. Filipinos loved to create nicknames, the more outlandish the better.

"Arf!" Homobono repeated. "She's in no pain at all, Mr. Watson. She'd have been better off spraining a wrist, the one she uses to lift a glass. But don't worry. That's not news anymore."

"With you, Sandy, I always worry."

"Not this time, Mr. Watson. 'Pro Bono' admires winners."

Well, true enough for tonight, Amos thought. Then would come the penalties for having won.

When Papaya returned to the front of the bandstand, everyone clustered around again.

"Okay," she said. "Last song. Everybody's favorite number one. Tomaso?"

A trumpet fanfare, just like on *Your Hit Parade*. Then the orchestra joined in and Papaya sang:

> *"There's a great day coming mañana,*
> *With a wonderful, wonderful dream . . ."*

Her clear, brassy voice was promising them everything:

> *"There'll be beer and pretzels mañana,*
>   *There'll be strawberries floating in cream . . ."*

Brad Stone put his arm around Judy Ferguson's shoulder and hugged her close to him.

> *"There'll be high times,*
>   *High-in-the-sky times . . ."*

Felix Logan had a satisfied look on his face. This was the right way to end the evening.

> *"There's a great day coming mañana—*
>   *If mañana ever comes."*

Papaya now let the band play the melody all the way through alone. She stood in front of them, swaying to the lively music, snapping her fingers, smiling, shaking her shoulders in a rhythm that also swung her breasts. You never just *stand* there during an orchestra interlude, she had explained to Amos, or the audience will get away from you. You really *listen* to that music. You show you can't wait to get back into the singing, and then the audience won't be able to wait either. Then when you finally come back in, they're right there with you.

And here she came. Without looking backward, she held out one hand to stop the orchestra. Only the drummer continued behind her as she belted out:

> *"There's a great day coming mañana!"*

Just the single line. Tomaso, seated beside her, repeated the notes on his trumpet. She sang it again, changing the notes slightly, and the trumpet repeated the change.

"There's a great day coming mañana!"

Soon it became a chant. Papaya could feel the crowd's rising excitement. She went with them, leading them, urging them. As she repeated the single line a dozen different ways, the trumpet following faithfully, she began to point to different parts of the crowd, sometimes with a finger, sometimes stretching out her whole hand. Yes, she was saying, you and you and you, each one of you, I promise you a great day.

The chant electrified not only the crowd but Papaya herself. Amos kept his eyes on her shining, exalted face. She was on a big roll, the crowd with her on every word, every note. He had seen it happen a few times before, the emotion so high that it seemed nothing could stop it.

"There's a great day coming mañana!"

But whenever she got on a roll like this, just when he thought there was no room for anything but the animal drive of her music, she always managed to find him in the crowd and send him a big wink, a personal message saying that, in spite of her excitement, she still had time to think of him. So he kept watching, and finally there it flashed, just for a second: the big wink, the special smile. He nodded to show he had caught it.

He knew it was about to end. Never let them get tired of it, she always said. She sang the line once more and then made a slight gesture to Tomaso. You had to be familiar with her work even to notice it. From the trumpet burst one high piercing note.

Papaya stretched her plump, bare arms as high as she could reach, up toward the nipa ceiling, up toward the sky beyond, and sang the last words of her song, and of this party and this night:

"If mañana ever comes."

⇥ 5 ⇤

Mañana

Mañana arrived on Monday, December 8, at 3:30 A.M. Pacific Time.

Sam Phipps was stuck on night duty again at the message center, but traffic was light, because back in Washington it was still the weekend. Some of the men were reading, and one was listening on headphones to shortwave radio from California. The first word of war did not, after all, come as Colonel Sampson had predicted—from Washington, or from one of their Luzon units, or from the navy.

Suddenly the man with the headphones ripped them off as he jumped to his feet. "Hey!" he yelled. "For Chrissake! They just bombed Pearl Harbor!"

Sam Phipps took a few seconds to confirm that the man could not possibly have misheard. Then he called Colonel Sampson, woke him up and told him.

"I'll be at the Calle Victoria office fast as I can make it," the colonel said. "Call there the minute you hear anything more. Anything, but especially confirmation."

By the time Phipps hung up, every man in the

message center had his headphones on. Phipps learned
later that the navy had got official word direct from
Honolulu half an hour earlier, at three o'clock, but
had not bothered to notify MacArthur.

———

Nine hours later, at 12:30 P.M., Major Jack Humphrey watched the defense of the Philippines begin—
and end.

High in the clear blue sky above the Zambales
Mountains, the Japanese bombers came sailing
straight toward Clark Field in two precise V forma-
tions. There must be fifty of them, he guessed, arranged in the neat, undeviating pattern of migrating
geese.

After last week's hostilities alert, his Scout battalion had moved out of barracks to bivouac in the field,
not far from the perimeter of Clark. Through his field
glasses, Jack Humphrey could see the hangars and
the workshops and the officers' mess and kitchen and
even the individual shapes of planes lined up along
the runway. American bombers and fighters had been
flying around earlier this morning, but not now. Now
they were all parked on the field.

Everybody had known, all morning long, about
the attack on Pearl Harbor. During the last few nights
at the officers' club, Humphrey had heard some of
the Junior Birdmen talking about Jap planes, presumably from Formosa, being sighted off Lingayen Gulf.
The Birdmen were full of their plans to move all their
B-17 Fortresses down to the big southern island of
Mindanao, where they would be safely out of range

if any attack came from Formosa. But as the Jap bombers sailed in, Humphrey could see a lot of B-17s still sitting there—and many, many other American planes as well.

He had seen newsreel pictures of the air war in Europe, the bomb bays gaping open and then the black clusters of bombs falling slowly down through the sky toward the distant ground targets below. Sometimes the films showed bombs exploding on the ground in silent puffs of white smoke.

It wasn't like that. As the earth shook from the first bombs landing, chaos erupted. His hands trying to hold the glasses steady, Humphrey could see planes and buildings burst apart. Dust and debris and flames. He saw a few P-40 fighters lift from the runway and escape into the air, but they were the only ones. Suddenly, an oil dump exploded and caught fire. A vast cloud of thick black smoke gushed up from the ground and spread across the battered field. A second long thundering wave of bombs fell behind the first. Then the last bombers passed over the field and, still in their migrating-geese formation, flew straight on to the south.

It was even worse when the Zeros, with the red balls painted under their wingtips, came screaming in after the bombers. They flew in low to the ground, cutting through the smoke. Their machine guns and cannons blew up everything that was left—every plane, every building, every shed and shack and tent that had managed to survive the bombers. In one frightful hour, Clark Field and everything on it was destroyed.

Looking at the terrible smoking remains, the burned corpse of MacArthur's air force, Humphrey thought to himself, Jesus, now what? Now how are we supposed to hit their bases in Formosa? Now how are we supposed to sink their ships and landing barges? How are we supposed to stop them at the beaches now? How could MacArthur let all his planes get caught on the ground?

———

Judy Ferguson was not afraid, she was furious.

The first few days of the war were exciting enough. After all the endless cocktail-party speculation of the last months, something was finally happening. On the third day, from the rooftop of her office building, she and most of her fellow employees watched the Japanese planes bomb the giant U.S. Navy base of Cavite. It was only a few miles south of Manila, so they had a sensational view. The planes kept coming in and in, and the pile of smoke kept getting bigger and blacker.

There didn't seem to be any American planes trying to stop them. Our planes must be off fighting somewhere else, Judy thought, but it was odd they weren't defending Cavite. All her navy friends, many of whom must be out there under all that smoke, claimed Cavite was the biggest, most important U.S. Navy base in the whole western Pacific. Dry docks, fuel tanks, supplies, ammunition—all that sort of thing. One of her occasional dates, Commander Bob Crutchfield, said Cavite was even more vital than any of the army bases, because it was the Pacific Fleet's home. Most men exaggerated the importance of their own work, but just the same, everybody agreed Cavite was special. She wondered if any of her friends were getting hurt.

The Japs bombed Nichols Field, too, even closer to Manila, and some of the bombs fell on homes in the southern part of the city. But that was a less spectacular sight.

What infuriated Judy was that the war spoiled everything else. Offices, including the export-import firm where she worked, started closing early, but since shops began to close even earlier, Manila afternoons were empty. But what really collapsed was the evening social life. All the army and navy officers were out of it, but that wasn't all. Parties and dinners and dances, events she had already written down in her date book, were canceled. Blackouts and curfews made it difficult to get around Manila at night. Even the big clubs and hotels began to limit their activities. For two nights in a row she had nothing to do.

Brad Stone hadn't called her since the day after the Polo Club party, a few days before the war began, but telephone service wasn't very good now, especially from out of town. She hoped he could get another pass to come to Manila, but passes for the military were rare, especially after the rumors floated that the Japs had made a couple of small landings somewhere in Luzon.

And all for what? This was not going to last. The United States was sending ships and planes and troops to help defend the islands and defeat the Japs. Some said the reinforcements had already begun to arrive, but you could hear anything in Manila these days.

Judy was more realistic. She knew it took time to move things across the Pacific. You couldn't just fly troops in by the Pan Am Clipper in a couple of days. Still, help was on the way, and when it got here, that would be that. She thought it ridiculous to stop everybody's pleasure while they were waiting.

Judy was so bored and lonely that she allowed Frank Otis to take her to lunch. The president of L.C.L. met several of Judy's standards. He was rich, prominent and virtually unmarried, since his wife had returned to the States last fall to get a divorce. However, Frank Otis had plump hands, a feature Judy disliked in men. He also had little bright eyes which, even before his wife's departure, were focused on every white female body in Manila, including her own. She did not mind sexual interest from men she didn't like. It was the across-the-board nature of Frank Otis's attention that offended her.

"I'll go," she said, "provided you take me to the Dixie Kitchen."

"That's not very romantic. I was thinking of something more secluded."

Romance and seclusion were not what Judy wanted. She wanted to see people—lots of them.

Frank's car picked her up and drove her to the famous two-story institution on the Plaza Goiti, not far from Manila's main business street, the Escolta.

Tom's Dixie Kitchen was the most popular spot in Manila—open day and night for a business lunch, for cocktails, for dinner before or after a vaudeville show, even for breakfast after an all-night party. Tom Pritchard, the Jamaican Negro who had run the

Kitchen for more than twenty-five years, served good food and drink at reasonable prices. On the rare occasions when Judy had to buy her own lunch, she often came here with one of the girls from the office for the one-peso special, the best fifty-cent meal in town. Unlike the clubs, the Dixie Kitchen was open to everybody, and everybody came: Americans, Filipinos, Spanish, businessmen, politicians, actors, soldiers, sailors. The noise level was high. Loud conversation in English, Spanish and Tagalog competed with the clatter of dishes and the clink of glasses.

But the Dixie Kitchen was not itself today. As she walked into the big downstairs room with its bright lights and its forest of ceiling fans, she could see business was much slower than usual. The two big round tables reserved for prominent businessmen were only half full. The noise was several notches below normal. The long lunch counter usually jammed with soldiers and sailors had mostly civilians, and not a full crowd at that. If the Dixie Kitchen wasn't crowded at lunchtime, Judy thought, what was this city coming to?

She climbed the stairs to the Oriental Grill. Its decor was not especially Oriental, and the food was mostly Southern American, with a few Filipino and Chinese dishes thrown in for atmosphere, but the tables were relatively quiet compared to downstairs. Judy had been here many nights for late parties, private dinners and dancing.

Today it was somber, with a number of empty tables. Frank Otis saw her enter, got to his feet and waved.

"Well, you're looking beautiful as always," he said

with his too-quick flattery. "I ordered you a brandy alexander to celebrate our first meeting alone together." He raised his glass, holding it in his plump white hand. "The first of many, I hope."

Judy didn't like sweet drinks before meals. She also thought it transparent for Frank to order this kind of milkshake drink, loaded with brandy and crème de cacao. No doubt he hoped she would have several. "I've never seen Tom's so deserted," she said.

"Cozy," Frank Otis said. Despite his hands, he was not bad-looking. He still had all his hair.

"This war," Judy said. "Nobody does anything."

"That's just why I decided we should get together today. I've always admired you, you know."

Judy thought it early for that kind of talk. They had not even ordered.

When the Negro waiter came, she said she would have just the strawberry shortcake, the Kitchen's most famous dish. Otis asked for the sliced luncheon steak, "to keep my strength up. And how about another round of these tasty brandy alexanders?" Judy had scarcely touched the first one, but she thought it easier to accept a second than to explain why she didn't want it.

Rather than let the conversation get personal, Judy clung to her least favorite subject. At least Frank Otis would have the latest inside information—business leaders always did. "Do you hear any good news? Things sound bad on the radio."

Otis nodded. "That's because the big battle hasn't started yet. It'll be fought somewhere north of the city, and that will be the key. However, I know something much more encouraging than that." He leaned forward across the table and lowered his voice. "Help is expected by New Year's Day. Big help. A lot of planes are coming in from aircraft carriers, and they'll make all the difference. Also troopships are on the way from Australia. This is extremely secret, but I think good cause for celebration. In fact," he added with what was meant to be intimacy, "I've told my office I'm taking the afternoon off."

First things first, Judy thought. She hoped the report about help was true. It was hard to know what to believe.

That afternoon, still bored and with nothing to do, she let Frank Otis take her to his house on Taft Avenue. Once there, he was troublesome, but nothing she hadn't handled before. Without protest, in casual thanks for the lunch, she let him kiss her, but when his soft hands started to touch her, she stopped him.

"Please don't, Frank. I have the curse," she lied.

"That doesn't matter. It doesn't matter to me a bit. In fact—"

"Well, it matters to me. I'm sorry, stop it."

"Then how about doing something nice for me?" He tried to move her hand onto him. "Come on, Judy. You know how much I want you. I'm really ready for you."

This was tiresome. His touch was more unpleasant than she'd expected, perhaps because no one had touched her at all since the last night with Brad. But she had a cardinal rule about men: don't burn any bridges, because you never know what might happen tomorrow.

When she finally insisted on going home, she left
Frank Otis disappointed, but optimistic for the future.

———

Brad Stone's company began to lose men during the
march north to Lingayen Gulf. At first he was glad
to be on the move from San Fernando, because he
thought it would give the men a stronger sense of
purpose than the dreary hours of training. The roads
were good, there was plenty of food, and the weather
was dry and warm but not blistering.

The morning after their first encampment, Paradiso reported to him after roll call. In front of the
troops it was "lieutenant" and "sergeant," but in private it was still "Mr. Stone" and "Paradiso," as it
had been the last two years at school.

The former head houseboy was short and stocky,
even shorter than most Filipinos, and his skin was a
darker brown. There was Igorot mountain blood in
his background. He had wide, strong shoulders. His
broad face showed the wrinkles of his age, and his
long black hair frizzled into gray curls above his ears
and at the back of his neck. His hair hung across his
forehead, almost to his eyebrows, in most unmilitary
fashion, but he was easily the most military man in
Brad Stone's company. This morning his bright
brown eyes were narrowed and angry.

"Mr. Stone, four men missing."

"Well, where are they? We have to take off in half
an hour."

Paradiso looked at him. "Not missing. Gone."

"What do you mean? Gone where?"

"Gone home, I think. To their families. Three of them were from the same town, Baliuag." He waved his hand over one shoulder. "It is the other way."

Brad Stone was disgusted—and embarrassed. Not one shot fired yet, and he had already lost four men. Desertion. And there was no time to go searching for them. He would surely catch hell from the regimental commander.

But he didn't, because his company was not alone. At the regimental officers' meeting just before the day's march, it turned out that twenty-three men had vanished during the night.

The colonel, an elderly West Pointer called back from retirement, was not as exercised as Brad thought he should have been. "I want heavy guard posted in every company tonight," the colonel said. "I want all the men reminded that the penalty for desertion in time of war is death. Just make sure everyone understands that. Death. There is to be no more of this."

But there was.

———

Felix Logan was trapped, but at least he was trapped in his favorite city. When the rest of the school returned to Baguio the day after Mr. Watson's Polo Club party, Felix had Dr. Clarke's permission to stay behind for dental work on his braces. Twice a year he had to have new bands put on his front and back teeth to anchor the thick wire that was supposed to be pulling his teeth into correct position. It took three appointments before it was all finished. By that time, when he was ready to return to school, his whole mouth ached—and war had begun.

He had been staying with the Millers, friends of his parents, and now it looked like they were stuck with each other for a while. He couldn't get back to Baguio, because the miltary had taken over all the transportation, and he couldn't get home to Cebu because the interisland steamers were no longer carrying civilian passengers. Now that the dental torture was over, Felix didn't mind too much. He had already missed two basketball games, one of them important, and Jane Barker would now get to edit the next issue of the *Gong*. On the other hand, he was also missing all his classes and all the preholiday tests. And he had these extra days in Manila.

Of all the cities he had lived in—Tokyo, Yokohama, Shanghai, Cebu—he liked Manila best. Of course, he hadn't actually lived in Manila, but he came here so often—on his way to and from school, for basketball games with American School, for special events like Mr. Watson's party—that he felt as though he had.

He liked the way the important buildings were spread along the bay—the Manila Hotel, the High Commissioner's Residence, the Polo Club, the Elks and the Army-Navy Club, the Bayview Hotel. Also the pretty green Luneta Park, with its grassy lawn and walkways and its white stone monument to José Rizal, the revolutionary martyr who had been shot by the Spanish right on this spot. From every one of these places you could look out across the crescent of Manila Bay, ringed by the mountains of Bataan.

Felix liked it much better than the Japanese cities where he had grown up. Quite aside from the war, he also liked the Filipinos much better than the Japs. They were friendlier and better-looking and more fun-loving. Their language was more fun, too, especially the curses and the dirty words, although he hadn't learned nearly as much Tagalog as he had Japanese. Having a Japanese amah and Japanese servants while you were little made a big difference in learning a language. Maybe if he'd had a French amah, he wouldn't be so close to flunking French.

The shoreline wasn't even his favorite part of Manila. The best was the Walled City, which the Spanish had built over three hundred years ago, dark gray stone walls forty feet thick so they could feel really safe. Inside the walls, the narrow streets and crowded little shops made it look like a medieval town, which is just what it was. In spite of the war, the streets were still jammed with automobiles and the new Austin minicabs that people said would soon replace the *calesas*. Felix hoped not. He preferred the picturesque two-wheeled wooden carriages pulled by the little Philippine horses, their long horsecocks bouncing up and down beneath them as they rattled over the cobblestone streets. Tough life for the horses, though. Filipinos weren't very nice to their animals. The *calesa* drivers relied on whips and shouts.

One afternoon when he was in the Walled City, he walked across Jones Bridge to the Escolta and dropped in at Mr. Watson's office to see his new friend Miranda.

She jumped up from her desk and gave him her happy gold-toothed smile. "Felix! But you are supposed to be back in Baguio."

He explained about being trapped by his dentist and then by the war. She worried about where he was living, and he told her that the Millers had taken him in.

"Mr. Watson isn't here," she said, "but he will worry about you"—which Felix very much doubted. "This war is very dangerous," Miranda said solemnly. "The Japanese are very wicked to us. You must be careful, Felix. Those bombs can drop anywhere."

Felix wished he were old enough and brave enough to ask her to see a movie with him, but she would laugh at him. Besides, she was engaged. He promised to be careful.

Amos Watson kept a large amount of cash in his steel safe at home, usually a hundred thousand pesos or more. The Philippines was the kind of country where the need for substantial cash could arise without warning—for a sudden business opportunity, for a payoff, for a "gift" to a worthy government official, or to help someone out of trouble in return for some future consideration. It was a country where, at the right moment, ready cash sometimes had much more than its face value.

In the last days before the war, instinct told him to increase his cash, just in case. He doubled it. And when the war did begin, he prudently increased it again. He had no experience with war—World War

I had scarcely touched the islands—but he knew it meant uncertainty, and uncertainty always meant business opportunities. With Germany and Italy jumping into the war behind Japan, there might be excellent real estate bargains if people got panicky. He could always put the money back in the bank if he turned out to be mistaken, but if things got difficult, he wasn't so sure he could always take it out. He had lived here too many years to trust in providence. Cash made him comfortable.

He advised Papaya to get cash too.

"Where am I supposed to keep it, in my evening purse? Everybody doesn't have a big safe."

"Safe-deposit box, if you like. But you must have some place at home." Amos had never been in the house Papaya bought for her mother, herself and her younger half sister when she began making good money from her records.

"Like some secret panel, no? You think every Filipino house has a secret panel?"

"Where do you keep your ruby necklace?"

"You think I am going to tell you that, Amos baby? Then someday if you get mad at me, you come and take it back."

"Good. Then you can put some pesos in the same hiding place."

"How many?"

"Many."

———

Sam Phipps knew nothing about military tactics and did not plan to learn, but he wondered why Mac-

Arthur wasn't sending his army to attack the Jap landings on Luzon, way up in Aparri and at Vigan and down south in Legaspi. They were reported to be small landings, and MacArthur, with more than twenty thousand U.S. troops and Philippine Scouts and another hundred thousand Filipino troops, could wipe them out. After all, the General had been saying for months that he would attack any invasion at the beaches. Here were the beaches. Where was the attack?

Phipps got his answer from the newspapers. MacArthur explained to reporters that General Homma's little Luzon landings were a transparent attempt to make him spread out his own army in three far-flung directions. He told the press, "The basic principle in handling my troops is to hold them intact until the enemy commits himself in force."

From the message traffic concerning the movement of U.S. troops to Lingayen, Phipps thought MacArthur must be pretty sure that was where things were going to happen. Never having seen Lingayen Gulf except on a map, Phipps wondered how MacArthur could be so sure.

———

By the time his company reached its assigned position above the beaches of Lingayen, Brad Stone had been strafed for the first time and had lost eight more men—only one of them to the strafing. On the road between Tarlac and Bayambang, a single Zero came over the Zambales Mountains to their left, swooped down on them, fired one long string of machine-gun bullets at the diving, scrambling troops and then flew on about its business, whatever that was. The string of bullets killed three men in Company B, but Brad Stone lost only a private named Gonzales, badly wounded in the right thigh. Because it was the company's first casualty, everyone tried to gather around to look at the wound and listen to Gonzales yell. Paradiso got rid of them with the warning that the Zero might return at any moment. Gonzales was sent back to the hospital in Tarlac.

Six more men simply vanished in spite of guards being posted every night. In fact, two of the disappearances were guards.

The eighth man was shot and killed by Paradiso.

"He was deserting," Paradiso explained, reporting the death first thing in the morning.

"How do you know that?" Brad Stone was shocked. "He could have just been headed for the latrine."

"He had his pack."

"That doesn't prove he was deserting. Maybe he was afraid someone would steal his stuff."

Paradiso's dark brown face was tough and expressionless. "He made trouble. He was no good."

"That doesn't change anything. If you were so sure he was deserting, you should have halted him and put him under arrest."

Paradiso shrugged and said nothing.

"I have to report this to headquarters."

"Why is that, Mr. Stone?"

"Because you can't just go around shooting our own men, that's why. For God's sake, Paradiso."

"What do you want me to do now?"

Brad Stone rubbed his hand over his forehead, thinking hard. Of course, he would have to report it. But he also didn't want to lose his sergeant. How could he put this to the adjutant in the best light for Paradiso? "What have you done with him?"

Paradiso smiled. "He is where he fell down. So everybody can see him."

After two years of daily contact, Brad Stone had thought he knew this man very well. Although Dr. Clarke had final say on everything at Simpson, he gave Brad the job of dealing with the large Filipino staff—the houseboys, cooks and gardeners. What this really meant was dealing with Paradiso, who ran everybody else. He kept good discipline and knew how everything should be done, because he could do it all himself. The school seldom had to call on a local carpenter or plumber or electrician, because Paradiso was all of these. Brad's job was light, because Paradiso was so easy to work with—polite, efficient and very smart. Now he had just shot a fellow soldier and was displaying the body as an object lesson to the rest of the company.

"Get him buried," Brad said. "Right away."

"Yes, sir."

Brad need not have worried about the adjutant. The adjutant was, in fact, delighted. "So we finally caught one of those deserters right in the fucking act. Good work, Stone. The colonel will want to spread the word to the other companies. We'll list him killed in action, of course. This is no time for a lot of paperwork."

Brad Stone had visited Lingayen Gulf twice before today. It was only a couple of hours by bus down the mountains from Baguio, so each year the school took a one-day swimming holiday at the Lingayen beaches, where the water was almost skin temperature.

The gulf was a deep rectangular scoop out of the Luzon coast, a huge tongue twenty-five miles wide and thirty miles long, lapping into the land. At the tip of the tongue and all along one side from Dagupan to Bauang lay the beaches, seventeen of them suitable for enemy landings, according to Colonel Ambrose. From the tip of the tongue to Manila, more than a hundred miles away, stretched the Luzon Plain, which had the richest agricultural land—rice, sugar cane, vegetables—and the best roads in the country. Only the extinct volcano of Mount Arayat broke the serene flatness of the plain.

On a bright sunny day like this, the water was pale blue-green against the dazzling sands. Behind the white, inviting beaches, the coconut palms arched gracefully into the sky.

———

Sandy Homobono enjoyed the discomfiture of the Americans. He was not allowed to print much of what he heard, but this did not lessen his pleasure. The Americans had made an incredible mess of Clark Field, letting the Japs catch all their planes on the ground, and because of that, the Americans had also managed to lose Cavite. Those bases were the perfect symbols of American colonialism, and it served the

Americans right that they had been the very first things to go.

It seemed to Sandy as though he had spent all his life waiting for Philippine independence, and it was still five years away. Four and a half, to be exact. July 4, 1946. The American Congress, as a final insult, had even foisted its own Independence Day on the Filipinos.

Many Filipinos felt as he did, and even more of them would if they understood the situation. Sandy acknowledged that his countrymen were still pitifully ignorant. Too many of them loved the Americans and all things American—the cars, the radios, the popular music, the sharkskin suits, the Hawaiian shirts. Even the comic strips. They had imported *Bringing Up Father* and rechristened Jiggs and Maggie Don Pancho and Doña Ramona. If it was American, it was good.

Filipinos didn't realize that the Americans owned and ran most important businesses—except those owned and run by the Spanish or the British or the Chinese or the Japanese. Any nationality would do, as long as it wasn't Filipino. Of course, the Americans claimed they were preparing the Filipinos for independence, but Sandy would have preferred quick freedom, even if it meant making a few more mistakes.

Maybe the Americans, now that they had made such a mess of the war's beginning, would speed up independence. Unlike old Amos Watson, Sandy Homobono didn't think the Japanese could take the islands. The Americans would pull themselves together after this initial shock. Already MacArthur was build-

ing new airstrips to receive the planes that were expected to arrive from aircraft carriers. Eventually
there would be troopships crossing the Pacific. But
Sandy heard Admiral Hart was moving U.S. Navy
headquarters from the Philippines to the Dutch Indies.
Maybe that was a significant step away from colonial
rule. Every little bit would help.

And even if the Japanese did invade the Philippines,
at least they were Asians, not white monkeys.

———

Major Jack Humphrey's Scouts were being held in
reserve outside Tarlac, almost fifty miles behind the
Lingayen beaches. It was, of course, an honor to be
picked as the reserve force, held in readiness for wherever they were most badly needed. It was a tribute to
the Scouts' tradition of excellence. Just the same,
Humphrey would rather be fifty miles farther north,
where the action was likely to begin. He wondered
where his two sergeants, Olivo and Dubang, were
stationed now. Probably right up there at Lingayen.
Now that war had actually begun, Humphrey was
going to have one hell of a time getting them back
from Master Sergeant Maxsie.

———

"I'm asked to dinner at Mr. Watson's," Felix told
Mrs. Miller. "He's sending a car for me."

"Felix dear," Mrs. Miller said, "you can't just go
out at night with this curfew. You won't be able to
get home. You know that. Now you just stay here
and study."

"Mr. Watson has a military pass," Felix said. "He can send me home by car."

"How can he have a military pass?"

"I don't know, he just has one."

"My goodness. Well, I guess it's all right. I didn't know you were such good friends."

"We aren't. His secretary thinks he's worried about me."

"He's supposed to have a lovely house. You keep your eyes open so you can tell me all about it."

Miranda had said it was to be informal, but Felix wore a jacket anyway.

Mr. Watson's driver picked him up in a black Buick and drove him out Dewey Boulevard, the broad avenue that ran along the rim of Manila Bay. Lots of soldiers and military trucks were on the street. In front of the High Commissioner's Residence, U.S. Marines stood guard at the closed wrought-iron gate.

Several blocks south the Buick turned in at a gravel driveway and deposited him under a porte cochere. The big old-style mansion was set well back from the boulevard and surrounded by green lawn and palm trees and tropical bushes. The thatch roof was steep. A veranda ran the entire length of the house, and behind it Felix could see that the walls were open to the breeze from the bay. Heavy wooden shutters, now pulled aside, could slide closed against the rains and the typhoon winds.

Felix walked up the wide front stairs, through a dark foyer and into the living room, which was only slightly smaller than the Simpson basketball court. Felix whistled through his braces, glad he had decided to wear a jacket. The high, open ceiling had long, thin rafters strung from one wall to the other. Air plants and orchids hung from the rafters by slender chains. The dark wood floor had only occasional scattered straw rugs to emphasize the color of the wood. Philippine floors were polished by a houseboy with his bare feet slipped into straps of split coconut husks so that he could skate back and forth, the coconut oil imparting its rich sheen to the wood, the harsh fibers polishing it. This gleaming floor must take a full day's skating.

The furniture was low and open-backed. No overstuffed American couches or chairs or cushions to hold body heat. Two gigantic rattan peacock chairs, the biggest Felix had ever seen, faced each other across the length of a narra-wood coffee table the size of his bed at school. A low bamboo couch stretched the length of the coffee table between the peacock chairs. The dark wood walls held no paintings, only an occasional woodcarving. Wall sconces with candle-shaped bulbs, now lighted against the darkening evening, ringed the entire room. It all looked like some Cecil B. De Mille movie about India, except for the absence of tiger skins.

And here, through the wide, open arch at the opposite end of the room, came the pukka sahib himself, followed by a Filipino houseboy about half his size, dressed in a white uniform. Mr. Watson wore a pale blue *barong* with short sleeves and white trousers that matched his bushy hair and eyebrows. It all looked so exactly right that Felix felt like clapping.

"Well, Felix," Mr. Watson said in his deep voice,

shaking hands, "so everybody got home from the party except you. Take off that jacket and be comfortable. What will you have to drink, and how do you like your steak done?"

Felix asked for a cuba libre and rare steak, if rare was all right with Mr. Watson.

"That's the reason for individual steaks. One rare, Carlos, and mine as usual. And I'll have a gin and *kalamansi* juice. Tell Ling dinner in half an hour."

They had their drinks sitting in the peacock chairs, and Mr. Watson asked him how he was getting along. When Felix said he hoped he could get home to Cebu for Christmas, Mr. Watson shook his head and said he doubted it.

At dinner, alone at the huge mahogany table, they had shrimp cocktail—the tiny Philippine variety— then shell steaks and a spicy rice ring with creamed spinach in the middle topped with slices of hard-boiled egg.

"You'd better have seconds on that," Mr. Watson said, "or my Chinese cook will be hurt."

It was so good that Felix had thirds. The steaks were wonderful, too, even better than at the Polo Club party.

When Felix had finally finished the main course, the houseboy Carlos brought in large cut-glass bowls of mango ice cream.

"How many years did you live in Japan?" Mr. Watson asked.

"Eleven. I was born there."

"Yes, I know. Miranda says you even went to a Japanese school for a while."

"Yes, sir, but just for a year in Yokohama. My father thought it would be a good experience."

"And was it?"

"I guess so."

"Do you speak Japanese?"

"Oh, sure. I mean, yes, sir. Not like I used to, but I can understand pretty much everything. I practice some in the Jap stores here and up in Baguio."

Mr. Watson looked thoughtful. "I don't think you should do that anymore."

"Why not?"

Mr. Watson spread his big bony hands. "People misunderstand. If they hear an American boy speaking Japanese in wartime, they might get very angry. Also . . ." He paused, thinking this over. "It might be useful to keep your knowledge of Japanese a secret."

The tone made Felix think this subject of the Japanese might somehow be the whole point of their dinner together, but he didn't understand why. "Why, sir? I mean, how could it be useful?"

This time the pause was much longer. Finally Mr. Watson said, "Well, let's just say that in a war you never know what's going to happen. Do you like coffee?"

———

The war was just under two weeks old when the message was passed on by the navy. On December 20, a U.S. sub had spotted many Japanese cruisers and troopships north of Luzon. Sam Phipps knew this must be what MacArthur had been waiting for, a serious commitment by General Homma. Now, after this quiet waiting period, MacArthur would at last be able to strike. Phipps was sure of it when the few surviving Flying Fortresses were sent to bomb the approaching Jap fleet. He was disappointed when they reported no hits on the troopships, but it probably didn't matter. MacArthur had always said he would repel any invasion at the beaches.

Three days before Christmas the Japanese landed just where MacArthur thought they would, just where he had planted his troops, on the beaches of Lingayen Gulf. Phipps was impressed by the General's foresight. Colonel Sampson and the other communications officers told Phipps that you could always count on the Old Man to guess just where and when an attack was coming.

As the junior officer in a nest of loyalists, Phipps decided not to ask how come the Old Man hadn't guessed about Clark Field two weeks ago. He'd had nine hours' warning, but his air force had been destroyed on the ground. Even with discreet questioning and careful reading of the message traffic, Phipps could not learn what had gone wrong. He could only guess. MacArthur being waked up out of a sound sleep in the middle of the night to learn he had a war on his hands. So much to be done, so many questions to be asked, so many decisions to be made with very little solid information to go on. Maybe the Old Man froze. Maybe he just forgot to think air force. Maybe, maybe . . .

Whatever it was, Phipps had not forgotten Colonel Sampson's explanation of that cable from Washington telling MacArthur not to "jeopardize your defense." It meant that no matter what, MacArthur was expected to protect his command. You didn't have to be a West Point officer, or even a Yale English major, to realize that he had failed to do that.

Sam Phipps couldn't believe what happened next—or how incredibly fast it happened. Even when he wasn't on duty, he took to hanging around the message center to keep track of what was obviously a collapse.

At Lingayen, facing professional Japanese troops, the raw Filipino units threw away their rifles and ran, some for the Zambales foothills, some back along the highways toward Manila, with the Jap army in pursuit. News from the field was so bad, and also so confused, that MacArthur drove out into the Luzon Plain to get accurate information from his field officers. At least the American troops and the Philippine Scouts were said to be fighting and delaying and trying to hold. Phipps couldn't tell what was going on. Somewhere a big pitched battle was supposed to be shaping up, but even with careful reading of all the message traffic, Phipps couldn't figure out where it was going to be. He wondered if war was always so confused.

Then bad, definite news came in. The Japs had made another big landing at Lamon Bay south of Manila and were driving straight for the city from sixty miles away. Two fast Jap armies were converging on Manila from two directions. The message went out by radio to every American and Philippine unit that could still be reached: War Plan Orange.

Even Phipps knew what this was, because Mac-Arthur had publicly derided it as "defeatist." It was the old Washington war plan to defend the Philippines by holing up on Bataan. Defeatist or not, two things were clearly wrong with it now: the American and Philippine forces weren't on Bataan, and all the supplies and food for a proper defense were in warehouses and depots far out on the Luzon Plain.

———

Christmas Eve in Manila. A calm, warm night with a bright moon shining down on the bay.

Felix Logan listened to the radio with the Millers, who always wanted to hear the latest shortwave war news from San Francisco. Felix did not pay close attention. This would be the first Christmas he had spent away from his family.

Sandy Homobono was writing a rush, one-subject column on what it would mean for Manila to be declared an open city, as MacArthur said was being considered. It was a difficult column, because he had little to work with except his imagination. Besides, he could not write what he really thought, that "open city" meant "I quit."

Papaya's mother was desolate because she could not attend a midnight Christmas Eve mass, as she had done every year she could remember. Papaya and her younger sister, Karen, tried to cheer her up by singing Christmas carols.

Amos Watson dined alone in his house, served by Carlos, who was uncharacteristically silent throughout the meal. As he drank most of his next-to-last bottle of the 1921 Château Ausone, Amos thought about what he must do and about whom he could count on. Among other things, he decided that in the next few days he would drink the last bottle of this splendid wine, although it would still be splendid twenty years from now.

Judy Ferguson, alone in her small room at the San Luis Hotel, cried for the first time since childhood, when a diagnosis of measles had made her miss a birthday party.

Sam Phipps, clutching his field pack and his one allotted suitcase, stood on the very crowded deck of the steamer *Don Esteban* as it chugged out to the island of Corregidor, carrying the General and his family as well as his staff. He had actually seen MacArthur walk up the gangplank. Since Corregidor was a fairly small island, he would probably encounter MacArthur face-to-face, but this prospect did not terrify him the way it once had. Because he had had only a few hours' warning and because he had been so excited, Sam Phipps was only now remembering several items he wished he had packed. He had even forgotten his razor.

The war was seventeen days old.

≡ 6 ≡

A Time for Choices

Brad Stone had eleven men left in his company when he reported to his regiment to learn about the surrender.

Colonel Ambrose was resigned in defeat. His troops had quit on him by the hundreds, and now he was quitting too.

"I have spoken to a General Ishita," he told his officers. "Through his interpreter, of course. He will accept our surrender at eleven hundred hours."

Nobody said anything. They all looked as ragged and hot and dirty as Brad felt. It was only twenty-four hours after the Japanese landing, which they had done nothing to oppose. Instead, they had watched their untrained men break away in a tide so large and swift that it could not be halted. Brad's company, what remained of it, was stationed at the left flank of the regiment on the far left corner of the beaches, below the mountains. It had not fired a shot.

"There is no alternative," Ambrose apologized. "We are completely cut off from our forces. Your men will be permitted to take their field packs. They will stack their rifles under those palm trees and then stand formation until further orders. I have the assurance of General Ishita—through his interpreter, that is—that we will be treated as honorable prisoners of war. Dismiss."

Brad Stone walked slowly back toward his company. He had been in uniform less than two months. Two months ago he was a history teacher, dancing with Judy Ferguson at the Fiesta Pavilion, and then making love to her through that long wonderful night. He wondered where she was now and what she was doing. Manila had been bombed. She could be dead. The way this attack had gone, Manila might easily be captured and he might never see her again, or might never even hear what happened to her.

This attack. Brad Stone was angry and ashamed—for his company, his army, his country and himself. The regiment had been so far to the left of the landings that he had not even had a chance to shoot at the enemy. The war had only just begun, and already he was told to surrender. For years he had been studying history and then teaching it, but it had never occurred to him that he might participate in history. Now that he had actually become a participant, his first act would be to surrender.

That was not why he had volunteered. Judy and many of his friends thought he was crazy, but Brad knew exactly why he'd done it. Because it was right. Because he knew he could help, could contribute. He had made up his mind and nothing could shake him. But now this. Now "honorable prisoner of war."

He stopped walking. No, he thought. Not me. By God, not me. I haven't even fought yet.

His step picked up. He knew absolutely what he was going to do.

His eleven men were seated on the ground in a rough circle under the shade of a cluster of palms. It was easy to pick out Paradiso, because his skin was a darker brown than the others'. They got to their feet at his approach.

"The colonel has surrendered," he said, angry at having to report the news. He looked at his watch. "In one hour we're to turn in our rifles and become prisoners." He looked at Paradiso's dark, expressionless face. "Sergeant, you will be in charge. I'm not going."

Paradiso's face did not change. "Where will you go, Mr. Stone?"

Paradiso had forgotten to call him lieutenant. Well, it didn't matter now. "I'll try to get back to Baguio." At least he knew the way there, and it had been his only home in the Philippines. He would find some way to survive in that familiar landscape.

Paradiso shook his head. "Too many Japs. You never get there."

Brad could see several of the others nodding. A white American officer would stand little chance crossing the lowlands to reach the mountain road up to Baguio. Maybe if he tried at night? He didn't know what else to do, where else to go. Manila was out of the question now. The only thing he was sure of was that he did not intend to become an honorable prisoner of war.

"Well," he said to Paradiso, "what do you suggest? I'm not surrendering."

Paradiso gestured with his chin, the way Filipinos often did, without using their hands. He was indicating the close green foothills over his shoulder. "Zambales. I come with you." He looked around at the others. "Who else is coming?"

A long moment of silence before one said, "Zambales Mountains is very bad country. Nothing to eat. And many serpents."

A bright-faced boy named Rosauro, who looked too young to be in uniform, said, "Oh sir, that is not true. Not too many bad snakes. I am born from Carabangay, right below the mountains. Very nice." He drew himself up. "I will come. I will be your guide. I will be the one."

"Good," Brad said. "Who else? We're going to fight the Japs, not look at snakes. Make it quick."

Six men elected to join Brad Stone and Paradiso and Rosauro. Brad was not surprised. These were the men who had stayed with the company to the end. They must have stayed for some reason other than fear of being shot by Paradiso. But now they must move out fast before anybody came looking for them.

"Packs and rifles and as much ammunition as you can carry," Brad said. "Two days' field rations."

"Mr. Stone," Paradiso said, forgetting the title again, "everybody carry two rifles. Plenty of food around here. We worry about food later."

Paradiso was right. Any kind of military operation would require as many rifles and as much ammunition as they could carry. Enfield rifles were lying all around the beach where they had been flung before the company disintegrated into flight.

"All right, everybody pick up another rifle. Let's move out."

———

Jack Humphrey knew his Scouts were in bad trouble when he saw the first Jap tanks rumbling and clanking toward him out of the early twilight. Through the thick dust cloud rising over the flat green Luzon Plain, he could see infantry following close behind. A major attack.

Until then his afternoon had been relatively quiet, broken only by the occasional appearance of one of the tiny Jap observation planes. He had used the time to dig in and strengthen his battalion's position on both sides of the gravel road leading south to Bridge 31, one of the lines of retreat toward Bataan. He thought he was ready to handle any infantry likely to be thrown at him, especially this late in the day. For serious work, the Japs usually preferred dawn and daylight. Humphrey had been ordered to hold here only until dawn tomorrow, when he and his men would themselves retreat across the bridge, after which it would be blown. However, that neat head-quarters plan had made no allowance for tanks.

He called in to report the attack and to ask for air support, knowing he couldn't expect any. The only planes over central Luzon these days were Japanese. He hadn't seen an American plane in three days, and he didn't know if there were any left. He didn't know whether there were any antitank field pieces within twenty miles of him. What he did know was that his own trench mortars and machine guns weren't going to stop those eight tanks. He gave orders to fire anyway, just to give the Japs pause, give them something to think about.

Through his glasses he could see that, as usual, half the old mortar shells were duds. Grenades had proved almost as bad. The mortar shells that did explode on the tanks had little effect. The tanks kept coming down the gravel road between the banana trees and the neat squares of the brilliant green rice paddies. Perfect tank country: flat, open, only an occasional river as a natural obstacle—and even the rivers were low during this dry season.

At half a mile the tanks opened fire. The muzzle blasts flashed orange in the gathering dark. The high-velocity shells screamed in.

Hunched down against the explosions, Jack Humphrey thought about prospects. Not good. No stopping the tanks with what he had. He could stay where he was until their position was overrun and the battalion obliterated, which would not take very long. But that waste wouldn't even accomplish anything. When it was over, the Jap tanks and infantry would have a clear run down to Bridge 31, where his own army's retreat was supposed to be going on all night.

He made up his mind. He sent word to his company commanders: Abandon position. Move out rapidly east and north to get well behind tanks. Then attack their infantry in full force from flank and rear.

He set the attack for ninety minutes from now, hoping that allowed enough time to get through the rice paddies and reach attacking position in what by then would be total darkness. His Scouts were well trained in night maneuver, and he was counting on darkness to add helpful confusion.

The attack took place on time, and after that Jack Humphrey got all the confusion he could possibly have asked for. The Jap infantry, moving confidently down the road in the thin moonlight behind the shelter of its tanks, was totally surprised to be hit from the rear in force. The return fire was scattered and demoralized. The Scouts' first wave drove the Japs off the road and into the rice fields. It was only a few mintues before Humphrey got the first result he was hoping for. The tanks stopped, swung around to meet the threat and began firing into the darkness. Luckily they couldn't see enough to do much damage. Humphrey pressed his attack.

At last came the second hoped-for result. The tanks clanked back up the road the way they had come, then turned into the rice fields toward the Scouts.

"Come on," Humphrey said out loud. "Come get us. Come chase us."

The tanks came churning through the paddies, still firing, their treads chewing up somebody's rice crop, the Jap infantry now forming behind its armor.

Communication between the frazzled Scout units across the soggy rice fields in dim moonlight while under constant fire from eight tank guns left something to be desired. By runners, Humphrey kept sending word: fall back, keep firing, stay in touch if you can.

All through the night they kept drawing the Jap

force into open country and away from Bridge 31, but in the process they backed into several U.S. units headed for the bridge. Nobody knew who anybody was in the darkness. Indiscriminate firing took place. Unfortunately, one of the retreating U.S. units was a Philippine Scouts cavalry troop, leading all its horses. In the black confusion of the night with gunfire spewing everywhere, the terrified horses broke loose and, snorting and screaming, charged wildly in all directions.

Jack Humphrey, trying to keep his battalion under some semblance of command, never knew when a berserk cavalry mount would come careening out of the night, eyeballs rolling and glaring white, hooves ready to cut and chop at anything it saw. The crazed horses were more terrifying than the tanks.

When sunrise came, Humphrey's scattered battalion was miles away from where it was supposed to be. He couldn't tell how many men he had lost as casualties and how many were only temporarily lost. A lot of each, no doubt. Wherever the battalion was now, it sure wasn't going to make it across Bridge 31 before demolition time. But the Jap tank assault never got there either. Humphrey's Scouts had saved the bridge.

After the endless night, Jack Humphrey was too weary to know what he and his Scouts should do next. He figured if they all just sat down for a few minutes and rested, somebody would find him and tell him where to go.

———

Ten thousand troops as well as many civilians were crammed onto the rugged three-and-a-half-mile-long island of Corregidor. Sam Phipps now saw Mac-Arthur every day. He even got used to it.

Early each morning, after spending the night in his hilltop quarters at Topside, the General marched into the underground communications center in the stone-arched Malinta Tunnel, the centerpiece of a labyrinthine system carved into the rock. Sometimes he spoke a quick good morning to the teams lined up at their field desks against the tunnel walls. More often, tall, grim and silent, he walked straight to his desk at the end of the lateral, not speaking to anyone. His khakis were clean and neatly pressed, his shirt open at the throat, his dark hair combed across his head. His four silver stars gleamed dully in the dim electric light.

From his desk poured an incredible stream of messages, instructions, recommendations, orders and exhortations. The General, maps constantly spread flat before him, smoking an occasional cigarette in his long holder, tried to yank and twist and guide his two reeling armies away from the Japanese divisions and into the citadel of Bataan.

Sam Phipps had never in his life worked so hard—or with such excruciating care. MacArthur's northern army had to hold and fight and delay and stall, constantly falling back to new positions, until his southern army could be moved past Manila, around the long rim of the bay and onto the peninsula. Only then would the northern army, if it still existed, be able to retreat to Bataan. After each carefully orchestrated fallback, bridges had to be blown up to delay the Japs again, but they could not be blown before MacArthur was sure each of his disheveled units was safely across.

Message after message. Hold here at all costs until 0600. Move here at 1600, bypassing this battalion on your right. Bridge 17 must be demolished at 1445 without fail, repeat without fail. You will be relieved in three hours and thereupon will take up new position with the following map coordinates. . . .

Sam Phipps drove himself and his radio and phone operators crazy, proofreading and rechecking each new order to make certain that every hour and every coordinate and every place name and number went out to the field exactly as dictated by the tall figure at the end of the tunnel. Sam Phipps had the delirious conviction that if one message went out containing one error, the entire maneuver would collapse and War Plan Orange would fail. If it was going to fail, it must not be because of a message error. At the end of each shift, exhausted, he would review the day's traffic, just to make sure one more time that no error had slipped past. Sometimes he would fall into his bunk in the dormitory tunnel without eating, then wake up starving after a few hours of sleep.

One morning he spotted something wrong in a message. A Philippine Scouts infantry unit was being ordered to withdraw immediately from Point A to Point B, taking up its new position in two hours. This *can't* be right, he thought. I'm sure that unit isn't at Point A, it's ten miles north of there. It can't possibly get to that new position on time.

"Hold that one," he said.

"But, sir, it says 'Immediate.' "

"I know, just hold it one second."

Hands shaking with impatience, he fluttered through yesterday's late-afternoon traffic, looking for what he thought he remembered. Yes, there it was! The Scouts unit was right where he thought.

"Don't send that," he said. "Give it to me."

He hurried to Colonel Sampson and handed him the two messages. "Sir, this isn't right. Look, that unit isn't where this new message says it is."

The colonel scanned the two brief orders. "Jesus, Eli. Wait here."

Colonel Sampson hurried to the desk at the end of the lateral, and Phipps could see him lean down to speak to the General. MacArthur looked up, listened, looked at the papers and then answered something back. Colonel Sampson turned away, but MacArthur called him back to say something more.

Christ, Phipps thought, I'm going to get the Medal of Honor.

Sampson came back to where Phipps was standing and thrust the message at him. "Send that, lieutenant. As is, and right this fucking second. And then the Old Man wants to see you."

Oh God, Sam Phipps thought, what did I do wrong? He had never before spoken to General MacArthur. And it would be the firing squad, not the Medal of Honor.

He watched to make sure the message went out exactly as written, then took the interminable walk to the desk and came to attention. MacArthur's head was bent over his maps. Phipps looked down on the thinning black hair.

Finally he said, in a voice hard to recognize as his own, "Sir, Lieutenant Phipps reports as requested."

MacArthur looked up, with the most piercing eyes Phipps had ever seen. The wide mouth was clamped shut in a severe, straight line. The curved nose pointed at Phipps like a scimitar. For several endless seconds of appraisal, MacArthur said nothing. Phipps could feel the sweat flowing under his arms. *I was not meant to be a soldier.*

"I understand, lieutenant," MacArthur said in his measured, resonant voice, "that you saw fit to question my order."

"Yes, sir." He was enough of a soldier to know that was all he should say.

"On what grounds, may I ask?"

He could hardly avoid answering, but at least he could keep it brief and take his punishment. "Sir, I thought the Scouts unit was in a different location."

"I see." The piercing eyes, from which there was no escape, seemed not to blink at all. "And why is that?"

MacArthur had to know the answer already. Sampson had shown him both pieces of paper. "Sir, I remembered a message from yesterday."

"In view of the volume and detailed nature of the traffic," said the General, "that would seem to indicate a prodigious memory."

Since no suitable comment occurred to him, Phipps kept silent.

"Calamitously for you, lieutenant, I have spoken

this morning with General Wainwright. Because of a ferocious Jap tank assault during the night, the Scouts were not only dislodged from their assigned position but driven far behind it. They are now in perilous circumstance, from which I am endeavoring to rescue them. An endeavor you have elected to thwart."

MacArthur spoke in words and cadences that might have come straight from literature—perhaps from Sir Walter Scott, or maybe Gibbon without the sarcasm. Yet he did not grope for his language. It just rolled out.

"On the other hand," said the General, and now he held up his right hand, hand, the long fingers pressed close together, as though to ward off not a danger but an intolerable affront to his presence, "it is conceivable, in such desperate operations as we are now engaged, that a mistake could have been made. That would be tragic." He nodded several times to Phipps, the eyes still piercing. "Tragic beyond measure."

Phipps thought it was a good moment to say, "Yes, sir," although MacArthur's tone indicated that such a mistake was extremely unlikely.

"Accordingly, every precaution must be taken. Every precaution we can devise. But next time you question my orders," MacArthur said with a sudden smile, a truly generous smile of reprieve, "you had better be right."

"Yes, sir!"

"I understand you are known by the sobriquet of Eli. Get back to work, Eli."

———

Amos Watson was putting together his team before the Japanese arrived in Manila. Once they came, it would be impossible to arrange things, so he was doing it now. He didn't know what kind of game his team would be in, or what the rules would be, but he knew he wanted to play. He hoped the others would join.

He softened up Papaya by feeding her a big lunch in his backyard pagoda. It wasn't really a pagoda, but that's what Marian had called it. An octagonal wooden structure with open sides, it had a thatched roof of nipa palm to protect the white wicker furniture from rain. He had built it of natural-finish wood to blend into the garden so that Marian would have a pleasant outdoor spot for small lunches or afternoon bridge. However, she preferred the Polo Club for both rituals. Amos used it occasionally for private business discussions away from the bustle of house and phone servants.

Carlos brought their lunch tray. The square, flat monkeywood plates held split avocados stuffed with fresh crabmeat and tiny shrimp. The basket of rolls had been home-baked by Ling this morning. The iced tea sprouted sprigs of fresh mint from the garden.

Papaya ate like a starved animal, with gusto. Three rolls with butter and strawberry jam, every speck of seafood, and every spoonful of the big ripe avocado. She still had room for the dessert of sliced oranges sprinkled with shredded coconut and the platter of chocolate cookies.

"I'm glad the war hasn't spoiled your appetite," Amos said dryly, as she finally put down her dessert spoon.

Papaya smiled. She was used to his teasing about her weight and appetite. "It takes energy to sing," she said.

She was simply dressed today. A plain short-sleeved blouse of coarse white cotton, open at the throat. No orchid in her black hair. No jewelry except two wooden bracelets. He wondered when he would see her next, and under what circumstances. Depending on the Japanese, this might be their last meeting for quite some time.

"Why do you need energy? You said you were going to retire when the Japanese came."

"I am. I will." She reached for the next-to-last chocolate cookie, nibbled it and smiled at him. "But they are not here yet."

"Yes. Well." Time to begin his pitch. "Papaya, I've been thinking a great deal about what is going to happen to all of us in the next few weeks and months. You, me, everybody. I don't think you should give up singing."

She was surprised. When it had become plain a week ago that Manila was bound to fall, they had discussed her retirement at length. She had enough money. Since she was a Philippine citizen, the Japanese would leave her and her family alone. No reason for her to go on working during Japanese occupation, when conditions might be unpleasant, especially for an attractive young woman.

"Why are you changing your mind, Amos baby?

I don't want to sing for those shitty little people."

Her directness made him laugh. He patted her hand with pleasure. Then he spoke seriously. "Let me tell you why I've changed my thinking," he said. "We're not just losing. We've lost."

She shook her head, also serious now. "The Americans are sending help."

"Maybe. Sometime. I don't know how soon, but I doubt that it will be soon enough to matter. By then the Philippines will be gone."

"Amos baby, like everybody said, you are too defeatist. You need more faith."

"Yes. Well. In any case, when the Americans do come, whenever that is, they will need information. About the Japs, everything about them. Troops, ships, supplies, defense—all kinds of information. I intend to help collect it for them."

"How are you going to do that? You said they would put all the Americans in prison camp."

"Yes, almost certainly. So it will take some arranging. And quite a lot of money, too, I suspect. But they won't intern the Filipinos, because you are their Asian brothers."

"Ha!"

"Yes, ha, but anyway you will be free, even though we Americans won't be. That means *you* can get information and pass it on."

She opened her eyes wide. "You mean"—she giggled at the thought—"you think I should be a spy?"

Amos nodded. "Yes. In fact, I think this whole country should become a spy. Also I think there will be many ways to make life difficult for the Japanese. Perhaps some of them very small ways, I don't know. But maybe some big ways, too."

He could see she liked the idea, as he had hoped she would.

Then she giggled again. "I don't know anything about this spy business."

"I don't either, but I've been thinking about it a lot. It seems like a good way to get even, or at least cause the Japanese a lot of trouble."

"That would be fun."

"Yes. Also dangerous. Extremely dangerous. Spies get shot, you know."

"That is in movies," Papaya said. "I was shot in a movie once, did you know that? At the very end, by my angry lover. It was terribly sad. I sang this last song and then I died. The audience always cried."

"Papaya, this is serious."

"Okay, I am serious. What do I do?"

"You go on singing. Once they get settled in, I'm sure the Japanese will set up their usual busy nightlife. Beer and scotch and saki. And always music. Night-clubs, hotels, cabarets, whatever. That's where you sing—and listen."

"Listen? You mean I am supposed to *talk* to the Japs?"

"How else will you learn anything? Yes, not only talk to them but be nice to them. And not just the army and navy officers. There'll be businessmen and engineers and government administrators. They'll all be far from home and, I am sure, very lonesome for pretty girls. If you sing them sentimental songs and smile a lot and act sympathetic, I'm sure they will pour their hearts out to you."

Flash of anger in the brown eyes. "Amos, I am not going to be some kind of spy whore and make *suksok* with those ugly little men. Get somebody else."

"Of course not. Singing and talking and listening don't mean screwing."

Papaya shook her plump shoulders, mollified. "Okay. So everybody is telling me their favorite big military secrets. Then what?"

"I don't know. I'll get you some help, but—"

He stopped, because Carlos was coming down the stepping-stone path through the warm garden sunlight to collect their lunch dishes. Papaya grabbed the last cookie just as it was about to vanish. Amos waited till Carlos was out of earshot.

"I haven't spoken to anybody else yet, but I'm getting others to help you. I don't know who they'll be. But that's where you have to promise me to be extremely careful. Papaya, you have to be very careful about whom you trust."

"It really is just like a spy movie."

"Papaya—"

"Okay, okay."

"I want you to be in charge, because you are smart and tough. I am going to give you a very substantial amount of money when you leave here today, and it is going to be up to you how to spend it."

"Like on what?"

"Again, I don't know. Whatever's needed, whatever we need to buy. Also paying the people who work for us."

"How much money are you talking?"

"Many, many, many pesos. Quite a fat suitcase."

Papaya was, as always, impressed by any mention of money in quantity. "How you know I won't just take all those pesos and retire like we decided?"

"Because if you do, when the Americans come back, I will hunt you down and cut your nice juicy body into little tiny pieces. Many, many, many pieces."

She laughed with delight. "Ooh. Very scary." Then she looked at him, a long steady look. He knew what was coming. She raised her eyebrows, a question and an offer.

"Yes," he said. He put his hands under both her breasts and raised her up. "I'd like to very much. If," he added, "you think you can manage it on such a full stomach."

Sex had always been lighthearted between them, never a solemn matter.

"Oh, I can manage. And I don't mind screwing an American. You sure you're not feeling too old and sleepy?"

In his bedroom, neither of them mentioned that this might be the last time for quite a while. It did not feel like that.

Afterward, when she had gone home in the car, carrying the brown leather suitcase stuffed with pesos, he showered and dressed. Then he told Carlos to follow him out to the pagoda. When Amos sat down in his wicker chair, Carlos stood with his hands clasped behind his back, a small, alert figure, still trim. His round, wrinkled face was, for a change, unsmiling. He knew something serious was coming.

Amos had already discussed with Carlos what was likely to happen as soon as the Japanese took Manila. Amos would be interned with other American civilians. This house would be taken over by some very high-ranking Japanese officer, an important general or admiral, the instant Amos was out the door. Since Carlos had run the house for the last seven years, the new Japanese occupant would surely be willing to keep him on if he wanted to stay. But Carlos, with his two oldest sons in the Philippine Army, sons who might by this time be wounded, dead or captured, was offended. He said he would not work for the Japs, and especially not in Mr. Watson's house.

Today Amos had a more attractive proposition for Carlos. However, it would not do to throw it bluntly on the table. The traditional courtesy between American master and Filipino head houseboy required a different approach.

"Carlos, how many years you work for me now?"

"Thirteen, sir."

"And how many as head houseboy?"

"Seven, sir."

"Everything satisfactory?"

"Yes, sir. Very satisfactory."

"Good. You know I'm very satisfied, too."

"Salamat po." Carlos allowed himself a slight smile of pride while expressing his thanks.

"I think then, since we are both satisfied, we should continue."

"Sir, as soon as Japs go, I work for you again."

Since this was offered as a solemn promise, Amos nodded his head in appreciation before he said, "That's not what I have in mind. How would you like to keep on working for me while the Japs are here?"

Carlos shook his head sadly. "Sir, alas that cannot be. I cannot leave my family and go in prison with you."

"I don't think they would let you in. But yes, it can be, and you won't have to leave your family." Amos could say something man to man to Carlos that he would have been embarrassed to say to Papaya. "I hate to lose to the Japs. I hate them to take over this country. And I hate them to take my house, as they will do. They will live in my house and sit on my furniture and eat at my dining-room table and sleep in my bed. If I didn't think I'd get it back someday, I'd almost rather burn it. Carlos, I want to get even, if I can. I want you to help me."

Carlos waited, not speaking, but Amos could sense the little man's excitement as he squared his narrow shoulders.

"What I want you to do is stay in this house. Be head houseboy to some big Jap general. Be very nice and polite to him, just the way you are to me."

Carlos's face fell.

"Wait a second. That is only so that you can do them great harm. All the time you are here, you listen to everything that's said and remember it. See what other generals come here. Find out what they are saying to each other."

"But, sir, I am not speaking Japanese."

Amos shrugged. "They will have to speak English or Tagalog to you. Maybe Filipinos will come here and the Japs will have to talk to them. Besides, many Japs speak English. Anyway, you will learn what you can, so that later we can tell the Americans."

Carlos was puzzled. "What Americans, sir?"

Amos wished he knew. "The Americans who will be coming to fight the Japs." He tried to sound more confident than he felt. "Till that happens, you must report whatever you learn to Miss Papaya. I have given her money and instructions about what to do. She will be the one." He could see this was popular news. Carlos not only liked Papaya but was proud that Amos had such a young and famous mistress.

"When you need extra money," Amos said, "she will give it to you. I think the Japs will be less generous than I am. But you must run the house for them, be pleasant to them, make them trust you. Hire any extra houseboys you need." Several of Amos's staff had already joined the panicked exodus from Manila. "But the most important thing is to keep everything secret. You must not talk to anybody except Miss Papaya. And maybe one or two others I'm considering. If the Japs catch you, they will shoot you."

"I am not afraid of them, sir."

"No, but if they shoot you, you won't be any help."

"Sir, what about Ling?"

"What about him?"

"He could help. He hates the Japs, too. Also he is very tricky."

Amos had thought of enlisting his Chinese cook but then rejected the idea. He had never been able to tell what Ling was really thinking. After a few moments, Amos said, "Let's wait and see. The Japanese are at war with the Chinese. They may not even want Ling as a cook. And Ling may not want to stay."

"He would stay for you, sir."

Amos felt mildly flattered, since Ling—unlike Carlos or his secretary, Miranda—had never displayed anything resembling personal loyalty. Ling's loyalty was to his culinary skill and his monthly pay.

"Well, I may speak to him. But I can count on you?"

"Always, sir."

"Good. Don't get shot."

———

Amos had to change his plans for Miranda when she said she was not going to stay in Manila under the Japanese. She was going to be with her family and her fiancé Benny's family in San Fernando. He did not try to dissuade her. An attractive single woman probably would be safer with her family in the provinces than alone in Manila. Besides, she might even be useful in San Fernando, a railroad and highway junction city some forty miles north of Manila and not too far from Clark Field. He gave Miranda two months' salary and told her that if she needed anything, she should get in touch with Papaya. She was tearful saying goodby. He gave Papaya Miranda's family address, just in case.

The last one he enlisted for his team, and perhaps the most enthusiastic of all, was his driver, Donato. There would be ample time in the weeks to come, Amos decided, to deal at leisure with Felix Logan.

With everything in place, or as much in place as he could arrange, Amos made a phone call to the special number he had been given for Enrique Sansone. He barely knew Sansone, a middle-aged Spanish playboy, a member of the Elizalde brothers' Tamaraw Club, an ardent but indifferent golfer, a dabbler in minor business ventures. Behind this idle façade, Sansone was also a key member of the secret intelligence group set up last year to contribute inside knowledge to the military.

"Yes?"

"Mr. Sansone, this is Amos Watson."

"Yes?"

"I hope in the months ahead to be in a position to send useful information to your group."

"Mr. Watson, I have no idea what you are talking about."

"Good, of course not. The person who will be my contact is the singer Papaya. As you are probably aware, I know her very well. She is totally reliable."

"Mr. Watson, I am delighted to hear such a nice character reference for this young lady, but it is of no interest to me. If you will excuse me, I am already late for a golf game."

"Of course," Amos said. "Don't forget: totally re-

liable, regardless of any appearance to the contrary.
Good luck."

———

On the last day of the year the fires started. Everything
of military value that could be demolished before the
Japanese arrival was being burned or blown up. From
his own backyard Amos could see the towers of black
smoke rising into the sky from the exploding oil
dumps along the Pasig River. He could hear the thudding blast of concrete bridges being blown. Stores and
warehouses were thrown open to the public on a help-
yourself basis. Carlos reported that looting was taking
place all over the city.

Amos could have gone to a number of last-gasp
New Year's Eve parties. With Manila an open city,
all the lights were on again. The hotels and clubs and
cabarets opened for the final fling. Peggy Ashburn
phoned Amos, urging him to join their group for the
dance at the Fiesta Pavilion.

"I'm going to wear an evening dress for the first
time since this war began," she said.

"Well, Peggy, that's hard to resist," Amos said,
"but I think—"

"Oh, Amos, come on. Last chance to show the
flag."

"What flag is that, Peggy?"

She didn't answer the question right away. "You
were right, weren't you? We've sure been whipped."

"Not much comfort to be right on that one."

"No, probably not. Hell with it. Join us, Amos.
It's New Year's Eve." And now she did answer his

question. "Last chance for old-time Manila to kick up our heels."

He did not want to say no to Peggy Ashburn, who at least was going down with banners flying. "I'll try to make it," he said.

"That means you won't. Probably spending the evening with your singer ladyfriend. I don't blame you. Happy New Year, Amos, you old goat."

"Happy New Year, Peggy."

Amos had dinner alone in his own home, celebrating New Year's Eve by drinking every drop of the final bottle of the 1921 Ausone. Damn good wine. Damn good house.

On the afternoon of January 2, the Japanese army—first the troops on bicycles with little Rising Sun pennants on the handlebars, then the cavalry with long saber scabbards curving down below the horses' bellies—paraded into Manila. The war was twenty-five days old.

≡ 7 ≡

The New Dawn

Her doorbell finally rang at four-thirty. Tired and tense after waiting all day, Judy Ferguson flung open the door, expecting to find herself face-to-face with her first Japanese soldier. But it was only the hotel manager, Mr. Obispo. He made a strange little embarrassed bow of his head.

"They are in the lobby," he said in a voice just above a whisper. He was frightened. "They say all Americans must come downstairs right away."

What right did Mr. Obispo have to be frightened? He was Spanish. The Japs weren't bothering with the Spanish. "What about our suitcases?" she asked.

"Yes, yes, they say bring your suitcase. I am sorry I have no boy to help you."

"I'll bring it myself," Judy said. She started to close her door.

"They say right away," Mr. Obispo reminded her.

"Yes, I heard you." She slammed the door.

Service at the San Luis Hotel, never outstanding in normal times, had deteriorated the last two weeks as members of the staff fled Manila or simply chose not to come to work. The dining room, even with a severely restricted menu, barely functioned. The last two mornings Judy had had to make her own bed. Of course, it wasn't just the San Luis Hotel. The whole city was falling apart.

Judy was scared, really scared. Everybody knew about the infamous Rape of Nanking, when the Japanese captured that Chinese city four years ago. That was rape in the broadest sense, the destruction of a whole city, but it included plenty of rape in the specific sense. Thinking about what the victorious Japs might now do in Manila, Judy wished for the first time in her life that she were a plain girl with an uninteresting body. She could only hope the Japs had different views of what constituted an attractive woman. She was scared—but she knew she must not let them see how scared she was.

She had packed this morning after the hotel got its orders from the Japanese. All American and British residents were to pack one suitcase with enough clothes for three days, then wait in their rooms until the Japanese came to collect them.

Residents had different interpretations of these instructions. Some thought "three days" meant they would be put through a lengthy registration and interrogation process. Then, depending on the results, they would be sent somewhere else, perhaps right back here to the San Luis Hotel. Others were convinced they were all going to be interned somewhere, beginning today, but that the Japanese, just arrived in Manila, hadn't had time to get organized. According to this theory, the three-day suitcase would be a sort of weekend introduction to internment, with the real event to take place later on when the Japs could arrange things properly. Everybody knew the Japs prized order and efficiency.

There were also rumors that the Americans and British at the luxury hotels had already been picked up yesterday and taken to—depending on which rumor it was—Rizal Stadium, the pier district, Santo Tomas University, Bilibid Prison or the huge Santa Ana Cabaret. Someone had heard they were all camped out in Japanese army tents on the Polo Club's polo field. Another had heard it wasn't the polo field but the North Cemetery. The most extravagant rumor was that these civilians had been put in chains and loaded onto Japanese ships bound for Formosa.

Listening to the speculation rattle around the lobby, Judy realized no one knew anything. She would make her own judgment. She decided that clothes for three days meant just what it said—three days. However, since no information was provided about where or how the three days would be spent, she pulled down her large suitcase, the one she had taken on last summer's southern-islands cruise, and filled it with a variety of garments, just as she would have done for a three-day weekend in a country house where she didn't know either the hosts or the schedule of activities.

Another important consideration in her selection was that looting had been extensive these last few days. She suspected that once all the Americans and British had left for wherever it was they were going, security in the hotel would collapse. She took every-

thing she could not bear to have stolen: her best evening clothes and slippers, all cosmetics, every piece
of her costume jewelry, including the carved wooden
Baguio bracelet that was her only memento from Brad
Stone. He had bought it for her one afternoon in the
Baguio open-air market for two pesos, all he could
afford. When she found she had overfilled the suitcase, she switched the jewelry to her large shoulder-
strap purse. None of this had great value, but she did
not intend to lose it. The clothes and shoes she had
to leave behind would be a less serious loss.

She decided to wear flat-heeled shoes and a sensible
lightweight cotton dress that wouldn't wrinkle. Now
she put on fresh lipstick and gave a final brush to her
short brown hair. She slung her purse over her shoulder and picked up her heavy suitcase. She left her
room without looking back, closed the door behind
her, walked down the hall and pressed the elevator
button. She heard the elevator clank up and down
twice without stopping at her floor. She tried not to
be nervous. Finally the elevator door opened.

Two middle-aged American men and a younger
American woman holding a small child in her arms
stared at Judy in resentment. Their luggage and a
shiny blue baby carriage occupied much of the floor
space. The child was crying in a weary, aimless fashion. Judy wondered what the Japs would think of the
baby carriage. She squeezed in without apology. The
elderly Filipino operator closed the sliding door and
the folding iron gate. The baby's cry was the only
voice as they rode down to the main floor.

The lobby looked like a bus terminal at Friday-

night rush hour. Everybody standing around waiting—men and women of all ages, a few bewildered
children—surrounded by suitcases of every size and
material: leather, canvas, straw. The space was
jammed with anxious, white-faced people who constantly checked to make sure they had all their belongings. The strangest thing was the silence. All these
people and yet no one spoke aloud. Around the edges
of the lobby Judy saw some Filipino hotel residents
and staff members, here out of curiosity or perhaps
to say goodby to friends.

And then, with a jolt, she saw what was behind
the hotel registration desk. There, in front of the rows
of empty mailboxes and the dangling room keys,
where she was used to seeing only Filipino faces or
occasionally the milk-pale face of Mr. Obispo, there
They were.

There were three of them. All wore peaked military
caps with stubby visors. One had thick horn-rimmed
glasses, just like in the cartoons. They were looking
at papers spread in front of them on the counter.
Apparently satisfied, the one in the center scooped
the papers together and shuffled them into a neat
stack. He gestured to Mr. Obispo, who scurried forward. Judy could not hear the conversation. Everybody in the lobby was watching.

The manager turned to face his clientele. He held
up his arms and said in a nervous voice, "Quiet,
please."

Judy stifled a laugh. It was hard to imagine a more
silent gathering.

"The officer says that you should go outside, where

there are trucks to transport you. Please take your suitcases."

The Japanese officer said something further to Mr. Obispo, who nodded and raised his arms again. "The officer says do not get into the trucks until your names have been checked off. Also, you are to remain quiet at all times."

As they lifted their suitcases and began moving toward the front entrance, everyone began talking to his neighbor about where they might be going. The officer reached out and banged the desk bell normally used to summon bellhops. He hit it half a dozen times in quick succession. The people fell silent. The officer nodded his approval of the silence and waved them toward the entrance.

By the time Judy got through the door, the narrow sidewalk in front of the hotel was crowded with people and luggage, stretching halfway down the block. The bright blue baby carriage was still part of the scene.

Three open-bed army trucks with slatted sides waited at the curb. A soldier with a rifle stood in the bed of each truck, looking down with impassive curiosity at the hotel residents who were about to become his passengers. Across the street, well away from the trucks, a small group of Filipino men and women watched to see what would happen. Otherwise the street was strangely empty in both directions.

The late-afternoon breeze carried the smell of all the fires that had been burning these last days. The air had the dusky quality of smoke.

The three Japanese soldiers emerged from the hotel. The officer who had spoken to Mr. Obispo still held his stack of papers. He spoke in a commanding voice in very good English. "Americans with names A to G go in the first truck, H to P in the second truck. All the rest, including British, in the last truck. Line up immediately. Wait until your name is checked before entering truck."

This led to great confusion, with people squeezing past each other on the narrow sidewalk, suitcases banging together, to get to their assigned trucks. The soldiers waited patiently, seeming neither angry nor amused. Then at last they began to load—one truck at a time.

All three Japanese stood beside the tailgate of the first truck. As each person gave his name and was checked off, he swung his suitcase onto the truck and climbed in behind it. Judy saw she would have an awkward time, but she knew some man would help her. Indeed, a young man reached down from the truck to pull up her suitcase and then to give her a hand.

When the truck was finally loaded, with everyone squeezed together standing up, the three Japs painstakingly checked their list all over again to make sure everyone was in. The tailgate closed, the soldier with the rifle took his place at the rear, and the three Japs moved down to the second truck to repeat the process. The loading and checking took well over an hour. It was almost dark when the three trucks set out across the city, crossing the Pasig River and heading north.

The passengers held on to the slats and to one another, trying not to fall over their own suitcases in the swaying vehicles.

"This is the wrong way to the Polo Club," somebody said, and a few people laughed.

Also the wrong way to the piers or to Santa Ana, Judy thought. Maybe they're going to take us out of Manila.

"It's the North Cemetery, like I told you," someone said.

"Yeah, or it could be Bilibid Prison."

But when their truck made a sharp turn onto a broad avenue, an older man's voice said, "This is España. We're going to Santo Tomas after all."

Better than the cemetery or the prison, Judy decided. She did not know much about Santo Tomas, just that it was a very old university started in early Spanish times. She had never heard of any American students going there. It must be all Filipinos and Spanish. At least it would be civilized.

Their truck turned in at a wide, closed gate and stopped. The horn honked. The gate swung open. Inside were spotlights aimed directly into their eyes and more Japanese guards with rifles. Judy could hear a jabber of conversation in Japanese. Then their truck moved forward into the university grounds. It was now too dark to see much, but Judy had an impression of spaciousness.

Their truck stopped at a huge lump of a building, which the headlights revealed was made of light-colored stone.

The tailgate clanged open.

One or two at a time they climbed out of the truck, reaching back to drag down their suitcases. The same young man helped Judy. The other two trucks were unloading behind them. Judy hoped a visit to the bathroom would be early on the schedule, but she did not want to say anything.

They were herded through the entrance into a very large open area, obviously the main hall. Three Japanese soldiers sat at tables facing the new arrivals. Behind the soldiers a broad flight of dark wooden steps rose to the second floor.

The officer who had been in charge at the San Luis Hotel stood before them. "American men line up at first table, American women and children at second table. All British men and women at third table."

"How about a trip to the men's room?" a man asked.

A chorus of agreement.

The officer held up his hand, palm toward them. "First, silence. Then, baggage inspection. Then, men's room."

Everybody groaned.

"How about some food?" a woman said. "My children are getting hungry."

Other voices rose in agreement. The officer glared. Then he folded his arms and pointedly turned his back until the voices died away. Then he motioned for the inspection to begin.

To Judy the arrangement seemed stupid. Only a handful of British subjects had to line up at the third table, while the lines at the two American tables were long.

Each person had to lift his suitcase onto the table and open it for inspection. The women also had to open their purses. It was like going through customs, except that the Japs' main interest appeared to be cameras and knives, both of which they confiscated. Judy noticed that a receipt was given for cameras. As each person cleared inspection, he had to carry his suitcase up the broad stairway, past two more guards, to the second floor.

The British line was soon finished. Instead of taking some of the Americans at the third table, the soldier there stood up and walked away, his duty completed.

Looking back down her line, Judy was amazed to see the blue baby carriage was still present, with the child now asleep inside it. How could the Japs have let that woman put the carriage in a crowded army truck? Strange people.

It was finally her turn. This time no young American male was available to lift her suitcase. She could not quite lift it to the table by herself, but on her third try, she got one end of it high enough to rest on the table, then was able to shift her grip and push it the rest of the way. The woman behind Judy, a stout middle-aged female with an angry face, made no offer to help. On the contrary, she said, "You shouldn't have brought so much stuff."

Judy told her to mind her own business. She opened the catches and raised the lid. The Jap, who had been appraising her while she was struggling with the suitcase, now began to rummage through her clothes. He took out her high-heeled silver evening slippers, held them up, looked at her, snorted and put them back. The snort was echoed by the stout woman behind Judy. Then the Jap went slowly through her cosmetics, opening each lipstick, opening her jar of cleansing cream and her box of powder and her perfume and her cologne, elaborately sniffing each one before closing it. He dipped his finger into the cleansing cream, then wiped his finger on the table. He kept looking up at her to watch her reaction. She knew he was playing some kind of sexual game with her. He had broad cheekbones and sharp, dirty little eyes. She could imagine him having a great old time at the Rape of Nanking.

Then he began to toy with her lingerie, picking it over, still glancing up at her from time to time, raising his eyebrows and pursing his lips. He started to hold up a filmy white brassiere for closer study.

Judy had had enough. She slapped it out of his hand. "I haven't got all day," she snapped. She closed the lid of her suitcase.

He stared at her in enormous surprise. He was very angry. No games now. He did not open the lid again, but for several fierce seconds he did not speak. Then he said something coarse in Japanese, some kind of abrupt command, and pointed to her purse. She took it from her shoulder and placed it on the table between them.

Instead of looking inside and feeling around with his hand, as she had seen him do with all the other women's purses, he turned hers upside down and dumped the contents on the table. All her costume jewelry cascaded out—everything—the rhinestone clips, the ruby-colored chunky glass bracelet, the capiz-shell earrings, the imitation-pearl necklace and matching earrings, the star-shaped copper pin, the mother-of-pearl pin, the purple choker of fake amethysts, the rings, the bangles, the beads that looked almost like coral—the entire Judy Ferguson Collection. Several pieces rolled off the table, and she bent down to pick them up.

"Hey, sister," said the woman behind her, "you figuring to open a jewelry store?"

On her hands and knees, groping in the shadow under the table to make sure she got everything, Judy was furious—at the Jap soldier, at the woman mocking her, at his whole degrading scene. Ah, there was the fluted pin with the imitation rubies, one of her favorites.

When she stood again, she saw that the soldier was picking up her jewelry one piece at a time and dropping it into an open drawer. "Hey, what do you think you're doing? Stop that."

The soldier grinned, said something unintelligible and continued to drop earrings and bracelets and pins into his drawer.

"Come on, let's move this line," some woman said.

"He's stealing my jewelry!"

"Serves you right," said the stout woman. "Bringing all that fancy stuff in here. What kind of woman are you?"

"Shut up," Judy said. She turned back to the soldier and grabbed his wrist. "Give those back."

He knocked her hand aside and spoke again—more gibberish.

"Where's that officer?" Judy asked loudly, addressing everybody in both lines. "Where's that officer, the one that speaks English?"

"Come on, let's go."

"Look, lady, everybody's tired. Save it for later."

"I'm not moving until—oh, there you are." The English-speaking officer had materialized beside the table. "Look at him," she said, pointing to the grinning soldier who had almost completed the rape of her collection. "He's stealing my jewelry!"

The officer glared at her for a few seconds. Then he slapped her hard in the face.

Judy gasped.

There was sudden, total silence in the hall.

"Japanese soldiers do not steal," he said.

Judy was determined not to rub her stinging cheek. "Then why is he—?"

"Silence." He spoke to the other soldier in Japanese. They exchanged several sentences. Then the officer turned back to Judy. "It is not appropriate to bring so many jewels to this place."

"But I'm not going to wear them. They aren't even real. I just want to keep them safe."

"They will be safe. They will be returned to you at the proper time."

The Japanese soldier closed the drawer on her jewelry. He had left nothing on the table but the wooden pieces, a necklace of ebony beads and Brad's monkeywood bracelet.

"Receipt," Judy said. "I want a receipt. Like the cameras. I insist on a receipt."

The officer lost his temper. "No receipt! No receipt! You have been defeated. America has been defeated. You cannot insist on anything. Now move on, move on." He shoved her shoulder so that she almost lost her balance.

"That's telling her," said the stout woman. She had light orange hair of a shade too unattractive to be anything but real.

The Japanese officer was not finished. He looked down both lines of Americans and raised his voice. "Everyone must understand. You have no rights. You will get only what His Imperial Majesty's Army chooses to permit. Is that clear?"

No one answered.

Judy put her remaining belongings back in her purse and slung the strap over her shoulder. She slid her suitcase off the table. As she climbed the broad stairs, lugging the suitcase that she now wished she had packed more lightly, she told herself, I'm *not* defeated. I don't care what he says, I'm not defeated. And not going to be.

The Jap guard at the top of the stairs pointed her down a long corridor. There were open windows on the left, looking out onto total darkness, and closed wooden doors on the right.

"Where is the ladies' room?" Judy asked.

The guard shook his head, not understanding, and pointed again.

She noticed that each of the doors bore an English message in chalk: "30 woman," "28 woman," "42 woman." Some kind of dormitory arrangement, although this building did not look like a college dorm. She passed open areas with stairs leading up and down. She could hear women's voices from behind the closed doors—American voices.

At the end of the corridor she had to turn left, and there at last was an open door—and still another Jap. He waved her into the room.

It was her worst sight in a bad day. A single overhead globe lighted the room, which had plainly been a classroom in university days. Two blackboards ran along an end wall. All furniture had been removed. The room was crowded with arguing women who were trying to carve out private territory for themselves, their children and their belongings. Judy recognized some women from the San Luis and from the inspection line downstairs. Others were total strangers. There seemed to be no space left in this jumble.

She backed into the corridor, intending to move to another room, but the guard stopped her. He pointed to the door with the chalk sign "35 woman" and indicated she must go inside.

All right, Judy thought, but first things first. She put her suitcase inside the classroom, showing that she was willing to obey. Then she said to the guard, "Ladies' room?" When he didn't respond, she tried, "Bathroom?"

The guard shook his head and shrugged.

"Toilet?"

The same signal.

Oh hell, Judy thought, I can't be squeamish about sign language. She lifted her dress slightly and pretended to squat.

The guard giggled. "*Ah, benjo!*" He pointed toward the end of the corridor.

Judy was grateful until she got there. It was an elderly tiled bathroom with two stall toilets, only one of them functioning. Three women were in line for it, one with a sniffling child in tow.

The second woman peered at her in the dim light coming from one naked bulb above the sink. "You're Judy Ferguson, aren't you?" She was a round-faced woman of perhaps forty-five or fifty, wearing a floor-length bathrobe.

"Yes," Judy said. "I'm afraid—"

"Oh, we haven't met. I'm Millie Barnes. My husband Sammy pointed you out once at the Fiesta. He said you were the most popular girl in Manila." She laughed, a nice cheerful sound. "A woman doesn't forget *that* sort of remark, especially when it comes from her husband."

The other two women turned around to look at Judy, who didn't feel like the most popular girl in Manila. She could not remember anybody called Sammy Barnes among her attendants. "Were you living at the San Luis Hotel?"

"Goodness no. We have our own house in Pasay— or we did until this morning, when they picked us up."

"You've been here all day?"

"All day. I'm a veteran. Actually, a whole lot of people were brought in yesterday. You just come in?"

"Just now, tonight."

Millie Barnes shook her head. "Well, welcome to World War II. All I can tell you is it's terrible. I haven't seen my husband since our baggage inspection. I don't even know where he is. By the way, I hope you brought some toilet paper."

"No, I didn't think—"

The older woman shook her head again. "Then you haven't traveled in the Far East as much as my husband and I have. We never go anywhere without taking our own soap and toilet paper."

Judy was going to ask if she could borrow some toilet paper, but it seemed quite an intimate request to make of someone she had just met. Then she remembered she had some Kleenex in her purse.

"When do they feed us supper?" the woman with the child asked.

The toilet flushed. A woman came out of the stall and the next woman hurried in.

"Supper—ha! We got one stale roll at four o'clock this afternoon. And I have a funny feeling that's it for today. These Nips don't seem quite ready for business, if you know what I mean."

Two more women walked into the bathroom and got in line behind Judy.

Millie Barnes entered the stall and was there only a few moments. When she came out, she said to everybody, "Cheer up, girls, the first fifty years are the hardest." Then, surprisingly, she shook hands with Judy and said, "So nice to have met you." She winked.

Judy realized that a few folded sheets of paper had been slipped into her hand. She closed her eyes. The sudden kindness at the end of this day came as a shock. Most women were not kind to her.

When she returned to her assigned room, it looked

even more crowded. There were at least half a dozen young children in there—did they count as part of the "35 woman" or were they in addition? Judy was too tired to count.

There were no cots or bedding, just the hard floor, although Judy saw that several women had had the foresight to bring blankets, now spread out to define their territory. All the places under the windows and along the walls were occupied. The stout woman with the orange hair who had been behind her in the inspection line—Judy thought of her as "the bitch"— had captured a corner spot. Judy would have to settle down in the middle of the classroom. Even there, no open space remained. She would have to make some.

She picked an area as far as possible from any of the children and carried her suitcase to it. When she put it down, a woman said, "You can't come here. This space is already taken."

Judy ignored her and laid her suitcase flat on the floor.

The woman's voice turned shrill. "You have to find another place."

"Look," Judy said, "I didn't pick this room. You find me a space and I'll go there."

She opened her suitcase. She would have to make a bed out of her clothes. Her quilted robe would be best. Unfortunately it was pastel pink and would show the dirt, but that couldn't be helped. Besides, if there was one thing you could count on in the Philippines, it was cheap, quick laundry. She would use a sweater for a pillow.

All around her she could hear a steady whine of

complaint as everyone tried to get arranged for the night.

"Why isn't there any food? I'm starving. . . ."

"Why aren't there any beds? . . ."

"Have you seen the toilet facilities?—Barbaric! . . ."

"This is ridiculous, all of us stuck in one room. It's a great big university—there must be lots of space. . . ."

"Why do we have to have all these brats in here? Women with children ought to be in a separate room. . . ."

"How are we supposed to get undressed? There's no privacy. . . ."

"You mean they expect me to climb over everybody and walk all the way down the hall in the middle of the night to empty Charlie's potty? They have to be kidding. . . ."

"Have you looked at those Jap soldiers? I mean really looked at them? They look like animals. . . ."

"Did you see one of them slap that woman? . . ."

Judy silently agreed with all the complaints, especially the last, but she did not join in. The company and conversation of women seldom interested her. She guessed she was stuck with this group for tonight, but surely tomorrow would be different.

The classroom door swung open—two soldiers, one holding a sheet of paper. A women in the midst of taking off her dress quickly pulled it back on. "Don't you know how to knock?" she snarled. Both soldiers smiled at her.

The one with the piece of paper said, "Answer name."

He then conducted a long, ludicrous roll call, mispronouncing names so badly that no one could understand what he was saying. When this happened, he would slowly spell out the first and last name, and even some of his English letters were difficult to understand. This took forever. When one woman did not answer, even after her name had been spelled aloud twice, there was consternation. The two soldiers jabbered at each other in frantic Japanese, plainly alarmed that someone was missing. What were they going to do, search the building? But just as the alarm seemed to be reaching crescendo, a tiny old woman appeared in the hall behind them and tried to get through.

"You Coomberlannee?"

"What?"

"Coomberlannee! Coomberlannee!"

"Cumberlane. Yes, I'm Mrs. Cumberlane."

"Late roll call!"

"What?"

"You late roll call."

"What roll call?"

But eventually they got it straightened out. When the last mispronounced name had answered "Here," the Jap folded his piece of paper and put it in his tunic pocket. "Now lights," he said. Then he spoke to the second soldier, who up to this point had contributed nothing to the ceremony except dismay over the momentary absence of Mrs. Coomberlannee. The second soldier flipped the light switch, putting the classroom in darkness. The door closed.

"Hey, turn that light on," somebody said. "I'm not ready yet."

After a moment someone reached the switch and the light came back on. Instantly the door opened. It was the second soldier, pointing to his wristwatch and expostulating in vigorous Japanese. Again he turned out the light.

"Ah, shit," a tired voice said.

That struck Judy as just about it. Groping in the dark, she arranged her robe, folded her sweater and lay down. Instantly she knew it would be impossible to get comfortable. The floor was too hard and her robe not thick enough. And she was used to sleeping nude, not in her clothes. She slipped off her shoes but did not want to take off her dress and be caught at dawn in her underwear in front of all these females. Whenever she rolled over, or whenever the women on either side of her moved, there was contact. If she stretched an arm or leg, she hit her suitcase or purse or another woman's belongings. It was hopeless.

But even if she could have been comfortable, the noise would have prevented sleep. Women were talking or arguing or complaining about each other's encroachments. When one child started crying, two others took it up. Women started calling "Hush!" or "Quiet!" in loud voices. It was impossible for anyone to thread her way unobtrusively through the darkness of this crowded room to get out to the bathroom, but someone tried it at least once an hour, stumbling over bodies, waking those who had managed to fall asleep, drawing angry protests.

Shifting and turning, trying new positions, then trying to hold still and sleep, Judy waited for dawn. Anything would be an improvement.

———

Amos Watson was several days late reporting to Santo Tomas. He heard the orders over the radio, and Carlos said that all the other Americans living in the big homes along Dewey Boulevard and Del Pilar and Mabini had already left for internment. Except for Filipino servants, the neighborhood was deserted. However, Amos was in no hurry. He would enjoy his home as long as possible.

He talked to Carlos and his driver, Donato, about how they might best keep in touch with him and Papaya and others who might be working against the Japanese. He told them how to find Miranda at her family's home home near San Fernando.

Amos emphasized how careful everyone must be. He set an example by not seeing Papaya or talking to her on the phone, just in case the Japanese were watching or listening. He did not leave his own house.

He spoke to Ling, guardedly, about staying on as cook for the Japanese, but in spite of Carlos's recommendation, Amos did not feel comfortable about inviting Ling to join his team.

Ling listened politely and carefully. Then he said, "Mr. Watson, I cannot, sir. I hate Japanese too much. Also Japanese hate Chinese. Too dangerous for me. I will leave the day you go."

"All right, Ling. But keep in touch with Carlos. I want to know that you're all right."

"Thank you, sir. Also Japanese do not appreciate Chinese cooking."

"Well, I certainly do. Now about dinner to-night . . ."

They came for Amos late that afternoon.

Carlos announced them while Amos was having his before-dinner cocktail. In fact, they followed Carlos directly into the living room without waiting to be asked. An officer wearing full uniform, including a saber, and a Japanese civilian in western suit and tie. They were the same height and looked about the same age, in their early forties.

When Amos stood to greet them, he towered over them. He had already chosen the role he would play. "Good afternoon," he said, bowing his head slightly in greeting.

Somewhat to his surprise, the civilian answered with a more pronounced bow, and the officer actually saluted.

"You are Mr. Watson, sir?" the civilian asked. "This is Colonel Iseda of His Imperial Majesty's Army. I have the honor to be his interpreter. My name is Takasaki."

"How do you do," Amos said. Takasaki's English was perfect. "Won't you sit down? Would you care to join me for a cocktail? Or some tea?"

This caught the interpreter by surprise, as it was meant to. He turned to his colonel to explain the offer. A good bit of back-and-forth discussion followed. Amos waited patiently. Carlos was far off to one side, interested but trying not to attract attention. Everyone remained standing.

Finally Takasaki said, "Colonel Iseda says to thank you for your hospitality to His Imperial Majesty's representative, but unfortunately he is here on pressing business. He asks, respectfully, why you have not reported to the University of Santo Tomas. This has been repeatedly ordered on the radio."

I wonder why they're treating me so nicely, Amos thought. "I don't listen to the radio," he said. "Have I missed something?"

Without translating for his colonel, the interpreter said, "All American civilians and other enemy aliens at war with the Japanese Empire have been told to report at once to the University of Santo Tomas for internment. This has been announced every day."

"Is that so?" Amos said. "Why wasn't I told?"

"Sir, everyone was told."

"Not me. Well, I hope I haven't done anything wrong. Am I to be punished?"

This provoked more discussion between the interpreter and the officer.

"Colonel Iseda says that because you had the wisdom and, in his opinion, the courage to predict that the Japanese forces would defeat the American forces in battle, there can be no question of punishment."

Oh, so that was it. At least somebody had paid attention to his warnings. Of course, since heavy fighting continued on Bataan, it was premature to speak so glibly of defeat, but Amos let that go. The important point was that the Japanese thought so highly of him. His fellow Americans wouldn't like it, but it might be useful. He wondered how far he could push it.

"However, you must please come with us now at once."

Amos shook his head, appearing to regret that he must disappoint them. "I'm afraid that will be impossible. Since I have made no preparations to leave my house, I can't do so on such short notice."

"But—" Takasaki began.

Amos held up his hand. "Also," he said, "as you can see, I was just having a cocktail. I have not yet had my dinner. At my advanced age, as I am sure Colonel Iseda can appreciate, it is extremely important for me to take proper nourishment. Perhaps tomorrow?"

Much more discussion. Then: "Colonel Iseda suggests that perhaps this evening after you have had your dinner—"

"No, no," Amos interrupted pleasantly. "After my dinner I always go straight to bed. It will have to be tomorrow."

"But Mr. Watson, tomorrow morning this house is to be occupied by General Miyama."

"Oh? I'm glad to hear it. I wouldn't want to leave this house empty with all the looting going on. I don't know this General Miyama, but I hope he will take good care of my things. Who is he?"

"General Miyama has been designated the administrative commander of this city. Colonel Iseda is his staff officer."

Bingo, Amos thought. Miyama should be a splendid source of valuable information—if somebody was around to hear it. "Good. My chief houseboy, Carlos, can show General Miyama and Colonel Iseda where everything is. He has run this house expertly for seven years." Amos gestured toward Carlos and then waited for Takasaki to translate. He didn't want to press Carlos's candidacy any harder than that. When the interpreter had finished and both Japanese had glanced at Carlos, Amos said, as though it were all settled, "Well, until tomorrow morning then."

Takasaki and Iseda conferred. Amos was amused to see some waving of hands by both parties. Finally Takasaki turned and bowed.

"Colonel Iseda says that because of his respect for your age, as well as for your well-known public position, he will make a most special concession. But you must be ready tomorrow morning, very promptly, at seven o'clock."

Amos could see from the expression on both their faces that they expected some show of gratitude. When he shook his head, their faces fell so far that he had to struggle not to smile.

"I'm afraid not," said Amos, who customarily rose at six. "I could not possibly manage such a major event in my long life so early in the morning. Perhaps nine o'clock?"

The interpreter said a single word to Colonel Iseda, who launched into a long, excited response. At the end of it, the interpreter asked a single short question. Colonel Iseda almost shouted his one-word answer.

Takasaki said, also not quite shouting, "Eight o'clock!"

Amos felt as though he had just won the war.

"Very well then," he said, seeming graciously to

accept this slightly unsatisfactory compromise. "Now are you sure you wouldn't like some tea?"

That evening, after especially enjoying his well-earned dinner at home, Amos said goodby to Ling. He warned him to be careful until things settled down. Carlos had heard from other Filipinos that some Japanese soldiers were beating up and even killing Chinese civilians. Ling had heard this too. As with Miranda, Amos gave Ling two months' salary as a farewell bonus and promised to hire him again as soon as the Americans returned. This was another of those undated promissory notes.

Then he gave Carlos final instructions. Because of General Miyama, the man who was going to run Manila, it was now even more important for Carlos to continue to run this house. He must do it—for the sake of his country, for the sake of the American and Filipino people, for the sake of his two brave sons in the army. Carlos, nodding at every sentence, needed little convincing, but Amos laid it on thick. There was no telling how much information Carlos and Donato would be able to collect and pass on to Papaya.

Then they talked about getting messages into and out of Santo Tomas. Other Filipino servants had told Carlos the Japanese were letting Filipinos deliver packages of food and clothing and laundry for their American friends. The Japanese inspected these packages, then let them go through.

As soon as Amos heard this, he told Carlos to prepare several straw baskets with false bottoms in which a message could be hidden. Tonight Amos said they must be very careful about the use of these baskets. Nothing must jeopardize Carlos's standing as chief houseboy for General Miyama. For the time being, no written messages whatsoever. They would test the system by concealing some innocuous item in the false bottom—a candy bar, a handkerchief, something that wouldn't matter even if it was discovered. Amos would do the same when returning an empty basket to the outside. If this worked, if the false-bottomed baskets went in and out without discovery, then it would be time enough to risk messages.

"And Carlos," Amos said, "if you get to stay here at the house, you must ask permission before sending packages to me."

"But sir, if they say no."

"I don't think they will. As you heard, I seem to be in good standing with them. But if they say no, then you must send me packages through someone else. The main thing is for you to convince the Japs they can trust you. You must show them you don't want to do anything wrong. You have to show you're eager to cooperate with them."

"It is very hard, sir."

"Carlos."

"Yes, sir, I will do it."

After they said good night, Amos undressed and put on his best pajamas, which Carlos, with his strong sense of the proprieties, had laid out for this occasion. They were a very light, very pale blue silk, hand-embroidered with intricate dark blue swirls on the lapels and on the vest pocket and the two side pockets. Amos considered pockets on pajamas useless except

as sites for decoration. He wondered if General Miyama, who would be sleeping in this bed tomorrow
night, had embroidered pockets on his pajamas.

In the morning he had his usual breakfast, a large
slice of papaya with *kalamansi* juice squeezed over
it, two slices of toast and cherry jam, three cups of
black coffee. He reminded Carlos that when mango
season began, he was to send mangos to Santo Tomas
the very first day they reached the market.

Having wrung the last possible concession from
Colonel Iseda, Amos would live up to his end. He
was tempted to play a few more games by pretending
to be delayed in the bathroom, an elderly gentleman
with unspecified intestinal problems, but it was better
not to antagonize the Japanese on the day they were
taking over his house and staff. So he shaved and was
fully dressed—white sport shirt, pressed khaki slacks,
moccasins freshly polished—and standing in the sunshine at his front door, a suitcase and a gladstone bag
beside him, Carlos next to him holding a rolled-up
tatami straw mat and a folded blanket, when the
black Packard drove up at five minutes to eight.

The interpreter, Takasaki, popped out of the front
seat beside the driver and opened the back door. It
took Colonel Iseda a little longer to emerge, because
he had to manage his saber. Bows and salutes.

"Colonel Iseda says he is most grateful that you
are ready on time. For him, this is a busy day."

Amos acknowledged the compliment with a slight
bow to the colonel.

"He will not be able to accompany you to Santo
Tomas, because he has many things to do here to

prepare for General Miyama. However, you are expected there, and the driver knows precisely where to go. Now if you don't mind, Mr. Watson . . ."

The driver, another Japanese soldier, opened the trunk of the Packard. Amos was certainly going in style. Carlos put the suitcase, the bag and the bedding in the trunk.

"Now when I leave," Amos had told Carlos after breakfast, "I'm not going to shake hands with you. The Japs would consider that too intimate. And Carlos, if you cry, the Japs will think you are too fond of Americans. Then they won't trust you. So we will say goodby now."

They had shaken hands, Carlos with tears running down his cheeks. They are so damn sentimental, Amos told himself sternly. He patted the little man's shoulder several times. Many years together.

Now he said, "Well, goodby, Carlos. Take good care of the house."

"Goodby, sir," Carlos said.

They did not look at each other. Amos climbed into the backseat.

On the way to Santo Tomas, he and the driver did not speak. The car went slowly, avoiding holes and piles of debris from the bombing. Amos had not left his own property since the day the Japanese marched into Manila. As the Packard drove up Dewey Boulevard, he saw an enormous Rising Sun flag flaunted from the flagpole at the U.S. High Commissioner's Residence, and Japanese troops guarded the wrought-iron gate where U.S. Marines used to stand. The boulevard itself was almost empty of traffic. As the car turned at the corner of Rizal Park, Amos could see another Rising Sun flag on top of the Manila Hotel, where MacArthur's penthouse was. He wondered what Japanese general was living in the penthouse today.

He was relieved to see that no Japanese flag flew at Rizal Monument, the forty-foot-high white stone pedestal and obelisk with the standing bronze figure of José Rizal himself, surrounded by lesser bronze friends. It was typical of the Philippines that this imposing monument stood in the wrong place, some hundred yards away from the spot where Rizal was actually shot.

Amos had never heard of any national hero so perfect as Rizal—and so perfect for the Filipinos. A novelist, a poet, a doctor but, above all, a patriot. He was handsome, fiery, brave and eloquent, although Amos had always thought anyone as eloquent as Rizal might have chosen better titles for his fierce political novels than *Noli Me Tangere* and *El Filibusterismo*. Young Rizal had certainly stuck it to the Spanish governors and religious orders that ruled his country, criticizing with violent passion their many abuses. The Spanish rulers committed many errors during their three hundred years in the Philippines but none more foolish than their final handling of Rizal.

They arrested him and brought him to trial in Manila for fomenting insurrection and forming a secret revolutionary society. Unlike America's hero Nathan Hale, who was hanged by the British for being a spy because that's just what he was, Rizal was innocent. His absurd trial ended in a death sentence: to be shot in the back as a traitor.

Nathan Hale made his mark by getting off one great line: "I only regret that I have but one life to lose for my country." It earned him his portrait on the half-cent postage stamp. José Rizal, whose picture was on many stamps as well as on practically everything else, did better. He spent the night before his execution composing a wildly patriotic poem to his country, and this time he got the title right: "*Mi Ultimo Adios.*" Fourteen stanzas long—he was nothing if not prolific. All Filipino students could, and did, recite at least the opening stanza, voices throbbing with emotion:

Farewell dear Fatherland, clime of the sun caressed,
Pearl of the Orient Seas, our Eden lost!
Gladly now I give to thee this faded life's best
And were it fresher, brighter or more blest,
Still would I give it thee, nor count the cost.

This composition would never have survived discovery by his Spanish jailers, so Rizal wrote it on tiny pieces of paper and hid them in the base of the oil lamp in his cell. After his execution by firing squad on December 30, 1896, the lamp was returned to his family along with his other belongings, and the poem was found. He was thirty-five.

As the Packard left the monument and park behind, Amos wondered what Rizal would have been doing today and how the Japanese would have handled him. About the same all around, he guessed, although it was early to tell.

On Calle España, the Packard turned in at the main entrance to Santo Tomas. As Carlos had reported, many Filipinos, both men and women, were standing in front of the iron fence, holding packages and bundles for friends inside. They stood back when the gate opened to admit the Packard. The driver spoke briefly to the guards and was waved waved through.

A square, flat campus of some sixty acres in the heart of the city, Santo Tomas was referred to by Manila Americans as the oldest university in the United States—twenty-five years older than Harvard, they said.

Amos had little use for ancient history. To him, useful history was what had happened during his own lifetime, like the execution of José Rizal, but preferably before his own eyes. From history like that, one could draw practical conclusions. Brad Stone claimed one could *always* draw conclusions from history, that that was the whole point of it. Amos didn't agree. He wondered where Brad Stone was now—fighting on Bataan? Still alive? No solid information about anybody or anything existed these days.

The Packard drove through a short entrance park, with trees, shrubs, green grass and walkways. The entry road went up one side of the park and back down the other. On the far side of the return road he could see a broad playing field, and behind it a large, low stone building that must be a gym. Off to the right, men in work clothes were digging some kind of excavation. With a slight shock Amos realized they were Americans. In the Philippines, Americans didn't do that kind of work.

The car approached a solid three-story building surmounted by a central tower, then stopped beside a one-story structure in the shadow of the main building. The driver turned to Amos and, without speaking, indicated he should get out. Amos pointed to the trunk, asking if he should take his things, but the driver shook his head. This must be some kind of check-in point, Amos guessed. He climbed out.

As he did so, four young American women, one of them a teenager, came around the corner of the building, saw him and stopped to stare in amazement. Amos had never seen any of them before. Their amazement must be caused by his arrival in a chauffeured Packard.

"Good morning," he said to them and went inside.

He found himself in a single large room. Whatever this building might have been in college days, it was now some kind of Japanese headquarters office, though not a luxurious one. A single desk stood in the center of the room. Behind it sat a slim, neatly uniformed Japanese officer with a pencil-line mustache. His hands lay folded on the desk, fingers tightly interlocked. Another Japanese soldier stood beside him, and several other soldiers ringed the room. One was seated at a smaller table, working on papers. Two file cabinets stood against one wall. It was all plain school furniture, with the officer's wooden chair distinguished only by the fact that it had arms—the teacher's chair.

In front of the officer's desk, lined up in a straight

row of armless chairs, sat three Americans, dressed like Amos in sport shirts and slacks. He knew all three extremely well. One was a friend turned enemy, one an enemy who had never been a friend, and one a presumed neutral. Billy Waters of Inter-Island Mahogany, Boris Cutter of American City Bank, and Carky Vaughan, who managed the warehouse and storage facilities at the piers. Billy Waters was growing a beard, half an inch of thick sandy whiskers lighter than his deeply tanned skin. He looked up when Amos walked in, stared at him briefly with his strong green eyes, then looked away.

Boris Cutter, always ready to think and say the worst, told Amos, "You are interrupting an important discussion." He looked less authoritative in an open-necked shirt than in his banker's suit, but no less sure of himself—and no less floridly unpleasant.

"I was told to come in," Amos said. He looked at the seated officer. "My name is Amos Watson. I have just arrived here."

The soldier standing beside the desk said something to the officer in Japanese. Then he said to Amos, "This is Major Omi, the commandant of Santo Tomas. You will please to bow to the commandant."

Amos duly inclined his head. The interpreter's English wasn't as good as Takasaki's. One would think the best available interpreter would have been assigned to Santo Tomas, where more English would now be spoken than anywhere else in Manila.

"Where is your baggage for inspection?"

"It's outside," Amos said. Then he added, for Boris Cutter's benefit, "In the trunk of the Packard that brought me here." Yes, that did annoy Cutter, who must have come by truck like everyone else.

More Japanese discussion. Then: "Major Omi says no inspection is needed now. If you swear no guns, knives or cameras."

"I swear," Amos said solemnly, deciding to overlook the pocket knife in his gladstone bag.

"Then you will at once go to the gymnasium immediately."

"That's where we've put all the old farts," Boris Cutter explained as Amos turned to leave.

Amos did not intend to carry his things all the way to the gym if he could help it, so he climbed back into his Packard as though expecting no less than door-to-door transportation. Apparently the driver was expecting the same. The car moved off in the direction of the low stone building beyond the playing field. In the few minutes Amos had been inside the commandant's office, a crowd of American women, some fifty or more, had assembled outside the main building, under the supervision of a Japanese soldier. He wondered what it was—a work group, perhaps. What sort of work would women internees be required to do? He did not have time, as his Packard rolled by, to see if he recognized anyone.

Amos had not missed Boris Cutter's baronial "we." He supposed he had walked in on some kind of conference between the commandant and a committee representing the American internees. Despite his personal troubles with Billy Waters and his dislike of Cutter, he thought the internees could do much worse than those three men. Billy was a practical, no-

nonsense fellow who saw directly to the heart of a problem and then couldn't wait to fix it. The fact that before the war he had entered into illegal contracts with Japanese investors in Mindanao might now be helpful in dealing with camp authorities, just as Amos's prewar warnings now seemed to be working for his own benefit. Boris Cutter was a pain in the ass but a master of detail and precision. If any question arose about internment camp money or finances, as seemed likely, his advice would be sharp, clear and valuable, though no doubt expressed without charm or courtesy. Carky Vaughan hadn't much imagination but was a good manager and an even better diplomat. Not a bad committee. Amos would not be invited to join it. That did not bother him, since he didn't like committees anyway.

The gym was right up against the tall fence that hid the campus from Noval Street. No guards in sight. Far down the side of the building Amos could see what appeared to be some presumably elderly males—"old farts," in Boris Cutter's phrase—sitting peacefully on the ground in the morning sunshine.

The Packard stopped before a large double door. Amos and the driver both got out, and the driver opened the trunk. Amos expected no help and got none. He lifted out his suitcase, bag and bedding and put them on the cement sidewalk. The driver climbed in the car, still without speaking, backed around and drove off. Amos tucked his blanket and rolled straw mat under one arm, picked up his bags and shouldered his way through the double door.

His new home was a basketball court.

Even though perhaps a hundred people were present, the first thing to catch his eye was the expanse of litter spread from one end of the wooden floor to the other, arranged in little private piles of ownership. A few cots and even fewer mosquito nets dotted the court. Everything else lay flat on the floor: bedding, stacks of clothes, luggage, an occasional box crate. The total vision was of one grand casual mess, and yet each man's individual area was neatly arranged, as though any sign of confusion or disorder might lead to a loss of ownership. Some men were parked on their floor areas, emphasizing their right of possession. Others sat talking to each other on the bleacher seats, as if waiting for the beginning of some game that would never take place.

A grizzled man in a blue T-shirt hopped off the bleachers and hurried toward Amos. It was Dewey Petitbon, a Manila old-timer from the very early 1900s.

"Hi there, Amos," he called, still halfway across the floor. "We heard you were coming."

"Hello, Dewey." He put down his bags and bedding.

Dewey had his hand stretched out in greeting while they were still twenty feet apart. "Welcome to the old folks' home." He laughed, showing he didn't really mean this. "How'd you manage to stay out so long?"

"I was busy. Have you got a room reservation for me?"

Dewey pretended to find this the funniest thing he had ever heard. Among his dozen or more careers in the Philippines, none of them successful, none of them disastrous, he had once managed a hotel. He was one of that early handful who had arrived in the Philippines right after the Spanish-American War and had had a chance to try his hand at practically everything. "Fully booked," he said. He laughed at his joke. "Fully booked. But I expect we'll find you a space. What you want, a room or a suite?"

Dewey always claimed his parents had named him after the hero of Manila Bay. Then when it was pointed out that he was much older than that event, he would explain that his parents had known Admiral Dewey back in the States, long before the famous battle. This was poppycock, but Dewey enjoyed it.

"Who's in charge here, Dewey? I hope not you?"

Dewey cackled and chuckled. He was a geezer, but a nice one. "Actually, Amos, I'm in charge in a way. I'm one of the gym monitors."

"What's that?"

"Oh, you know. Take roll call. Keep things quiet. Keep the Nippos happy."

"Is this really the old folks' home?"

"Sort of. Just men, of course. No *dalagas* for us to play with, but we're working on that." He laughed at the prospect of getting women into the gym. "And I don't know what you mean by 'old.' I'm sixty-nine myself, of course, but we go all the way down to the fifties and some forties."

Amos knew Dewey was well over seventy but let it pass. "Where are the other men?"

"It's all organized." He waved his hands with enthusiasm. "Not by the Nippos but by us. I tell you, Amos, first few days it was so fucked up around here you'd think nobody was in charge. No food, everybody all mixed in all over the place, and hundreds of new folks coming in every day in the trucks and buses, all of them hopping out yelling, 'Where's lunch? Where's the crapper?' And no lunch and half the crappers don't work. I tell you." He shook his head. "Now it's all straightened out. Took us Americans to do it, though. Now we got women and girls in the Main Building, women with little kids over to the Annex, young guys in the Education Building, and us over here. And we—us Americans—finally talked the Nippos into letting the Red Cross come in and feed us, not much but something. Got to stand in line for it, though. Longest, slowest line you ever saw. 'Course it's all still a fucking mess, but better organized."

"How many of us?"

"Altogether? Couple of thousand by now, I guess. All I know for sure is the number we got in here, and you're one more. Come on, better find you somewhere to flop. There's a little space down to that end, not too popular 'cause it's right on the way to and from the crapper."

"You always ran a decent hotel, Dewey."

An appreciative cackle. Then Dewey asked, "Say, Amos, you didn't slip any booze in with you by any chance?"

"Not a drop. I was told it wasn't allowed."

"Well, that's the Nippo rule. No booze, no sex. But we're working on it."

⩵ 8 ⩵

Hanging On

The first time Sam Phipps had to write a communiqué for MacArthur's headquarters on Corregidor, he was scared to death. It happened because the regular information officers were down with malaria. Colonel Sampson, now Brigadier General Sampson, came up to Phipps's desk in the message-center tunnel and slapped down several pages of the daily status report.

"Here, Eli. You're supposed to be an English major. See if you can turn this into English. Today's communiqué."

"You mean *write* it? Sir, I don't know how to write a communiqué."

"Sure you do—you read them every day. In any case, you got sixty minutes to learn. The Old Man wants you to do it."

Sam Phipps thought that highly unlikely. It was much more probable that Colonel Sampson—General Sampson—had to find a substitute and had just grabbed the nearest body. But MacArthur would see the result—in fact, would no doubt rewrite the whole thing and raise hell about incompetence. Oh, shit.

Phipps glanced through the papers Sampson had left him. All the usual stuff, gathered from the commanders on Bataan: hospital and casualty reports, food supplies, medical supplies, estimates of combat effectiveness of our own troops, analysis of enemy position and movement and intention. Nothing was good, but worst of all was food.

Back in early January, when the army had been on Bataan less than a week, the daily ration had been cut in half, only thirty-six ounces a day for Americans and thirty-four ounces for the smaller Filipinos. But now, in early March, it was cut to less than fifteen ounces a day, and most of that was rice. Part of the problem was that there were twenty-five thousand civilian refugees on Bataan who couldn't be allowed to starve.

Meat was pretty much gone. All the wild carabaos, and the farmers' work carabaos as well, had already been shot, along with every discoverable wild monkey and iguana. The horses and pack mules of the Scouts Cavalry had already been eaten. Not much was left in the meat line these days except canned salmon, of which, thanks to some mysterious quartermaster logic, Bataan had been supplied with over two million pounds. Looking at the food reports, Phipps saw that as usual the front-line commanders complained that their troops weren't getting even the allotted fifteen ounces per man. Between Jap bombing and artillery fire, terrible roads and fewer and fewer functioning vehicles, it was getting harder and harder to move the food up to them. Fifteen ounces a day was less than a quarter of the normal peacetime ration, and yet those men were expected not only to fight but to fight in jungle terrain and in intense heat.

The Bataan hospital report said quinine was virtually gone. Only serious malaria cases could now be given any quinine at all. The two hospitals near Mariveles on the southern tip of Bataan were already jammed with sick and wounded. A true malaria epidemic, with a predictable impact on combat effectiveness of all units, was feared if quinine supplies did not arrive promptly from the States. Since nothing had arrived from the States in three months of war except some lies from Roosevelt about help being on the way, Phipps saw no reason to expect quinine.

For a while back in February, the military situation had not seemed too bad. True, the American and Filipino forces had been driven south from Mount Natib, but only after inflicting heavy casualties, and they had fallen back in good order to the planned second line of defense across the middle of the peninsula. In fact, after the Japs had been licked in their attempts at end runs down the coast and had lost severely when some of their units had been cut off in pockets and wiped out, General Homma had actually called a halt to action in order to regroup and get reinforcements. MacArthur's communiqués had been almost jaunty. But now Homma was ready again, and still no help had come from the States.

However, none of this could be put in a communiqué that would be released to newspapers and radio stations all over the world. Phipps stared at his problem. In a way, it was like one of those essay questions on a college exam where you didn't really know the

right answer but knew enough to bullshit your way
through the minefield. And, as with a college exam,
there was no time to screw around. He had read all
MacArthur's previous communiqués. This was just
one more.

He began to write. As he had learned in college,
and even at prep school, once you start writing, something is bound to happen. Anything is preferable to
staring at blank paper. Sir Walter Scott could never
have written all those novels if he had brooded about
blank paper. The phrases and words came to Phipps,
some of them original, many by now familiar. He
had not only read the communiqués but listened to
the Voice of Freedom radio broadcasts from Corregidor. Out the phrases came: the citadel of Bataan . . . the bastion of Corregidor . . . the gallant
American and Filipino troops . . . determination to
hold at all costs . . . Japanese forces kept at bay . . .
brave men in hospital wards eager to return to their
units . . . the holy camaraderie of battle-tested soldiers . . . staunch . . . steadfast . . . indomitable . . .

When he finished, he employed one more device
learned during his long exam experience. He handed
in his paper to General Sampson five minutes before
deadline, thus indicating serene confidence. General
Sampson looked at his watch and raised his red eyebrows but made no other comment.

Sam Phipps's grade came back much faster than it
ever had at Yale: A + .

In twenty minutes Red Sampson was back at Sam's
desk, shaking his head and smiling. "Eli," he said,
with none of his customary sarcasm, "the Old Man

asked me to tell you that was first-class. He'll tell you himself when he has time. You know how often the Old Man uses that term? First-class? About once every other war."

This encouraged Phipps to ask his boss an improper question. "General, did he really assign me to this?"

Sampson smiled, the relaxed smile of a successful conspirator. "Not exactly. I volunteered you, Eli, and he said good idea. But next time it'll be his idea. You watch. Damn good job."

When that day's communiqué was issued, Sam Phipps grabbed a copy and took it to the latrine to study in privacy. As far as he could tell, reading and rereading it, only a single change had been made in the text he'd handed in. "The gallant American and Filipino troops" had become "MacArthur's gallant American and Filipino troops." Phipps would remember that if there should be another occasion.

Later the General did find time to speak to him. He said Phipps had "captured the essential spirit of our stand." Another phrase worth preserving for future use.

That week Phipps wrote two more communiqués in addition to handling his normal message-center duties. He was also promoted to captain, although he had no way of knowing whether this was because of the communiqués or because of his message-center performance, which Sampson told him had been excellent. A captain, after only a year in uniform. If Bataan and Corregidor could hold out a few more months, no telling what he might become. Major?

Lieutenant colonel? Maybe that would please his parents when Bataan and Corregidor finally fell.

He wondered why the General never visited Bataan. It was only a couple of miles and a few minutes by PT boat from Corregidor, but MacArthur had gone there only once, way back in January. Everyone knew that on Bataan the troops were calling him Dugout Doug. It would be such an easy situation to correct, another visit to show that MacArthur cared about them, but Phipps couldn't possibly suggest it to anyone.

On March 11, under orders from Washington so secret that Phipps had never even heard the subject discussed, MacArthur left Corregidor at night by PT boat for the southern island of Mindanao, and then on by B-17 bomber to Australia, where he would assume command of the Pacific forces. He took with him his wife, Jean, his young son, Arthur, and his son's Chinese amah. He also took with him in the tiny fleet of three PTs a select group of staff officers, of whom Sam Phipps was by far the lowest in rank and by far the most astonished to be chosen.

The trip was so rough and so fast that Phipps was throwing up all the way to Mindanao. It made him realize, between spasms, that as little as he might belong in the army, the navy would have been worse.

———

To avoid thinking about a cigarette, Jack Humphrey was composing a letter to his wife, Sara. He had no paper and pencil, so he had to write the letter in his mind. Even if he'd had paper and pencil, there was no way to mail a letter from Bataan—and never would be. He found himself saying more or less the same things over and over, but it kept his mind occupied. Cigarettes were now five dollars a pack, if you could find anybody to sell you a pack.

Except for three days in the hospital at Mariveles with malaria, he had been on one defense line or another ever since the retreat to Bataan, now more than two months ago. His Scouts battalion, which had lost so many men during the retreat, was augmented by soldiers from the Scouts Cavalry, now useless in the thick jungles and steep mountains of Bataan, their mounts long since devoured by the starving army.

With all the shifting and combining of units, Jack was proud that his Scouts battalion had never been absorbed into some other command. Instead, the remnants of other commands had been absorbed into his. His men still had the spirit of the original group, and his biggest challenge was to make sure they kept it, in spite of everything. He had been promised a medal and probably a unit citation for their nighttime defense of Bridge 31, but that was a long time ago, before they even reached Bataan. Now they would all prefer a good meal or a pack of cigarettes to a citation, but he doubted they would get either, the way things were going.

His Scouts were moved from one position to another, never a very long move because the jungle of bamboo forest and thick vines was so impenetrable. There they waited for the next Jap assault, received it, stopped it and then, always, struck back through the jungle. Humphrey insisted on the counterattack, no matter how limited in scope or success. Not only did it tell the enemy that the U.S. Army was still dangerous, still aggressive, but it instilled in his own men, including the new recruits, a pride in their indomitability. They were Humphrey's Scouts, by God, so look out. He wondered how long they could keep this up.

Dear Sara,

Well, we're still hanging on. I don't like to worry you, but things don't look too great. One good thing though, I've lost a lot of weight—thanks to the heat and this strict rice diet we're on. No bathroom scales out here in the jungle, but when they weighed me at the hospital a few weeks ago, I was down to 210. I've certainly lost more since then—maybe down to my playing weight at the Point. I could sure use some of your steak-and-kidney pie. I think I could eat a whole one all by myself. Not eating makes you feel dizzy, especially in the morning. At first I thought it was the malaria coming back, but finally realized it was not having enough to eat. It's hard to get going in the morning.

The Scouts have been terrific. Good troops, I'm very proud of them. They don't complain, and they still find things to smile at, even joke about sometimes. They all have jungle rot or malaria or wounds that won't heal properly in this heat, but nobody wants to go to the hospital if he can help it. We've lost a lot of men, first when we were fighting our way onto Bataan and now trying to keep from getting pushed all the way back into the ocean. We've held on, though—haven't lost a yard of ground since we took up this position nine days ago. Nine? Eight? A hundred and three? I get a little hazy about the numbers.

Speaking of numbers, how is Terry doing on his math? Keep him at it. He'll never get into the Point without good math scores, although right now I'm not so damn sure I'd recommend the army as a career.

We're over on the west side of Mount Samat, dug in pretty well. The jungle is awful to live in but good to defend. All bamboo forests and vines—you can't walk ten yards without using a bolo to cut your way through. Hard for the Japs to attack through that stuff. Then when you do come to a clear space in the jungle, what you get is cogon grass, which can tear your skin if you aren't careful. The other side of Mount Samat, the east side over toward the coast, is said to be nicer country—small farms, rice fields, even a few little towns. Flatter land but harder to defend. I guess we'd rather be where we are, although I'll never grow really fond of it!

I miss you and the boys very much, especially you and especially at night. I hope you all had a good Christmas with your folks, but that's so long ago now that you've probably forgotten it. Wish I'd been there. We'll make up for it next Christmas. Write when you can.

Love, Jack

———

Brad Stone and his forty-five men came down from their hillside camp above Carabangay in the late after-

noon. Paradiso himself was carrying the dynamite and
fuses.

Night would have been safer, because then there
would be no danger of a Jap patrol plane spotting
them, but it was impossible to follow these narrow
mountain trails at night. Even after two months of
practice it was easy to lose one's way. Besides, Brad
and his men had to reach the town of Bamban and
the ammunition dump during moonlight hours, so it
was necessary to risk coming down in daylight. They
came down in groups of threes and fours, using different trails. Some of the men lived with Brad and
Paradiso in camp in the hills, some lived in Carabangay and the other towns below the Zambales foothills, collecting information on where the Japs were
and what they were doing. Some came and went between camp and town, and some would suddenly
disappear altogether, perhaps for a week, perhaps for
good. Maybe they had decided to live somewhere else,
maybe they were dead. Despite Brad's efforts, it was
a very loose organization. It would have been even
looser without Paradiso. The stocky sergeant knew
how to make men jump. And he spoke not only Tagalog and Ilocano and English but useful bits and
pieces of other dialects, so Brad had at least one man
who could talk to everybody.

Down from the hills, they remained separated into
small groups that would not attract attention. Until
it got dark they could not use the main road. They
kept out of sight behind the towns, walking through
the cane fields and rice paddies and small vegetable
farms.

Moving through the countryside was far less dangerous now than in the weeks right after the Jap landings. Back then, Brad and Paradiso had had to keep to the hills as they carefully made their way south down the Zambales mountain chain from Lingayen to Carabangay, picking up other army stragglers on the way. There had been Jap units everywhere then, not just infantry but tanks and artillery. Now the fighting on the Luzon Plain had ended. If any fighting was still going on, it was way down on Bataan.

The Japs were still around, of course, especially at Clark Field, only a few miles south of Bamban. They were fixing up Clark as their own major air base. Brad Stone would have loved to mess up Clark Field for them, but it was so heavily guarded that any guerrilla action would have been suicide. Instead, they had stuck to bite-sized adventures—until this one tonight at Bamban. The most that could be accomplished at Clark Field these days was for the hired Filipinos to do slow, sloppy construction work, which was just what they were doing.

When it got dark, Brad led his three men out of the fields to the main road, where walking was easier and faster. As always whenever he came down from the mountains, he wore his farmer's conical straw hat to conceal the fact that he was white. His skin was now so deeply tanned from outdoor life that he could easily pass for a Filipino—except for his bright blue eyes and red-blond hair and thin, sharp nose. The hat kept these features hidden.

One of the things the Japs had done was to solve the Philippine traffic problem. There wasn't any traffic. No gasoline worth mentioning was available, and you had to have a permit to go anywhere by private car. During the day the roads were empty of automobile traffic, except for Jap military vehicles, mostly army trucks. Filipinos traveled by carabao cart and horse cart and bicycle. At night almost nothing moved.

Tonight the road was clear. They walked toward Bamban at a good pace, rifles slung from shoulders, bolos tucked in belts. The bamboo-and-nipa huts in the barrios they passed were dark—everyone observing curfew and saving kerosene or candles. Dogs barked at their smell, then quieted as they walked on. Whenever they saw headlights coming, which at this hour could only mean a Jap vehicle, they quickly stepped off the road and dropped out of sight in the darkness.

Even when the half-moon came up, they saw none of their colleagues along the road. That was as planned. Paradiso had suggested that each small group keep to itself, staying out of sight, until everyone reached the meeting place at Bamban.

Their information for this attack came from Rosauro, the bright-faced boy from Brad Stone's original company who looked too young to be a soldier. Now he looked too young to be a guerrilla. His friendliness and his air of happy innocence made him an excellent collector of detailed information. Having grown up in Carabangay, he knew everybody in the town. He also knew the nearby countryside from Angeles up to Tarlac.

Rosauro drew the sketch for Brad and Paradiso.

The dump was half a mile off the main road just this side of Bamban. It was a big tin shed, a former warehouse, in an open field behind a thick banana grove. The new barbed-wire fence that surrounded it had a steel gate and was patrolled at all times by at least two guards, sometimes more. Maybe a hundred yards away from the fence was a concrete guardhouse where the Jap garrison lived.

They talked it over. It was far more ambitious than any of the little actions they had attempted, both on the way down from Lingayen Gulf and after they had established camp above Carabangay. They had the explosives and fuses they had found in the abandoned chrome mine in the mountains. Getting in through the steel gate was out of the question, so they would have to cut through the fence to reach the shed. That meant they would have to dispose of the two patrolling guards without alerting the guardhouse. A handful of men might accomplish all that, but Brad and Paradiso decided they needed a big enough force to defend themselves and fight their way out if the guardhouse woke up. They would need enough light to see what they were doing. The best time of night, Rosauro said, would be around ten or eleven o'clock when some of the soldiers were patronizing Bamban's combination beer joint and whorehouse, while those back at the guardhouse should be getting sleepy. Brad calculated the night and hour when the moonlight would be most in their favor.

Their assembly point was the thick banana grove at the edge of the open field. As soon as Brad's group entered it, Paradiso came up to him. The grove provided good concealment but made it difficult to count noses in the dark. There were supposed to be twelve groups of three or four men each, but after Brad and Paradiso had waited the full half hour, only ten groups were present.

"I wish they'd hurry," Brad whispered.

"We cannot wait longer," Paradiso said.

"Where do you suppose they are? It wasn't that hard to find this place."

"Maybe in the whorehouse. Maybe they change their mind. It doesn't matter. We must start."

Paradiso had already spaced the men along the edge of the grove facing the open field. Now he passed the word for them to lie down in prone firing position, ready to cover both the fence area and the more distant guardhouse. Everybody was nervous.

From here they could see the big tin shed directly in front of them and the square concrete guardhouse off to their left. The wire fence was invisible in the pale moonlight, but its location was outlined by the occasional passage of a figure, one of the Japanese patrol guards. The steel gate, Rosauro said, was on the opposite side of the fence, hidden by the bulk of the shed.

Ramon and Despido, the two men Paradiso had selected, must now cross the open space between here and the fence without being seen. A long crawl. Then they must hit the guards, one at a time, in total silence. The two men with wire cutters must then come in right behind. And finally Paradiso and his one helper would follow with the dynamite and the fuse cord.

They all watched Ramon and Despido set out. The two men scrabbled quickly on hands and knees, then dropped to a flat crawl whenever one of the guards came in sight. The night was quiet, no breeze, no sound. It was hot in the banana grove. Brad wiped the perspiration off his face with his sleeve. It seemed to take Ramon and Despido a long time to crawl within striking distance, but it was probably only a few minutes. Finally Brad watched them lie down flat. Once they stopped moving they disappeared. When Brad looked away and then looked back, he could not tell where they were. Good.

A guard appeared around the corner of the fence, walking slowly. He reached the point where Brad thought the men were lying and kept on walking. Suddenly two figures sprang from the ground behind the guard and darted forward. The guard didn't even have time to turn. From across the open field, Brad heard the slap of a sharp, heavy bolo hitting flesh. It was the only sound. Now the figures formed a close group in the moonlight—Ramon and Despido dragging the guard's body away from the fence so it wouldn't be seen. Then the figures disappeared into the dark ground.

Beside him, Brad heard Paradiso whispering to the wire-cutting team, telling them to be ready.

It seemed a long time before the other guard appeared. He reached the same spot and kept walking, a little faster than the first one. Again the two figures jumped up and ran toward him. But this time the guard heard something. He stopped and turned toward the bolos. A short, loud cry—of surprise, of fear? They hit him. Another short cry, not as loud as the first. Silence.

"*Sige na*—hurry!" Paradiso said.

The two men with the wire cutters sprinted across the field. Paradiso and his helper followed quickly behind them with the explosives. They had timed it beforehand back in camp. Once the fence was open, which should be a matter of only a few seconds, it took three minutes to plant the two bundles of dynamite, light the long fuse and run.

Brad Stone saw a sudden square of light off to his left. The guardhouse door had opened, and a figure walked out. Let him just be taking a leak, Brad prayed. The figure walked a few steps, stopped and called something. Getting no answer, he came on toward the fence. Maybe he would go around the other way to check the gate. If not, if he came to this side, the four men at the fence would have heard his call and would be ready for him. Yes, the figure was coming to this side. It stopped to call again.

From so close beside Brad that he jumped, a rifle cracked. He just had time to think, Oh Christ. Then, after a few bare seconds of silence, other rifles fired from the grove. The figure turned and ran back to the guardhouse, shouting the alarm as he fled.

"Hold it! Stop!" Brad told his men, but he was far too late.

In a few seconds armed Jap soldiers poured out the guardhouse door and ran toward the shed, firing into the darkness.

Brad looked for Paradiso and the others. He could

see men running back toward him, trying to reach
the safety of the banana grove. One, two—four. Paradiso and his helper must still be inside the fence. No,
here came a fifth man.

From in front of the guardhouse he suddenly heard
the terrifying chatter of a machine gun. Where had
that come from? He couldn't remember Rosauro saying anything about a machine gun. The men running
toward him hunched over as the bullets raked the
field.

"Fire at the gun!" Brad yelled. What the hell was
the Tagalog for "machine gun"? What was the Tagalog for "fire"?

The first four men crashed back safely into the
grove.

The fifth man didn't make it. The machine gun
caught him a good twenty yards away. There was no
sixth man.

Now the soldiers from the guardhouse had found
the bodies of their companions and the gaping hole
in the fence. Brad saw some go through the hole to
check the shed. Others knelt to fire at the banana
grove.

Brad Stone was trying to decide whether they
should leave or stay, and what they could accomplish
if they did stay, and whether or not Paradiso was still
alive, perhaps hiding from the Japs somewhere inside,
when the shed blew up. A sudden great flash. A tremendous boom that hurt the ears. The tin roof lifted
straight up in the air, then twisted and buckled as it
fell back down. A series of resonant bangs and booms,
and then lesser rattling explosions of small-arms am-

munition going off. A huge rising pall of smoke and flame. The Jap soldiers simply weren't there anymore. Neither, of course, was Paradiso.

Brad Stone watched for a few moments in silent amazement. He couldn't believe they had brought it off—or that the cost would be so high. Paradiso. Jesus, Paradiso. Then he shook himself. They had to get away from here. "Let's go," he called up and down the line. "Go back in the same small groups. And look out for Japs. They'll be all over the roads looking for us. Let's go, let's go."

The trip home took much longer than the trip down. When he and his three-man group got back to the main road, Brad decided he could not risk using it. Not only would the Japs be out in force, rushing troops up from Clark Field and God knows where else, but they might well plant ambushes along this road to catch anybody moving. It would be much slower but much safer not to use the road at all. Wishing he had thought of this when he had all his men together back in the banana grove, Brad struck out into the fields.

Even with the help of moonlight it was a long, hard hike back to Carabangay. All the way back he thought about how much he had relied on Paradiso. He wondered if he could hold his guerrilla band together without Paradiso's skill and leadership. The sergeant had been the glue in this group ever since Lingayen Gulf.

Maybe it would be best to merge with one of the other guerrilla outfits. There were several in the Zambales neighborhood, notably the Quintano Marauders, who sounded as though they had been named out of a comic strip. They were led by a man who called himself Major Julio Quintano, although that rank was surely spurious. It was said to be a considerably larger group than Brad's, but all guerrilla numbers were suspect. Maybe he should promote himself to Major Brad Stone. It was all so phony. But tonight's ammunition dump wasn't phony.

They finally reached the outer edge of Carabangay. Because this was Rosauro's home, the town was friendly to Brad's guerrillas and supplied them with food. They would have been welcome to spend the night in town, but Brad did not want to risk compromising the townspeople. The Japs would surely be on a rampage tomorrow, searching the entire area, town by town, and questioning everybody. Better if the townspeople knew nothing. Brad skirted the town and took his men onto the slopes of the foothills. That was as far as they could go in the dark. They would spend the night here in the open and then, at first light, before any Jap patrol plane could spot them, find the trail back to the main camp. As a result of this decision, Brad Stone didn't learn until morning that Paradiso was still alive.

≡ 9 ≡

Welcome to STIC

Everybody Judy knew was in Santo Tomas—along with a great many people she didn't want to know. By the first of April more than three thousand men, women and children clogged the university buildings and grounds. The population was almost as big as her Indiana hometown's—and much more varied. More than two thousand were Americans, but there were also British, Canadians, Australians, French, Dutch, Poles, Norwegians—even a Nicaraguan.

Every profession, trade and occupation seemed to be represented—bank managers, lawyers, doctors, corporation heads, engineers, miners, teachers, merchant marines, builders, prostitutes, carpenters, nurses, plumbers, electricians, civil servants, office workers like herself and, most abundant of all, housewives. More than five hundred of them. Judy had had no idea so many American and British housewives were in Manila, and now she had to live with them.

But living was much better than during that horrible first week. Now that the mothers with young children were exiled to a separate building, Judy no longer had to live among diapers, potties and squawling brats. The classrooms converted to dormitories were still jammed, but with more buildings and more rooms put to use, they were less crowded than at the beginning. Still it was a shock to have to live with so many women. The only time in her life Judy had ever shared a bedroom with anyone was with a sorority sister in college. Now she had twenty-one roommates.

She changed rooms the second week. Millie Barnes, the woman who had befriended her with toilet paper the first night, saw her in the morning breakfast line— what Judy thought of as the mush line, since mush and coffee were all they were given to eat.

"Well there, Judy Ferguson." She sounded cheerful, in spite of the unappetizing plate of mush she was carrying. She was wearing a loose blue cotton dress, short-sleeved, that made her look dumpy. Her light brown hair, short and curly, was neatly brushed. She was a pleasant-faced woman, but homely. Homely women usually avoided Judy. "Everything shaking down? How's your room?"

"Terrible," Judy said. "How's yours?"

"Oh, terrible," Millie Barnes agreed, but with a big round smile. "Everything's terrible, of course, but ours is better than some. Look for the bright side, I say—there's bound to be one, if you look hard. We're on the first floor, at least, and we get a breeze. Doesn't matter now, but that will really help, come the hot season. Just wait till April and May."

"Our room doesn't get any breeze at all," Judy said. "Also we have a couple of awful women who don't shower."

Millie Barnes shook her head, laughing. "Just what you'll want in the hot season, right?" She found the situation funnier than Judy did. "Say, you want to move to our room? There's a space open today—or there's about to be when old lady Hochster transfers to hospital."

"I'd love to," Judy said, "but I'm sure they won't let me."

"Oh, pooh," Millie Barnes said. "Of course they won't let you if you ask. Just do it. I'll tell them you're supposed to take Mrs. Hochster's place, and you tell them the same thing. You have to convince these monkeys that it's all settled." She leaned forward and lowered her voice to a whisper. "Both their monkeys and our own monkeys." Then she laughed aloud. "They'll just think you're obeying somebody's orders, without stopping to ask whose. Come anytime after siesta. Goodness now, excuse me. I have to eat this porridge before the flies do."

It was as easy as Millie said. Judy packed up, told her most officious roommate she had been transferred and carried her suitcase down one of the back stairways to the first floor and into Room 6.

"Ah yes, there you are," Millie Barnes greeted her, taking everything for granted. "That's your space over there. Put your things down and I'll introduce you."

By evening roll call, after a certain amount of back-

and-forth confusion, Judy's name was on the Room 6 list.

Room 6 was a definite improvement, although the toilets and washing spaces were no better on the first floor than on the second. Not nearly enough of either one. Everybody had to stand in line, and the water came on only at certain hours. Judy hated undressing and washing in front of other women, but as everybody said, "If you want privacy, close your eyes."

Fortunately, now that the very hot weather of April was here, the showers, washbasins and water supply had improved greatly, but no thanks to the Japs. The men internees, with tools and supplies from the Philippine Red Cross, rebuilt the Santo Tomas plumbing system and installed additional showers, basins and laundry troughs. Everybody's favorite plumbing gadget was an ingenious double-headed shower installed outdoors above an old-fashioned bathtub set on a wooden stand. With this device two women could wash their hair simultaneously and without having to take off their clothes.

Judy thought the men were wonderful when it came to building or fixing things. Some expert always knew about pipes or electrical wiring or cooking stoves. The men were far less wonderful when it came to rules and regulations. The Japanese encouraged the internees to set up their own system of government, subject only to the approval of the commandant. The men did so with a vengeance. Santo Tomas Internment Camp, or STIC as everyone now called it, was a jungle of bureaucracy. Executive committees, advisory committees, operating committees—everybody who was anybody was chairman of something.

At the top was the Triumvirate. Judy knew the three Manila businessmen by sight and reputation—Billy Waters, Boris Cutter and Carky Vaughan. They were the last word on what must be done or not done. Because the theft of her jewelry still rankled, Judy made several formal appeals to get it back, but she was finally ordered by Boris Cutter, through the chairman of the Discipline Committee, to stop causing trouble. She did, but in protest she always wore Brad Stone's carved monkeywood bracelet, wondering if she was wearing the two-peso gift of a dead man. Perhaps Brad was alive on Bataan or Corregidor, where they were still fighting.

The Triumvirate's word was law. Back in January, for instance, there had been an election of room monitors. Judy thought that was all right—somebody had to be in charge of each room, if only to settle territorial disputes. She helped elect Millie Barnes monitor of Room 6. But it was not enough to have room monitors. Each floor of each building also had to have a floor monitor, who was elected by majority vote of the previously elected room monitors. And even that wasn't enough to satisfy the Triumvirate's lust for organization. The monitors also had to elect one overall building monitor.

The Triumvirate also established classes for both grammar school and high school, partly to continue the children's education and partly to keep them occupied. The few textbooks were carefully passed around according to an elaborate schedule. Judy was glad not to be a teacher.

And the rules! Judy didn't like rules, especially for herself, but she was willing to grant that in a community as strange and crowded as STIC, there had to be a few rules and regulations. But surely this was excessive. At first, women were not allowed to wear shorts. Then shorts were permitted. Now the rule was that only girls ten years or under could wear shorts. Ridiculous, especially if one had good legs. The rule was supposed to preserve a high moral tone by avoiding random sexual stimulation, but since two White Russian whores from Shanghai were doing steady if surreptitious business on the first floor of the Main Building at two pesos a crack, it seemed rather silly.

Elaborate rules also governed the building and use of the shanties, which had become enormously popular in the past month. Anybody who had the money, as many internees did, could build a private little getaway hut out of bamboo, cheap lumber and nipa or sawali thatching, all of which the Japs allowed to be brought into camp. You didn't even have to build it yourself but could pay someone to build it for you. Most shanties cost only a hundred or two hundred pesos, although it was said that Boris Cutter and his wife spent fifteen hundred for their shanty mansion.

The shanties became a way to escape the overcrowded dormitory rooms, a place to be by yourself, to read or smoke in peace and cook your own food over a charcoal stove. Everybody longed to have one. So naturally the Triumvirate started laying down shanty laws. Now there was a Shanty Department and a list of Shanty Regulations. You must get permission in writing for a shanty building site. Your proposed shanty design must be approved. Shanty owners must pay a monthly charge of one peso into the general welfare fund. Shanties could be occupied only during daylight hours. Above all, shanties must be so constructed that there was a clear, uninterrupted view of the interior at all times.

This last rule was accurately translated by the internees as No Sex in Shanties. Or, as Millie Barnes put it, In Shanties Keep On Panties. Like STIC's other no-sex rules, it was subject to evasion. The various shanty areas spread around the campus were too large to be fully patrolled, although the risk of a passing guard, either a Jap or an internee policeman, was always there. More important, a large loophole existed in the requirement about an uninterrupted view of the interior. In case of rain, shanty owners were permitted to close shutters to protect their belongings. When rain came, there was a concerted rush to the shanties. At this time of year, of course, rain was rare, but many people, and not just husbands and wives, looked forward to the arrival of the rainy season a month or so from now, when the shutters could be closed frequently.

Judy did not have enough money to afford a shanty. Nor did she have enough money to make proper use of the Package Line. If you had money and Filipino friends, you could have almost anything sent in through the Package Line. Even laundry was sent in and out. Everything was permissible except liquor, and even this rule could be subverted by bribes to the Jap guards or by concealing the liquor in medicine bottles. Peggy Ashburn, the old socialite in Room 5, boasted that she was drinking as much in STIC as she ever drank at the Polo Club, although no one thought this was possible. Judy couldn't afford either the liquor or the bribes.

Judy also did not have enough money to patronize the coffee shops, bakeries and "restaurants" that the Japs allowed to flourish in the corridors of the Main Building, some of them run by internees, some by Filipinos, some by Japs. The "restaurants" were mainly stalls. The food might be nothing special, but it was much better than what was available from the STIC kitchen on the regular food line.

The commandant, Major Omi, was quite lenient, as long as camp rules were obeyed. When they weren't, he could be ferocious. No one had forgotten what happened in February when three internees escaped by climbing over the wall at night. They were captured next day, severely beaten, court-martialed and, by order of the Japanese High Command, sentenced to death. Everybody thought the High Command was overreacting because fighting still continued on Bataan and Corregidor, but protests were useless. As a lesson, the men's-room monitors were made to watch the execution in the city's North Cemetery. One of them told Judy the three men were blindfolded and forced to sit on the edge of a grave that had been dug for them. When shot, they toppled into it. Since then, no attempted escapes.

Having no money bothered Judy no more than

usual. Men outnumbered women in STIC, and as
Judy had known ever since sophomore year of high
school, where there were men, there were opportunities. Her first choice was single men with money and
a decent role in the STIC heirarchy. This eliminated
many of the younger, more attractive men, but times
were hard.

An obvious candidate was Frank Otis, who had
paid for her last restaurant lunch at Tom's Dixie
Kitchen. Frank had a nice shanty and was eager to
be of service. Because of hard times, she let him. Frank
was happy to share with Judy in his shanty the del-
icacies he received through the Package Line. She also
let him buy her doughnuts and hot dogs and pastries
and good coffee in the Main Building "restaurants."

But this was only for subsistence. She would not
spend time with him in the evenings before lights out
on one of the many broad, dark stairway landings
that ran between the three floors of the Main Building.
The landings provided popular subversions of the rule
against any physical contact between the sexes, but
here Judy drew a firm line. She told Frank she did
not dare risk being caught, which was almost true.
Frank, like everyone else in STIC, was losing weight,
but his hands remained unpleasantly soft and plump.
He talked about the approaching rainy season and
the possibilities of closed shutters in his shanty, but
Judy vowed that by then she would have made some
other arrangement. Right now, day-by-day was all
she could cope with.

Old Amos Watson was another possibility, although in a very different way. She was surprised that

anyone so rich and with so many years in the Manila aristocracy wasn't a camp leader, perhaps even a member of the Triumvirate, but he seemed to be out of things. He had looked her up in the early weeks, the first time she had seen him since the Simpson School party at the Polo Club—her last night with Brad.

"I heard about your jewelry troubles," he said, coming up to her after one of those awful Red Cross meals. "And I heard a Jap officer slapped you. I'm very sorry."

It occurred to Judy immediately that Amos Watson had been deprived of his mistress, Papaya, and might be hunting around for a replacement, but he didn't have that look. He seemed nothing more than gruffly sympathetic. She thought him good-looking for his age, tall and craggy with big strong lines down his face and bushy white hair and eyebrows. His khaki shirt and pants were casual, compared to the embroidered *barong* he'd worn the last time she had seen him. She was pleased, but of course not surprised, that he remembered her.

"I'm still trying to get the jewelry back," she said.

He nodded, giving no encouragement. "Have you heard anything from our friend Brad? The Coach."

The last reference struck her as odd. Was that how Amos Watson thought of Brad, as the Coach? Judy didn't think of Brad that way.

"Nothing," she said. "Nothing since your party." She held out her arm. "This is his bracelet, actually. It's all they let me keep."

Amos Watson inspected the circlet of soft yellow-brown wood with its simple crosshatched design. "Very nice," he said generously. "Well, let's hope he's all right."

Judy wasn't sure she could afford to hope.

"Let me know if you hear anything," he said. "I'll do the same."

"How would I hear anything? I don't even know where he is. Or even if he's alive."

"Oh, he's probably alive. Most people don't get killed, you know, even in a war."

"We're going to lose, aren't we?"

He nodded. "We've already lost. All they can do on Bataan is make it expensive."

"But suppose we get help?"

"Yes," he said. "Well." He seemed to dispose of that hope. "Speaking of help, do you need anything?"

Judy thought quickly. Amos Watson didn't seem to have much influence in camp, but he had been a very important man in Manila. Maybe he could still get things done on the outside. "I brought all the wrong clothes," she said. "As you can see." By camp standards she was overdressed. "I wish I could get some things from my hotel room. I suppose they're all gone now."

"Maybe," he said. "Why don't you give me a list?"

Three days later she received her first shipment through the Package Line, a straw basket filled with the clothes she needed. When she thanked Mr. Watson, he said it was nothing and told her to call him Amos.

Maybe he *was* hunting around. Judy didn't intend to become any man's mistress, but she wouldn't mind being Amos Watson's friend. He was old, of course, over sixty, but still attractive. And Brad Stone had liked him very much.

Judy did not restrict her company to single men. If the woman was willing to accept her, she enjoyed sharing shanty privileges with couples. There weren't too many couples where the woman was agreeable. Fuzzy and Anita Cummings, who had given the farewell dinner for Brad at the Fiesta Pavilion, invited her to their shanty in Froggy Bottom. Each shanty area had a name too cute for words: Jungletown, Glamorville, Toonerville, Jerkville. Most shanties had bare-board or bamboo floors, but the Cummings shanty had comfortable mats and even chairs. Anita, unlike most plain women, had never been jealous of Judy. Perhaps money provided its own brand of security.

Judy also had shanty privileges with Millie and Sammy Barnes. Millie's husband was gray, stocky and as homely as his wife. He owned a profitable firm that did accounting work for the many Manila businesses too small to have their own accounting departments. He liked flirting with Judy, which Millie didn't seem to mind.

"Listen," Millie said, "if I can't trust Sammy after all these years, it's too late to worry about it."

The three of them were sitting side by side on the crude shanty bench that Millie called "the sofa." It wobbled every time anyone shifted weight. They were sharing a bag of fresh coconut cookies a Filipino friend had sent in through the Package Line this morning.

"I'm not sure I like being trusted," Sammy said. He winked at Judy.

"Well, I certainly don't trust you," Judy said. She gave him her best, fullest smile with a lot of eye sparkle behind it. "I don't trust any man."

Sammy Barnes was delighted. When he had to leave for a meeting of the Labor Committee, he told Judy to be sure to stay until he got back. Millie's eyes followed him, fondly but not sentimentally, as he walked down the narrow dirt path between the shanties. Then she turned to Judy.

"You know," she said, "I just love to see you operate."

"Operate how?"

"With men. It's really a treat."

"I don't know what you mean."

"Oh, I bet you don't." She laughed. "Judy, you're just a pro, that's all there is to it."

Judy did not care for this comment. "Not at all," she said stiffly. "I happen to like men."

"Who doesn't? That's not what I'm talking about. You just have some kind of automatic instinct. Everything you say or do pulls the men right in. You're like flypaper."

"That sounds—"

"Oh, goodness, accept a compliment from an old lady to a young one."

This was obviously so well meant that Judy relaxed. "You're not that old, Millie. And anyway, I'm twenty-four."

"Twenty-four—with probably ten years' practice

tying boys and men up in little knots. Have another cookie."

"I can't. I'm stuffed."

"Well, I am too, but one more for the road. You know, I wasn't but fifteen when I figured out I was never going to tie any boy in knots with my looks. No face, no figure. So I said to myself, 'Look here, Millie old girl, you'd better go all out for personality.' That took a big load off my mind, I can tell you. I didn't have to worry about my boobs anymore. I just started plugging away, not looking in the mirror too much, smiling and laughing and having a good time, and helping everybody else have a good time too, and one day there was Sammy Barnes, and that's the way it's been ever since. But I always get a kick out of watching the pretty ones at work. Especially if they have a little brains and style to go with the big fluttery eyes. Tell me something, Judy—how come you're not married?"

With Millie, Judy found she somehow didn't mind direct questions that she would have resented from another woman. "I just haven't got around to it, I guess."

"Sammy and I couldn't figure it out. Did you come out here to find a husband?"

Judy was slightly insulted. "I didn't have to come to the Philippines to get a husband."

"No, I suppose not. With your looks and style, you wouldn't have to hunt very far."

"I came here for fun and adventure." Judy gazed out over the shabby shanty area. "And look what I got."

"Yes, it's not a young woman's dream world, is it?"

"Why did you and Sammy come?"

"A less glamorous reason. Employment. Things were so tight in the early Depression years, Sammy couldn't get any work in the States. I mean, who needs an accountant if your business has just gone bust? But through friends, we heard one of the banks out here was looking for an American CPA. We caught the next boat and never looked back. Once we got here and Sammy had time to look around, he realized a lot of Manila firms needed accountant service, so he went into business for himself. We've never regretted it. At least not till now."

"This is a terrible life," Judy said with conviction. "A really awful life."

"Sure," Millie said cheerfully, "but what the hell. They'll come back and rescue us sooner or later, and meantime Sammy and I are alive and still together. I like the old goat. How many men have you been in love with?"

"You mean have I gone to bed with? Just a few."

"No, I do not mean that, although if you want to get something off that beautiful chest, Aunt Millie's always game to listen. No, I really mean in love."

Judy thought about it. "Once for sure. In college. I got pinned and everything, but it didn't last." She thought some more, remembering her good times with Brad Stone that now seemed long ago. "And maybe once here in Manila."

"Is he here? In Santo Tomas?"

"No, he's in the army. Maybe on Bataan. Maybe

dead by now, for all I know. It's better not to think about it. I wouldn't have married him anyway."

"At least it's not that Frank Otis. You've had me and Sammy wondering."

"Oh, Frank. He's just—I don't know, a convenience."

"Well, that's something you pretty ones can afford. Oh look, here comes my convenience. It must have been a short meeting."

Sammy Barnes came back down the shantytown path and rejoined them on the bench. "You waited for me," he said to Judy.

"Of course I did. What took you so long? I've been miserable."

They all smiled, and Millie held up a circled thumb and forefinger.

"Any cookies left? All we had to do was approve the work hours we already set at the last meeting."

Sammy's Labor Committee was in charge of making sure everyone did a fair share of camp labor. Like everything else at STIC, the rules were meticulous and elaborate. Men between the ages of seventeen and forty did two, three or four hours a day, depending on whether it was hard physical work like ditch-digging and garbage disposal, or medium work like sweeping and patrolling, or light work like guard duty and toilet supervision. Men forty-one to fifty did two or three hours of medium or light work, and men over fifty did two hours of light work. Women sixteen to thirty-five did two hours a day, and women over thirty-five did one hour a day.

By far the biggest chore for women was food preparation for the camp kitchen, especially peeling and chopping vegetables. Because she had worked in an office, unlike all the housewives, Judy was able to escape the vegetable line and work in the internee record office. She helped keep records on everything from camp population and supplies to new regulations and the levy of fines. It was boring, but better than vegetables.

"Sammy," Judy said, "why did they put you on the Labor Committee? Why aren't you on the Finance Committee?"

"Because finance is Boris Cutter's specialty, that's why, and I'm an accountant, not a banker. Of course, if I'd been an accountant at American City Bank instead of an independent, I'd probably be on Finance."

"Why isn't Amos Watson on anything?"

"Oh, Amos," Sammy said. "He's in very bad odor for something or other with both Billy Waters and Boris Cutter. Some kind of feud. They don't like him. You watch—they'll never let him into the big tent. Besides, Amos used to go around saying we could lose this war."

"Well, we're losing it, aren't we?"

"That's it exactly," Sammy Barnes said. "Hey, Judy, did you miss me?"

———

Amos Watson's assigned job, two hours a day because he was sixty-two and therefore classified for "light work," was to hand out sheets of Red Cross toilet paper at the men's toilet. He had volunteered to plan or manage construction work, because that was something he really knew from his early days, both in California and in the Philippines. The first two fortunes he had made out here were in cement and pipe, so he knew he could help. However, the word came back down that other, younger experts were available and that he was "not needed." Instead, he got toilet-paper duty. Demeaning punishment, from Billy Waters and Boris Cutter, of course.

Amos didn't mind. He could have made a fuss, refused the job, perhaps even tested his standing with the Japs by appealing to the commandant's office, but he decided not to let Boris Cutter have that satisfaction. He gave helpful ideas and advice to the "younger experts" in charge of construction and plumbing, and they brought problems to him for discussion. Except for not being able to give on-site orders, it came to practically the same thing as being in construction.

As for toilet-paper duty, he was amused. So were others. Women with this job were called Miss Issue Tissue. He had spent too many of his early years in construction camps with outdoor latrines to be put off by the relatively civilized setting of the gymnasium. And of course it was, as the young member of the Labor Committee told him with a straight face, "a grave responsibility." A supply shortage existed in Manila, so each man was allotted only eight sheets per day.

"And," said the committee member, "we can't have cheating. We can't have somebody getting eight sheets in the morning, and then coming back for another eight sheets in the afternoon."

"Of course not," Amos said.

"So when you give out paper, you have to check each one off on the daily list and pass it on to the next man on duty."

"That makes sense," Amos said. "How much paper do we use up by keeping a daily list?"

"Very little. Look, see here, we have boxes for four weeks for forty people printed on both sides of a piece of paper. So it's only one piece every two months."

"Wonderful," Amos said. "What about people who bring their own toilet paper?" The camp paper was not the highest quality.

"What about them?"

"Do they get eight sheets a day too?"

"Of course not."

"They could conceal their own paper and take the handout and maybe sell it."

"Now, Mr. Watson—"

"What about diarrhea?"

"What?"

"Suppose somebody has diarrhea? Does he still get only eight sheets a day?"

"Absolutely. Otherwise, there's too much opportunity for cheating. A person could get extra toilet paper by claiming he had diarrhea when he didn't."

"Couldn't you check?"

"What?"

"I mean you could have a diarrhea inspector. You know, to see if a man really has diarrhea or is just pretending to have it."

"You start this afternoon, two to four."

It was a harmless chore, one way to get to know

all the men, although he had known most of them before.

He had become an old hand at his work, a veteran, and he happened to be on duty the morning the columnist Sandy Homobono came to do his story on STIC. It would appear in the *Manila Tribune*, the Jap-run propaganda paper that circulated throughout the city and even inside Santo Tomas.

Amos had heard that Sandy, now writing for the Japs, was coming. By this time the camp was so well organized that both the commandant and the Triumvirate could see benefits from a story about how the "enemy aliens" were getting along. The Americans were so proud of their organization that they wanted to see it written up. They hoped a newspaper story might somehow get back to the States, or at least to Bataan and Corregidor, to reassure worried friends and relatives. The Japanese wanted recognition among Filipinos, and perhaps in the wider world, for treating their prisoners decently. It was understood, without being discussed, that none of the more serious problems would be reported.

Amos had not expected Sandy Homobono to visit the gym toilets, but he had always been a thorough reporter, and here he was, looking just about the same. Same rumpled black suit, but no tie this time, perhaps in deference to the informality of an internment camp. Cigarette in the corner of his mouth, eyes squinting against the smoke. As usual, no notebook, relying instead on his memory. He was accompanied by the commandant, Major Omi, with his interpreter, and Carky Vaughan of the Triumvirate.

"Hello, Sandy," Amos said. He had his checklist on a clipboard, and the stack of toilet paper beside him, divided into handy piles of eight.

"Hello, Mr. Watson. I asked if I could visit you."

"Well, here I am. I guess it's safe at last to give you an interview. What would you like to know?"

The interpreter was translating in a low voice to Major Omi. Carky Vaughan was looking slightly embarrassed.

"Nothing special. I just wanted to see how you were."

"I'm touched. As you see, I have a good job. I see you have a good one, too. How do you like writing for the *Tribune*?"

"Very much," Sandy said. "Besides, everyone has to make a living."

"Why is that?"

Sandy ignored this. He said carefully, "I see some of your old Filipino friends from time to time. They seem to be doing fine. They sent you their best, if I happened to see you."

"I think we should be moving on," Carky Vaughan said.

Amos decided to give everybody a parting shot. "Hey, Sandy," he said, "would you like to take a crap before you go?" He waved his hand expansively. "It's on the house. Normally we allow eight sheets of toilet paper, but for a distinguished *Tribune* columnist, I'll make it ten."

The interpreter stopped translating. Major Omi knew something was wrong but couldn't tell what. Carky Vaughan looked stricken. Only Sandy handled it.

"Very funny, Mr. Watson. Maybe some other time. I'll tell everybody you haven't lost your spirit."

The conducted tour went off to see finer things, leaving Amos alone in his domain.

Amos had kept up to date on Papaya, by notes from Carlos slipped in through the Package Line. Sometimes oral messages were brought in by one of the Filipino shanty-builders who was Donato's cousin. Before the Japs got themselves organized, Amos had been able to walk down to the main gate and see Carlos or Donato almost daily. They could smile and wave to each other and sometimes exchange a few words, even though the rules forbade conversation. Then the Japs covered the high open fence with sawali thatch so that the internees' view of the outside world was cut off.

Only when the Package Line opened at eight in the morning and at three in the afternoon was it now possible to get a glimpse of an outside friend. The outsiders entered through the main gate and handed over their packages for inspection. Internees had to stand well back from the inspection tables, but during these moments one might exchange a wave or smile. It was hardly worth the trouble, but, seeing how much it pleased Carlos, Amos continued to stand there.

Their notes moved back and forth easily in the false bottoms of the straw baskets. At first the notes were innocuous, as Amos had ordered, but when no discovery occurred, they began to exchange real information, although still being careful about what they said and how they said it. Since the Japs per-

mitted simple written messages, provided they were
informational and not emotional, Amos and Carlos
always pinned an open message to the outside of the
basket for the Japs to read and approve. This would
say something like "Buy me aspirin and toothpaste,"
or "My daughter Lisa had her baby." The most complicated of these open messages dispatched Donato
to the San Luis Hotel to persuade the manager, Mr.
Obispo, with a few pesos if necessary, to take Judy
Ferguson's clothes out of storage and give him the
ones on her list.

The important messages were the hidden, cryptic
ones: Carlos accepted as head houseboy to General
Miyama. Still living in servants' quarters with family. . . . General Miyama speaks some English, learns
more fast. Very smart man, very strict. . . . Staff officer Colonel Iseda lives in number-one guestroom.
Civilian interpreter Takasaki lives home with family
but comes to house every day. Old study now Miyama
office. . . . Biggest headache for Miyama is Manila
garbage. Sanitation trucks either wrecked in bombing
or taken for army use to carry supplies to Bataan.
Garbage all over streets. Very smelly. Many flies. Miyama worrying about epidemic, trying to get trucks
back. . . . Miyama changing curfew from 8:00 P.M.
to 10:00 P.M. but keeping blackout. . . . Papaya living
home with mother, sister, all okay, send love. No
entertainment because of blackout but will sing when
nightclubs open. She's in touch with others but being
careful. No news Ling. Miranda message fiancé killed.

Amos felt very sorry for Miranda. So many being

killed. He had information of his own to send out through Carlos to Papaya for whatever use she and "others" could make of it. Since most news in Santo Tomas was either common knowledge or unfounded rumor, about half of each, Amos often had little to report. However, he did have one source that even the Triumvirate didn't have, the commandant's office.

When he arrived in Santo Tomas, Amos had tried at once to find Felix Logan. "Tall boy with thick glasses and braces on his teeth? About seventeen? He's at Simpson School. His parents live in Cebu." Nobody had heard of Felix. Even the teenagers didn't seem to know him. With three thousand people getting settled all at once, it was understandable. Then Amos remembered Felix had been staying with a couple called Miller. He did not know the Millers, but he found someone who led him to Mrs. Miller, who said, "Oh, yes, Mr. Watson, Felix is here. He's in the Annex, the second floor. He'll be so glad to see you. He had *such* a nice dinner in your lovely house." Amos escaped before she could tell him what he and Felix had eaten that night.

That afternoon, right after the siesta quiet time, he found Felix by trial and error, going room to room through the second floor of the Annex building. He thought the young man looked rather forlorn. It must be difficult for someone his age to be thrown into such a strange environment with neither family nor school friends for support. His parents were still in Cebu, and all the Simpson kids were interned in Baguio.

This room was too public for what Amos had to

discuss. He asked Felix to join him for a walk outside. Felix seemed to welcome the attention.

After perfunctory questions about his parents ("no news yet") and his general welfare ("all right, I guess"), Amos came to the point. "Does anyone here know you speak Japanese?"

Felix shook his head. "No, sir. You told me I ought to keep quiet about it."

"Good man," Amos said. That was an excellent start. "Can you understand what they're saying?"

"Pretty much. Not every word of course. I think one or two of the guards must be Koreans or something. They speak funny. Excuse me, Mr. Watson, but what's the point?"

Amos stopped walking and looked down into Felix's eyes, holding his attention, not answering right away. Then he said, with solemn emphasis, "Felix, you could become the most important young man in this entire camp."

That certainly got his interest. Amos had not forgotten Dr. Clarke's comments about this boy, that he was class president, that the other kids called him Felix the Fixer, that Dr. Clarke sometimes wondered whether he ran the school or Felix did. That kind of boy, now lost in Santo Tomas, was the perfect candidate.

"Are you good at keeping secrets?"

Felix nodded. "Yes, sir."

"This is an extremely important secret. Any mistake could be serious. Quite serious. In fact, fatal."

Felix nodded again.

"I am collecting information for our friends on the

outside. Useful information about what the Japs are up to. How would you like to help?"

He watched Felix's eyes widen behind the thick lenses.

"Oh, boy," Felix said.

"That's just how I feel," Amos said. "It's a way to get even. Perhaps a small way at first, but it could become very useful."

"What would I have to do?"

"Get close to the Japs. Listen to them talk. Remember what they say and tell me."

"You mean be *friends*? Talk Japanese with them?"

"No, no, they must not know you can understand them."

"You mean just hang around with the guards?"

"Actually, I had something more than that in mind. You could work for them."

"Where? How?"

"In the commandant's office."

"Oh, nobody wants that job," Felix said scornfully. "That's where you have to bow all the time."

"Well, you know how to bow, don't you?"

"Sure. In Yokohama we had to bow every morning to the teacher. Or even when we met a teacher in the hall."

"Well, then."

"That was different. Here everybody gets out of bowing. Especially all the kids. Whenever we see one of the Japs coming, we turn some other way so we don't have to bow to him."

"You'd have to change that, of course. You'd have to bow the way you did in Yokohama. I suppose you might have to stand a little kidding." Amos thought it could be worse than that but didn't want to discourage him. "If you were working in the commandant's office, you'd learn things nobody else in camp would know. Nobody, not even the Triumvirate. You'd be *the* expert on the Japs. It could be invaluable." He held the boy's eyes again. "Felix, you must do this. Many people will be counting on you."

"I guess I can try."

"Good man."

Since, indeed, none of the internees wanted the humiliating job of sweeping and straightening the commandant's office every day, bowing right and left whenever a Jap entered, Felix had no trouble getting it. In fact, when he suggested the change to the previous jobholder, the man thought Felix was hunting for a payoff and gave him twenty pesos to trade places.

So Amos had his source.

When he first learned from Carlos that Papaya was "in touch with others," Amos wondered who they were but did not dare ask for names. That would be the message the Japs stumbled on. This morning, after Sandy Homobono's visit, he'd wondered if the columnist could be one of them. He was a patriot of sorts, to the extent that he had always gone out of his way to criticize American government and business, and he had supported Quezon's false-hearted cries for "immediate and total Philippine independence." Independence would have wrecked the country's economy, as Quezon well knew. Sandy was smart enough to know it too.

What side would he be on now? His own side, of course, switching to the *Manila Tribune*, as he said, "to make a living." But then what? Hard to imagine him turning to the Americans, especially now, on the edge of defeat. But would he like Japanese rule any better? If he really wanted Philippine independence, as Amos thought he did, where did Homobono think it was going to come from? Would he work for the Japanese or against them? Or both? Amos couldn't decide. He told Felix to keep his ears open for any Japanese conversation about Homobono.

Next day he forgot all about him when the dreaded news was broadcast by the Voice of Corregidor. It was heard on the secret radio hidden in the Education Building basement and then passed quickly throughout the camp. All Santo Tomas was shaken and subdued. Long faces everywhere one looked, almost no conversation, and a terrible sense of lost hope.

After three brave months, Bataan had fallen.

BOOK TWO

SURVIVAL

≡ 10 ≡

The Long Walk

When the word came through on April 9, Jack Humphrey sat down on the ground and took off his helmet. It was over. He was too weary and too hot to know what he felt.

For a week he had known it was coming, ever since Good Friday, when the incredible last barrage began. Six straight hours of heavy Jap artillery, most of it to the east of Mount Samat, but enough of it here on the west to deafen and terrify Humphrey and his men. When the infantry attack came, his Scouts held position.

But by the next afternoon word reached Humphrey that a lot of ground had been lost to the east. From then on, the trickles of news got worse and worse. Whole units were breaking up and collapsing and retreating. Finally it became what every commanding officer fears most: a rout, a complete rout, pellmell flight all the way down the whole east coast. Surrender had to follow.

Now the guns were silent. While waiting to learn

what would happen to them next, Jack Humphrey
thought up another letter to his wife.

Dear Sara,

*You've probably heard, we lost. No great surprise,
I guess. Not one bullet or man or plane came from
the States since this all started four months ago. The
battalion did its best, which was damn good. We gave
up only a hundred or so yards this whole last week.
We're still here in position, waiting for the Japs to
come tell us what to do. I hope they have food and
medicine for us. Everybody's in pretty bad shape.
They're going to have to take us to some kind of
POW camp. I hope it's by truck. Nobody's fit to walk
very far. I'm all right, no wounds. The malaria comes
back now and then, but the doc says I have to expect
that without quinine. Maybe the Japs will have some.
Mostly I'm hungry—starved, in fact. But now that
it's over we'll be getting food. I guess I won't be seeing
you for quite a while, but I'll write as soon as they
let me. Give the boys a hug.*

Love, Jack

———

From Cabcaben, on the southern end of Bataan, it
was less than sixty miles on level roads, up along
the coast of the peninsula and then across the flat
plain, to the junction city of San Fernando. From San
Fernando to the tiny railroad station of Capas, it
was only twenty-five miles by train. And from the
Capas station to the unfinished bamboo-and-nipa bar-

racks of Camp O'Donnell, it was less than four miles.

For Jack Humphrey, who did not even have to travel the full distance because he was already halfway up the peninsula, it was the longest trip of his life.

It started well enough. The slim, precise Japanese major, too neatly dressed to be anything but a staff officer, was courteous and clear, one professional officer addressing another. He spoke English and took pains to make sure Humphrey understood the orders.

"Twenty-one officers in your group," he said. "You are senior officer and will command. You know the Bagac-Pilar road?"

Humphrey nodded. They had been forced to retreat across it. It was a small gravel road not far away, the only decent east-west road on Bataan.

"And Balanga?"

"Yes, the town just north of Pilar."

"That is assembly point. You and your officers will report there. At Balanga you will receive food and rest. Also again at Orani and at Lubao. It is arranged."

Orani was another town at the top of the peninsula, but Lubao was out on the Luzon Plain, on Route 7. "Is Lubao our destination?"

"No, no, only food and rest. Sleep."

"Where are we going from there?"

"There will be—facilities."

"I'd prefer to stay with my men."

"That is not possible. Americans and Filipinos must be separate. But your men will also be going to Balanga. All troops go to Balanga. It is arranged."

He looked at his watch. "You leave at once, major. You should fill your canteens, since the day is hot. Also we give you rice because there is no food until Balanga."

"I'd like to say goodby to my men."

"I am afraid no time."

"Two minutes."

The Japanese major raised his eyebrows in surprise. "Okay, two minutes."

Humphrey returned to the open area of burned-down cogon grass where the Japanese had ordered his bedraggled men to wait. Long ago the weary army of Bataan had given up the formality of standing in the presence of an officer. Most of his men were sitting on the ground or squatting on their haunches. The sickest were lying down. They no longer looked like soldiers. Torn, ragged clothes, scarcely uniforms. Many of the men were shirtless, many wore bandages, some were barefoot. They were only tattered survivors. They gazed up at him without expression as he approached.

Jack Humphrey knew how to give orders, but he was no good at speeches. He didn't try. He halted in front of them, banged his heels together and came to stiff attention. Then, formally and precisely, just as in West Point days, he raised his right hand to salute them—and held the salute.

The men began to scramble to their feet. One by one, they were all getting up, some quickly, some very slowly. Two men were helping one of the very sick, supporting him under both arms. Another of the sick rose to one knee, the best he could do.

Everyone who could rise was now standing at attention to return his salute. A man with his right arm in a sling was saluting with his left. Humphrey could see tears rolling down brown faces. He felt his own face working, and his arm began to tremble, but still he held his salute. Finally he brought his arm down. He did a parade-ground about-face and walked away. The end of his command.

He knew most of the officers in his group, some of them very well. Up in this territory, they were all combat infantry. They looked terrible. He supposed he did too. Bud Osmondson looked too sick to walk. Probably dysentery. They said quiet hellos as they filled their canteens and accepted the small packet of boiled rice that a Japanese soldier handed to each of them. Humphrey filled the two canteens hooked to his web belt.

He had discarded his steel helmet the moment the fighting stopped and picked up a pith sun helmet, much lighter and cooler in the hot sun. The others wore sun helmets or fatigue caps or garrison caps. One had a handkerchief knotted over his head. One still wore a regulation steel helmet—maybe he thought hostilities were going to break out again. It was very hot.

"You must leave now," the Jap major told Humphrey.

"Will anyone accompany us?"

"That is not necessary for officers."

Good, Humphrey thought. We'll be on our own for a few hours, at least. "That officer," he said, "is much too sick to walk. Can you send him by truck?"

The Japanese spread his hands, palms up. "I am sorry. There is very few transportation. We must still fight your Corregidor."

"He may not be able to make it."

"I am sorry."

They set off, walking slowly in the heat, all of them weak from months of not having nearly enough to eat. They took turns supporting Bud Osmondson. The tall dead shape of Mount Samat, the last battle-ground, loomed off to their right as they walked the gravel road. When they came to a small river, Humphrey said if anybody wanted a bath, now was the time. Weak though they were, most joined him in sliding down the bank to the river. They stripped naked and lay flat in the shallow water. Afterward, their bodies dried quickly in the hot sun. They ate their packets of rice. Climbing back up the bank to the road was harder work, but all felt better.

The closer they came to the east-coast road, the worse the countryside looked. This was where the main attack had come. The flat land was torn by artillery fire, and even from the road they could see shattered vehicles and bloated bodies. They had to stop frequently for Osmondson, either to let him rest or to let him pull down his pants and endure the ravage of his bowels. After one such stop, a captain named Freddy Collins told Humphrey, "We ought to leave him."

Jack Humphrey looked at him. "We can't leave him. He'll die."

"He's going to die anyway if he has to walk the rest of the way. All the way to Lubao, the Jap told you? At least if we leave him, somebody might pick him up."

"Like some passing ambulance, you mean? Come on, Freddy. We're not so far from the east road. There'll be doctors at Balanga. Your turn to give Bud a hand."

Freddy Collins looked ready for mutiny but probably hadn't the strength. "Okay," he said finally, "but it's a waste of energy. You know that."

"I don't know any such thing. Let's go, captain."

"Don't chickenshit me, Jack. War's over."

It was late afternoon, just after five but the day still steaming, when they came around a bend and saw the east-coast road ahead of them. They all stopped and stared.

The road was jammed with people, not only the blacktop road itself but the dirt shoulders on both sides.

"What's all that?" somebody said. "A parade?"

"I doubt it," Humphrey said. Whatever it was, they would have to join it, since this was the only road up to Balanga.

As they came closer, Humphrey saw that the people on the road were his own army, Americans and Filipinos in separate groups, moving slowly northward in ragged columns, long stretches of open space between the groups. Watching on either side were silent Filipino men and women and even children, probably from the nearby coastal town of Pilar. Closer still, he could see Jap army guards patrolling alongside the edges of the columns.

When Humphrey's group reached the intersection,

they had to wade through the townspeople, who
turned in surprise to see American soldiers appearing
from behind them. As he led the way, a woman
pressed a ripe mango into his hand. He said thanks
and slipped it into his shoulder pack. He hadn't had
a mango since the end of the season last summer. It
was going to taste wonderful. He saw Filipinos passing pieces of candy and fruit to some of the other
officers as they came through onto the blacktop road.

Right away one of the Jap guards saw them and
started yelling at Humphrey. He had a rifle with bayonet attached and carried an unsheathed Philippine
bolo at his belt. Humphrey shrugged and held out his
hands to show he didn't understand. The guard yelled
some more, pointed toward the slow-moving column
and gave him a hard shove on the shoulder. Even
after all the weight he had lost, Humphrey was too
big to be much affected by the shove.

"Don't do that," he said.

The Jap's voice rose a notch as he pointed again
to an open space in the column.

"All right," Humphrey said. "We get it." He
turned to the other officers. "We join the line. Hang
on, Bud. Only a mile to go."

But it took more than an hour to reach Balanga,
and Bud Osmondson didn't get there. The march was
painfully slow, sometimes barely more than a shuffle.
Every now and then it would stop completely for no
apparent reason. Even out in the open country between Pilar and Balanga, silent Filipino civilians stood
at roadside, staring sadly at the marchers. If no guard
was watching, they would quickly try to give a

marcher some food, a little morsel wrapped in a banana leaf, a tin cup of water. Some made surreptitious V signs with their fingers.

A sudden blaring of horns from up ahead announced approaching vehicles. Three Japanese army trucks were headed south, no doubt for the attack on Corregidor. Soldiers standing in the open truck beds leaned out to jeer at the Americans and slash down at them with bamboo sticks. The marchers tried to get off the road, away from the trucks and the slashing. Some men fell down. The officers dragging Osmondson dropped him to get out of the way. Humphrey dodged one blow but caught another on his shoulder, only partially deflected by his sun helmet. The soldiers in the trucks were having a good time.

When the trucks had passed and the column was ready to move again, they tried to pick up Bud.

"No," Osmondson said weakly. "I can't walk anymore."

"Yes, you can, goddamn it," Humphrey said. "We're almost there."

Osmondson still didn't want to get up. The two officers holding his limp arms looked at Jack Humphrey. They had Bud halfway up, his legs still dragging on the road.

"Come on, Bud," Humphrey said. "On your feet."

A Jap guard with rifle and bayonet approached, yelling loudly, plainly furious that this particular little group was not moving.

In explanation, Humphrey pointed to the slack, dangling figure of Bud Osmondson.

The guard looked at Bud, made a noise like

"*Hunh*!" and bayoneted him in the chest. Osmondson didn't make a sound as the astonished officers let him fall. The guard stepped back, grinning, waving his bayonet back and forth as though to say, Who's next? Then he gestured that they should roll Osmondson's body off the road and get moving again. In silence, they did. Humphrey took one of Bud's dog tags, not knowing quite what he intended to do with it. He would have died anyway, Humphrey thought, but shit.

Toward sunset they arrived at Balanga, once a town of five thousand people, now badly wrecked by the fighting and bombing and shelling. This, the Jap major had said this morning, was "the assembly point—food and rest." There was a long period of standing around, waiting for the Japs to herd each cluster of marchers to its overnight location.

Humphrey's group was directed to a fenced-in schoolyard with a battered school building behind it. A water faucet from an artesian well was still functioning, or at least trickling, so with patience officers could refill their canteens. There were over a hundred men in the small yard. One corner of it was the latrine. Men with diarrhea and dysentery had made it horrible. Humphrey wondered how many days it had been in use to get like this. And if this was officers' country, what was it like for the enlisted men?

After an hour, when it was getting close to dark, the Japs rolled in a small wagon containing a barrel of boiled rice mixed with a few vegetables. The officers stood in line with mess kits or canteen cups to collect their portions. Jack Humphrey thought about the mango in his pack. It wouldn't keep forever, so he would eat it for dessert. It would be his tastiest meal in three months on Bataan, better even than the two days when they'd had a little fresh mule meat, courtesy of the Scouts Cavalry.

He looked for a place to sit, far from the latrine, where he and his mango would have a little privacy. Over there against the fence.

As he started to sit down, he saw a man a few yards away leaning stiffly against the fence, one hand behind his back. Even in the fading light Humphrey could see the large birthmark blotch on the man's left cheek, starting just below the eye. There couldn't be two like that in the whole Philippines. Master Sergeant—what was his name?—Maxsie, that was it, the one who'd stolen two of his best men. He wondered what had happened to them. And furthermore, what was a sergeant, even a master sergeant, doing here in the officers' compound?

Still holding his mess kit, Humphrey walked over to him. "Sergeant Maxsie? Major Humphrey."

Maxsie studied him for a long moment. "Major," he said, "I owe you two sergeants."

"That's right. Dubang and Olivo. Where are they?"

"They're both dead."

"Shit. How?"

"Yeah, damn fine men. Olivo killed during the retreat from Samat, if you can call that a retreat. He stayed there to buy a little extra time for all those fuckers who were running away. Dubang caught it just day before yesterday, on the march up from Cabcaben. Tried to keep his stripes a Jap wanted for a souvenir. Jap shot him and cut the stripes off his body. So I let him take mine." Maxsie showed Humphrey the ragged holes cut in his sleeves.

"Jesus." Humphrey shook his head. "I'm going to sit down and eat my supper. You've had yours, sergeant?"

"Yes, sir. It's lieutenant, by the way. My outfit ran out of officers."

"Congratulations."

"I guess. Better pay, if I ever get paid again, but that's about it. Battlefield demotion, I see it. Once you got master sergeant, there's no rank better till you get up to one-star general. The Japs drove our generals up from Cabcaben by truck. Where were you, major?"

Humphrey sat down and leaned back against the fence. He began to eat the gluey rice and vegetables with his spoon. You'd think a country that lived on rice could cook it better than this, he thought. "We were on the west side of Samat. And still there at the end. Nobody ran."

"The Scouts," Maxsie said with respect. "Few more regiments of them, the Japs'd still be trying to take Bataan."

That was just how Humphrey felt. "Sit down, sergeant—lieutenant."

"Thanks, I'm better off standing."

Humphrey looked up at him. It was getting hard to see, but Maxsie was still standing stiffly, one hand against his lower back. "You wounded?"

"Not exactly. I got hit by a rifle butt today. Still hurts."

"What'd you do?"

"I refused to bury a man."

"That doesn't sound very smart."

"No, I guess not. But he was still alive."

"My God."

"Yeah, that's how I saw it. Soldier falls down the side of the road, couldn't get up, Jap tries to stick a shovel in my hands and wants me to bury him. He's still trying to get up. I shake my head, Jap hits me with the butt, then he turns around and smashes the guy's head in. He's sure dead now. Jap gives me the shovel again, and this time I do like he says." Maxsie lowered his voice. "You want a cigarette, major?"

Humphrey couldn't believe the offer. "You have some?"

"A few. Way this march is going, I may not get to finish them. Here."

He held out a half-empty pack and Humphrey reached up to take one. A real genuine American cigarette. "I'll trade you half a mango," he said. They were about the same age, and Maxsie was now a fellow officer. And besides, Maxsie appreciated the Scouts. "My name's Jack."

Maxsie laughed. "I haven't been a lieutenant long enough to call a major Jack. I'll call you what your men called you. Dubang and Olivo. They called you the Hump."

"I never heard that." He didn't know his Scouts thought of him as anything but Major Humphrey.

"Yeah, the Hump. They talked about you a lot, pretty boring after a while. Here's a match, Hump."

Humphrey took the box of matches and, hands trembling a bit, lighted the cigarette. Best thing he ever tasted.

"How come you're wearing that ring?" Maxsie said.

"It's a West Point ring."

"Shit, I know what it is. Big Jap souvenir. How come they didn't take it?"

"I don't know. Maybe they didn't see it. We just joined the march late this afternoon."

"We been walking three days. Every time they switch guards, the new ones check our stuff, looking for goodies. Bet you there's not a watch or razor or ring left between here and Cabcaben, unless it was really hidden. Put it in your boots or underwear, if you want to keep it."

"Thanks, I will."

"You got any Jap souvenirs?"

"Nope, I'm not much for souvenirs." This really was one of the best cigarettes ever, although it made him slightly dizzy. He was smoking in small puffs to make it last.

"Good. Japs find anybody with souvenirs, they figure they had to come from their own soldiers' dead bodies. They cut your head off. Even if it's just Jap money. They're big for cutting off heads. Did you say something about a mango?"

"Sure did. As soon as I finish this smoke. What's your first name?"

"I don't use it. Just Maxsie."

"A pretty bad one, huh? Two more puffs and we'll have the fruit course."

Humphrey held the short butt carefully between his first two fingers. There was barely enough sticking out for him to get his lips on it. The smoke came hot this close to the burning tip, but it still tasted good. One more drag. He burned his fingers a bit, but it was worth it.

The schoolyard was dark now. Most of the men were lying down, using their packs as pillows. It was still hot.

Humphrey felt around in his pack to find the mango and his mess-kit knife. He could not see the mango, but he knew just how it looked: oblong, slightly pointy at one end, golden yellow skin with speckles of brown. Inside, the fruit would be a brilliant dark orange. Finest mangoes in the world, better than in Panama or Puerto Rico. He placed the mango in his mess kit so that any juice would be saved, dug the dull point of his knife through the skin, a quarter-inch off center, slicing carefully along the edge of the flat seed. He did the same on the other side so there were two equal pieces plus the half-inch center.

"Here," he said, holding up one of the pieces to Maxsie.

They ate in silence, slowly and with total concentration, scraping the ripe fruit out of the skin with their teeth. Humphrey leaned over his mess kit so that any juice he spilled would drip into it. When the melon skin was finally as empty as his teeth could make it, he tore it into pieces and chewed them one by one to capture the last of the juice. The taste, the

experience, was incredible. That Filipina would never
realize what she had done for him, not just the life-
giving fruit but the gift itself. Just knowing that they
cared.

As he ate, he thought about the problem of the
seed. "Maxsie?"

"Yeah?"

"You finished?"

"It was terrific. Better than pussy."

"Now about the seed—"

"You eat the seed. I've had enough."

"No, we're both going to have the seed. It's my
mango and I'm a major, so I get the meaty side. You
get the slippery side, okay?"

"You don't have to do this."

"I know I don't, but since you haven't yet run out
of cigarettes . . ."

With his teeth Humphrey pulled the strip of skin
away from the seed section and gnawed his way thor-
oughly down the edge of the seed. The meat came
away in small, delectable bites. Maxsie's side would
taste as good, but he would be getting stringy pulp,
not real bites. Humphrey had never taken so long to
eat a mango. At last he gave the now slippery seed
to Maxsie, both of them using two hands to make
sure it didn't fall into the dirt. Humphrey drank the
juice in his mess kit.

"That made a real difference," Maxsie said. "I can
face tomorrow."

"You going to stand up all night?"

"No. Have to lie down now, I guess."

Humphrey climbed to his feet. "Here, I'll give you

a hand." Together they got Maxsie down flat with only one gasp of pain.

————

In the morning two officers lay dead in the schoolyard. Maxsie knew one of them. "That's old Herrold. He had malaria real bad and now he's been on the road three days in the heat. Just ran out of gas, I guess."

They didn't know the other man, a young lieutenant. His body was so thin it took almost no effort to lift it out of the way.

Humphrey told the officers who had come with him yesterday what Maxsie had said: get rid of any Jap souvenirs, hide anything you hope to keep, especially rings, watches and metal bars and oak leaves—"if anybody still cares about insignia."

Freddy Collins, who had suggested dumping Bud Osmondson yesterday afternoon, felt more protective about his gold Point ring with its clear red stone. "This hasn't been off my hand since graduation day," he said. "I'll just turn it around so it doesn't show."

"Suit yourself," Humphrey said. He hadn't realized Freddy was so sentimental about the Point—or about anything, in fact.

"What makes him the expert?" Freddy Collins said. He was staring over at Maxsie, who was leaning against the fence and massaging his sore back, which had stiffened during the night on the hard ground. The ugly purple-red birthmark stood out in the bright morning sun.

"He's been on the road longer than we have. All the way from Cabcaben."

"Are we meant to be impressed?" Freddy asked. But he turned his ring so that the stone was hidden.

The Japs herded the officers back to the blacktop road. A long delay in the already-hot sun as Jap officers and guards tried to organize the several thousand troops who had spent the night in Balanga, some in open fields, some in barbed-wire enclosures. They were breaking them up into groups of about a hundred, all Americans in this one, all Filipinos in that one, and then assigning officers to lead each group.

Humphrey asked Maxsie, whose back was plainly bothering him, "You going to be able to walk?"

"Bet your ass," Maxsie said. "Anybody don't walk today ain't never going to walk again."

Humphrey thought carefully about the day and the heat and the march ahead before he said, "Want me to carry your pack?"

Maxsie grinned at him. "Want me to carry yours? I got mango energy today. Stick together, Hump, see if we can get in the same group. I'll spell you if you get tired."

Before the march began, they filed past a row of big steel drums from which Jap soldiers ladled dollops of rice into canteen cups or mess kits or open hands. At the end of the line of drums, two soldiers with rifles stood guard, eyes sharp, watching everyone. They were identically dressed in khakis, wool puttees wound in spirals, and shapeless woolen field caps with short visors, a star on the front and a piece of white cloth hanging down behind for sun protection.

Humphrey and Maxsie were close behind as Freddy Collins came off the rice line, already beginning to eat by hand from his canteen cup.

One of the sharp-eyed guards stopped Freddy and reached for his right hand. Freddy drew back. The guard spoke to him in a fierce voice, pointing to his hand.

Well, that didn't take long, Humphrey thought. There goes Freddy's ring, Class of '34. He was glad his own ring, Class of '27, was tucked into his jockey shorts.

The guard hit Freddy in the face so hard that he staggered and dropped his canteen cup, the rice spilling out on the ground. The guard grabbed Freddy's hand, a knife blade flashed in the sun, and before Humphrey realized what was happening the guard was holding Freddy's severed finger. He removed the ring, looked at the shiny red stone with satisfaction, and tossed the finger aside.

Freddy, staring at the bleeding stump of bone and gristle, gave a short, hoarse cry. Two other officers moved quickly to help bandage the hand. It was very bloody.

In dead silence Humphrey and Maxsie collected their portions of rice. When they had moved past the two guards, being careful not to meet their eyes, Maxsie said, "There's times it's better being an enlisted man."

On that day's march along the coast to the village

of Orani, and the next day's march across the Pampanga Plain to Lubao, the weather gave no mercy. Still the height of the dry season, it was blistering hot. Jack Humphrey plodded along, hour after hour, trying not to think about when he would next resort to his canteen. The longer he could wait, the more he could think about something else, the better his chances.

Dear Sara,

This morning we finally left Bataan and crossed over into Pampanga. We could tell the exact spot because even after all the fighting, there's still a cement road sign on Route 7 saying Pampanga Province. No difference in the road or the heat, but at least we're off Bataan. Hope I never see it again the rest of my life.

Japs guards have pored over my pack three different times but I didn't lose much. My ring and watch are tucked in my shorts, and my pesos and your picture are inside my boots. The searching isn't all that thorough. I guess the guards figure all the good loot has been taken.

I've seen some awful things on this march. I don't even want to tell you about them. But the strange part is that everything, whether it's the worst damn sort of horror or a lucky break, seems like an accident. A random event. At the Point they used to teach us about random numbers. You toss a coin, heads or tails, and it's going to average out fifty-fifty. You can count on it, it's predictable. But then you can hit a streak where it comes up tails eight, nine, ten, a dozen

times in a row, totally unpredictable. That's the way
the Japs treat us—random behavior at its scariest. In
almost every village or barrio there's one of those
artesian-well standpipes where the people get their
water. Sometimes the guards will let a few of us fill
our canteens, sometimes not. Filipino civilians stand
along the road, wanting to give us a little food, maybe
a chunk of sugar cane, maybe a banana. Sometimes
a guard will look the other way and let us accept.
Sometimes not. Sometimes a guard, if he catches a
Filipino trying to help us, will shoot the poor bastard
or bayonet him. Sometimes not. It's a total crapshoot,
a roll of the dice, except that you're rolling your life.
I've been lucky. I got a mango the first day, some
sugar cane to chew on the next day. I even ate a raw
turnip that an old Filipina gave me, and you know
how I feel about turnips.

We move terribly slowly because the road is so
jammed and the men are so weak or sick. Malaria,
dysentery, plain old starvation—you name it—and
always the heat. The Japs sometimes let us rest every
hour or two, but it depends on the individual guards.

I don't think they had any idea what bad shape
we were in. Or how many of us there were going to
be, not just the soldiers but all the thousands of civilian refugees who fled to Bataan with us and now
are trying to go back to their homes. The Japs didn't
even have any food lined up until Balanga. That was
no big problem for our group, since we got there the
first night, but it was a disaster for the men who had
to walk all the way from Cabcaben. You can look
these places up on the map. You'll see it's no great

distance—if you're healthy. Pretty bad if you're not.

But the worst is the water. In this heat you want a drink all the time. I never used to think about water. If I was thirsty, I'd think about a beer or a bourbon or even iced tea. Water was something that came out of a tap. Now we think about water every minute, and there's never enough. Every day we see troops dive off the road to get a drink of water at any dirty little stream, even a carabao wallow. You try to stop them, the water's polluted, and you know they're going to get dysentery or some other tropical disease, but they don't have the discipline to say no, I can't drink that. Especially the younger guys and the Filipino troops. They don't know any better or they just don't care.

I have a new friend, man named Maxsie. "Friend" is too strong a word—we've only spent a few days together. He's old army infantry, joined up at the start of the Depression and worked his way up to master sergeant. You know what that means. He got promoted to lieutenant on Bataan, but kept his stripes and rockers, at least until a souvenir hunter cut them off. I asked him why was that, and he said the war made him a lieutenant, but he made himself a master sergeant. A good guy, like me a big admirer of the Scouts. We take care of each other.

We'll be coming into Lubao tonight. A fair-sized town, and it's in Pampanga instead of Bataan, so it ought to be better than the last couple of stops. I hope so. Say hello to the boys.

Love, Jack

They could smell the campsite at Lubao before they came to it, the terrible, now-familiar stench of dysentery stools in open latrines.

"Jesus," Maxsie said, "that really gives a man an appetite. I can hardly wait for supper."

The camp was surrounded by a fence with a sign announcing the National Rice and Corn Corporation. Just outside the entrance was the line of steel drums containing the evening meal. In spite of the stench, everyone got out his kit or cup. Humphrey was grateful that in addition to a generous rice ration each man got a packet of salt. It would make the rice taste better and it would help those suffering heat prostration.

The fence enclosed a flat hundred-yard-long area. Off to one side was the main source of the stench, an open-air straddle trench. Humphrey knew from experience it would be crawling, swarming with maggots, a sight so revolting that many men could not use the trench without vomiting. A very long line of men waited in the late-afternoon sun to fill their canteens at a single faucet. In the center of the yard stood a sheet-iron warehouse that must, not so long ago, have held rice and corn.

"Looks like we got here late for the water line," Humphrey said. "Let's eat first."

Fat green horseflies buzzed at their food. By the time they finished eating, the open area was crowded, and still more men were filing through the gate. Plainly there was not enough space.

Instead of halting the flow and sending new arrivals to some other camp area, the Jap guards began herding men into the warehouse, Humphrey and Maxsie among them. Humphrey held up one of his canteens, the empty one, and shook it, indicating the water line. The guard nodded his understanding, pleasantly enough, but pointed to the warehouse. Then he pointed again to the warehouse and to Humphrey's canteen and nodded quickly three times: there was water inside the warehouse.

"Want to bet?" Maxsie said. His back ached again after the day's march. He was not optimistic.

The empty warehouse had a concrete floor and a high ceiling with dim bulbs. The daylight that came through the open doors would not last much longer. The air was stifling. But, yes, there was a water faucet. A line had already formed in front of it.

"Give me your canteens," Humphrey said. "I'll fill them." When Maxsie started to argue, Humphrey said, "You find us a good space, over against that wall. Before it all gets taken. Here, take my pack, lie down and spread out, save us some room. I'll get the water."

"Fucking majors," Maxsie said, but he took the pack and handed over his canteens.

Jack Humphrey joined the line. It moved slowly, as slowly as the water trickling from the single faucet. The daylight faded, the doors darkened, and he was still in line. He was very tired and hot. When he drank the rest of the water in his second canteen, it made him sweat heavily. The tinkling sound of empty canteens banging against each other was all around him as the line inched forward. The air, thick and hot to begin with, took on the odors of feces and of filthy men.

As he was nearing the head of the line, a man slumped to the concrete floor and rolled over, dead. One less man ahead of me, was Humphrey's only weary thought. The man right behind grabbed the dead man's canteen, then quickly patted the pockets to see if there was anything worth taking. There wasn't. Might as well leave him right there. Let the Japs worry about it when they find him in the morning.

It took Humphrey almost ten minutes at the slow faucet to fill all four canteens to the brim and cap them. As he walked back to find Maxsie, with his arms full of precious cargo, he could see in the dim light that the water line was even longer now than when he had joined it. Patient, tired, silent men waiting, waiting for the water that might or might not keep them alive. Humphrey supposed some of them could be there all night. The sad tinkle of empty canteens was the only sound from the long line.

———

Jack Humphrey dreamed that the rains had come at last. In his dream he even heard the raindrops pounding noisily on the sheet-iron roof, but when he awoke he saw through the doorway that they were in for another day of bright sunshine. Maxsie claimed his back was better for having slept on the hard concrete floor. Humphrey didn't see how this was possible. His own back was sore and stiff.

This morning of all mornings, the Japs were slow getting started. Until they could move men out of the yard area, creating some open space, they wouldn't let anyone out of the warehouse. The temperature was already unbearable, the sheet-iron walls and roof seeming to magnify and concentrate the day's heat. The canteen line was still there, still shuffling toward the faucet.

At last the guards stood aside, allowing the men to escape the inferno. By now they were so used to the stench that it did not seem as bad as last evening. After another meal of rice and salt, they were on the march to San Fernando.

The blacktop road between Lubao and San Fernando had buckled and broken under the weight of Japanese tanks and trucks. It was difficult, painful walking, especially for all the men who no longer had combat boots. The heat of the crumpled blacktop came right through worn sneakers or the scraps of clothing men had tied around bare feet.

San Fernando was the railroad and highway junction city for rich Pampanga Province. Starting at the outskirts, the streets were lined with civilians, more than Maxsie had seen anywhere during the entire march from Cabcaben. The same sorrowing brown faces, the same stealthy gifts of food when the guards weren't looking, the same surreptitious V signals, sometimes the quick little pats on the shoulder, the touches of friendship, but many more than ever before. There were also more Japs patrolling both sides of the column.

Every now and then as they wound through the

city, Humphrey would see a Filipino soldier seize the chance to slip out of line and vanish into the thick civilian crowd. Most of them escaped successfully, but he saw the guards catch one.

Instantly the column was halted and guards took up position facing the crowds on both sides of the street, waving their rifles back and forth in menace. The captured Filipino soldier began to scream and cry for help as three guards wrestled him to the pavement. He begged the guards for mercy and at the same time shouted for someone to save him, save him, *Jesus, Maria, Joseph*, save him.

The guards held him face up, arms and legs spread. A fourth guard began to bayonet him, thrust by careful thrust, in the groin, in each arm and leg, in the stomach, but just shallow jabs, very expert, making sure not to kill him. The soldier's shrieks and sobs filled the street. Answering groans and prayers and curses came from the crowd. Humphrey's eye was caught by an attractive young Filipina with short black hair standing only a few yards behind the atrocity. Her eyes were bright with horror and her mouth was so wide open and so rigid in a silent scream that he could see one of her front teeth was gold.

Finally—the guards had no more time to waste on this particular object lesson—a bayonet stroke was delivered straight down through the soldier's head. Leaving the body in the street, the guards got the column moving again.

Humphrey wondered how many Filipino soldiers had escaped into the crowd to make up for that one poor bastard. He hoped a lot.

They spent the night in a large open shed that had been the city's cockfighting arena. Although it was still very hot, the arena was a definite improvement over the Lubao warehouse. They were given a relatively generous meal—bits of fish mixed in with the rice and vegetables, and even a cup of weak tea.

Maxsie was delighted. "Hump," he said, "when I write my guidebook about all the places and meals and latrines on this fucking march, Cabcaben to wherever we wind up, I'm going to give my top grade to San Fernando."

"Yeah," Humphrey said. "And how about bayonet practice?"

"You can't have everything," Maxsie said.

They left town at ten o'clock the next morning—by train. Maxsie couldn't believe their luck when they were marched to the railroad station and ordered to wait on the platform. They quickly grabbed a place where Maxsie could lean his back against the station wall.

"I told you San Fernando was top-grade," he said. "We're finally going to get a *ride* to wherever it is, just like the generals."

But it wasn't at all like the generals. While they waited in the sun, more and more soldiers arrived. They were all worn down to the nub, exhausted by the long hot days, but spirits picked up as they realized the marching was over. The long straight lines of the rails stretched before them, south down to Manila, north up to Lingayen Gulf. It didn't matter which direction, they were going by rail. Finally a train came chugging into the station from the south.

"I guess that's us," Humphrey said. "Wonder if we're going right back to Stotsenburg, where I started from. It's only fifteen or so miles."

"That'd be good," Maxsie said. "I'll buy you a drink at the officers' club. Maybe we can get in a little polo."

It was less funny when they saw how they would travel. Behind two passenger cars reserved for the Japanese, the train was made up of battered old box-cars, completely enclosed by corrugated steel. A single sliding door in the center of each side was the only opening. Jap guards began to load the prisoners, counting off a hundred men to each boxcar, jamming them in. Everybody had to stand erect. Once inside, the men tried to keep away from the scalding hot walls, but it wasn't always possible. When the loading was finally done, the guards walked down the length of the train, closing and sealing the doors.

With the doors closed, no air circulated. At last the train began to move. As it picked up a little speed outside the station, the swaying motion threw men against the steel sides, burning their skin. Soon men began to faint standing up and had to be supported by friends. Some died in place and were allowed to slump to the floor.

The twenty-five-mile trip lasted four hours, with halts and delays and countless stops at small nameless stations. At each station the guards opened the doors to let in air, but no one was allowed to leave the boxcars. When the doors opened, Filipino civilians waiting at the stations, knowing by now what these trains were, threw fruit and pieces of sugar cane over the heads of the guards and into the cars. For once, the guards made no effort to stop them.

Pieces of fresh fruit came flying through the air to be caught by desperate hands: mangos, papayas, chicos, chunks of the round, deep-green Philippine watermelon, bananas of every size and color—the square yellow *latundan*, the little yellow *lakatan*, the green *balangon*, the tiny *señorita*, the stubby, fat red *morado*, a cooking banana but as welcome today as any of the others.

Of course, you had to be lucky enough to be standing in the center of a boxcar somewhere near the door. And more food was thrown into the boxcars opposite the station building, where most of the Filipinos were, than at the extreme front and rear of the train. Jack Humphrey, who happened to be in one of the middle boxcars, and who happened to have been packed in fairly close to the door, and who also happened to be tall enough to outreach other clutching hands, managed to capture four pieces of fruit during the journey. Random numbers, random variables.

There was no way to tell how much difference that fruit made to him and Maxsie. All he knew for sure was that when the train finally reached the last stop, he and Maxsie were still alive, while some others were not. Wherever they were, whatever came next, at least they could leave the train.

Maxsie, whose back was crippled from four hours of standing in the swaying train, had to be helped to the ground. He took one look at the tiny station sign—"Capas"—and said, "Oh, shit, I know where we're going. Sorry, Hump, no polo."

While they waited for all the other boxcars to finish unloading, Maxsie said they must be headed for Camp O'Donnell—O'Donnell, with the accent on the last syllable. He had heard about O'Donnell when he was stationed at Cabanatuan, back last fall when he was guarding those warehouses full of rice and trying to train his Filipino draftees to be soldiers. O'Donnell was three or four miles outside the village of Capas, a training camp for an entire Philippine Army division. Maxsie had heard he might be transferred there when it was ready for troops. "It was a long way from finished when the war started," Maxsie said. "What you want to bet it still is?"

The long tattered column moved out of the Capas station and crossed the tiny main street lined by native houses—nipa thatch roofs, bamboo floors resting on bamboo stilts, children's solemn faces peering out of the deep shadows underneath the flooring to watch the defeated army pass in silence.

A narrow gravel road, dusty in the dry heat, led them westward out of town under the crisscrossing branches of tall trees. When they passed the last of the shacks and huts on the outskirts of Capas, they came to open country. There, just to the left of the road, was a handsome stand of trees—avocado, mango, santol.

Men broke from the column to reach the fruit. The guards clubbed them back to the road, and clubbed two of them to death, but a few managed to seize an avocado or a mango before rejoining the column. Humphrey, who still had the precious security of half a banana tucked in his pocket, knew that those few,

who could just as well be lying dead beneath the trees,
not only had food to sustain them but also the miracle
of their own good luck. Random variables.

Several miles up ahead, hazy blue-green in the
shimmering heat, stood the long chain of the Zambales Mountains, stretching all the way down to Bataan. Around them was nothing but cogon grass, tall
and brown in the dry season. No farms or rice paddies
or fruit trees this far out of town. Empty country.
Empty until at last they reached the barbed-wire fence
and the guard towers.

Humphrey and Maxsie looked at each other, then
shook hands. Whatever awaited them, they had made
it.

Inside the camp they were taken to an open-field
area in front of a vacant speaker's platform and told
to remain standing.

"What do you suppose that's for?" Humphrey
asked.

Maxsie had both hands behind his back, massaging
hard. "This is where they give us the VD lecture," he
said, "so we don't get in trouble with the local girls."

They had to wait an hour in the sun under the eyes
of the guards. A few hundred yards away they could
see the barracks they would be living in, the usual
bamboo-and-nipa construction.

At last two figures approached the speaker's platform. One was a Filipino in a clean white shirt and
neatly pressed khaki shorts. The other was a portly
Japanese officer, perhaps fifty years old. The two men
mounted the platform and stood side by side. The
officer had a mustache and big horn-rimmed glasses,

leather boots and baggy shorts hanging to his knees. He put his fists on his hips as he studied his latest group of prisoners. Then he spoke in Japanese in a shrill voice, while the Filipino translated.

"I am Captain Yoshio Tsuneyoshi. I am the commandant of this Camp O'Donnell. The Filipinos and the Americans live in separate areas of the camp. You will have nothing to do with each other. And why is that? Do you know why is that? It is because you evil Americans deserve only each other. You have lost the war! The Japanese Empire will now rule all of East Asia. You are finished. You have proved that you are an inferior race. I do not consider you prisoners of war. *You are my captives.*"

Captain Tsuneyoshi was getting worked up. His shrill voice grew louder as he talked, and he began to wave his arms in excitement.

"I was told to expect twenty thousand captives in this camp. Perhaps as many as thirty thousand. That was the plan. And do you know how many you are? You are sixty thousand. Do you know what this means? It means there is not enough food. It means there is not enough water. There are not even enough buildings. Do you think that I care? I will tell you. I do not care. I do not care if you live or die. You are animals. American animals. Inferior American animals. Anyone who does not obey orders will be executed. Anyone who tries to escape will be executed. Anyone who tries to communicate with our enemies outside the camp will be executed."

"I don't think he likes us," Maxsie whispered.

Captain Tsuneyoshi's arms thrashed the air. "You

Americans are our enemies. We will fight you and fight you and fight you. You will be destroyed."

With a final gesture, an angry shake of his fist, he turned and left the platform. In amazement the prisoners watched the stumpy figure march furiously away.

"Not too promising," Maxsie said.

≡ 11 ≡

Zorro and Peanut

After the fall of Corregidor, Papaya went back to singing.

Corregidor was so sad, the final end of everything. She watched the day the Japs brought all the Corregidor prisoners to Manila by landing craft and then marched them up Dewey Boulevard in a long victory parade. Right past the High Commissioner's Residence, where the Japanese flag now flew and where General Homma now lived. So very sad.

With Corregidor gone and the fighting finished, the Japs would surely let Manila nightlife start up again. The blackout had been lifted even before the fall, and the movie houses had already opened. Nightclubs and hotels could not be far behind. She would follow Amos's orders: sing for the Japs, be nice to them, find out things and pass them along.

The morning after the parade of prisoners she met with Jorge Esteban. Jorge had been her agent and manager for seven years, ever since her appearance in the music festival at Rizal Stadium when, as sixteen-year-old Carmen Despensayang, she sang with her high school band, the Santa Mesa Swing Kings. Next morning she became Papaya, thanks to a gushing newspaper review: ". . . a voice and a body as ripe, plump and sweet as a perfect papaya. . . ." And that afternoon Jorge Esteban introduced himself.

Jorge, now in his fat fifties, wore his trademark pink sharkskin suit, the way President Quezon always wore his specially designed black-and-white tango shoes for dancing. Jorge was an excellent manager. He was aggressive and imaginative and demanded high fees. He even had a reputation for being fairly honest, which in the Manila entertainment world was rare. However, Papaya had her suspicions. When she became Amos Watson's *querida*, she asked him to look over Jorge's contracts and financial statements. Amos told her most of it was fine but to challenge Jorge on several items that struck him as fishy, particularly the skimpy record royalties.

Jorge did not bluster or deny or pretend to be deeply wounded. Instead, he shrugged and smiled. "These things happen," he explained.

Papaya smiled back. "Yes, but not to me, Jorge. Not anymore, okay? There are other managers. There is only one me."

"Actually, little Carmen, there is only one me, also."

This was true enough. But from then on, Amos never found anything fishy in the financial statements, and Papaya made sure Jorge knew she was paying close attention.

This morning she told him she wanted to go back to work.

"Good," Jorge said. "Only engagements, though. There won't be any records or movies. Not for a long time."

"Okay, engagements. Let everybody know I am available so I get the best spots. And the best price."

"Obviously. But it isn't going to be like with the Americans."

"Why not? Don't the Japanese have money?"

Jorge looked at her. "You mean you would be willing to sing for the Japs?"

"Jorge, this is business. You are always telling me I should decide things on what is best for business, long-run and short-run."

"I'm not sure this would be good long-run."

"In war maybe there is no long run."

Jorge considered this. "What would you sing?"

"How do I know? Filipino songs, Spanish songs. American songs on request, maybe. I can learn Japanese songs if I have to. You get the money, I'll worry about the music."

Jorge thought for a while. He seemed reluctant. Then he said, "They are taking over the Army-Navy as an officers' club, but I don't think there will be singing. I suppose I could ask. I hear Lopez is turning his Mabalinga into some kind of private supper club, with new Jap partners. There is supposed to be a small band."

The Mabalinga had been a popular restaurant on Mabini Avenue, within walking distance of both the Army-Navy Club and the Manila Hotel, now the Jap military headquarters. Papaya knew it well. A good big room, although the ceiling was not quite high

enough for the best acoustics. She also knew Aurelio
Lopez, the mestizo owner. It was just like Aurelio to
go into partnership with the Japs, protecting himself
against any difficulties with liquor licenses and other
necessary permissions. Oh well, she thought, it is a
time of adjustments for everyone.

"That sounds good."

Jorge nodded. "I'll try." Then he thought of something. "Is it all right if I use Mr. Watson's name?"

"For what?"

Jorge, who was never embarrassed, actually looked
embarrassed. He said in a stiff voice, "For negotia-
tions. I think his name might be good for business."
Then he shook his head and laughed. He was too
irrepressible to be embarrassed for more than a few
seconds. "When you started with him, it was very
good for business because he was so rich and everybody knew him. Lots of gossip, many newspaper
items, very nice publicity. Then when he predicted
we would lose a war with Japan, it was very bad for
business. It was awkward for you to be connected
with him. But now I think he will again be good for
business, at least with Japs. They think he was the
one true American prophet."

Papaya knew Amos would have been delighted
with this. In the old days, only six months ago, she
would have made a wonderful story out of it, acting
it out in their suite at the Bayview, embellishing here
and there. She knew how to make Amos laugh. "All
right," she said, "you can use his name."

"People are going to ask why you are singing for
the Japs."

Yes, indeed, Papaya thought, but that can't be helped. "Tell them it is for the usual reason. Money."

Her mother and her half sister, Karen, found that hard to believe, and they didn't even know about her hoard of Amos Watson's pesos. Her Spanish father, when he heard about it, found it impossible. He telephoned her at once. He had always been proud of her, she thought perhaps he loved her more than any of the children of his marriage, but now he was angry.

"Carmen, they have destroyed this country. They have killed our friends. You cannot sing for them."

"Papa, I'm not singing for them, I'm singing for money."

"You don't need it."

"Yes, I do. The expenses of this house—"

Her father knew better. "You have always been smart about money," he interrupted. "You have made much more than I ever did, and I know you haven't just lost it somewhere. And then your—profitable—liaison with Mr. Watson." Her father had been impressed by her affair with Amos and admired his gifts, especially the ruby necklace. "I know you, Carmen, you are rich. But if something strange has gone wrong, something you have not told me, I can try to give you and your mother additional money." A pause. "Although these are very difficult times."

"Thank you, Papa, you have always been generous. Don't worry, it will be all right. I can't just sit around the house, you know. I have to work or go crazy."

"It's fine to work, but work for your own people,

the Spanish and the Filipinos. Sing for them, not for those Japs."

The Mabalinga kept its name and its choice location on the corner of Mabini Avenue, but almost everything else was different. What had once been a formal restaurant with starchy white tablecloths and napkins and a long continental menu printed in almost illegible italic script became a more casual, more intimate club. The single large room was broken up by private alcove tables along two walls. In one corner, where a piano player in a dinner jacket had provided discreet music, there was now space for a trio. The Japanese military forbade public dancing by their army and navy personnel, but civilians were under no such restriction.

The two new menus included nothing remotely continental or American. One was traditional Japanese—sushi, sashimi, tempura, beef—and one was Filipino to provide local color, but only "safe dishes," Aurelio Lopez explained. Shrimp, fish, the usual *adobos* and a variety of the sweet Filipino desserts, but "nothing risky," like the pungent *bagoong* paste, or *kare-kare*, oxtail and tripe cooked in peanut sauce. "My partners," Aurelio said, "don't want the customers to have too much adventure."

Membership in the new Mabalinga Club was, Aurelio said, strictly up to his partners. All army and navy officers willing to pay the fee were automatically acceptable. Papaya was pleased to learn there were many more high-ranking officers—generals and admirals—than lieutenants. Many Japanese civilians were also members. Engineers, businessmen, a recently arrived symphony conductor—new Jap civilians were coming in every week, now that the war in the Philippines was over.

The partners also welcomed certain non-Japanese members. The new Filipino puppet government officials, the mayor and all his opportunistic gang, were given a discount on the entrance fee, much to Aurelio's disgust. His guiding principal as a major restaurateur was the same under the Japanese as under the Americans: profit. He could not see why the puppet officials should get a break. "They are all thieves," he said. "They can afford the full rate." Leading members of the German business community were also urged to join, though not at a discount. So were Spanish businessmen, if they were important enough, but there were few Spanish takers.

On opening night, on the long ride down to the Mabalinga in her horse-drawn *calesa*, Papaya worried how she would feel when she sang for the enemy, and how they would feel about her.

She also worried about how much information she could get in the months ahead and what she would do with it if she got it. The *Manila Tribune*, published by the Japs, listed seventeen acts that were punishable by death. Number three was the one that interested her: "any person who commits acts of espionage, collects or betrays vital military secrets to the enemy." Well, nothing to fear so far. She didn't know a single vital military secret and might never know one.

She wished she could still use her car and driver, but everybody except the military had to have a special automobile permit these days. The *calesa* had a

comfortable swaying motion, and she liked the
rhythmic clop of hooves on the pavement, but it was
a slow trip from her home in Pasay, giving her too
much time to fret.

When her carriage finally drew up to the Mabalinga, she saw cars parked for two blocks on both
sides of Mabini. Many were military cars, but others
were not. Some people were getting automobile per-
mits. At least she would have a decent crowd for her
comeback. She was angry at Amos for making her go
through all this.

It was crowded inside. All the tables on the big
floor were filled, as were all the alcoves and the long
bar. Thick cigarette smoke. Japs everywhere. She had
never seen so many Japs in one place. But also a
number of Filipino faces. She must not judge the Filipinos too harshly. She didn't approve of those who
had become club members, but she knew some were
invited as guests of Japs and didn't dare refuse.

Her Filipino trio—saxophone, clarinet, upright
piano—was playing soft, indiscriminate music in the
corner where she would soon be singing. They were
all right—in fact, better than all right. Experienced
band members all over Manila had little opportunity
to play. Because few could afford to turn down a job,
Aurelio had been able to pick and choose. Unfortunately, her own trumpet player, Tomaso, refused to
work at a Jap club. Papaya was proud of him but
couldn't say so and couldn't tell him why she was
singing here. Trust no one, Amos had said. Damn
Amos anyway. She was very nervous.

She squeezed her way between the tables, holding back the skirt of her orange evening dress so that no one stepped on it. This was her most conservative costume, bright in color but with long sleeves and a high neckline that covered her bosom and shoulders. It felt strange to walk through a crowded room and have so few people recognize her or even look at her. Even the Filipinos she knew seemed like strangers tonight.

At the front of the room she found Aurelio Lopez, looking trim and dapper in a white *barong*. His little black mustache bristled with pleasure as he surveyed his opening-night crowd.

"Well, what do you think?" he asked. "Isn't this something?" His heavily pomaded black hair, combed straight back from his forehead, lay sleek and flat against his skull. His self-satisfaction was intense. "Everybody is here," he said. "All the Japanese brass. My partners are very pleased."

"Is General Homma here?" Papaya asked. She was curious to see the general who had conquered the Philippines and now lived in the High Commissioner's residence.

"No-o-o," Aurelio admitted reluctantly, but then brightened at once. "You can hardly move without running into a general or admiral. General Miyama is here in person."

"Where? Which one?" She was even more curious about Miyama, who lived in Amos's house and slept in Amos's bed. She already knew a lot about him from Carlos and Donato.

"I'll point him out later," Aurelio promised. "It's time for you to go on. One of my partners will introduce you."

"Couldn't you do it?" she asked. Aurelio, whatever his drawbacks, was at least a Filipino.

"No, no. Introduction has to be in Japanese. Come on."

She stood beside the piano, a frozen smile on her face, while the partner in black suit and white shirt talked about her to the crowd. She understood nothing of what he was saying, but his singsong voice had no animation. He might be a smart businessman, as Aurelio claimed, but he knew nothing about warming up an audience. When he stopped, applause was perfunctory.

She bowed anyway and went immediately into "Cielito Lindo," a safe, pretty song, like all the numbers she had planned. Conversation went on around the room throughout her half hour in front of the microphone, as she mixed Spanish and Filipino lovesongs, all of them chosen for melody, since most Japs could not understand the words. Light, polite applause—not what she was used to. This was a tough audience.

When she finished, she smiled and bowed and stretched out her arms and said thank you, thank you, but there was no reaction here to be milked.

As she prepared to walk off, a Japanese civilian called from the audience in perfect English, "Would you sing 'Oh, Susanna'?" Must be one of those California college Japanese, UCLA or somewhere, showing off to his friends.

Papaya looked at her trio and shrugged. It wasn't her fault someone had asked for an American song. They shrugged back. It wasn't their fault, either. The piano player grinned and tinkled a few bars.

"Faster," Papaya said. If they were going to do an American folksong, they would do it right. The piano player speeded the tempo. First fast song of the evening. Papaya hit it bright and strong:

> *"Oh, I come from Alabama*
> *With a banjo on my knee . . ."*

To her surprise, most of the conversation stopped. Maybe out of curiosity over this strange song? When she finished, there was actually some genuine applause, especially from Filipinos but also from Japs. Well, if they liked "Susanna," then . . .

She turned to the trio. "Okay," she said, "now that they woke up, let's do 'Deep in the Heart of Texas.' And keep it going till I say stop."

The piano player pounded a few fast chords. The sax and clarinet joined in on the simple, bouncy tune that was almost a march.

> *"The stars at night*
> *Are big and bright . . ."*

Papaya clapped her hands sharply four times. At the same moment the piano player banged the side of his instrument four times in perfect synchronization. They had not practiced this. Everybody in music knew those four claps. They were what made the song.

> *"Deep in the heart of Texas."*

On the second verse, a few Filipinos in the audience began to clap along with her. Papaya gave them a big smile and beckoned them all to join in—yes, all you Japs, too. If there was anything she knew, it was how to bring an audience into her act.

> *"The rabbits rush*
> *Around the brush . . ."*
> (Clap-clap-clap-clap!)

Many more joining in now, even Jap officers. As with any song she let the audience participate in, the result was erratic. Some people clapped three times or five times instead of four, and many did not quite catch the rhythm. It did not matter. Papaya was clapping her hands right into the microphone to lead them. They were all playing a noisy game together, and apparently it didn't matter that it was an American game.

She gave them a good long string of verses but stopped before they could tire of it. This time her applause was real. Even the partner smiled at her when she walked off.

Aurelio was, as usual, less than the perfect gentleman. "You had me worried there for a while," he said. "But you pulled it out at the end."

She ignored this. No one had to tell her she had given the crowd something to enjoy and talk about. Aurelio and his partners would consider her a valuable property. It was time to begin her real work. "Now you can introduce me around," she said. "I want to meet all the big important Japs."

"I wouldn't use that word here."

"What word?"

He lowered his voice. " 'Japs.' They don't like it."

"Okay, so introduce me to the important Japanese. Then maybe I will get to drive down here in my car."

Aurelio got hold of a civilian who could serve as interpreter. The three of them made their way slowly through the busy room. She was introduced to a number of generals and admirals as well as civilians. Few spoke any English, but they acted friendly. No hand-shaking, but a bow of the head, a smile, a few complimentary words on her show. She would bow and smile back, then move on to the next table.

Two officers stood out. General Miyama, of course, and not just because he was so important. He was in one of the alcove tables, sitting across from Mayor Vargas and his wife. Vargas, Quezon's personal secretary for many years, had been left behind when Quezon fled to Corregidor and been told to cooperate with the Japs. He was certainly cooperating tonight, but Papaya scarcely glanced at him.

Miyama had a lean, serious face and sharp black eyes. He looked austere. However, when Papaya approached his table, he lightly clapped his hands four times, just the right rhythm. As Carlos said, this general was very bright. She knew he was still learning English, but he wasn't shy about trying the new language.

"Hello, Miss Papaya. I am liking your songs."

"Thank you, general. It is fun to sing again."

"You not sing before?"

"Not since the war."

"That is bad." Miyama had a thought that was

apparently too complicated for him to say in English. He spoke rapidly to the interpreter in Japanese. In Japanese, his voice had the snap of authority.

"General Miyama says he hopes he will have the opportunity to hear you again. He enjoys music and likes to listen to different kinds."

Papaya bowed her thanks. Aurelio indicated it was time to move on, but Papaya thought this was a favorable moment. "General Miyama," she said, "I will be singing every night for this fine Japanese club. Can I get a special pass to drive here in my own car?"

Mayor Vargas gasped. So did Aurelio. Miyama looked at the interpreter, who translated her request.

Miyama's face was austere again for a few seconds. Then he shrugged, reached inside his jacket pocket and took out a card. With a fountain pen he wrote several Japanese characters on the back and handed it to her. A nod of the head told her it was now most definitely time to move on. She would not have a chance to ask how General Miyama liked living in Amos's house. Firmly clutching the card in her fist, she followed Aurelio to the next table.

The other officer she could hardly help remembering was Admiral Buto. He spoke perfect English and he criticized her, although she could tell he was attracted to her. Besides, his name was a Tagalog word for prick.

Buto sat at a corner table with two other naval officers and the Filipino Minister of Public Works, Paredes, who was responsible for restoring the piers and the port of Manila for the use of the Japanese navy. The three officers were in white uniforms, and

Paredes wore a white linen suit. An all-white table. Buto had a shaved head and black mustache, just like the pictures of Premier Tojo. But he was a much better-looking man, with deep, mournful eyes and a sensual mouth. His voice, too, was deep, almost a bass.

"You sing extremely well," he said, "but you should not sing enemy songs."

"I was asked to," Papaya said. "By a Jap—anese."

The admiral shook his shining bald head. "Nevertheless, it is not appropriate."

"Oh, music is not politics," she said airily, "and anyway, those weren't war songs." She decided to pull a little rank. Admiral Buto might be in charge of the port, but General Miyama was in charge of the whole city. "As General Miyama told me a few minutes ago, he likes hearing different kinds of songs. I think all music is for everybody." She smiled innocently at the Public Works Minister, hoping to embarrass him. "You agree, Mr. Paredes?"

But Paredes was an experienced Manila politician. "Don't ask me about music. I cannot even carry a tune."

"You should learn some Japanese songs," Admiral Buto said. "Some of them are very beautiful. Very sad." His mournful eyes passed approvingly across her bosom, which even the orange dress could not conceal.

"I intend to." His admiring gaze led her to risk a rebuttal. "By the way, admiral, you speak the enemy language extremely well."

His eyes lifted from her bosom to her face, regarding her thoughtfully. "It is useful in enemy territory," he said at last.

Papaya deliberated staked out a wounded position. "Enemy territory?" she said. "The war is over. I thought the Japanese and the Filipino people were supposed to be friends now. At least that is what Mr. Lopez and I are trying to do. Isn't that right, Aurelio?"

"But of course. That's why this club has opened."

"Yes," Buto said. "We shall see."

Papaya sang a second set of songs and spoke to many other Japs, both military and civilian. She also spoke to Sandy Homobono, who was covering the Mabalinga opening for the *Manila Tribune*. But at the end of the long evening, riding home in her *calesa*, she realized that the only "military secret" she had learned was that American and Filipino guerrillas were giving the Japs trouble north of Manila. Everybody knew that. All she really had to show for the evening was Miyama's card. She would have to do much better in the future.

But the day after Sandy's puff piece on the Mabalinga appeared, with a short but favorable comment about her singing, she got a phone call at home from Enrique Sansone. Amos had told her that Sansone was an important part of a very small, secret intelligence group and that she might be hearing from him. But that had been six months ago, and she had heard nothing. She assumed he had been killed in the fighting or had gone somewhere else, and that in any case the group must surely have broken up with the defeat.

Over the phone he gave his name, made no mention of Amos and asked if she would meet him for tea that afternoon. He sounded charming. He gave her the address of a café in Ermita and told her how to get there by streetcar.

"I can use my own car now," Papaya said with pride. She had not ridden in one of the *tranvia* streetcars since the earliest days of her success.

"Streetcar," Sansone repeated. "Or *calesa*, if you like, but not a private car. And don't dress up. It's a very modest place."

Papaya lied to her mother, saying she was going to meet Jorge Esteban for a business conference. Lying to her mother made her feel like a real spy for the first time.

"You aren't going dressed like that?" her mother asked.

"It's only Jorge, Mama." She was wearing her around-the-house clothes, a loose blouse and cotton skirt, bare legs and sandals. She took a brimmed straw hat that ought to prevent recognition on the streetcar.

The Hut-Nut Café was indeed a modest establishment, set in the heart of Ermita's red-light district. Since it was only four in the afternoon, no whores sat at the dozen or so wooden tables, but it looked like the kind of place where at nine o'clock in the evening there might be lots of them. Right now only a couple of tables were occupied, by Filipinos drinking orange soda and beer.

A man stood up at an isolated table in the rear and waved her over. He wore a short-sleeved white sport shirt hanging outside his trousers. His bare arms were tanned, but his face showed he had a very white, almost delicate skin. He remained standing until she reached the table, then took her hand and bowed low over it. Not quite a hand-kiss, but decidedly more gallant than a handshake. It was a gesture no Filipino could have made so naturally and that no American would have made at all. As she knew from her own father, Spanish gentlemen were different. He held a chair to seat her.

"Sorry about this," he said, waving a hand at the room as he sat down opposite her. "But it's a quiet place to talk, and the owner is very discreet. Actually the food here isn't as bad as you might think. Especially these peanuts."

He held out a monkeywood bowl of salted peanuts with the red skins still on. Papaya took some. She loved peanuts with skins, even though they were bad for her weight.

"And there really is tea, if you'd like that. Or something else?"

He was drinking San Miguel beer, so she said she would have one too. There went a few more ounces. When the owner, whom Sansone addressed as Nino, had poured her beer and left them alone, Sansone leaned forward, crossed his arms on the table and smiled at her. "Well now," he said in a cheerful voice. "Mr. Watson says you are totally reliable. Tell me all about your marvelous Mabalinga Club." He gave a funny little sideways twist of his head, getting rid of a crick in his neck.

Papaya thought he was very nice-looking, not at all handsome but quite aristocratic. He had merry blue eyes and a long thin nose that turned up at the very tip, like an afterthought. "What would you like to know?" she said. "I haven't learned anything useful."

"Oh well, you can't be sure of that. Just tell me what it's like."

Papaya described the club and the people in it. Sansone was a good listener, nodding his head to encourage her, asking questions to spur her on. Were the same people there on other nights who had been there on opening night? What was the proportion of Japanese army and navy officers to civilians? What was the mood of the officers? What did they say about their victory in the Philippines? What was their attitude toward her? Which ones had she talked to? Who was interesting? Who seemed important? Did she think she could talk to them again? What was their attitude toward Filipinos in general? Toward Americans? Was anything said about the prison camps? Had anybody mentioned Camp O'Donnell?

They had another beer and a second bowl of peanuts. Sansone seemed so interested in everything she had to say that he made her feel her information was more important than she had thought. When he had finally exhausted the Mabalinga, he started on Santo Tomas Internment Camp. He approved of the way she and Amos were sending messages in and out of camp through Carlos and Donato and the Filipino shanty builder. But he suggested that because of Carlos's important role in General Miyama's household, perhaps he should not risk any more personal deliveries to the Package Line. It might be wiser to have Donato or even a third party make the deliveries.

When she told him about Felix Logan's job in the commandant's office, he said, "Splendid! Splendid!" as though she had just given him a special present. He was surprised to learn that she was also getting occasional messages from Amos's former secretary in San Fernando. He thought that Miranda might be useful in getting information to guerrillas, which was proving difficult.

But when Papaya tried to ask Sansone some questions of her own about his group and how they worked, he politely cut her off. He held up his hand and smiled. "It's best to keep things separate," he said. "Then if somebody gets caught, there's not much to tell. If it's necessary for you to work with some of the others, as I'm sure it will be now and then, I will let you know. For now, you and I will talk just to each other. That reminds me. You will need a name." When she looked blank, he said, "A code name."

"What for?"

"Oh, you know." He gestured vaguely and gave that little twist of his head. "When I talk to anyone about you, I don't want to use the name Papaya. Or if I have to call you or send you a note, if I use your code name, you'll know it is from me. Everybody has a name. For instance, I decided to be Zorro." Using his forefinger as a sword, with three quick strokes he slashed a Z and made a sword-through-the-air swishing noise, "*Wht! Wht! Wht!*—the Mark of Zorro. Isn't that delightful?"

He looked down at the nearly empty bowl, then smiled at her. "I think you will be Peanut."

Coach and Sergeant

The morning after the ammunition dump, Brad Stone lost his command for the second time. But this time he could accept the reason.

At first light he and his three men climbed the hill back to camp and found Paradiso waiting there. The men had all known for certain that Paradiso had died. His reappearance was magic. They sat on the ground eating a breakfast of rice and bananas and drinking bad coffee. The circle of dirty faces ranged from light tan to brown, some even lighter than Brad's own, which was deeply tanned from life in the hills. Paradiso's face was the darkest of all—he had the blood of the Igorot mountain tribes. The stocky sergeant told them what had happened, switching back and forth from English to Tagalog to one of the other dialects so that everyone could understand the story.

When the rifle fire began from the banana grove, Paradiso said, he was just about to light the fuses. With the shooting, his helper tore back through the fence the way they had entered, to be cut down by the Japs as he tried to cross the field. From the first

rifle shot, Paradiso realized the field would be a poor
bet. He carefully lighted the fuses, waited to make
sure they were burning, then ran through the shed to
the front gate, away from the firefight.

The steel gate was closed by a heavy horizontal
bar. Paradiso got his shoulder under the bar, put his
back and legs into it and lifted with both hands. It
was very heavy—probably took two or three Japs to
lift it. When he got it raised to vertical, the gate swung
open. He slipped through and ran like hell. He was
two hundred yards away when the shed blew up behind him. The force of the blast knocked him down
but didn't hurt him. He stayed flat so as not to be hit
by exploding ammunition. His ears ringing, he got
up and kept running until he was far enough away
to be safe from roaming guards. Then he had to make
a wide loop through unfamiliar territory. By the time
he finally circled back to the banana grove and then
to the main road, everybody else was gone. "So I
walk home by myself. Long night." He smiled at them
all, and they all smiled back, immensely pleased with
him. Brad was smiling too. He thanked God he hadn't
lost Paradiso.

Then Paradiso squared his shoulders and sat up
straight. "Also a big night," he said, looking from
face to face around the circle. "A very big night for
us. A beautiful night. *Maganda*!"

The men clapped and cheered and smiled at each
other over their shared success. "*Maganda*—beautiful," they agreed.

Paradiso wiped his hands on his shorts and stood
up. He put his fists on his hips and stared down at

the circle—his tough sergeant look. Then he turned to Brad. "Lieutenant," he asked, "who fired first rifle?"

Brad shook his head. "I don't know. It was dark." He felt guilty about not knowing.

After a long moment during which his face was expressionless, Paradiso glared down at the men. "Ramon and Despido could kill that one Jap, just like they killed the two guards." He looked for confirmation at Ramon and Despido, who nodded. It was obvious to Brad that Paradiso had already spoken with them. "Instead of one more dead Jap we get many live Japs everywhere shooting at us. And a machine gun. Rosauro, how come you don't know about that machine gun?"

Young Rosauro, who had collected so much accurate information to make the raid possible, was stricken. "I am not knowing, sergeant. Maybe they just now bring it in."

Paradiso snorted. "Huh. Maybe. So one man shoots his rifle, we lose two men dead. Maybe more— four still not come back. We almost lose *me*. I want to know. Who did it?"

Brad could feel the almost physical power of Paradiso's voice. The weight of it hung in the still morning air.

A man finally raised his hand. "I am the one, sir."

Paradiso nodded. "You lose your rifle. We talk later about what else." He turned to Brad. "I must see you private, please."

The way he said it reminded Brad of the days back at Simpson School when Paradiso, as head houseboy,

would come to him bearing bad news about something—a gardener who had to be fired, a breakdown
of the school bus too serious for Paradiso to fix himself. He would never ask what to do—he always knew
that—but only for the authority to do it.

He and Paradiso walked away from the men. The
top of Paradiso's head, with its curling gray hair at
the back and sides, came to just below Brad's shoulder. In Brad's tiny hut—not really even a hut, just a
shed—they sat down together on the crude bamboo
platform, a bed high enough to stand clear of rain-
water.

Paradiso turned a little sideways to face Brad. His
dark brown face and eyes were solemn. "Mr. Stone,"
he said, "this does not work."

Brad said nothing, waited for him to go on.

"This is not American army anymore. Everything
is different. It does not work this way. Mr. Stone, I
must be the leader. I *am* the leader. You see it too."

To Brad this was a shocking thought—but not a
preposterous one. It was true that all the men looked
to Paradiso for leadership. They had ever since basic
training at San Fernando. After last night, even more
so. It had really been Paradiso's show and would have
failed without him. If Paradiso had been there in the
banana grove, no one would have fired without his
permission. The man was a presence. Brad had to
admit that Paradiso was capable of making most decisions himself. But Brad Stone was an American and
an officer in the U.S. Army. Paradiso was a Filipino
and a sergeant.

"That's impossible," he told Paradiso.

"No," Paradiso said, and this time without a "sir." "I have long time to think last night walking home. It is the right way. I give the orders. That must be."

"What the hell am I supposed to do? Go somewhere else? Join some other group?"

"No, no," Paradiso said, shaking his head. "You are a very smart man, Mr. Stone, you give good advice. Figure out two weeks ahead what time the moon will be right. I cannot do such things. Also very important to have an American officer. It gives us much face." He nodded to himself. Then he smiled to show goodwill. "I tell you what I think. I think you will be the Coach, just like at school. That is very important, you be the Coach. I listen to everything you say, Coach. But I will be the one."

And that was how they settled it. Brad warned Paradiso that the U.S. Army would probably court-martial him for mutiny. Paradiso said he would worry about that later. The U.S. Army wasn't around anymore.

———

The Japanese went berserk over the ammunition dump. Their fury cost Filipino lives. For a week afterward the army was all over the countryside. Observation planes flew back and forth trying to spot guerrilla encampments in the hills. Paradiso made everyone stay out of sight beneath the protective foliage. Trucks loaded with Japanese soldiers crisscrossed the entire area from San Fernando south of Clark Field to as far north as Tarlac and as far east as Mount Arayat. So many radio-equipped foot patrols combed the Zambales foothills that Brad persuaded Paradiso to pack up everything important and be ready to abandon camp on a few minutes' notice if a patrol came too close. "We could handle one patrol," Brad argued, "but they'd call in others by radio."

Everywhere the Japs visited, they hauled out the local officials, lined them up and asked questions. The worst treatment was reserved for Bamban, the site of the ammunition depot. The Japanese were convinced the sabotage could not possibly have taken place without the knowledge of the Bamban townspeople. After severe questioning that produced no information because no one in Bamban knew anything, the Japanese publicly beheaded five citizens. When that failed to produce information, they beheaded five more, including a woman, before deciding that the townspeople really didn't know anything.

Everyone grieved for and sympathized with the victims and their families, but Filipino fatalism acknowledged that undeserved tragedies were bound to happen, especially in war. The dominant emotion throughout the countryside was not grief or sympathy but elation.

Look at those Japs, running around like crazy! When Japanese troops were present, asking their frantic questions, Filipino faces and voices were solemn, stolid, willing to cooperate. But as soon as the troops left, everybody broke into smiles and laughter. Oh, how badly these Japs hated to lose all that ammunition!

It soon became known, and word was quickly passed, that this had been the main ammunition storage depot for the defense of Clark Field. Now the Japs would have to build a brand-new dump, maybe several new dumps to spread the risk. They would have to bring in much new ammunition—maybe all the way from Japan, some said. And many new guards and lots of fences and big gates and watchtowers and many machine guns, because the guerrillas had shown that even a well-guarded, well-fenced building could be destroyed.

It was no secret which guerrillas those were. The men whose families and girlfriends lived in Carabangay could not help boasting privately of what they had done. No other guerrilla group in central Luzon, large or small, had accomplished anything like it. In Carabangay the word passed quietly from house to house—*our* guerrillas did it, the ones we are helping.

And from Carabangay, the word was carried just as quietly to the nearby barrios and towns and finally even to the cities. In Mabalacat and Dau, in Capas and Angeles and Cabanatuan and San Fernando, people learned that the ammunition dump had been the work of one particular guerrilla group hidden somewhere in the Zambales Mountains. No, one cannot say just where, but it is a small group, not a big one. It is led by an American officer and a Filipino sergeant. No, one cannot say the names. They are simply called Coach and Sergeant. Some say Sergeant uses the code name of Paradiso, but one cannot be sure. Naturally all has to remain very secret.

———

They were famous, Brad realized. And they were not
so small anymore. Because of what they had done,
new men sought to join them, and even some members of other guerrilla groups from as far away as
Arayat were eager to serve under Coach and Sergeant.
So many new recruits offered themselves that Paradiso appointed Rosauro and Despido to screen them.
He did not want to accept just anybody, and neither
did Brad.

The guerrilla movement was loose and disorganized. Some men were serious, some were not. Some
guerrilla groups were little more than a collection of
bandits, terrorizing the civilian population for food
and supplies and even women, while contributing virtually nothing to the battle against the Japanese occupation.

Paradiso would not accept such men. He would
not let his own men steal food. Food must come as
a gift, which the farmers and townspeople of Carabangay and neighboring barrios were proud to contribute. Brad even gave receipts for what they
received, tiny slips of paper signed "Coach, Lt. USA."
Brad wasn't so sure these would ever be redeemed,
even if the Americans came back, but the receipts gave
their benefactors something to cherish—and perhaps
someday they would be honored.

As for women, Paradiso was equally strict. "You
can make *suksok* all you want," he said, "but only
if the *dalaga* wants to." This restriction did not im-
pose an impossible hardship on his popular men. The

Philippines took a genial attitude toward matters of sex.

Quite aside from matters of behavior, there was the risk that someone might try to become a guerrilla only to sell information to the Japs. There were such men.

Rosauro, with his friendly contacts in all the nearby towns and barrios, and Despido, who was too mean to be fooled, were usually able to get a good line on a candidate's character and reputation. When they could not, or when they heard anything compromising or suspicious, the candidate was rejected. Far more were rejected than were brought to Paradiso and Brad for final approval. A man stood a better chance if, along with a good reputation, he could bring a rifle or pistol or a supply of ammunition.

But in spite of all the screening, their group grew rapidly. When it grew to more than two hundred active members, Brad and Paradiso decided to split the camp into several groups in different locations so that it would be harder for the Japs to find them. And still they grew.

One day Paradiso came to Brad with a proposal. Two proposals, in fact. "Coach," he said, "we are very big group now. Too big for me to be Sergeant."

Brad was amused but did not show it. Filipinos loved rank and ceremony. "What did you have in mind?"

"I should become officer."

"What kind of officer?"

"I am thinking captain."

"Hhm." Actually this was a fairly modest title by

guerrilla-leader standards. A few miles north of them were Quintano's Marauders, led by "Major" Quintano. Brad had even heard of "colonels" and "generals."

"Captain is not too much," Paradiso said. He obviously liked his idea but wanted assurance.

"No, not too much," Brad agreed. "Paradiso, what do you think of all these guerrilla leaders with high rank? Major Quintano, for instance?"

Paradiso spat. "Fake."

"Yeah, me too. Everybody knows they are fake."

"Yes, but I am real."

"That's right. But if you are suddenly captain, you will be fake too."

Paradiso thought that over. "Lieutenant then? To start?"

"What about the fact that everybody already knows about you? They know you as Sergeant. If you're a captain or even lieutenant, you're somebody else. Someone no one knows."

"They will get to know me," Paradiso said with utter confidence. Then he added what was really bothering him. "Sergeant is very small."

That gave Brad an idea. "Have you ever heard of a man named Napoleon?"

"Yes," Paradiso said. His education in everything but practical matters was extremely limited, but he had heard of Napoleon. "Big general."

"Right. Very big general," Brad said. He was back in history class. "Probably the greatest general who ever lived. And not just a general. He went on to become Emperor of France, and he conquered so many other countries that he was practically Emperor of Europe. Like Charlemagne."

Paradiso shook his head. "I don't know him."

A natural mistake for a teacher to make, Brad thought. He waved his hands. "We're not talking about him anyway. We're talking about Napoleon. You know how he started in the army? He was a corporal."

"Corporal!"

"Yes. And he was very short, shorter than you are, so they called him the Little Corporal. Later, when he became a general and then the Emperor, you know what his troops called him? They were proud to be his soldiers because he was such a great leader, but they never thought of him as a general or emperor. They still called him the Little Corporal."

Paradiso laughed with delight at the story. Although he had a sharp sense of humor, he seldom laughed out loud. "Only corporal," he said. "Not even sergeant."

Brad said nothing. He let the story sink in.

Paradiso was silent for at least a full minute. Then he said, "I have other idea. I think you will be captain."

"What for? That would be fake too."

"Different. Lieutenant is the lowest." Paradiso grinned. "Not like sergeant. For signing the receipts, for the food. We will need more food for so many men. Captain is—captain will be—"

"More impressive?"

"Yes, more impressive."

Brad Stone was amused. Would a receipt signed

"Coach, Capt. USA" have more value than one signed
"Lt."? To the Filipinos, who cared so much about
titles, perhaps yes. To the U.S. Army, who could say?
The subject had never come up in ROTC training.
"Who's going to promote me?"

Paradiso jabbed his own chest with his thumb.
"Me."

Brad laughed. It was certainly a different way to
achieve rank. Why not? So let it be.

———

A large part of their guerrilla life consisted of gathering information about what the Japs were up to.
Hard, reliable information was difficult to come by.
All communication was by word of mouth, and
rumor and exaggeration were as much a part of Filipino life as rice or bamboo. Paradiso's men were out
in the fields and roads and barrios every day, talking
to people, observing Japanese activity, trying to pin
down facts and numbers.

It was frustrating to receive conflicting reports
about practically everything. The Japs were doing
this. No, the Japs were doing that. This happened last
week. No, it will happen day after tomorrow. The
discrepancies were not deliberate. Everybody meant
well and was trying to be helpful, but everybody
seemed to see the same event in his own individual
way.

It made Brad wonder how history could ever sort
itself out. Who could decide, of all the different versions presented, what actually occurred? The trick,
he realized, both for history and for guerrilla activity,

was to collect as many versions as possible and then hope that some pattern of truth, or at least of probability, would emerge.

For one event in their own area, such a pattern was unmistakable. It was a pattern of horror. Their own town of Carabangay was only a few miles south of Capas. Capas, everyone agreed, was the final stop in the long journey of the Bataan survivors. During the hottest days of April, many people had witnessed the arrival of the freight train at the Capas railway station. They had watched the doors of the steaming boxcars slide open. They had watched the broken men, the American and Filipino soldiers, crawl down from the cars onto the platform.

Everyone agreed that the sight was the same with every train that disgorged its pitiful cargo. Gaunt, scarecrow men, battered by thirst and starvation and disease and defeat, many on the brink of death, they stood there on the Capas platform in the blazing sun. Then, one behind another, with armed Jap guards prodding them along, they shuffled down the dusty gravel road to a place called Camp O'Donnell.

Brad realized that he and Paradiso and Rosauro and the other men from his company could easily have been among those scarecrows. Instead of being stationed at Lingayen Gulf, where the invasion cut them off and gave them the hasty choice between surrender and flight to the Zambales Mountains, they could have been placed anywhere else on the Luzon Plain and wound up on Bataan. If that had happened, would Brad have survived to reach the Capas station?

About O'Donnell the reports were once again con-

fusing and contradictory. He could not be certain
what conditions in the camp were really like, but they
sounded bad. He made up his mind.

"Paradiso, we have to try to help those men."

"How can we help prisoners?"

"I don't know. We could be prisoners in there
ourselves."

Paradiso shrugged. Such things were fate.

"Anyway," Brad said, "we have to try."

"No, we don't."

"All right, put it this way. I'm going to try. I'm
going to go up there and see what's possible. Maybe
something can be done."

Paradiso thought about this. When he was thinking
something over, his face was always expressionless.
Brad could not tell what was going on in Paradiso's
mind. It could be anything. He waited.

"Okay," Paradiso said. "I go with you."

= 13 =

Jesus Doesn't Live Here

From the first day at Camp O'Donnell, men began to die. They did not have to be killed. They made it on their own.

Humphrey and Maxsie were in the same bamboo barracks as the adjutant who kept the records on all the Americans. Nine thousand came to O'Donnell, the adjutant figured, and during the seven weeks of the camp's existence, fifteen hundred died. One out of every six. Nobody was keeping records on the far greater number of Filipino soldiers in the other camp. The adjutant only knew that thousands and thousands of them were dying. When he said nobody would ever know how many, Humphrey believed him.

Dear Sara,

I wish they'd let me write you, but this will have to do. At least I can say some things I couldn't put in a real letter.

This place is godawful—worst I ever saw. We all thought when the march from Bataan was over, things would have to get better, but they didn't. Lot of guys who barely made it through the march had nothing left when they got here, and they just started keeling over. What we all need is food and medicine, but this Tsuneyoshi bastard won't give us anything. He won't even let anybody else give us anything. Yesterday two guys came in the barracks crying. Grown men, tears running down their faces. They'd been on work detail at the main gate when a whole string of trucks drove up the road from Capas. Philippine Red Cross, all the way from Manila, loaded with food, medicine, clothes, blankets, mosquito nets—everything we need. Tsuneyoshi turned them away! He said if he let them in, it would lead to smuggling!

You remember Freddy Collins? He was at Fort Benning with us, wife named Nancy. Real cynical guy, drank too much, not a bad officer, though. Anyway, he's flipped. He lost a finger on the march, Jap soldier cut it off to steal his class ring. It pushed Freddy over the edge—or maybe it was the malaria or starvation or whatever. He's become a Jesus nut. Talks about Jesus all the time. He even talks to him. It drives the rest of us in the barracks crazy. Can you imagine Freddy Collins with religion?

Lot of men dying every day, dysentery is the worst. But don't worry, I'm not going to be one of them. Maxsie says hello. I've told him a lot about you and the kids. He says I'm worse about you than Freddy is about Jesus! Give the kids a hug.

Love, Jack

Their barracks scarcely deserved the name. Like all the others in the camp, it was a long bamboo hut with a thatched nipa roof. No water, no toilets. The floor and the walls were bamboo poles lashed together with rattan. The double-decker bunks were flat racks of split bamboo. The barracks had been built for Filipino soldiers who were used to sleeping on bamboo, but Jack Humphrey could never get comfortable. His big frame, even after all the loss of weight, seemed to feel every bump. Although he was worn out, he never got a solid night's sleep.

All the others had trouble sleeping too, so they talked a lot in the darkness. They talked about home and families and the war, but, unlike any other barracks Jack Humphrey had ever lived in, they almost never talked about sex. Nobody had enough strength or lust for it. Most of all they talked about food. Food was the one fantasy that could relieve their desperation.

They would be lying in the darkness and someone would begin. "I remember one time in New Orleans . . ." And they would be off. No one interrupted the man describing his great dinner, course by course. A good food-talker could hold the barracks for fifteen minutes. They soon got to know who was best, and sometimes they would call on an officer to "Tell again about your night at Antoine's," or "How about that crab dinner at Ernie's in San Francisco?"

Jack Humphrey was at his best on Sara's home-cooked meals. Her steak-and-kidney pie was his specialty. "It comes to the table," he said, "in a big round earthenware dish, steaming hot. Sara has to carry it with potholders because it's so hot. And I can see it's heavy, so I'm worrying if she's going to drop it, but she sets it down in front of me. I can smell it, because she's poked little holes in the crust to let the steam out. It smells like—well, it smells exactly like steak-and-kidney pie. Now that crust is golden brown, and it curls over the edge of the dish all the way around. And it's crisp. I know when I dig into it with the serving spoon, some of that edge is going to flake off and fall on the tablecloth, but it won't make a stain because it is pure, dry crust. I could serve it sitting down, but I always stand up so I can look right down on that perfect circle of crust.

"I pick up the spoon—you need a long-handled serving spoon with a fairly deep scoop so it will hold the gravy, but a ladle wouldn't be good because you couldn't cut through the crust without making a mess. Well, I wait just a couple of seconds, admiring it, and Sara says, 'Hurry up, Jack, before it gets cold.' The steam's still coming out of it, and she's worrying that it's going to get cold. Actually, what she's really worrying about is if it's going to be as good as last time. So I hold that spoon over the pie—in some ways, this is the best moment of all—and then I dig that first hole through the crust. It's thicker than the crust of a dessert pie, but it's cooked through just right. It doesn't fall apart into little crumbles. I can cut it into pieces so that everybody gets a piece. But before I serve the first plate, I pick up a little piece of the outside crust off the tablecloth and eat it. 'Jack!' Sara says. 'Serve your guests first.' And I say, 'I'm just testing to see if it's fit to eat.' She throws her head back and sticks her chin out at me. 'Well?' And I say,

'I think it will pass,' and then I start serving. Along with a section of crust, I give each person some chunks of cubed steak, a couple of spoonfuls of the rich gravy, and some sliced-up lamb kidneys. One of the secrets of steak-and-kidney pie is that you have to trim the kidneys very carefully to get rid of the veins. The veins aren't just tough, they also give the kidneys a bitter taste if you don't get them out. What Sara does, she takes a small, very sharp knife . . ."

Humphrey could run this story on for another five minutes before he got to the excruciating moment when he put the first bite in his mouth.

On the subject of food, Maxsie was a listener, not a talker. One night Humphrey called out to him, "Hey, Maxsie, what's the best meal you ever ate?"

But Maxsie declined. "I'm straight steak and potatoes," he said. "I never ate a French meal in my life. I'll just lie here and listen to all you fairies talk about your frog food."

There was a moment of silence while everyone thought about this accusation. Humphrey decided Maxsie had made the transition from enlisted man to officer with a minimum of shyness. The silence did not last long.

"Speaking of frogs," somebody said, "the best frogs' legs I ever ate . . ."

In the daylight, they confronted their real food: boiled rice, or the watery rice soup called *lugao*, or boiled *camotes*, the Philippine sweet potato. At least they got something to eat three times a day. Sometimes *camote* greens or *pechay* or another vegetable

was added to the rice. The best job in camp was to
work in the kitchen, where you could occasionally
steal something extra.

The challenge was to eat your food before the flies
landed on it. The fat flies buzzed straight from the
open latrines to the mess area. Jerry Baron, the medical officer, warned that the flies spread dysentery and
other diseases. He taught the men to carry a piece of
cloth—a T-shirt, a handkerchief, any scrap would
do—and spread it over the mess kit as soon as the
rice was ladled in, then slide one hand under the cloth,
grab some food and stick it directly into the mouth
before the flies got to it.

Dysentery, along with malaria, was the scourge
of O'Donnell. So many men caught dysentery that
a separate hospital ward had to be established for
them. Everybody called it Zero Ward, because there
was little hope for any man sent there. Humphrey
visited Zero Ward just once, when he heard that a
fellow Scouts officer was a patient. He would never
go again.

As he approached the low bamboo building, the
stench was so strong that he gasped and held his nose.
Then he looked inside.

Men lay stretched out on the floor, silent and
dying. Many were naked. Everybody in camp, including Humphrey himself, was scrawny and under-
weight, but these men were mere bones covered by
tightly stretched skin. Their eyes were hollow and
staring. Too weak to get up and relieve themselves,
they lay in their own filth. The appalling feces of
dysentery, mixed with blood and mucus torn from

the dying men's intestines, spread in pools on the floor. Humphrey could see ulcers, great raw patches, on bony hips and shoulders. Maggots crawled in the open sores. Flies swarmed and buzzed in the silent ward.

Humphrey left without looking for his fellow officer. He could not bear to walk from body to body, peering into those shattered faces. As he turned the corner of the building, he saw a stack of naked dead bodies, half a dozen of them, waiting for the next burial detail. Even though the bodies were wasted away, the living were so weak themselves that it took four of them to carry each corpse to the graveyard outside the barbed-wire fence.

He told Maxsie what he had seen. Maxsie listened, his pale blue eyes showing nothing. When Humphrey finished, Maxsie said, "We got to get ourselves out of here. That Tsuneyoshi's going to kill us all."

"Escape? We can't do that. They'll kill us if they catch us, and if they don't catch us, they'll kill ten guys in our place. Ten for you, ten for me." This standard Japanese punishment for escape kept prisoners where they belonged.

"No, I don't mean escape. I mean we got to get outside this camp, get on one of those work details that'll take us away from here. Maybe get some different food. Do something different. At least *see* something different. You could go crazy in here, sit around watch guys die and listen to that fucker Freddy talk about his blessed Jesus."

"Yeah, how are we going to do that? That's all up to Tsuneyoshi."

"Same way I got to be a master sergeant," Maxsie said. "Volunteer."

"Volunteer? Didn't they teach you anything? What about the old army law, 'Never volunteer for anything'?"

"It's bullshit, always was. You want to get ahead, get a few stripes, you better volunteer. Especially," Maxsie said, "if you got something like this on your face." He touched the ugly purple blotch on his cheek. It was the first time he had ever mentioned it.

Humphrey knew he had to acknowledge that Maxsie had spoken about his birthmark. He wasn't sure what he ought to say, but by now he knew Maxsie pretty damn well.

"What thing on your face?" Humphrey said, trying not to smile. "Oh. Oh, that. I guess I never noticed it before."

Maxsie laughed, a short happy bark. "You fucker," he said.

Two days later Maxsie walked back into the barracks, rubbing his hands together. He was grinning with self-satisfaction. "Okay, Hump, it's all set. We go out tomorrow morning. Bridge repair in Capas."

Humphrey tried to decide how he felt. He wasn't in such great shape for heavy work, but at the same time the prospect of getting away from O'Donnell, even for a few hours, was too pleasant to resist. "You volunteered?"

"Just went up to Tsuneyoshi's office and told that little lieutenant, the skinny one, that you and I wanted to do some special work. Both of us. You're in charge, of course."

"How come they gave us a bridge?"

"It's just a little bridge," Maxsie said. "Thirty-man detail, no more than a couple days' work."

"I never repaired a bridge. I wouldn't know where to begin."

"Yes, you would," Maxsie said. "I told the lieutenant you were an engineering officer."

"You didn't."

"How do you think we got the job? Listen, half the things I've volunteered for in this army I didn't know how to do till I did them. The worst time, I guess, was mess sergeant." He laughed at the memory. "Lots of guys pretty pissed off the first week in that mess hall. Cheer up, Hump, we'll figure it out. It's just a bridge."

And in fact, it did not prove too difficult. They set off next morning in a captured American two-and-a-half-ton truck with construction tools, thirty enlisted men and three armed Jap guards.

Driving past the sentries and through the barbed-wire gate was the nicest experience Humphrey had had in a long time. It was a beautiful morning, not too hot because the rainy season had finally begun. Behind them were the Zambales Mountains, and far across the plain ahead of them stood the solitary volcanic cone of Mount Arayat, almost the same sight he used to see every morning at Stotsenburg, twenty miles away to the south.

On the brief drive to Capas and then through the town, Humphrey drank in the scenery—especially the trees. He'd never thought he would enjoy the sight of trees after those months in the mountain jungles of Bataan. But there were no trees at O'Donnell, no shade, nothing but cogon grass, so this morning the trees along the road seemed beautiful. So did the faces of the townspeople who stopped to stare as the truck went past and sometimes risked a smile and a friendly wave.

Maxsie spent the drive taking a quick survey of the enlisted men in the detail. By the time they reached the little bridge on the far side of town, he had identified three men with previous construction experience.

"They'll be your advisers," Maxsie said.

"*My* advisers?"

"Well, you're the engineer, aren't you?"

One of the guards counted the men aloud in Japanese as they climbed down from the bed of the truck. Then the three guards sat down in the shade of a mango tree, rifles resting between their legs, and waited for the Americans to fix the damaged bridge.

It was a simple single-span wooden bridge across a shallow stream. Heavy planks formed the roadbed. One of the main timbers supporting the roadbed had rotted away underwater and collapsed, twisting the planks into a jumble and splintering several of them. It looked like more of a mess than it was. Humphrey and his advisers checked the other main timbers and found them sound. Even Humphrey could see they would have to remove the planks, install a new supporting timber and then put the planks, including several new ones, back in place. Maxsie organized the men into work teams.

The work went slowly because the men were weak, and most of them had no experience with construction tools. But it was a commonsense job, and progress was measurable. By noon, with crowbars and carrying teams, they had removed the twisted planks and laid them on the road at the near end of the bridge. A small group of Filipinos squatted on the bank of the stream to watch. The guards, who seemed indifferent to the whole project, made no objection.

The great surprise was lunch. At noon a small truck drove out from town and unloaded their food. Because they were doing hard physical labor, and perhaps because the food came from Capas instead of from camp, Americans got the same meal as their guards. There was a generous portion of rice with little pieces of real meat mixed in, tough enough to be carabao but no less tasty. Each man also got a piece of fruit.

As they were about to return to work after their best meal in a very long time, a young Filipino boy approached the guards with a large straw basket of sweet cookies. He offered them to the guards, who each took one, and then indicated he would like to give some to the Americans. The chief guard nodded permission. As the boy walked among the men, holding out the basket, he kept smiling and whispering to each one, "Good luck, Joe. Good luck, Joe."

The cookie Humphrey nibbled was made of rice flour so packed with sugar that it was almost unbearably sweet. The hell with the taste, it was solid energy. He remembered the many times during the march from Bataan when some Filipino had risked his life to give an American a bit of food or a cup of water. They just might be the nicest people in the world.

The cookie made him thirsty. He took a careful swig from his canteen, holding the water in his mouth and swishing it around before he swallowed. They had all learned to make water last. When they first reached O'Donnell, there had been a single water spigot and endless lines to get to it. Now there were three spigots with a much stronger flow, but men still had to get by on one canteen a day. In the first days, despite all the doctors' warnings and the officers' efforts, many thirst-crazed men drank from the sluggish, muddy river below the camp, polluted by seepage from the latrines. It was a dysentery death sentence, but some men, mainly the younger ones with no training or discipline, drank from it anyway. Humphrey screwed the cap back on his canteen before he could be tempted to take a second swallow. Back to the bridge.

Humphrey and Maxsie managed to stretch the bridge project to four days. Two and a half days could have done it, if the guards had pressed them, but the guards did not care. The Jap officer who came to inspect the work at the end of each afternoon was satisfied that it was going well. Meantime Humphrey and Maxsie and their crew were eating one decent meal a day, followed by the Filipino boy with his basket of rice cookies.

They lost two men from their crew. One fell dead while helping to carry a heavy plank back to the roadbed. He was very young, eighteen or nineteen. The good lunches had not arrived soon enough to overcome all the months of never getting enough to eat. The other man had a recurrent malaria attack on the afternoon of the third day. He lay on the ground shaking and shivering, even though the other men piled their shirts on him to try to keep him warm. He was still alive when they drove back to camp but died during the night.

For Jack Humphrey, chief engineering officer, the bridge project was a success. A change of scene, a touch of the outside world, better food and, above all, something to do. By the time they finished, he had grown rather fond of the little bridge. He hoped the new supporting timber would last long enough to prevent them from being punished for sloppy construction work.

The only bad result was Maxsie's back. Four days of bridge work crippled him. When he began having spasms of pain at the bridge, Humphrey told him to stop doing physical labor. "You're an officer, you're supposed to supervise." Maxsie would nod, then when a little extra help was needed, he would pitch in.

The day after they finished, Humphrey urged Maxsie to go see Jerry Baron. Maxsie resisted. "The only time you go see an army medic," he said, "is when you're goldbricking. If there's anything really wrong, you go find a civilian doctor."

"Jerry's a civilian doctor," Humphrey said. "He's only in the army because he got drafted. And anyway, what civilian doctor were you planning to see?"

Maxsie finally went to see Jerry Baron. He came back discouraged.

"What's he say?"

Maxsie sat down carefully on his bamboo bed, supporting his back with one hand. "Nothing wrong that can't be fixed," he said grimly. "After the war, by surgery."

"What do you have?"

"Well, he can't be positive without X-rays and other tests, but he's pretty sure I have—get this—a 'post-traumatic disk protrusion.' "

"What the hell is that?"

"Yeah, my exact words. 'Post-traumatic' means what's left after something bad has happened. In my case, that Jap fucker's rifle butt hitting my back. Because of that I've got a disk, one of those little soft things between your backbones, sticking out from where it's supposed to be. Baron says it probably needs surgery to fix it right."

"What are you supposed to do till then?"

Maxsie's grin was savage. "Well, I shouldn't do any heavy physical work, and I have to be careful how I bend down and stand up, and I shouldn't sit too long in one place without moving. My favorite part is I should avoid emotional tension. Baron's a very funny guy. He says the best way to handle it is to kick off, the way everybody else is doing. Otherwise, he says, I just have to live with it. Some advice."

"No more construction work."

"I guess not. I guess not." He sounded both depressed and angry.

That afternoon while they stood in the chow line, it started to rain. Nobody at O'Donnell could afford to miss a single meal, so they all stood in the rain,

waiting their turn. It was not a cold rain, but they
were soaked by the time they returned to barracks.
Those who had spare shirts or shorts stripped and
changed, but most sat or lay down in their soggy
clothes. The gray light of a late rainy afternoon fil-
tered through the open walls.

Freddy Collins chose this miserable moment to
launch into his favorite subject. He put his palms
together in front of his face and looked around the
barracks at his fellow officers. "There is only one hope
for us," he announced in a loud voice.

Several men groaned. Jack Humphrey could remember not so long ago when Freddy Collins had a
dry, ironic voice. That was as recently as Bataan,
before he lost his finger. Now it was shrill—what
Humphrey thought of as Freddy's preacher voice.

"And that hope is Jesus!" Freddy cried. "We must
all pray to Jesus. He is watching over us, and if we
believe in Him, He will save us."

"Ah, please, Freddy, not tonight," somebody said,
but in a hopeless tone.

Freddy paid no attention. "Jesus is sorry for us.
He knows what we have to endure." He was standing
now, clutching his hands tightly in front of him. "He
is testing us. Aren't you, Jesus?" Freddy looked up at
the nipa roof. His thin face had a fanatic confidence.
"You are just testing us. You are waiting—just waiting—for us to come to You." Again he looked around
the barracks. "I tell you men, every one of you, if you
don't speak to Jesus, you will never see your homes
or families again. Come on, pray with me to Jesus."

Freddy's lanky frame folded like some great bird

coming to roost as he knelt down on the bamboo floor. Once again he lifted his eyes to the ceiling. "Jesus," he began, "dear Jesus—"

Maxsie swung his legs carefully over the side of his bunk, and with both hands pushed himself to a sitting position. "Hey!" he said in the parade-ground voice of a master sergeant. "Knock off that Jesus shit."

Freddy was shocked into silence, but just for a moment. Then he said, "Don't talk like that. Don't talk like that about dear Jesus. He is your only hope."

"Hope!" Maxsie said. His voice was scathing.

He pressed his hands hard on his knees to push himself to his feet, the way he always did when his back was hurting. As he rose, he inched his hands up from his knees to his thighs until he had finally brought himself erect. One hand behind his back, he took the few steps to where Freddy Collins knelt on the floor. He looked down at Freddy.

"Hope!" he repeated in scorn. "You still don't get it. Listen, this is O'Donnell. Your buddy Jesus is *gone*. Jesus doesn't live here. He is off-duty, understand? He is on leave. Maybe he's in Manila or Australia or some place like that, but he sure isn't here. He never heard of O'Donnell. He's never going to hear of it. He doesn't *want* to hear about it. It's off-limits."

Maxsie winced and shifted his weight. Humphrey could tell he was hurting like hell, but it didn't stop him from tearing into Freddy. "All those poor fuckers in Zero Ward shitting their lives out. You think Jesus knows about them? Nineteen dead yesterday. Two hundred this month. Stacked up outside the death shed like little white sticks, waiting for somebody to haul them off to the boneyard. You think Jesus cares about them? You think he even knows about them? Man, listen, wake up. This is O'Donnell. Jesus is somewhere else. You looking for hope, you got to find it some other way. It's no use calling for Jesus. He can't hear you. He isn't listening. He's nowhere around. This is O'Donnell."

Maxsie turned and hobbled back to his bunk. The barracks was silent. Even Freddy Collins, still on his knees, was quiet. Humphrey could hear the rain dripping from the eaves.

Dear Sara,

As "a present from the Emperor" we got issued razors and scissors. I guess Tsuneyoshi got tired of looking at all us scruffy prisoners. Maxsie says Tsuneyoshi doesn't care if everybody dies, just so we don't look too ugly while we're at it. Anyway we've all been busy shaving and giving each other haircuts. I thought about growing a real beard, but the bugs would get in it. And that time I grew a mustache, it made me look like a cavalry officer, so that's out too. Everybody looks even thinner without long hair and whiskers.

The Red Cross finally persuaded the Japs to let some medicine into camp, but Jerry Baron says it isn't nearly enough. He's furious. His own hospital orderlies stole some of the medicine and have been selling it around camp on the sly. For twenty pesos you can get three quinine tablets. Luckily my malaria hasn't been acting up recently—knock on bamboo.

If I needed it, I'd have to sell my ring to one of the Japs to get cash. There's still some money in camp, believe it or not. Some guys managed to keep personal stuff that they sell to the guards. Also a little money gets smuggled in, usually through the truck drivers who go into Capas for supplies.

I'm going out on another work detail tomorrow. Jerry Baron's so desperate about the dysentery situation that he's going to try the Filipino remedy, which is boiled guava leaves. So I'm off with a small work party to collect guava leaves, this time without Maxsie. His back's too bad. Jerry doesn't know if the guava leaves will do any good. What he really needs is sulfa pills, but he can't get any. Even if the guava doesn't help, I know it'll do me good just to get out of camp. It always helps to be doing something different. Give the boys a hug.

Love, Jack

He had no idea just how different it was going to be.

≡ 14 ≡

Contact

Going back to Manila made Miranda nervous. This was her first time back since the early weeks of the war, but she could not avoid it. She must talk to Papaya face-to-face.

During the years she worked for Mr. Watson, she'd made this train trip two or three weekends a month to visit her family and her fiancé, Benny. But those were happy trips. Now Benny was dead, killed in the first days of the invasion. Since she and Benny had been lovers, she felt exactly like a widow.

The trains ran better and faster under the Americans. The Japanese didn't care about any passengers but their own soldiers and officials. She had to ride with other Filipinos all crowded together on the roofs of the freight cars.

Manila felt sad and strange to her. It was always a dingy, shabby city, once one got away from the bay and the big boulevards. The streets were lined with little stores, beauty parlors, auto repair shops with stacks of used tires on the sidewalks, record and radio shops, tiny tobacco stalls with fat old women sitting on packing crates to sell cigars and cigarettes. Slum shacks were patched together out of sheets of tin, pieces of wood and cardboard, and parts of old signs with faded lettering.

But it was always a bustling city. She loved it during the years she worked for Mr. Watson, living with three other secretaries in a single rented room. It was a rotating group, with one secretary passing her place on to another when she got married or changed jobs. Miranda stayed. She could have afforded a better room on the salary and bonuses Mr. Watson paid her, but she always made a cash contribution to the family farm, part of the price for living in Manila.

The girls had kitchen privileges for one hour every evening, after the landlord's family finished their own dinner. The girls took turns cooking and washing up. Then often they went out together into nighttime Manila. It was so different from Miranda's quiet life on the farm outside San Fernando, where everybody went to bed early.

Manila's streets were jammed with automobiles and horse-drawn *calesas* and *caramatas* and *caretelas*. Day or night, it was always dust and noise, gasoline fumes and horse dung. Honking horns competed with the clanging brass bells of the *calesa* drivers. Every other block had its own yellow Magnolia ice cream cart. Drying laundry hung from windows on thin strings. At every stoplight intersection, skinny street urchins in ragged T-shirts and shorts busily wiped windshields, hoping for a tip, or slithered between the lines of cars, selling newspapers and cigarettes and bananas or just begging for a few centavos. Manila was always alive.

Now, Miranda thought, as she rode the streetcar out to Papaya's home in Pasay, it seemed dead. The city was not empty, but it was so quiet. Many shops were closed. The few automobiles and military vehicles looked lonesome in the once-busy streets. Along the sidewalks and in the gutters were clumps of building materials—stones, chunks of cement, mounds of dirt—unfinished business of some kind that looked as though it would never be finished. The city made her cry. She was glad she lived back home with her family in San Fernando.

Papaya's house was as American in style as Mr. Watson's was Filipino. A woman servant answered the doorbell and invited Miranda into a living room filled with overstuffed American chairs and sofas. "Miss Papaya says she will be right here and would you like coffee? Or real Coca-Cola?"

"Oh, yes please, a Coke."

Papaya appeared before the Coke did. She came hurrying into the room wearing a long pink dressing grown and wrapping a big white bath towel around her head. "Oh, Miranda, I am so very sorry for you. Poor Benny. Those horrible Japs." She tucked the end of the towel in place to make a turban and then gave Miranda a warm hug and a kiss on each cheek. She smelled of nice expensive soap.

Miranda liked Papaya very much. Papaya had never been snooty to her, not even when she first became Mr. Watson's *querida*. There could have been a huge gulf between Mr. Watson's secretary and his mistress, especially when the mistress was not only a mestiza but rich and famous. But from the first week Miranda was invited to call her Papaya, not Miss Papaya. Miranda knew from other secretaries that a mistress could be far more demanding than the boss himself, but Papaya rarely asked for anything. She was appreciative when Miranda did anything special for her, like sorting out her record collection. They were not friends, but Papaya was always friendly.

"Come on," Papaya said, "we sit in the music room where nobody will interrupt us."

She led the way, walking in her quick, light steps. Her broad hips filled the pink dressing gown. Miranda thought Mr. Watson would be disappointed to learn Papaya had not lost any weight because of the war.

"Angela!" Papaya called out to the kitchen. "Where are the Cokes? *Sige na.*"

The woman came into the music room right behind them, carrying a brass tray with two glasses, a bowl of ice and two pale green frosty bottles. Papaya shooed her out, closed the door and poured the drinks herself.

The bookcases were filled with Papaya's enormous record collection. Much of it was popular American music, but there were also many Spanish and Filipino songs. Miranda had helped Papaya organize the records like a library, all properly indexed by nationality and orchestra and vocalist. The labels pasted on the front of the bookcases were in Miranda's clear, neat printing.

There were two victrolas. One was a gigantic Magnavox, a radio and victrola combined. When its intricate mechanism was functioning, it could play a stack of a dozen records one after another, automatically turning each record over so you could listen to the other side. It was fascinating to watch the prongs and metal arms in action. Unfortunately, the machinery was so elaborate and had so many moving parts that it often needed adjustment or repair. Papaya kept an ordinary one-record victrola to use whenever the Magnavox was "sick."

"So tell me everything," Papaya said when they were seated with their drinks. "It's so terrible about poor Benny, but is your own family all right?"

"Yes, all fine, thank you," Miranda said. "My parents and my brothers —everybody. On a farm, things change less than in the city." She wanted to get to her subject, but it would have been impolite not to go through the ritual exchange of family information. "And your mother and Karen?"

Papaya shook her head. "Mama is not too happy, mostly about me singing for the Japs, but other things too. And Karen is bored. But at least they are healthy."

"And how is Mr. Watson?"

Papaya brightened. "Oh, Amos is wonderful. Always sending out messages and instructions. He wants to know about everything. He will want to know how you are and what things are like in San Fernando. How are you really, Miranda? He will want to know."

That was all the invitation Miranda needed. She

had rehearsed what she wanted to say, and how she wanted to say it, but instead it just poured out.

"I want to go to work for you. You and Mr. Watson. Real work, not just send you a letter once a month. Papaya, I *saw* that death march. Those poor men walked right through San Fernando day after day. Our own soldiers and the American soldiers, too. They all looked—oh, so terrible. Like they were dying. I came into town and stood on the street to watch them go by. I cried when I looked at their faces. And then—and then—"

Miranda put her hands over her eyes as she felt her tears begin, the way they always did at this memory. Papaya was silent.

After a few moments Miranda rubbed the tears from her cheeks and said, "I'm sorry. It's just that— I saw something I can't forget, ever. One of the Filipino soldiers tried to escape into the crowd—you know, slip away—but the Japs caught him. When they threw him down on the street, I recognized him. He was a San Fernando boy, Petronilo Diaz—Pete. I knew him. I knew Pete. Benny and I both knew him. I used to *dance* with him. He was coming back into his own hometown. He tried to escape, get back to his family. They—the Japs—they did awful, awful, awful things to him. Right there in the street, as close as I am to you. With a bayonet. And Pete screamed and begged and—I couldn't bear it, but I couldn't look away either. It was like—I don't know, it wasn't like anything. It was just—Then when he was dead, they all marched on to the train station. When they were gone, people picked up poor Pete, what was left, and carried his body home to his family. I cannot forget."

"Of course not."

"Or forgive, either."

"Why should you?"

"The church say— It doesn't matter, I can't help it."

"Why do you try? Maybe someday it will all feel different."

Miranda shook her head. "I don't think so. Not about Pete. I'm sorry, but I tell you so you know why."

"Why what?"

"Why sending letters is not enough. They killed Benny. They tortured Pete and killed him. I want to do more."

"Like what?"

Miranda could see Papaya turn businesslike. Her eyes, which had been wide with sympathy, narrowed. Her voice sharpened. That was fine with Miranda. She had thought it all out before boarding the train for Manila.

"Help our prisoners. Help the guerrillas."

"How can you do that?"

"I don't know. Mr. Watson told me he would give you many pesos to do good things, and I should come to you. I could bring things, deliver things—money, food, messages, anything. I can get to places. The train, and also I can take a horse and cart from the farm, go anywhere. Everybody say prison camp at Capas is very bad, terrible. Many are dying. Suppose Benny was alive in that camp. Maybe we could bring

nice things to those poor soldiers. Also to the brave
guerrillas in the Zambales Mountains. Everybody is
talking about guerrillas in the Zambales Mountains.
We could help them. They are the fighters."

"Yes," Papaya said, "but even Amos doesn't have
enough pesos to help everybody. We have to choose.
For instance, which guerrillas?"

"My brothers say many groups are in Zambales,
but they hear most about two. The biggest is called
Marauders. The boss is Major Quintano, very handsome and flashy. The other group is smaller but very
famous because they explode a big Jap warehouse full
of ammunition and bombs. They don't have a name.
They have two bosses, an American officer and a
Filipino. They have funny code names, Coach and
Sergeant, and Sergeant even has a second code name,
Paradiso. My youngest brother thinks he will become
a guerrilla and join them, even though they are very
strict."

"Well, I will send word to Amos. I don't know
what he will want to do. But maybe he will say yes.
Are you sure you want to try these things?"

"Yes, very sure."

"It is dangerous."

"Tell Mr. Watson hello for me."

———

Since it was the first typewritten message Amos Watson had received from Papaya, he thought at first
glance it must be fake. Then he read that Papaya was
dictating this to Miranda, who would type it because

it was so long. Amos hadn't realized Miranda was in Manila.

The letter came concealed in a tube of bamboo, delivered to Amos's shanty by Papaya's most trusted messenger, Federico the shanty-builder.

Amos waited until no one in his shanty area was looking his way before he extracted the letter. He sat down in the folding bridge chair Carlos had sent in through the Package Line and read the letter carefully, twice. Then he set a match to it and dropped the flaming sheet into his charcoal cooking stove, which had also come through the Package Line. In the Philippines, war or no war, money still worked.

Watching the paper char and then crumble to black ash, he wondered if what he was thinking could possibly be true. Almost any American officer could have adopted the code name of Coach. It was a natural, normal American title but also one that all Filipinos knew and understood. Perhaps a number of American officers had actually been coaches in civilian life or on a military base. Just the same, Amos knew of only one officer who was definitely called Coach. And this guerrilla group was in the Zambales Mountains, not all that far from Brad Stone's last known whereabouts, an army camp outside San Fernando.

Amos always assumed Brad's unit had played some part in the hopeless defense of the Luzon Plain. He told Judy Ferguson the odds were that Brad's unit had managed to make the retreat into Bataan along with the bulk of MacArthur's army. If so, he would be a POW in a prison camp, possibly right here in

Manila at Nichols Field or Bilibid Prison, or else at
the big camp outside Capas. That was still the likeliest
possibility, but Judy Ferguson wouldn't let herself
think so. Amos could tell she thought Brad was dead
and that the best thing to do was forget about him.
But suppose Brad was neither dead nor a POW? Suppose he was Coach? Wouldn't that be something?
Now *there* would be a guerrilla unit Amos could support with conviction.

Amos rubbed his hands together. There was that
business about Sergeant, too. Of course, there must
have been several thousand Filipino sergeants. But
Amos remembered how enthusiastic Brad was about
some sergeant who had once been a Simpson houseboy. Well, it was all speculation, but just suppose . . .

Other things in Papaya's letter pleased him. He
was delighted to have Miranda in his network. It was
what he had hoped for all along—at least until she
announced she was leaving Manila to return to the
family farm in San Fernando. She was not as smart
and shrewd as Papaya, but she was practical and
charming. Like Donato, she was one of those people
everybody seemed to like. And above all, she was
loyal. She might indeed make a very useful courier,
the kind of nice-looking, smiling young woman no
Jap could possibly suspect of anything.

Amos didn't know what to do about the POWs.
Papaya and others managed to get some food and
clothes to the military prisoners here in Manila, but
not much was known about the big camp at Capas,
surrounded by barbed wire and carefully guarded.

Felix Logan said the guards in the commandant's office were constantly congratulating each other on being stationed here in Santo Tomas instead of at Capas. Filipinos in the fields outside the camp at Capas reported that burial details carried bodies out to a hillside every day. Even allowing for exaggeration and inaccurate information, things must be very bad up there. There must be some way to help those men, but he would have to know more. Maybe Miranda could learn something. Maybe Papaya could get further information from Enrique Sansone.

That afternoon when siesta time was over, Felix Logan came by Amos's shanty to make his daily report and to collect his reward, this time some canned tuna fish. Felix was better looking since he'd persuaded a dentist to take off his braces, but Amos felt sorry for him, cut off from his parents in Cebu and his Simpson friends up in Baguio, and isolated still further by being the flunky in the commandant's office. Amos knew he took a ribbing from other teenagers. It couldn't be helped. Felix needed a lot of shoring up to convince him that listening to the Japanese conversations was important. Sometimes it was, more often it was not. Even when Felix had something, it was usually less interesting than the tidbits Papaya picked up from generals and admirals at the Mabalinga Club. Still, Amos insisted that Felix report every day while his memory was fresh. Today he had nothing.

While they were sharing the tuna, spread on rolls from the STIC bakeshop, Amos asked, "What was the name of that sergeant who used to be a houseboy at Simpson? The one who wound up in the same outfit with Coach Stone."

"Head houseboy," Felix corrected him. "Mombak. Sergeant Mombak."

"Mombak?"

"Yes, sir. I think it's an Igorot name. Paradiso Mombak."

Amos Watson took a great wolf-bite of his roll.

———

The telephone, which had been ringing for four days without an answer, was picked up on the first ring.

"Yes?"

"Zorro, this is Peanut." She could not suppress a giggle at the silly names. "I've been trying to get you."

"Sorry, I've been away. How would five o'clock be?"

"That's fine."

At the Hut-Nut Café, the owner acted as though he had never seen her before. He just pointed to the rear table where Enrique Sansone was waiting. Papaya was unaccustomed to being treated like everyone else.

Over beer and a monkeywood bowl of salted peanuts, Sansone gave no explanation of where he had been. He had told Papaya that if he was not there himself, his private number would not answer. She wondered where that telephone lived. Was it in his home, perhaps in a separate room? Maybe locked in a closet? Or was it in an office somewhere? Could it be in a back room right here in the Hut-Nut? Although she had an active curiosity, she knew better than to ask.

She reported Amos's decision to give aid to a guerrilla group. "He told me check with you," she said. "Make sure it's okay."

Sansone's friendly smile did not change temperature. "Ah, guerrillas," he sighed.

"What's the matter?"

"Nothing. You know the trouble with most guerrillas?" he asked. He leaned forward on his crossed arms as though to tell her a special little secret. "They always want to *do* something."

"What's wrong with that? Everybody wants to do something."

"Yes, I know. Everybody wants to play cowboys and Indians. Bang-bang, shoot 'em up." He laughed at his own image. "So they decide it's time to kill a few Japs, or cut down a few telephone lines, or practice a little sabotage. Nothing big, you understand, because they aren't really an army. And what happens?" Sansone spread his hands, long delicate fingers stretched wide. "Our Japanese hosts get stirred up and decide they have to teach somebody a lesson. A few reprisals. So they torture and execute some Filipinos in return and make life more difficult for everybody else." He shrugged. "In the end, it probably comes out about even."

Papaya could not understand why he was so cheerful. He always sounded casual and carefree, as though nothing really mattered. "Well, what are the guerrillas supposed to do? Just sit around doing nothing?"

"Oh, no. The real value of guerrillas is collecting information. They can see what is going on, troop movements, troop strength, supplies, weapons"— he waved a hand—"all that sort of thing. And then pass along what they learn, just as you do at the Mabalinga."

"Yes, but guerrillas don't have anybody to pass it along to."

"Oh, yes, there are ways."

"And anyway, what good is it?"

"Are you the only Filipina who doesn't think the Americans will come back? You don't believe MacArthur is going to return, as he promised?"

She knew he was mocking her, but her answer was serious. "I think they will come back. So does Amos. But I also think Australia is very far away."

He nodded. "Yes, everybody must be patient. But when they come back, and even before, they will need to know what is going on here."

"Amos has a special guerrilla group he wants to help. Maybe you hear of them. The Coach and the Sergeant."

"Oh yes, well, fine. They're said to be quite good."

"Amos thinks he knows who they are."

"Is that right?"

Sansone sounded quite uninterested. Or perhaps he already knew?

"They blew up an ammunition warehouse. Wasn't that important?"

"The ammunition itself? Not terribly. There's more where that came from, as they say. But as a symbol, yes indeed. It was something for everybody to talk about and be proud of. And everybody knows it was done right under the Japs' noses—armed guards, wire fences, machine guns, all that. Oh yes, very nice."

"Well, Amos wants to help them."

"Why not?" Sansone twisted his head to get rid of the crick in his neck, or maybe just to move on to another subject. "So what is happening at your jolly club?"

Papaya giggled. "Admiral Buto is sweet on me. He has asked me to join his table twice."

"Really? That's good."

"He is teaching me a Jap lovesong."

"That's very good. I hope you encourage him."

"He wants me to sing it at the club."

"Good work," Sansone said. "Wonderful."

Papaya was not so sure.

———

When Rosauro walked into the hillside camp, he was soaking wet from the afternoon rain, and he was smeared with red dirt where he had slipped and fallen during the climb up from Carabangay.

The red lacterite soil of the Zambales Mountains did not turn to mud during a rain, but it became so slippery that it was difficult to walk, especially up and down hills.

"Why you not wait till morning?" Paradiso asked, as Rosauro approached the "headquarters" shed. Brad and Paradiso had been discussing their food supplies, which were low again.

"It is because," Rosauro said.

As Rosauro spoke, Brad could tell the young man was excited. He ducked his head to crawl into the shed beside them and squatted on his heels on the bamboo floor. His bare feet, which in this slippery terrain worked better than boots, were smeared red. His long wet black hair hung over his forehead.

"Coach," he said, obviously pleased with his news, "you have a visitor in Carabangay."

Brad and Paradiso exchanged looks. In the guerrilla world no visitor from outside was welcome. Only people you knew well were acceptable, and sometimes even they were not safe.

Rosauro saw the look. "It's okay," he said with his big smile. "It's a *dalaga*—a woman."

The only women Brad Stone knew must now be in prison camp, either in Manila or up in Baguio. "What woman?"

"She says you don't know her but she has very important messages."

"Well, what messages?"

Rosauro shook his head. "Only for Coach, she says. Nobody else."

That made Brad even more skeptical. Thanks to the ammo dump, he and Paradiso were by now pretty well known around the countryside, at least by name and reputation. If the Japs were trying to get to them, this would be one obvious way. Send a woman, with a message "only for Coach."

"She's a fake," he said, "whoever she is."

"I don't think so. Very nice."

Brad knew that Rosauro, who screened all their recruits, was almost never taken in, but this was a

woman, not a would-be guerrilla. Rosauro was un-
derstandably popular with all the young girls in Carabangay. Brad did not trust Rosauro's antennae for
women the way he did for men. "Where's she come
from?"

"She lives San Fernando. But her messages come
from Manila."

"Make her give them to you," Paradiso said. "Or
tell them to you."

"I already try hard, Sergeant, but she says only
Coach. She says that is her orders, only Coach. In
person."

"What's her name?" Brad asked.

"Miranda."

"I never heard of her."

"She says tell you two names, then you will know
she is all right. One name is Amos. She was his secretary until the war. The other name is Judy."

It took Brad a few moments to absorb that, to
translate it. My God, he thought. He had tried hard
not to let himself think of Judy Ferguson these past
months. Every time her image entered his thoughts
or dreams, he quickly banished her. He didn't know
if she was alive, but even if she was, he had no conceivable way to reach her. And the only Amos he
knew was Amos Watson. Where were Amos and
Judy? Maybe they were free somewhere, and this Miranda could take him to them. He was so excited by
the thought that he had to calm himself before he
could answer.

"You're right," he said. "I'll talk to her."

"You know those names?" Paradiso said.

"Yes, very well. There can't be a mistake. Rosauro's right. She has to be okay."

Paradiso was suspicious of women, especially in his present trade. "You can't be sure," he said.

"I'm positive."

"Maybe she's okay herself but somebody followed her. I don't like it, Coach. You can't go down there to meet a stranger."

"I have to see her."

Paradiso thought about it, his dark face expressionless. He thought about it a long time. Then he turned to Rosauro. "Bring her tomorrow. Make sure nobody follows you. Make somebody watch behind."

Brad was surprised. Paradiso never allowed women in the camp.

Early next morning when the slopes had dried, Rosauro went back down to Carabangay. Brad watched him leave, ragged white undershirt, khaki shorts. His figure soon disappeared into the thick foliage. Brad stayed close all morning, even though he knew it would be a long time before Rosauro returned. He kept checking his watch. Time passed slowly. A hot, slow morning.

At last Rosauro appeared on the trail, emerging from the forest greenery. When he saw Brad, he waved and smiled to say everything was all right. He carried a straw basket that he had not had when he left. Behind him came a Filipina carrying her *bakias*, wooden sandals, in her hand. She did not look tired from the long climb.

Paradiso appeared at Brad's shoulder. Together they waited. When Rosauro and the woman reached

camp level, she stopped to slip her feet into her *bakias*.
She wore a dark blue shirt and a loose skirt, lighter
blue—nondescript clothes that would not attract attention.

Rosauro was all smiles. "Okay, Sergeant. Nobody
follow."

"How sure?"

Rosauro made a circle with thumb and finger.
"Two men watching. It's okay. And here is Miranda."

She stepped forward, a little nervous but pleased.
She stared at Brad. "Sir, you are Coach?"

"Yes."

"Excuse me, I am supposed to ask. Will you please
take off your hat?"

Wondering what this was about, Brad took off the
straw hat he wore out of habit, even in camp, so that
no one could spot him as an American.

She looked into his blue eyes and then up at his
red-blond hair. She smiled and then put her hand over
her mouth, the way Filipinas did whenever they were
embarrassed, whenever they had done something
slightly impolite, like staring. "Oh yes," she said,
"you are the one." She turned to Paradiso. "And you
are Sergeant, right?"

She had a delightful smile, very full and friendly,
revealing one gold tooth among all the bright white
ones. Her black hair was cut short, in almost boyish
style, much shorter than most Filipinas wore their
hair. Her skin was a light tan. Her round cheeks came
down to a small, firm chin.

"Where is she?" Brad said. "Judy Ferguson."

"Sir, she is in the internment camp. In Santo

Tomas, the same as Mr. Watson. They are all right."

"How do you know she's all right?"

"Mr. Watson sends messages."

"Coach," Rosauro said, "maybe Miranda is hungry."

"No, I am fine," she said. "But maybe we sit down?"

No chairs, stools or benches existed in camp. In bad weather everyone sat on the bamboo sleeping platforms under the shelter of nipa thatch. In good weather like today everyone sat on the ground.

The four of them sat in the deep shade. Paradiso and Rosauro squatted on their heels. All Filipinos, even old women and little children, seemed to find this a comfortable, natural position. Brad Stone had learned to sit that way when he had to, when a group of the men were talking something over in conference, but this wasn't one of those times. He sat crosslegged. So did Miranda, facing him. Paradiso told one of the men to bring rice cakes and water gourds. Brad was tired of the bland rice cakes, fried in coconut oil, but they were good for energy and could be carried easily when the men were on the move. He waited impatiently while the gourds were passed around.

"What does she say?" he asked Miranda.

"Sorry? I don't understand."

"Judy Ferguson. Didn't you bring me a message? Or a letter?"

She shook her head. "Mr. Watson did not tell her about you yet. He wanted to make sure who you were."

Brad hid his disappointment. "Can I send a message back with you?"

"Yes. But everything has to be very careful. Mr. Watson say we cannot write names or anything that tells the Japs something. Just in case. And it takes a long time." Then she cheered up. "But I have a message from Mr. Watson. Also a special present."

She reached for the tattered straw basket that Rosauro had carried up the hill for her. It was an open-top basket the size of a large purse with big straw handles. She began to take out pieces of women's clothing, laying them on the ground beside her, one after another until the basket was empty. Brad saw nothing that looked like a special present.

Reaching inside the basket, she fiddled with something for a few moments. Then from somewhere she brought out a piece of paper. She smiled and handed it across to Brad. It was a single sheet of blue-lined paper, torn from a spiral notebook. No salutation and no signature. Brad glanced at it, then read it aloud.

" 'Glad to hear you are alive and doing so well. Your girlfriend is also well. I'd like to help you in your new career but don't know exactly what you need. Let me know. Meantime, here are my best wishes.' "

Not much of a letter, Brad thought. Amos Watson was certainly being careful. It told him nothing about Judy or even about Amos himself. He looked up.

Miranda was smiling and holding out a thick stack of peso notes bound together with a rubber band.

"This is Mr. Watson's 'best wishes,' " she said. "One thousand pesos, Mr. Stone—excuse me, Lieutenant Stone."

"Captain Stone," Paradiso corrected her. "This money is all for *us*?"

"Yes. Mr. Watson say you will know how to spend it."

The three men looked at each other in delight. A thousand pesos was five hundred dollars, a very sizable sum of money, especially out here in the countryside where a family could live on a few pesos a month. Today, under the Japanese occupation, real pesos had even greater value.

Brad could think instantly of half a dozen good ways to spend it. Clothes, shoes, food, tools, building materials—even additional weapons or explosives. If you had money, everything was for sale these days, much of it stolen from the Japs. Maybe some of the money should be used to redeem food chits. If he bought back some of those slips signed "Coach, Capt. USA," supposedly not due for payment until the American army returned, it might do wonders for their credit with the farmers. He was sure some of the farmers did not expect to be paid at all, even when the Americans came back. He could imagine the farmers marveling to each other that a guerrilla outfit was willing to pay its debts. Well, some of its debts.

Miranda said, "Mr. Watson hopes you can do something for those poor army prisoners. The ones at Capas."

"Yes, Camp O'Donnell," Paradiso said. "Coach and I went there to look. Many guards and barbed wire. But now we have money, maybe we can do things."

"We *will* help them," Brad said. "We could have been prisoners there ourselves, all of us. We'll find some way."

"Yes," Paradiso said. "Maybe."

"No maybe."

Paradiso was angry for a moment, then laughed. "Okay, Coach." He turned back to Miranda. "This Mr. Watson, can he get us medicines?"

"What kind?"

"Quinine. And also anything for the infection. Skin infections. Anything."

"I will ask. What else?"

"Cigarettes. Good ones. For bribe."

"Flashlights," suggested Rosauro, who had often complained that no one in camp could move around in the dark. "And batteries."

"Next time I have to come in a truck," Miranda said with a smile.

"How soon is next time?" Brad asked, thinking of Judy.

"Maybe two, three weeks." She noticed the disappointment on his face. "It takes time," she explained. "All the back-and-forth, very slow. I do my best. I think maybe I should start back now."

They all got to their feet. Brad said, "I'll give you a note to take. Two notes."

"Yes, sir. Remember not to put names. Much safer."

Brad wrote Amos Watson a carefully innocuous short note of thanks. To Judy, after trying to think what he could possibly say, he wrote, "Glad you are safe and well. So am I. Until next time, all my love." He did not sign either note.

Miranda put the notes in the hiding place in the bottom of her basket, then took her time folding the clothes and laying them carefully on top of each other. When she was packed, she politely shook hands with Brad. Her hand was small and firm. "Mr. Watson will be glad it is really you."

Brad said, "You are a very brave woman."

She blushed and said, "Oh, no, sir. You are the brave ones. You are the heroes. You are the fighters."

The admiration in her liquid brown eyes was so naked, so direct, that Brad was embarrassed. He did not think of himself and his band in such romantic terms.

"We are grateful to you," he said. "Very grateful."

"It is nothing. I am glad to help."

"Just the same." He touched her shoulder, a small gesture of friendship. "We thank you. And I hope we'll see you in two weeks."

———

While the men of his work detail were collecting guava leaves and the Jap guard, rifle between his knees, was dozing under a shade tree, Jack Humphrey walked off by himself. It was a pleasure to be alone, just to have the brief illusion of privacy and freedom.

In a gully below the hillside of guava trees, he came to a bamboo thicket. It reminded him of the days on Bataan, where the thickets were so impenetrable you

needed a bolo to cut your way through. That seemed
very long ago.

As he stood there by himself, the only person in
sight, two men stepped out of the thicket. Filipinos,
obviously. One, who wore a big cone-shaped straw
hat, was almost as tall as Humphrey. The other, bareheaded and much older, was short and stocky, with
dark brown skin. Jack Humphrey's first thought was
that they might have food to give him.

Then the taller one spoke to him in what was un-
mistakably an American voice. "Hey, soldier," he
said, "you trying to escape?"

For a wonderful moment Humphrey thought of
saying yes, and then vanishing into the thicket with
the two men and never seeing Camp O'Donnell again.
"I can't," he said. "They shoot ten for every one who
escapes. Who are you?"

"An American officer. We're guerrillas. This is Sergeant. I'm Coach."

"Humphrey. Major Jack Humphrey, Philippine
Scouts."

"Where's your guard, major?"

"Last I saw, he was asleep."

"We'd better hurry anyway. Listen, sir, is there
any way for us to get supplies into your camp? Somebody who goes back and forth? We can bring things
to Capas, but is there a safe way to send them in?"

Humphrey thought quickly. The only regular visitors to Capas were the men who went into town
every other day to pick up food supplies, mostly rice
and a few vegetables. He did not know the group

well, but he remembered one man who looked responsible. "Yeah, there's a Corporal Santini. He's one of the men who goes into Capas by truck to pick up our food. But there's always a Jap guard."

"That doesn't matter," the one called Sergeant said. "What does he look like? This corporal."

"Short, very thin. Black hair. Big black mustache."

"We know the place they go. The bodega near the church. You trust him?"

"I guess so. How do I know? Are you two really American army?"

"Yes," the tall one said. "The Filipinos who load the truck, we'll work through them. But you'll talk to this Santini? Tell him to look for things we put in the load? Make sure he takes them when the truck gets back to camp?"

"Sure," Humphrey said. "What kind of things?"

"Whatever we can get for you."

"I'll tell him. Look, I'd better get back before that guard wakes up and starts hunting for me."

"Wait a second," the tall one said. He reached into the pocket of his shirt. "Major, here's fifty pesos. Spread it around, wherever you think it will do the most good. We'll try to have more."

Humphrey took the money, thinking of the various ways it could be used.

"Are you out here every day, sir?"

"For the time being. When it's not raining."

"Maybe we'll meet again, sir. But you'll talk to that corporal?"

"Right away. This afternoon."

"By the way, major, do you smoke?" He held out an unopened pack of real Chesterfields.

Humphrey's mouth watered. "Not recently," he said.

"Well, here. You'll spread them around too?"

"I sure will," Humphrey said, thinking of twenty men who would be unexpectedly happy tonight. "You don't happen to have any matches, do you?"

———

Amos Watson had to look all over camp to find her. She was not at the Barneses' shanty, and Millie Barnes had no idea where she might be. He tried the shanty of Frank Otis, but no one was there. Maybe she was in her room. He asked another woman if she would mind checking for him, but she was not there either. He finally found her in one of the small canteens, where she was drinking coffee and laughing with two young men. The men were plainly annoyed at his interruption.

"I have to see you," Amos said.

"We're just having coffee," she said. "Will you join us?"

The two young men liked that even less.

"No thanks. Come outside for a minute."

"Hey now," one of the men began.

Amos glared down to shut him up. "It's important," he told her.

"I'll be back," she said. She got up, taking her tin coffee cup with her, and followed Amos outside to the plaza area in front of the Main Building. When

Amos kept on walking her away from the building,
she said, "My goodness, Amos, what's this about?"

He stopped when they were beyond earshot of any
of the people crossing the plaza. He turned to face
her.

"Judy, I have very good news. He's alive. And not
just alive but free."

"Who is?"

"Brad. He's with the guerrillas."

The cup dropped from her hand. Coffee splashed
over their feet.

"How—how do you know? When— Are you
sure?"

He reached in his pocket for Brad's note and held
it out to her. She stared at it as though she didn't
understand, or perhaps didn't believe. Then the big
gray-green eyes looked up at Amos for confirmation.

He nodded. "Take it," he said. "It's for you."

Her arm, with Brad Stone's cheap monkeywood
bracelet around the wrist, was shaking as she reached
for the slip of paper. Amos would not have thought
she would be so moved. He was certain Brad Stone
was more serious about her than she was about him.
Perhaps it was just the surprise. She closed her eyes,
then opened them and read the brief message. She
read it twice before she looked up. "This is really
from him?"

"Yes, don't you recognize the handwriting?"

"No," she said, shaking her head. "Actually, no,
I don't."

"Well then," Amos said, "you'll have to take my
word for it. It's Coach. It really is Coach."

=≡ 15 ≡=

Days of Anger

Captain Eli Phipps, who by now thought of himself as Sam only when he wrote home to his family, was glad to be moving north—at last. North to Mac-Arthur's new headquarters at Brisbane, halfway up the east coast of Australia, twelve hundred miles closer.

Ever since the escape from Corregidor, it had been south, south, south. First by PT boat to Mindanao, then by B-17 to Darwin on the north coast of Australia, then by DC-3 to tiny, miserable Alice Springs in the center of the huge, miserable Australian outback, then by endless train all the way down to Adelaide, and finally by still another train to Melbourne on the southern tip of the continent.

Damn near five thousand miles of retreat, with the General furious a large part of the time. Furious at being ordered by Roosevelt to desert his men on Bataan and Corregidor. He had talked of resigning, taking off his stars and going over to fight on Bataan as a volunteer, but everybody talked him out of it. Furious at Washington, which had not sent him a single

man or plane since the war began. Furious at the navy
and air force, which he blamed for lack of support.
Furious at the transportation. The B-17s from Mindanao were so decrepit they barely got off the ground,
and the primitive narrow-gauge train from Alice
Springs took three days to reach Adelaide. Furious to
find there was no army waiting in Australia for him
to lead back to the Philippines, and that Washington
was slow to do anything about it. Furious that when
he drafted his arrival statement to the press at Adelaide, Washington asked him to change his words
from "I shall return" to "We shall return." Phipps
thought MacArthur was being more megalomaniacal
than usual when he refused, but everybody else liked
it just the way the General wrote it.

Furious at General Wainwright a month later for
the surrender of Bataan without a final doomed and
hopeless attack. Furious a month after that at the fall
of Corregidor, although he did issue one of his pur-
plest statements about it: "Through the bloody haze
of its last reverberating shot, I shall always seem
to see a vision of grim, gaunt, ghastly men, still
unafraid."

To Phipps, who usually liked literary allusions,
this sounded ludicrously like Edgar Allen Poe's ra-
ven, that "grim, ungainly, gaunt and ghastly ominous
bird of yore." Surely that was where the well-read
General had filched his adjectives. Was it deliberate
plagiarism? Or unconscious plagiarism? Or perhaps
MacArthur took the position that it simply did not
matter what Poe had written, that all colorful words
in the English language belonged exclusively to the

General. If so, how arrogant. It was one of those questions about MacArthur to which Phipps knew he would never learn the answer. Phipps also thought "still unafraid" was pretty silly. The poor guys on Corregidor had probably been scared shitless by all that brutal Jap artillery and bombing in the final days.

The one group spared MacArthur's fury were the few officers who had come out of the Philippines with him. In the General's view they were hallowed men. Phipps was proud to be one of this little "Bataan Gang," even though he was its most junior member and even though, like most of the rest of them, he had never even been on Bataan.

MacArthur was hipped on Bataan. He named his personal plane *Bataan*. Telephone operators at headquarters were told to say, "Hello, this is Bataan." He persuaded the Aussies to call their new destroyer HMS *Bataan* and had his wife, Jean, christen the ship. When Roosevelt and Marshall awarded him the Medal of Honor, MacArthur said it wasn't meant for him personally but was "a recognition of the indomitable courage of the gallant army which it was my honor to command." Everybody pronounced Bataan as though it were two syllables, instead of three in the proper Filipino way.

Well, Phipps thought, the General had every right to be proud of it. Though MacArthur had done a lot of screwing up in the early days of the war, Bataan was the one spot in the Pacific that had held out. As General Red Sampson told Phipps, "Eli, if it hadn't been for Bataan and Corregidor, the Japs would have grabbed New Guinea, and by now they'd be all over

Australia. The Old Man really saved this country."

Whether Australia had actually been saved wasn't all that clear. The best Australian infantry troops finally came home from the Middle East to defend their own country, and two American divisions arrived. But the Aussies were still talking about withdrawing to "the Brisbane Line," letting the Japs take all the northern part of the country. MacArthur said that would guarantee defeat. Quite a feisty comment from the man who had himself withdrawn to Bataan.

When they moved up to Brisbane, Sampson made Phipps a deputy message-center chief, over the heads of two other captains. Phipps was still being called on to write occasional communiqués, a task he came to enjoy. Having learned his lesson on Corregidor, he used the General's name freely and frequently whenever he sat down to the typewriter. And now that MacArthur was Commander in Chief, Southwest Pacific Area, with the unwieldy and unpronounceable acronym CINCSWPA, additional flourishes were called for. The communiqués now quoted MacArthur references to "my navy." Eli Phipps wondered when the word would be passed down that it should now be referred to as "my war."

———

As her final number Friday night, Papaya sang the Japanese lovesong Admiral Buto taught her. She had no trouble learning the plaintive melody—she could pick up almost any melody the first or second time she heard it—but she had to memorize the Japanese

words syllable by syllable. Admiral Buto told her
what they meant.

> *"Each night*
> *I go alone*
> *To my quiet bed.*
> *My hero is far away.*
> *In the silent moonlight*
> *I often wonder*
> *If he will ever return.*
> *Will the blossoms bloom again*
> *Outside my window?*
> *Will spring ever come again?"*

She thought it sounded better in Japanese. In its
quiet way it was as sentimental as a Filipino lovesong.

Admiral Buto, standing at his table, his bald head
gleaming in the light, led the applause after the song,
but all the Japs were clapping. Some of them were
tearful, so she must have done it right. Aurelio Lopez
complimented her as she left the stage.

"*Very* good," he said as the clapping continued.
"They really liked it. How many more do you know?"

"Zero."

"That's too bad. You'd better learn some more.
And Admiral Buto says please come to his table."

Admiral Buto, or Admiral Prick as she thought of
him to herself, wasted little time. She had barely sat
down beside him, had not yet ordered a drink, when
he looked at her with his big mournful eyes and put
his hand firmly on her thigh. She could feel the squeeze
of his strong fingers against her flesh.

"I want you to come home with me tonight," he said in his deep, almost-bass voice.

Papaya moved his hand away. She received many propositions, it was to be expected in her business, but this was the first from an enemy officer. It made her angry. "I sang your song," she said. "That is enough."

"No," he said, "not enough." His hand did not return to her leg, but he stared into her eyes, slowly shaking his shaved head. "You are beautiful, and you sing beautifully."

"That is all I do. I sing. I must go now."

He did not object. "If you say so. But I will be here again tomorrow night."

When she reported this conversation to Enrique Sansone, he did not share her anger. In fact, his smile remained as charming as ever. "He's such an important man," he said in mild protest. "The whole port of Manila under his command. He would know so many interesting things." He waved a hand vaguely. "Ships coming and going, troops, supplies—all kinds of interesting things."

Now she was just as angry at him as at Buto. "I am supposed to listen to what people say. Nobody ever said I was supposed to fuck Jap admirals."

He ignored her vulgarity. "Oh, well," he said, and shrugged. "You mustn't take it so seriously."

"It's not *your* cunt," she snapped.

"Well, hardly." A charming little laugh.

"I am serious. What do you think Amos would say?"

"I don't know, Peanut. Why don't you ask him?"

She did ask him, in a carefully and delicately worded message that she made Federico repeat several times before she sent him off to Santo Tomas. When the shanty-builder came back, the reply was far less definite than she had expected. According to Federico, Mr. Watson had thought for a long time before he said, "Tell her to explore the possibilities."

"What else?"

"That is all, mum."

"That can't be all."

"Yes, mum. Nothing more."

She wondered what that meant. Was she supposed to play Admiral Buto along? Talk to him? Flirt with him? Go to bed with him? Whatever it was, it made her angry at Amos, too. What kind of lover would send instructions like that?

––––––

Sandy Homobono was amused by his new assignment for the *Manila Tribune*. He was to find out everything about the illegal radio station, the Voice of Juan de la Cruz, and then write a story denouncing it and offering a reward for information. The assignment came, as usual, from the paper's Filipino editor, Billy Bilisang, but this was fiction. All assignments except social notes and the weather really came from the *Tribune*'s Japanese "adviser," Mr. Shugi. On a story as sensitive as this one, the assignment had to come direct from General Miyama, the administrative commander of Manila.

"How big is the reward, Billy?"

"We haven't decided yet," the editor said, meaning

that Mr. Shugi had not told him. "We can fill that in when you write your story."

"Maybe I'll collect it myself."

"There's a bonus if you do a good job."

"I always do a good job. How much bonus?"

"We haven't decided yet."

The Voice of Juan de la Cruz had begun broadcasting shortly before the fall of Corregidor and the disappearance of Corregidor's own radio station, the Voice of Freedom. Juan de la Cruz was the Filipino common man, like the Americans' John Doe or the British John Bull.

The Japanese ordered the removal of all shortwave antennas and declared that listening to any shortwave radio station was a punishable offense. Whoever was running the voice of Juan de la Cruz, whose longwave broadcasts could be picked up by any set in Manila, obviously had a functioning shortwave set, for much of the material was a repackaging of the news from KGEI in San Francisco. The announcers boasted of it. The rest of their material was simpleminded patriotic propaganda—denunciations of the Japanese occupation and emotional calls for resistance. The voices were young. The performance was amateurish. But to the Japs the mere existence of the station was maddening.

Sandy put in a request to interview General Miyama for the story. He believed in polishing his contacts at the top, but this time there was another reason. If Miyama had ordered the story, as he must have, talking to him was the best way to get it right. Within hours General Miyama agreed to see him in his private office in Amos Watson's old house. The main administrative offices were downtown, but Miyama preferred to work alone, keeping in touch by telephone and messenger.

Sandy Homobono had never set foot in this house when Amos Watson lived here. Well, old Amos was now tucked away in Santo Tomas, and this was Sandy's third visit to see Miyama. Fortunes of war. The door was opened by Watson's former chief houseboy, whom Miyama had sensibly kept on. The houseboy had been sensible, too. These days in Manila, running a house for a high-ranking Jap officer was a very good job. Not as good as reporting for the *Tribune*, of course, but a very good job for a servant.

"I'm Mr. Homobono," he told the houseboy. "General Miyama is expecting me."

"Yes, sir." The little man stepped back to hold the door wide open.

"I know where it is." But the houseboy followed behind anyway.

Sandy walked through the grand living room to the office area. A junior officer took him into what had been Amos Watson's library, where General Miyama sat behind a narra-wood desk. On Sandy's first visit here, an interpreter had been present. On his second visit the interpreter had been standing by in the room next door. Today there was no interpreter in sight.

"Be seated," the general said with a minimum of warmth.

Sandy sat in the straight chair across the desk from the general. Miyama looked severe, businesslike. Last time when Sandy asked permission to smoke, the general had said no in such a way that Sandy knew there was no point in asking again.

"What would you like to know?"

"I would like to know, sir, what efforts are being made to find the station. Why can't we find it?" He used "we" to indicate that everybody was out hunting for the station, Filipinos as well as Japs.

"The army is using direction finders, of course. It takes some time to"—Miyama paused, searching for a word—"pinpoint a radio signal. It is clear that the sending station is being moved from place to place around the city."

"Very ingenious."

Miyama did not respond.

"What about the shortwave set they're using to get their information?"

"What about it?"

"Are efforts being made to find it?"

"A receiving radio cannot be—detected."

Sandy knew this perfectly well but wanted to hear the general admit it.

"I've heard the broadcasts. Those men are amateurs."

"You are not supposed to listen to that station. It is illegal."

"I can't write about it without listening to it. Sir. It also sounds to me as though they are very young men." When Miyama said nothing, Sandy asked, "Would you agree, sir?"

Miyama nodded his head. "Yes. Very young. And very foolish. They will be caught and executed."

"Can I write that?"

"Yes, you *will* write that."

Homobono hated to be told what to write. It didn't matter who told him—the Japs, the Americans, Filipino officials. President Quezon had been more tactful, putting his requests in the form of suggestions. Miyama had no such delicacy.

The little old houseboy came quietly into the office. He placed a silver tray with a porcelain teapot and a single matching teacup on the general's desk. "Pour tea, sir?"

Miyama nodded without looking. "Is there anything else?" he asked. Without quite waiting for Sandy to answer, he said, "Very good then."

General Miyama nodded his head in dismissal and turned to his morning tea.

Sandy was certain the general would read his story before it was published.

———

Amos Watson already knew from Felix that the Voice of Juan de la Cruz was giving the Japs conniptions. Even mild-mannered Major Omi was incensed. But it wasn't until the message from Carlos, delivered with his laundry, that Amos knew how deeply General Miyama resented the radio station.

Carlos managed to overhear most of the conversation between Miyama and Sandy Homobono while preparing the general's tea. Amos wondered if in the old days Carlos had overheard his private conversations in that same house. Probably. Head houseboys made a point of knowing their masters' affairs. Partly out of native curiosity, partly because it helped them anticipate their masters' likes and dislikes.

If the Voice of Juan de la Cruz bothered the Japs that much, perhaps Amos should try to help the station. Those young men, whoever they were, must need money and information to get away with what they were doing. Amos was impressed by their daring, but he wasn't sure how to go about aiding them. The station was a closely kept secret. Maybe his young driver, Donato, could ask around among his friends and learn what could be done.

Amos also had to wonder about Manila's former leading columnist. Just what was going on in Homobono's devious mind these days? Which side was he on? Of course, he was always, first and last, on the side of Sandy Homobono, but how did that translate? Sandy hadn't liked the Americans, but at the same time he could do business with them, letting them buy their way into or out of his column.

Surely he could not like the Japs better than the Americans? But there he was, working for the Japs' propaganda newspaper, taking their money and writing their stories. The Japs circulated the *Tribune* in Santo Tomas, so Amos was familiar with everything that appeared under Sandy's byline. Sandy was as critical of the Americans as ever, referring to them as "enemy aliens," but never a word against the noble Japs. Of course, he could not criticize the Japs even if he wanted to, but did he want to?

That afternoon after siesta, Judy Ferguson came to Amos's shanty with the revised version of her letter to Brad Stone. She was still angry at him, not just because he had insisted on reading the letter but because he had torn up the first version. "If that letter was found," he told her, "they would know it came from Santo Tomas. They could learn who wrote it and maybe even find out where Coach is. You have to be much more careful."

She went away mad. She didn't like taking orders, but if she wanted to write Brad, she had no choice.

"Here," she said, as she held out the new sheet of paper. Her big gray-green eyes were snapping mad. She wore no makeup—very few women even had lipstick anymore—but her face was clean and her short brown hair was brushed. She had not gone sloppy like so many other women. "See if this is any better."

"I hope so," Amos said. He ignored her sarcasm. He was glad to see her so full of spirit. Many of his fellow internees had become listless and bored by their captivity, once things had shaken down. Not Judy. She was full of fight. She stood with arms folded under her nice breasts, waiting impatiently while he read her letter. Her pencil handwriting was jagged, with large up-and-down strokes, distinctive and quite hard to read.

I'm happy to know you are alive and having such an exciting time. I wish I were. There's not much excitement here. Lots of old friends from before the war. Also a lot of very dull, bossy people [That means me, Amos thought] *and too many rules. I wish we could see each other soon, but that doesn't seem likely. I miss you and I miss the good times. I'd give*

anything to get all dressed up and go to a big dance.
Take care of yourself.

"Yes, that's better," Amos said. "Much safer."

"Good." A real snap to her voice.

Amos thought about Brad Stone, way up there in
the Zambales hills. "You know," he said with a smile,
"it wouldn't be dangerous to add that you send your
love. Or something like that."

"Now you're telling me what to put in as well as
what to take out?"

"No, just a thought."

"That's none of your business, Amos."

"Quite right."

She was somewhat mollified. "When will he get
it?"

"Hard to say. It's not like the post office."

"Well," she said. Then, grudgingly, "All right,
thanks."

After she left, he got out his own pencil and paper
from the bamboo cupboard in the corner of his
shanty. He practiced for a few minutes to duplicate
the slanting, jagged handwriting. Then, at the bottom
of Judy's note, he carefully added, "Much love."

It looks close enough, he thought. He folded the
note and hid it in his cupboard. He would send it out
tomorrow through the Package Line.

———

Felix Logan, at Mr. Watson's suggestion, was pretending to learn a few simple Japanese phrases. Although Felix hated his job cleaning the commandant's

office, he liked this part because Mr. Watson made it a game.

"What you want to do," Mr. Watson said, "is give them the impression that you're trying to be friendly. You're showing that you want to pick up their language. But at the same time, you can't afford to look too smart. Eager but a little dumb, okay?"

"Sure," Felix said. "You mean I should make a few mistakes?"

"Exactly. They'll like you for trying. People like to hear a foreigner trying to learn their language. It makes them feel superior, especially when you fuck up."

One of the things Felix liked was that Mr. Watson treated him like a fellow adult. Felix couldn't remember any other adult using the phrase "fuck up" in conversation with a teenager.

"I suppose the place you should start is 'Good morning.' How do you say 'Good morning' in Japanese?"

"*Ohaiyo gozaimasu.*"

"What?"

"*Ohaiyo gozaimasu. Ohaiyo*, pronounced just like the state of Ohio. Literally it means 'There is morning,' said in a polite way."

"Well, you don't want to say it too correctly, at least not at first. How about saying 'Oh-hee-oh'? And what's the other word?"

"*Gozaimasu.*"

"So how about 'gozzymassy'? 'Oh-hee-oh gozzymassy'?"

Felix laughed. "Sure. They'll think it's funny."

"And what about 'Good evening'? Do you say 'There is evening'?"

"No, sir, for some reason you say, 'In regard to the evening.' *Kombawa.*"

"I'll leave that to you to butcher any way you like. How about 'Kombowwow' or 'Kambaba'?"

"Why not give 'em both?"

"Why not? And how do you say 'It's a nice day'?"

"Kyo tenki wa ii desu ne."

"Too complicated. You'd better save that one for later on. How about 'Thank you'?"

"That's easier. *Domo arigato.*"

"Okay, I'm sure you can work that one in. Say 'Homo avocado,' or something like that. How do the guards and the other officers address Major Omi? What do they call him?"

"Omi-san."

"Oh, I know *san*. That means 'honorable,' right? But wouldn't it be Major Omi-san?"

"No, sir. You could say 'Major-san' or 'Omi-san,' but not both."

Mr. Watson shook his head in wonder. "Very interesting," he said. "All these different ways of being polite."

Felix was pleased that he could impress someone as old and important as Mr. Watson. "My favorite," he said, "is the way the Japanese would say 'Drop dead.'"

Mr. Watson smiled. "That's a Japanese expression, too?"

"No, sir, but some American figured out just how they'd say it."

"What would they say?"

"*Shinji-mai*. That's the short version. It's a contraction of *Shinde shimate kudasai*. It means 'Please give me your complete dying.' "

" 'Complete dying'—that's very nice. *Shinji-mai*. I guess you'd better not throw that one into the pot. Stick to the simple, everyday words. And be sure you don't get the pronunciation too perfect. They'll correct you, but don't let them think you're learning too quickly. Keep stumbling over things. They mustn't think you're really learning."

"That's easy. I was never too great a student."

"Neither was I," Mr. Watson admitted. "I barely got through engineering school. Classwork just didn't interest me at all."

"Me neither!" Felix felt a sudden bond with Mr. Watson, who hated school but still had managed to make all that money.

"How are you doing in your classes here?"

"About the same as at Simpson. A little better, I guess, because here it's something to do. And of course the teachers aren't as strict, and there aren't many textbooks, so I don't have to do as much reading. I'll graduate, and then it's all over."

"What about college?"

"You mean after the war? My parents want me to go, but I think it's a waste of time and money, and they don't have much money. Maybe I can get out of it."

Mr. Watson was shaking his head. "That would be a mistake."

"But you said yourself you didn't like school."

"That's right, I didn't. But I still managed to learn something, and a college degree is very useful."

"I'd rather get a job. Here in Manila, go right into business. To tell you the truth, Mr. Watson, what I'd mostly like, really like, I'd sort of like to be rich."

Mr. Watson laughed. "Very commendable. Very American. Greed is important in business, provided you don't overdo it. For instance, well, do you know anything about our big gold boom?"

"No, sir. You mean the gold mines up in Baguio?"

"Well, that's where the mines are, but the boom was in the stock market here in Manila. From 1932 to 1937, quite a long time for a boom to last. What happened was that Roosevelt raised the price of gold and guaranteed it. And here we were in the Philippines with all that gold sitting in the mountains around Baguio. The country went crazy. Everybody invested in gold stocks. Not just businessmen, everybody."

"Did you?"

"Certainly. Quite a lot, in fact. You could bet on the big existing mines, like Benguet and Balatoc, or on mines that hadn't yet been developed. You could also bet on mining equipment and mining leases. It was a real spree. Greed. One day—it's quite a famous day, July 13, 1936—over seven million shares were traded. A record. After the exchange closed, a group of us were having celebration drinks at the big round businessmen's table in Tom's Dixie Kitchen. But something told me, sitting there at Tom's big wooden table, something reminded me what I'd learned years before: everybody can't be a winner. Some instinct told me, if everybody's so happy, something is wrong. Sometimes you have to move away from the crowd, be alone. So I got up, said good night, and next morning I sold out everything I had in gold."

"Oh boy," Felix said. "And you were right?"

"Oh no. The boom lasted into the next year. I made a great deal of money selling when I did, but I didn't sell out at the top. A few people did. But many of them, most of my business friends and practically all the ordinary investors, wound up holding a large empty bag."

"Were you sorry you didn't stay in a little longer?"

Mr. Watson shrugged. "How much is enough?"

"I really like hearing about business," Felix said. "Especially now, when there's nothing to do."

Mr. Watson's face, which had been smiling when he told the gold-boom story, suddenly turned stern. "Felix, I don't want you to think you have 'nothing to do.' Just remember that what you're doing is important. Extremely important."

"It doesn't feel that way."

"No, I suppose not. But don't get discouraged. I count on you."

That made Felix feel better. "That reminds me," he said. "Some of the kids ask me how come I talk to you so much. What should I tell them?"

"Can't have that." Mr. Watson thought a minute. "Tell them I'm looking after you because your parents are in Cebu. Tell them I'm an old friend of your parents."

"But you don't even know them."

"I don't think that matters, do you?"

Next morning in the commandant's office when he made his formal bow of greeting, bending properly from the hips, Felix gave them a spirited "Oh-hee-oh gozzymassy." Several of the Japs stared at him blankly, but Major Omi raised his eyebrows and smiled, and then several of the others smiled too. Omi's interpreter laughed out loud. They tried to teach Felix how to say it correctly, but he was very stupid, unable to pronounce the strange words to their satisfaction. They all had a good time with the lesson.

Just before he started to empty the wastebaskets and sweep the floor, one of the guards gave him a cigarette.

———

Corporal Santini drove a tough bargain with Jack Humphrey. He took half of whatever the loaders managed to hide in the supply truck, and said it must be left to him to decide how to share it with other enlisted men. Humphrey got the other half to share with his fellow officers. They split everything down the middle, whether it was a few cans of beef or fish or a small bunch of bananas or some pesos or cigarettes. The one thing Humphrey insisted on was that whenever there was any medicine tucked away beneath the sacks of rice and bags of coconuts, it must go straight to the medical officer. Jerry Baron was grateful and asked no questions, but there was never enough medicine. Nor was there ever enough of anything else.

Dear Sara,

Sorry to tell you it's getting worse. The early part of this month we were losing twenty or so men a day. That's just American dead. God knows how bad it is in the Filipino camp. Then one day last week we went over thirty dead for the first time. Mostly dysentery and malaria, but an awful lot of it is just plain simple starvation.

Tsuneyoshi is not just a bastard, he's an incompetent bastard. The place is very badly run, and he doesn't have the sense or the authority or whatever it takes to arrange for supplies. I never trusted reserve officers in our own army, but Captain Tsuneyoshi must be the worst reserve officer in any army. He doesn't even look like an officer. He walks around with his fat ass and baggy shorts and this fierce look on his face and just ignores every complaint or request for better treatment. He gives us all something to hate—those of us who still have the strength.

Yesterday the dead went over forty for the first time. Everybody who can still walk and do a little digging helps out on burial detail. Lucky the bodies don't weigh much. We carry them out to the hillside and drop them into long trenches, whole bunches of them all dumped in together. In the rains the trenches fill up with water and the bodies float like little sticks. We have to push them under with poles and hold them down until dirt can be shoveled over them.

Remember my telling you about Freddy Collins, the Jesus nut? Maxsie and I helped bury him yesterday. It sounds awful, but it's a relief to have him gone. We were all getting so we couldn't stand that

*endless jabber about being saved by Jesus. The Japs
are finally letting us have a little wood to make
crosses, so at least Freddy has a small cross over his
grave. When we were walking back from the cemetery, I tried to think of something nice—after all, I've
known Freddy a long time. So I said, "Maybe Jesus
will like him better than we did." Maxsie said, "I
doubt it."*

*Thank God we're getting some help from outside
or even more of us would die. The guerrillas I met
that day are slipping a few extras into the supply
truck. The Jap guards have been bought off, so they
look the other way. It's never enough to go around,
but at least we know somebody is trying to help us.
That truck is the only thing we have to look forward
to. That and being alive tomorrow morning.*

*Tell Terry and Jeff hello for me. Tell them nobody's
going to whip their old man.*

Love, Jack

———

In the evenings at Santo Tomas, after supper but before curfew, people gathered in the plaza outside the
entrance to the Main Building to listen to records over
the loudspeaker system. Record collections from all
over Manila had been brought into camp, some by
their previous owners, some donated by Filipinos and
neutrals who still lived outside. So many records were
now in Santo Tomas that a different "concert" was
held every evening. Half an hour of opera followed
by half an hour of popular music followed by half an

hour of symphonic music or perhaps a solid half hour of Bing Crosby. It was the best time of the day. People brought stools or deck chairs from their shanties, but many sat on the ground. Friends assembled in familiar groups and familiar spots to talk in low voices and listen to records interspersed with announcements from the commandant or from the Triumvirate.

Amos Watson, stretched out in his deck chair with his eyes closed, listening with considerable boredom to excerpts from Wagner, did not see Felix Logan looking through the crowd for him. A tap on his shoulder took him away from the noisy music.

"Oh, hello there, Felix."

The boy was excited but kept his voice low. "Mr. Watson, I need to talk to you. Someplace quiet." He ran his hand through his rumpled hair.

Amos got up, prudently folded his chair and took it with him so that it wouldn't disappear during his absence. They picked a path through the crowd, trying not to distrub the listeners, until they were almost out of reach of the music. It was beginning to get dark.

"So, Felix?"

"I heard some real news for a change. They're closing that place, Mr. Watson. That Camp O'Donnell. The Japs are closing it."

"How do you know?"

"Major Omi was talking about it this afternoon with the colonel, the one who comes here on inspection. I mean the colonel was talking about it. He said it was closing. Because too many prisoners are dying."

Well, thank God, Amos thought. Somebody finally paid attention. "Where are they moving the prisoners?"

"There's going to be a brand-new camp. Just for the Americans, no Filipinos. At Cabanatuan. I don't know where that is. They didn't say."

"It's east," Amos said. "The other side of Mount Arayat." Immediate difficulties began to occur to him. Cabanatuan was a much greater distance from Brad Stone's Zambales camp. It would be harder to send help. On the other hand, the railroad ran to Cabanatuan, and good roads led there. Miranda could probably . . . Well, it would all have to be worked out. "Is it the same commandant?" he asked Felix.

"Uh-uh. The colonel said that guy is in disgrace. He's already been relieved."

A little justice at last, Amos thought, although too late for many American soldiers. But now he must compliment Felix. He put his hand on the boy's shoulder. "Good man," he said. "That's very important news, Felix. You see what you can learn by listening? That's really important."

In the near darkness he saw Felix bow to him, Japanese-style. "*Domo arigato*," Felix said, with real pride in his voice. "*Domo arigato, Watson-san.*"

The day before Humphrey's group was scheduled to leave for Cabanatuan, sixty-four men died, including two from his barracks. But not even that terrible figure could keep the survivors from celebrating. The despised Tsuneyoshi was gone, gone out of their lives forever, and they were leaving hated Camp O'Donnell at last.

That last night in camp, while they were playing "My Favorite Meal" with revived spirits and some faint but unextinguishable sense of hope, Maxsie joined in for the first time.

"The best meal I ever ate," Maxsie's voice came out of the darkness, "was a grilled steak."

"Aw, what's so special about that?" somebody said.

"You listen, fucker, and I'll tell you. Most steak is just plain old beef. It can be thin or thick, rare or well-done or medium rare, the way I like it. It can be a sirloin or a T-bone or a porterhouse, but it's still just beef." Maxsie had been listening all these nights and had the patter down cold. "Now, my steak was *not* beef."

He paused. Everybody was curious.

"No, sir, my steak was grilled Tsuneyoshi."

A sudden rattle of laughter through the barracks.

"Now some guys like a Tsuneyoshi rib steak, other guys like a Tsuneyoshi loin chop. I've even heard tell there's guys from Texas who like Tsuneyoshi balls."

Humphrey grinned to himself, remembering Captain Tex Cobb's description of eating prairie oysters around a mesquite fire on the open range.

"There's a cut for everybody," Maxsie went on. "Everybody to his own taste. But the most important thing, no matter what part you like, it's got to be *fresh*."

Humphrey heard happy chuckles in the darkness.

"Now there's fresh and there's real fresh, because

when it's real fresh, that's when it's tender and tasty. What you do, you take your Tsuneyoshi and you tie him down, like to one of these here soft bamboo beds we're lying on. Facedown. He doesn't like it much, he's a little worried, so he starts to squeal a bit, like a pig. A Jap pig. You just ignore that. You tell him it won't do him any good to complain. Now you take your carving knife, the best kind is a long thin knife with a good sharp edge, and you—oh, I forgot to say what part I like best."

Everybody waited.

"The part I like best, the tenderest, juiciest part, is that big fat Tsuneyoshi ass."

"Yeah!"

"Oh, yeah!"

"Well, you take your knife and you carve off a few slices, depends how hungry you are. Or how many guests you're having for dinner. Not too thick, I'd say maybe half an inch. You got to do it slow and careful so the slices come out even."

"What's Tsuneyoshi doing now?"

"I got to tell you, he doesn't like it much. He starts to holler a bit. Pretty noisy. Then he says, 'Maxsie, you are inferior race. You can't do this to member of Imperial Japanese Army.' "

"And what do you say?"

"Come on, Maxsie, what do you say?"

Maxsie's voice was savage with pleasure. "I say, 'Hold still, fucker. It's my turn.' "

Our Town

Brad Stone watched Miranda, led by Rosauro, coming up the hill toward the new camp.

Japanese patrols, invading the mountains in force last week, had compelled the guerrillas to draw back into the mountains. Their old camp was discovered and burned flat. No great loss. Unlimited bamboo and nipa thatching were available, and they had enough men and enough bolos to rebuild the simple structures they lived in.

They had two days' warning, both from Carabangay and from Mabalacat near Clark Field, that the Japs were mounting a large antiguerrilla offensive into the hills, supported by portable radios and search planes. That meant plenty of time to put their longstanding emergency plan into action.

Brad had had to persuade Paradiso it wasn't enough for them just to escape. They must salvage all their food supplies, cookpots, clothes, weapons and ammunition, tools, utensils—everything. Each man should have a specific assignment, and they should practice moving out of camp at high speed.

This sort of work, perhaps in the end totally unnecessary, held little appeal for Filipinos.

"It's the difference," Brad said, "between professionals and amateurs. Every great general in history paid careful attention to how he moved his troops and supplies from one place to another. Look at Julius Caesar."

"I don't see him," Paradiso said.

"The Romans even had a word for it, *impedimenta*. When Caesar wrote about his campaigns, he always talked about moving his *impedimenta*."

"Napoleon too?"

"Napoleon wasn't much of a writer, but damn right he paid attention. He had to if he was going to keep on winning battles."

Paradiso thought about that. "Okay, Coach," he said. "But not too much practice."

"Filipinos never like to practice. That's why Simpson beat them in basketball. We practiced plays every day. All the Filipino boys liked to do was dribble and shoot."

"Huh," Paradiso said. "Simpson boys were taller."

"But Filipinos are faster, so that part came out even."

"Okay, some practice. But not too much."

As a result they lost nothing in the move. Except that Miranda had to wait two days in Carabangay with Rosauro's parents until the dust settled and Rosauro could lead her up to the new camp. And that meant Brad had to wait two more days to find out if he was going to hear from Judy. But here came Miranda at last.

Even after the steep climb she was smiling. She waved gaily as Brad and Paradiso went forward to meet her. Brad's heart sank. This time she had no straw basket. Did that mean no messages?

"Good morning, sir," she said, slightly out of breath. "Good morning, Sergeant."

They all shook hands.

"Didn't you bring anything?" Brad asked.

"Oh, it is all safe in Carabangay," Rosauro said.

"I came in my family's horse cart. My brothers built a box underneath. You can't see it if you don't know it is there. Many nice things."

"There's a flashlight!" Rosauro said. "And it works!"

"No notes? No letters?"

Miranda's smile relieved him. "Oh, yes, Captain Stone. I did not forget."

She reached in the pocket of her skirt and fished out two folded pieces of paper. "These are both for you. But I think maybe this is the one."

Brad deliberately opened the other one first because he did not want to appear too eager in front of the others. Amos's note was brief:

I'm pleased you were able to help our poor friends up north. Hope you are well. Send back all the news you can.

Then he unfolded the other note. The creases and wrinkles made the unusual handwriting even harder to read. In spite of all his experience deciphering the scribbles of teenage students on tests and papers, he still had to pick it out word by word. It was really Judy—after more than half a year. He would read it again in private, over and over, but he already knew the two most important parts. "I miss you," and "Much love." Even during the few times they had been in bed together, even in their moments of highest excitement and most intense pleasure, Judy had never used the word "love." And now suddenly, right here in his hand, it was "Much love."

Brad Stone felt on top of the world. Even the war did not seem too bad this morning, because someday, some long-distant day, this war would be over, and she would be there.

He refolded the papers and put them in his shirt pocket.

Miranda was looking at him with concern. "Is everything all right then?"

He laughed aloud. "You bet," he said. "Oh, you bet." Then, because he had no other way to express his delight, he threw his arms around the messenger and hugged her.

For a moment she was stiff with surprise. Then, knowing she must have brought him happiness, she hugged him back before she stepped away, giggling and blushing. It was for only a moment that he had felt that soft, supple woman's body pressed against his, soft breasts against his chest, soft thighs against his. He had not held a woman in—how long? How many months? My God, he thought in confusion, Judy's wonderful note secure in his pocket and this lovely young Filipina smiling up at him.

"What are the messages?" Paradiso asked.

Brad tore his eyes away from Miranda's. He cleared his throat. "One's personal," he said. "A woman I knew before the war. The other's from Mr. Watson. He says thanks for helping the prisoners and to send him all the news." He risked another look at Miranda. "What does that mean?"

She did not seem as flustered as he was. "You are supposed to tell me everything about what the Japs are doing. Mr. Watson say this is more important than anything else. But no writing, it is too dangerous. I will remember and tell everything to Manila."

"To Mr. Watson? How can you do that?"

"No, no, I cannot go in Santo Tomas. I will tell others."

They told Miranda all they had seen and heard and learned in recent weeks: the strength of the Japanese in their area, the manner of attack against the guerrillas, the new airstrip and antiaircraft installations at Clark Field, the roadblocks and checkpoints, the Jap weaponry and vehicles. Miranda paid close attention, concentrating hard, sometimes asking for an explanation of something she did not understand.

Between his roiling thoughts of Judy and Miranda, Brad's own concentration was poor, but he was scarcely needed. Paradiso and Rosauro traveled through the countryside much more freely than he did and they saw more of the Japs' activities. Both had good memories for what they had seen. Paradiso, in particular, described things in a clear, orderly way, not cluttering his account with unnecessary detail, as Rosauro sometimes did.

"How are you going to remember all this?" Brad asked at one point, trying not to stare at her.

"For four years," Miranda said with pride, "I am Mr. Watson's secretary. He makes me learn to remember things. When I go back to San Fernando today, I will think about it all the way home. I repeat to myself over and over. Don't worry, I won't forget. Oh, maybe some little things, not important ones."

When Paradiso and Rosauro finished their report on the Japanese, they turned to the subject of the American soldiers who had recently been transferred from Camp O'Donnell to their new prison at Cabanatuan.

Miranda asked, "How will you help them now?"

Paradiso shook his head. "We can't. It is too far."

"Two days' walk," Rosauro said. "And two days back."

"Mr. Watson will be so disappointed. He wants you to help them."

"So do we," Brad said. "Maybe by horse cart?"

"Too far," Paradiso repeated. "Too much danger." He turned to Miranda. "Maybe you find other guerrillas closer to prison. Maybe they help."

"I don't know how to do that," Miranda said. "Maybe my brothers will have ideas. Oh, my youngest brother. He say, can he join you? Be one of your men? Hilario is a very nice boy, very strong. My mother is nervous, but I think she will say okay."

"Strong is good," Paradiso said. "I don't care about nice."

"Will you take him? What should he do?"

"Tell him come talk to me," Rosauro said. "Not

here. In Carabangay. Maybe you bring him next time."

"I do not promise," Paradiso said. "I have enough men."

"You will see," Miranda said with assurance. "Now, who are the American prisoners you know? Mr. Watson will want to know which ones to try to find and work with."

"There are two," Brad said. "I don't know if they're still alive. An awful lot of them have been dying. One is a corporal named Santini. Thin little guy with a long black mustache, very smart. Our people saw him the last time we sent stuff into O'Donnell, so I guess he's alive. And I guess he went to Cabanatuan with the rest of them. The other one Paradiso and I saw only once, so I don't know about him. A Major Humphrey. Jack Humphrey. We met him—"

Brad stopped because of the sudden expression of surprise on Miranda's face.

"But Mr. Watson knows him! I have talked to him myself! A big fat man, yes?"

"Well, he's big, taller than I am," Brad admitted. "But not heavy. There weren't any fat men in O'Donnell—except Japs."

"But it is the same. It is the same. Mr. Watson knows him. Humphrey. He had a son in your Simpson School."

It was Brad's turn to be surprised. "Humphrey. Sure, Terry Humphrey, I remember him. One of the younger kids. I never had him in any of my classes."

Paradiso was nodding, too, and smiling. "Very bad

little boy," he said. "Always get in trouble. Too much smoking. Dr. Clarke tell him next time is goodby."

"Well, he is the one. Oh, Mr. Watson will be very happy to know his friend is still alive."

"If he is," Brad said. He got up. "You go ahead talking. I have to write some notes for Miranda to take back."

While he was composing his letter to Judy, his mind kept slipping back to those few wonderful nights he had spent in bed with her, the best in his life. As well as to the more immediate feeling of Miranda's soft body against his. While he tried to express to Judy how he felt about her note, he knew he would find some pretext to hug Miranda goodby.

———

Rosauro brought the news of the rape. A fourteen-year-old Carabangay girl had been not only raped but beaten by two of Quintano's guerrillas. Everybody knew who the men were, the Tatloc brothers from Bamban.

Carrying rifles, they had descended on the Kalinga farm and demanded food supplies. They also demanded to be fed and to be given a jug of rice wine. The frightened family gave them all they asked for. The girl served them. They finished the meal and got drunk on the wine, then took the girl into the sleeping room, one at a time, and raped and beat her. The other brother stood guard over the family with his rifle. The Kalingas could hear their daughter crying and shrieking until one of the brothers stuck a cloth in her mouth. When they had finished, they picked up their gift of three chickens and disappeared into the night.

"How is the girl?" Brad asked.

"I didn't see her. The Kalingas don't want anybody to see her."

The men listening to Rosauro's story muttered angrily to each other. Paradiso's face was black with fury.

Sex in the Philippines was lighthearted, Brad knew. Boys and girls often had sexual experiences at an early age and sexual favors were given and received with goodwill. Young marriages and young pregnancies, not always in that order, were commonplace, especially in the barrios and villages. But, perhaps because of this cheerful attitude, rape was considered unforgivable. And rape accompanied by needless brutality was a particular outrage.

"Where are those men?" Paradiso asked, his voice blunt and hard.

"Nobody knows," Rosauro said. His handsome young face was full of the Kalinga family's pain. "Maybe back in Quintano's camp. Maybe gone home to Bamban. Maybe anywhere. What are we going to do, Sergeant?"

"Punish them."

"First you have to find out where they are," Brad said.

Paradiso looked at him. "I will ask Quintano."

That sounded preposterous. Quintano's guerrilla force was much bigger than theirs, and by his reputation he was not likely to give out information about his men. Or even to take the matter of this rape very seriously.

"I don't think that's a good idea," Brad said.

"Listen, Coach." Paradiso's eyes were dark. He tapped his chest with his thumb. "Carabangay is *my* town." He glared around at the other men. "Our town. All of us. They feed us and help us. They are our friends. Quintano's men cannot come in our town and demand food. Or anything else. They need food, they go ask in Santa Ignacia or Camilling. Their own places. Not here. They cannot hurt our people. Quintano knows that. It is not his town. Or his people. Those two men must pay."

A chorus of approval came from the circle. Most did not know the Kalinga girl or her family, but Paradiso had called her their responsibility, and they accepted.

"We'd better talk about it," Brad told Paradiso.

Julio Quintano, Major Quintano by his own proclamation, ran the largest guerrilla group in the central Zambales, although that too might be a matter of proclamation. It was impossible to tell the true size of any guerrilla group. Even the leaders did not know for sure, and they always exaggerated.

Guerrilla groups, large and small, organized and disorganized, existed all over central Luzon and, Brad supposed, all over the Philippines. Sometimes they talked to one another, exchanging information. Sometimes they fought one another, competing for territory and supplies. Brad knew there were quite a few American soldiers like himself, both officers and enlisted men, who had managed to escape from the Japs and join up with Filipinos. Sometimes Americans were an important asset because of their training and experience. At other times they were a danger and embarrassment because they could be too easily spotted by the Japs. He had heard of Americans actually being expelled from guerrilla groups and sent off to live as best they could, totally dependent on Filipino hospitality. No formal organization or network existed between the groups, though from time to time attempts were made by one group or another to claim dominion over others. It was hard to tell how successful such efforts were, or how long success might last.

It was also hard to tell how much any guerrilla group had actually accomplished. There was as much lying about achievements as about numbers. Quintano's camps were scattered through the hills within striking distance of the main road between Lingayen and Tarlac, a good position from which to harass Jap traffic up and down the highway. Whether his forces were harassing the Japs more than they were harassing the native population was questionable.

"Look, Paradiso," Brad said when they conferred alone, "we can't take on Quintano. He's too big. Besides, we're supposed to be fighting the Japs, not each other. I have a suggestion. Why don't we put the word out through all the towns that we are looking for the Tatloc brothers? Everybody will understand why and be on the lookout. Sooner or later they'll turn up in Bamban or somewhere else, and we'll hear about it and deal with them."

Paradiso shook his head. "That could be long time, maybe never. Anyway, it is Quintano's blame also. He has to make the rules. Like me."

"Maybe he doesn't have rules. Or can't enforce them."

"Then I do it for him."

"He won't let you."

"We find out. And *agad-agad*—right away."

Brad Stone began to feel slightly desperate. Paradiso was in one of his unshakable moods. When he was like this, it was almost impossible to sway him. Perhaps if Brad pointed out some possible consequences? "You're going to take our whole gang up there and confront him? We can't move that many men all that distance without being spotted. You want the Japs to catch us when they couldn't find us on their own?"

"I don't take everybody. I go see Quintano myself."

This was even worse. "He'll kill you."

"I don't think so. He knows then somebody kill him sure."

"What makes you think he'll even see you? Why should he listen to you?"

"Because I am Sergeant," Paradiso said with supreme confidence. The man's ego was extraordinary.

"You'd be crazy to risk anything like that."

Paradiso shrugged. "It has to be. So that is it, Coach."

Paradiso's mind was clearly made up, so Brad made up his own mind. "Then I'm coming with you."

"No."

"Yes. You came with me to O'Donnell. I'm going with you to Quintano."

"What for?"

Brad followed Paradiso's lead. "Because I am Coach. We go together. Quintano knows about both of us. If we're both there, he'll know we mean it."

Paradiso smiled for the first time all morning. "You are *loko*, Coach. Quintano eat you up."

Brad smiled back. "Don't worry, I'll take care of you."

———

It was impossible to reach Quintano's camp by walking across the mountains. The forested slopes, cut by deep ravines and waterfalls and small rivers and streams, were too steep for passage. The few old hunting and mining trails through the Zambales ran east to west, while they would have to go due north. They had to descend to the lowlands before turning up toward Lingayen Gulf.

They kept away from the roads, where they might encounter Japs, and instead hiked through the cane fields and rice paddies and the tall cogon grass, now green in the rainy season. They were reversing the route they had taken months ago when they fled south from the debacle at Lingayen. They wore native clothes and carried neither weapons nor canteens, which would attract notice. In small shoulder bags they carried enough food for the journey. Rosauro also carried a gourd of drinking water, although the streams coming down from the mountains would probably supply all the water they needed.

When Paradiso told the men what he and Coach planned, everybody wanted to come along, fully armed and ready for action, but only Rosauro was able to talk his way into the expedition. Having grown up here and driven a local bus route, he knew the country and the villages north of Tarlac, as Brad and Paradiso did not. More important, he might know some of the men in Quintano's band and could persuade them to take him to the "major." He even had cousins in Mamali at the foothills of Quintano's territory. Besides, he said, while Paradiso might consider Carabangay his town, it really was Rosauro's town, and the Kalingas were *his* people—he had known them since childhood.

All the way north they made plans. If this happened, then they would do this. If that happened instead, then they would behave another way. Rosauro was much more interested in Brad's various contingencies than Paradiso was.

They reached the small town of Mamali the afternoon of the second day. Rosauro set about finding his cousins—or what was left of them. There were three brothers, all of them drafted into the Philippine Army in the last year before the war. One had been killed during the invasion, and one was still missing. But the oldest brother had escaped and returned to Mamali and his wife and children. He was happy to see Rosauro and his friends.

While the wife cooked a simple supper, Rosauro explained the reason for their visit. The cousin's face darkened at the story. "Bad men," he said. Brad thought he meant the Tatloc brothers, but it turned out he meant Quintano's guerrillas in general. They were not all bad men. Some were true patriots, but many were little more than bandits. The cousin thought it might be dangerous to visit Quintano but promised to help. He and his wife found space for them to sleep inside the already-crowded little house.

It was the first time Brad had slept in a home since war began. He lay awake for a while, thinking how easy it would be for them to be captured here if Rosauro's cousin wanted to sell them to the Japs. But sense of family was so strong in the Philippines that this was virtually impossible. He slept well on the hard floor. It was more comfortable than sleeping out in the mountains.

In the morning the cousin told them to stay out of sight until he could find someone to guide them.

He was gone a long time—almost two hours. Long enough to be getting in touch with Japs. Long enough to make Brad begin to wonder about the sanctity of Philippine family relationships. He wondered what the market price was these days for an American officer. One who was also a well-known guerrilla leader. And what would be the combined price for Coach and Sergeant? The cousin was a poor man.

Unlike Brad, Paradiso and Rosauro waited with stoic patience in the dark little room. The cousin finally returned with a young man Rosauro's age who said he could show them where they wanted to go. Brad Stone was embarrassed by his suspicions. When he tried to give the cousin a few pesos for his hospitality, the cousin was offended. He put his hand over his heart and said passionately, "Oh no, sir, you are my guests."

They climbed silently into the hills, single-file through the morning heat. The heat did not seem to bother the three Filipinos, but Brad was grateful for the shade of his big straw hat. His hair and face and body were damp with sweat. They met no one.

After forty-five minutes they came to an open patch of cogon grass, and their guide said this was as far as he would go. Another five or ten minutes up the trail they would probably find somebody. He turned back down the hillside. They all drank from Rosauro's water gourd. Could be my last drink, Brad thought.

Paradiso took the lead. His stocky legs pushed up the hill at a fast, steady pace. Brad had no trouble keeping up, but he would not want to have to follow Paradiso through the mountains all day long. Igorot blood was mountain blood. Fifteen more steamy minutes passed before a man with shaggy black hair and an Enfield rifle with a broken sling barred the trail.

They halted. They all looked at one another.

"Where is Quintano?" Paradiso asked.

The man said nothing.

"We come many miles to see Quintano," Paradiso said in a louder voice. "Where is he?"

After long seconds of silence the sentry said, "He is not here. *Umalis kayo*—go away."

"Listen—" Paradiso began.

Rosauro stepped forward. "Hey, *kaibigan*," he said. "Hey, friend. Look, no weapons." He smiled and spread his hands wide to show he was unarmed. "We are guerrillas like you. We just want to talk to your famous Major Quintano."

"He is not here."

"Okay you say, but all the same he will want to see us. Look, this is an American officer. He is Coach. You hear of him, no? And this is Sergeant. You hear of him too?"

Brad removed his hat so the sentry could see he was an American. The sentry stared at him in surprise. Finally he lowered his rifle and said, "Wait. Sit. No move."

He did not move himself until Brad, Paradiso and Rosauro were all seated on the ground. Then he turned and vanished up the trail into the forest.

While they were waiting, Paradiso said, "He should have looked in our bags. We could have pistols."

Half an hour passed before the sentry came back with two more men. One had a bolo strapped to his web belt by a rope thong. The other carried a one-shot *paltik*, a primitive rifle whose barrel had to be unscrewed each time for loading, then screwed back on. Both men studied Brad with open curiosity. Then the one with the *paltik* patted each of their shoulder bags to make sure they had no weapons. Satisfied, he motioned them to precede him up the trail. The sentry stayed behind.

The camp they reached after a short, steep hike lay spread out on a large, uneven plateau under the protective umbrella of tall trees. Crude bamboo huts, grass shacks, lean-tos, an occasional sheet of canvas stretched between tree trunks. Shabby men stood to stare at the visitors. Shabby women looked up from squatting positions beside small cooking fires. The whole camp, which they walked straight through at the command of the man with the *paltik*, was bedraggled and filthy. It made their own rough camp seem clean and carefully organized.

At the far edge of this main area, another trail led off between the trees. Here a better-dressed guard with a holstered .45 on his hip awaited them. He, too, stared at Brad before patting their bags once again. Then he said, "Come, Major Quintano is waiting."

After a hundred more yards the trail opened into a clearing. There, to Brad's astonishment, stood a six-man pyramidal U.S. Army tent, its side flaps stretched out parallel to the ground and held in place by slim bamboo poles and guy ropes. Compared to the squalor of the camp, this was impressively neat, even grandiose.

So was the figure that now emerged from the entrance. Dressed in clean blue fatigue trousers and a starched khaki shirt with short sleeves, the man wore a visored khaki cap with the gold maple-leaf insignia of a U.S. major pinned in the center. Brad wondered where he had found that. And if he had found a silver eagle instead of a maple leaf, would he be Colonel Quintano?

The guard who had delivered them saluted. Quintano did not bother to return the salute. Instead, he carefully studied his visitors. He was rather tall for a Filipino, trimly built, with good shoulders and a narrow waist. He was also extremely handsome. He had wide cheekbones, clear tan skin and flashing brown eyes. There was almost a movie-star look to him.

"I am Major Quintano," he announced. No trace of an accent; obviously an educated man. His voice was strong, resonant—a voice born for giving speeches or making pronouncements. He smiled easily—flashing his white teeth. "And who are you?"

Quintano knew perfectly well who they were. If the sentry had not passed on their names, they would not have been admitted to his presence. Brad looked at Paradiso and then said, "I am Coach. United States Army. This is Sergeant. And this is our colleague Rosauro. I think you may have heard of us."

"Perhaps." Quintano smiled again, all perfectly friendly. "Come inside."

They followed him into the big tent. A canvas army cot with a mattress and pillow stood along one side on the bamboo flooring. Near it a small wooden table held a pile of papers kept in place by the weight of a half coconut shell. A large carved cabinet with two doors presumably held clothes and other belongings. Quintano seated himself in a wooden armchair and removed his cap to reveal thick, wavy black hair, glistening with oil. He indicated two folding metal chairs opposite him. The guard with the .45 remained standing at the entrance.

"My home and office," Quintano said with the same friendly smile. "Sit down, sit down."

Brad and Paradiso took the chairs. Rosauro sat on the floor.

"I suppose you want to join my Marauders," Quintano said.

Paradiso snorted.

Quintano's eyebrows went up as he looked briefly at Paradiso, then turned back to Brad. "What is your rank, Mr. Coach?" His voice was tinged with a faint amusement.

"Captain," Brad lied.

"Captain Coach?"

"No, just plain Coach."

"Ah, a nickname then. Well, Coach—"

"We come here for justice," Paradiso interrupted. His plain, solid voice held none of the grace of Quintano's.

This time Quintano's gaze did not shift from Brad's face. It was as though Paradiso had not spoken.

It had been agreed that since Brad was an American officer and spoke more easily, he would state their case. "Major," he said, "our guerrilla group is located near Carabangay some thirty miles south of here. The town furnishes us with our principal support, especially food. A couple of days ago two of your men came to Carabangay and forced a farmer's family to give them food and wine. Then they raped the daughter. They both raped her and then they beat her up very badly. We want those men."

Quintano did not answer at once but continued to look at Brad. At last he shrugged and said, "I have many men, Captain, as you have just seen. In fact, I have three other groups north of here almost as large as this one. Obviously I can't be responsible for the behavior of everyone. Many of them are not even known to me."

"We know who these two men are," Brad said. "They were recognized, and they've boasted of belonging to your group. Their name is Tatloc. They are brothers from Bamban. They had no business in our territory in the first place, much less to steal and rape."

"Then perhaps you should look for them in Bamban. They probably aren't even my men. Many people boast of being Marauders when in fact they are not. I wish I could help you, of course, but—" He held out his hands, palms upward, to show that he had no control of this unfortunate situation. "These are difficult days. No one can predict what will happen in such times."

"*Our* men do not rape young girls," Paradiso said.

"I am delighted to hear it," Quintano said with complete indifference, still not looking at Paradiso.

Brad knew they were making no progress but decided to try again. "We want your help, Major, both as a fellow officer and as a fellow guerrilla commander. We ask you to find those men and turn them over to us."

"But, my dear Coach, I have just explained—"

"Two tommy guns," Paradiso said.

He had caught Quintano's attention. "What?"

"Two tommy guns. One for each brother. You give us two men, we give you two tommy guns. U.S. Army guns."

This was an extraordinary offer. Brad and Paradiso

had been most fortunate to capture three of the precious weapons from a Japanese cache. They were very scarce, almost impossible to come by. Their value in a close fight with infantry was immense.

Quintano's eyes narrowed. Brad could almost see the greed begin to rise. "Ammunition?"

"You find your own ammunition. Like everybody else."

Quintano shook his head. "Ammunition is scarcer than guns," he said truthfully. "Guns have no value without—"

"Two hundred rounds," Paradiso said.

"That is more interesting. Where are the guns? If you give me the guns, I will do everything I can to help you find those men."

Now Paradiso shook his head. "You bring men to Carabangay, you get tommy guns. If you do by five days, you get ammunition."

"Two hundred rounds each gun?"

"No. Two hundred rounds."

"Not enough. Tommy guns shoot very fast." With his hands, Quintano pretended to point a Thompson submachine gun at them and swung it from left to right. "*Brr-r-r-r-r-r.*" He smiled. "Bullets all gone."

"You find more," Paradiso said. "Easy if you know how. And not afraid of Japs."

Brad thought Paradiso had gone too far, but Quintano threw back his head and laughed. He had a wonderful wide-open laugh. "Sergeant, if you join my Marauders and find me lots of bullets, I'll make you a captain too." He turned to Brad. "You know, Coach, people are still going through the old battle-fields, trying to find rifle bullets. All dirty and moldy. They clean them off, dry them out in the sun and then sell them. No one knows if they will still fire, but they buy them anyway."

Brad had indeed heard this, but he decided it was time he gave Paradiso active support. Quintano was not the only one who could boast. "We find it's easier, Major, to get ours direct from the Japs. They've got all the U.S. guns and ammo. It's less trouble and better ammo."

Quintano laughed again. "Very good," he said. "Very good. Tell me, how did your group make out when the Japs ran off their big attack?"

"Fine. We just moved farther back in the hills for a while. No casualties. How about you?"

"Oh, the Japs did not attack here. I do not think they would dare."

A ridiculous claim. The Japanese had the forces to attack anywhere in the Philippines that they wanted to. The truth was that their greatest concern was the whole Clark Field region, and Quintano was way north of that. Brad thought of saying that perhaps the Japs didn't consider Quintano's Marauders a se-rious problem, but since they were unarmed visitors in Quintano's stronghold, he thought better of it.

"Well," Quintano said, "if I should happen to find these bad fellows you are looking for, how will I get in touch with you?"

"Oh, sir," Rosauro said, speaking for the first time

since they had entered the tent, "if you bring them to Carabangay, we will know at once."

"So." Quintano rose from his armchair. The interview was over. "I will do my best to help you." He shook hands with Brad. "Think about joining my group. Together we could be very powerful. I understand you have some contacts in Manila that might be helpful to me. If you join my Marauders, we would control all central Zambales."

Meaning Quintano would control all central Zambales. "We'll certainly think about it, Major."

"Five days," Paradiso said.

Quintano pretended not to hear him.

———

On the fourth afternoon word came up the hill from Carabangay.

Paradiso took far more men than Brad thought necessary. Although no Japs were stationed in Carabangay, Brad and Paradiso had long agreed it was not desirable to risk attracting attention by moving too many men around at one time. One man could have carried both tommy guns, with another to carry the boxes of ammunition. But Paradiso was designating more than twenty men to join them.

"Why so many? There's no danger."

"Not for danger," Paradiso said. "Everybody will see we are the ones."

"Who? The townspeople? They'll know we arranged it. All we have to do is tell them."

"No, Coach. This time we show them."

It was late afternoon before they reached the market square. Brad saw there was no need to tell anyone what was going on. Many people were standing around the square. Paradiso sent Rosauro to collect the Kalinga parents and bring them to the small plaza outside the church where Quintano's men were waiting.

Brad and Paradiso and the men carrying the tommy guns and ammunition arrived first. Two very frightened men in their early twenties with hands bound behind their backs sat on the ground under an acacia tree, guarded by four of Quintano's scruffy guerrillas.

One said, "I am to count the bullets."

Paradiso grunted. The ammunition boxes were opened and Quintano's man painstakingly began to count aloud. He had reached one hundred seventy-three before Brad saw Rosauro coming across the plaza accompanied by a man and women.

"Hundred seventy-four, hundred seventy-five . . ."

When the couple reached the acacia tree, the mother shot one terrified glance at the two bound men, then lowered her eyes and stared at the ground in front of her feet. She was a frail figure, worn by hard work. The father, a sturdy man in his thirties, had the strong shoulders of a farmer. He glared at the two prisoners with a steady hatred.

"Are these the men?" Paradiso asked. One of the men tried to turn his head away, but Paradiso grabbed his hair and made him face Kalinga.

The father nodded.

"Hundred eighty-eight, hundred eighty-nine . . ."

"*Sige na*—hurry up," Paradiso said.

When the count was finished, the bullets were heaped back in their boxes. Paradiso handed over the two guns. Quintano's man looked them over with pleasure and patted the stocks. "Good," he said. "All done."

"All done," Paradiso agreed. "Tell Quintano his men don't come back here. This is my town."

"Tell him yourself." The man slung one of the tommy guns over his shoulder and handed the other to a second man. He told a third to pick up the boxes of ammunition. "We go now."

"That's right," Paradiso said. "You go."

When they had left, Paradiso ordered the Tatloc brothers to their feet and told his men to guard them closely. He told the Kalinga parents to follow him to the square. The mother, eyes still downcast, said something to her husband in a low voice. He answered back. They began to argue.

"What are they saying?" Brad asked.

Rosauro said, "She does not want to come. She wishes to go back to the daughter."

When the father insisted and then spoke sharply, the mother obeyed. All the way from the church plaza to the market square, she kept her eyes on the ground.

Paradiso said to Brad, "Coach, you stay out. This is Filipino business."

Brad nodded.

When the group entered the square, a prolonged murmur ran through the crowd. Then silence.

Rifles prodded the Tatloc brothers to an open space in the middle of the square. One moved quietly, the other tried to drag his feet and had to be encouraged with a rifle barrel.

Paradiso motioned the townspeople to step back, to leave more space. Then he ordered his men to form two lines a dozen yards away from the central group—Paradiso himself, Rosauro, the two guards, the two bound prisoners.

The square was very quiet. Brad, standing in the front row of the crowd, could hear each word Paradiso spoke to his men. The Kalingas stood a little apart from the rest of the townspeople. The woman did not lift her gaze.

Now Paradiso raised his voice and motioned with one arm. "Kalinga!"

A little hesitant, the father came forward into the open part of the square. The mother remained where she was. The father came to a stop beside Paradiso, facing the two prisoners. He was inches taller than the stocky sergeant.

"These are the men?" Paradiso asked in a loud voice so that all could hear.

Kalinga nodded. He was not used to being the center of the town's attention.

"The men who stole your food and wine?"

Kalinga nodded again.

"The men who insulted and beat your daughter?"

"Yes," Kalinga said.

"Good," Paradiso said. He stretched out his arm toward one of the lines of his men, then toward the other line. "We bring them back to you," he said. "For your justice."

Kalinga looked at Paradiso, not understanding.

"They are yours," Paradiso said.

Kalinga seemed puzzled. He whispered something to Paradiso, who nodded. He whispered again. Paradiso nodded again.

Kalinga hesitated. Then, his face working, he stepped forward and, with the back of his hand and all the strength of his big shoulders, struck one of the prisoners a tremendous blow in the face. The man reeled. Kalinga hit him again. Then he turned to the other one, who tried to dodge away. Kalinga seized him by the shirt and, with his fist, smashed his mouth.

Brad could see the blood gush from the broken lips. The man whimpered, trying to pull away. Kalinga let go of the man's shirt and stepped back. Massaging his hands, he looked at Paradiso.

"Is that all?" Paradiso asked.

Kalinga nodded.

"That is your justice?"

Kalinga made no response. Without another glance at the prisoners, he left the group and walked back to where his wife was standing, still staring at the ground. He did not touch her but simply took his place beside her.

Paradiso's eyes traveled once around the silent square. "Here is my justice," he said in a loud voice.

He walked over to one of the lines and took a service revolver from a man's belt. He broke it open to check the chambers. He walked back to the group.

"Make them kneel."

The two brothers were quickly wrestled to their knees.

"Prayers," Paradiso said. "Short prayers."

He waited ten seconds before he shot each man in the back of the head.

= 17 =

Get in Line

By the time she reached the head of the food line, Judy Ferguson was, as usual, steaming mad. The Triumvirate and the multitudinous internee committees had organized all of STIC life into one endless line or another—the food line, the toilet line, the shower line, the laundry line, the shopping line, the medical-treatment line. One as tiresome as another. And when you finally made it to the front of a line, what did you get?

"Ticket please," the checker said.

Judy handed him her meal ticket, a two-by-four inch piece of cheap buff paper with the days of the month printed on it in four parallel lines, days one to fifteen, A.M. and P.M., and days sixteen to thirty-one, A.M. and P.M. Her name and room number were handwritten on the ticket, which also had a stamped number and the signature of the chairman of the Meal Ticket Committee. Across the middle was printed "STO. TOMAS INTERNMENT CAMP MEAL TICKET, MANILA, P.I." Was this for the benefit of internees who had forgotten where they were imprisoned?

The checker punched her ticket for nineteen, P.M. "I see you been missing a lot of meals this month," he said, trying to be friendly. He was a garrulous old man who managed to slow down the food line by having a word with everybody. "What's the matter, young lady, don't you like our food?"

Without answering, Judy returned her meal ticket to the pocket of her skirt and collected her plate: rice mixed with slivers of chicken, a spoonful of the hard little brown mongo beans, flavorless without salt or bacon, and a heaping portion of talinum, the spinachlike vegetable grown in vast quantity in the camp gardens. Judy didn't like spinach even when it was real spinach.

She found a small open space at a plank table in the outdoor eating shed, crowding in between two women she did not recognize. With more than three thousand people in camp, many were still complete strangers to one another. But these could also be new internees, who were still arriving in camp from time to time from the provinces. It didn't really matter. She ate her meal in silence.

No, Judy did not like "our food." It was better and more plentiful than in the early months but still unappetizing. The Triumvirate had finally persuaded the Japanese to provide a food budget for the internees—all of seventy centavos, or thirty-five cents, per person per day.

At first she had eaten here as seldom as possible. She took advantage of the generosity of friends who got food through the Package Line or at the little shops, stores and bakeries that flourished in camp.

By happening to be in the right spot at the right time of day, she often got herself invited to a meal, or at least a snack, with Millie and Sammy Barnes, or Fuzzy and Anita, or Amos Watson, or Frank Otis, or practically any single man with a bit of money.

Judy could still smile and flirt and flatter. This had been second nature since sophomore year in high school. It was a skill, once learned, that a woman never lost. But in the boredom and monotony and the blank sterility of internment life, Judy was discovering a depressing truth about her relationship with men, especially attractive single men. More and more often, it felt empty.

Empty of anything except talk, and usually talk about the same old things, the food and the Japs and the restrictions of camp life and the far-distant possibility of liberation. Boring, boring, boring. No dances, no parties, no pretty clothes, no dinners in glamorous restaurants, no clubs, no tennis, no swimming, no weekends driving up to the Baguio mountains or to lovely Lake Taal. All that was gone. All the life she had loved and enjoyed with men was lost. And, as a result, the men, too, seemed empty.

Even though she could still arrange to be fed or treated by someone, she found herself more and more frequently joining the moneyless masses on the food line. The line itself might be maddening and the food poor, but at least she did not have to be charming. Still, she sometimes felt sad, eating at the plank table between people she did not know.

The shower line was usually shorter than the food

line, but in other ways it was worse. The idle chatter of bored females waiting their turn to bathe was excruciating. They exchanged interminable banalities about clothes and food and children and camp conditions. The worst topic, and the one that came up for more and more discussion as normal inhibitions and taboos eroded, was women's periods. Because of the bizarre camp diet—and, according to the doctors, because of the stresses of confinement—women's periods became very irregular, which seemed to fascinate everybody but Judy.

Another staple topic in the shower line was the problem of lice and bedbugs. It was bad enough to live with them, Judy thought, but why did the women have to talk about them all the time?

Standing impatiently in line one morning, clad in her bathrobe and wooden *bakias*, her towel slung over one shoulder and clutching her bar of the camp's homemade, latherless soap, Judy tried to shut out the drone of conversation.

"Would you believe it, I caught fourteen bedbugs this morning. . . ."

"They get in the cracks of the wood. . . ."

"They get in the lining of my mattress. . . ."

"They like to hide in the mosquito nets, too. . . ."

"I always shake my net out and do a real close inspection before I get into bed. . . ."

"Look at my arm. Eight bites last night right on this one arm. . . ."

"Huh. You're lucky it's your arm. I've got bites all over my poor little fanny. . . ."

"It's not all *that* little, dearie. . . ."

"Well, if you ask me, I can stand the bedbugs better than those lice. Nasty creatures. . . ."

"If you keep clean, they'll leave you alone. . . ."

"Why do you think I'm standing in this line? . . ."

"Listen, it's not enough to stay clean. My very own daughter. . . ."

"They get in your hair, and do they ever itch. . . ."

"Well, you can always do what some women do. You can shave off all your body hair. And I mean *all* your hair. . . ."

"Yeah, but that looks so *ugly*. . . ."

"The only thing uglier would be if a man did it. . . ."

Giggle, giggle, giggle.

I'm going to scream, Judy thought. Someday I'm going to scream.

Instead, standing there in the line, only four places from her turn to shower, she began to cry. The sudden welling of tears astonished her. She never cried. She had not even felt the tears coming, and yet now they were running down her cheeks.

"Hey, dearie, what's the matter with you?"

Judy shook her head. She couldn't answer. She didn't know the answer. She put her hands over her face to hide it from the other women. She felt her hands wet with the tears that would not stop. Her shoulders began to shake.

"What's she crying about?" a woman asked.

"Beats me."

"Listen, dearie, tell us what's wrong. You aren't pregnant, are you?"

Judy shook her head again. And then, because the tears would not stop, and because she could not endure them all looking at her and wondering and asking, she left her place in the line where she had been standing for a whole hour and, hands still trying to hide her face, walked back to her room.

It was midmorning and Room 6 was deserted except for the two women whose turn it was to sweep out today. She looked at the long rows of crude beds and lumpy mattresses, the dingy brown mosquito nets hung on rickety poles, the boxes and cartons of clothes and other belongings shoved under the beds to preserve what little walking space there was.

This shabby room. This shabby life.

It took a while for the strange tears to stop, and she felt no better when at last they did.

When the women trooped into Room 6 for siesta, Judy could tell that the story of her shower-line behavior had been passed around. Some women stared with frank curiosity. Others, the kinder ones, avoided looking at her. Only Millie Barnes dealt with it directly.

After siesta, Millie took her aside and asked, "Judy, what's all this about your crying jag?"

"I don't know. It just happened."

Concern was written all over Millie's plain, round face. "That's not like you."

"I know it isn't."

"Well, come on, there must be some reason. Anything Sammy and I can do to help?"

Judy shook her head. "Thanks, but it isn't anything particular. I'd rather forget it. Please, let's forget it."

Then, because Millie was still looking that way, she added, "I just felt sad. Everything is so sad."

———

But at least now there was Brad. At first she could hardly believe he was still alive. She envied him. Out there in the mountains, free to come and go as he pleased, without rules and regulations. No Jap commandant and guards. No bowing to anybody. No Triumvirate. No committees. And no lines to stand in. Once again, Brad Stone, with no money and no practical sense of how to make life better for himself, had lucked out. Amos said Brad was leading a hard, dangerous life, but Judy refused to believe it. After all, Brad was free.

It was hard to picture him as a guerrilla. Now that she knew he was alive, she let herself remember him in many different ways. She had no trouble recalling the very bright blue eyes, the strong, sharp nose, the wavy red-blond hair. Or the way he moved, with that natural balance and grace of an athlete. Or the way he made love—strong hands, all that energy and drive and stamina. In bed, she once told him, he wasn't such a damned idealist. They should have spent more time in bed—and could have, too, if he hadn't insisted on being a Baguio schoolteacher and then a volunteer soldier. He could have gone into business right here in Manila, and done well at it, too.

But what was he like as a guerrilla? Hard to imagine.

Amos said she must not talk about him, must not give anything away, that Brad was leading a very hazardous existence dependent on total secrecy. What nonsense. She didn't know anything to tell.

She liked Amos, but he was too busy trying to run things and run people. The way he made her rewrite her letter to Brad—just like a censor. On the other hand, the only way she could be in touch with Brad was through Amos. Judy compromised. She would tell Millie Barnes but no one else.

"I'm meeting Sammy down at the shanty," Millie said. "Come along, we can talk there."

"It's a secret. I don't want Sammy to know."

Millie's pale eyebrows went up. "You better not tell me then. I always tell Sammy."

Judy hesitated.

"Judy, he's an *accountant*. They never tell anybody anything. Not even their own clients."

So she wound up telling them both. She kept her voice low so that the couple in the next shanty could not hear what she was saying.

"You remember you once asked me how many times I'd been in love?" she reminded Millie.

Millie nodded.

"And your answer was twice," Sammy said, also keeping his voice low. "Once for sure and once for maybe."

So she really did tell him everything, Judy thought. "Yes. Well, I've found out the maybe one isn't dead after all. He's alive."

"Terrific," Sammy said. "How do you know?"

"I got a message."

"Where from?"

"Well . . ."

"Oh, Sammy, for goodness sake. Can't you see that's part of the secret?"

"No harm asking. Go ahead, Judy. This guy who's my rival, so where is he?"

"He's a guerrilla. I don't really know where. Somewhere in the mountains."

"Wonderful," Millie said. "Every girl needs a guerrilla lover, I always say. Wish I had one. Some of us have to make do with what we have." She gave Sammy a playful slap on the shoulder. "So now how do you feel about him?"

"I'm not exactly sure. It's very exciting to hear from him, of course, but I don't quite know."

"Then there's still hope for me?" Sammy said. "You haven't made up your mind?"

"Oh, Sammy, you know how I feel about you. If we could just get rid of this wife of yours."

"Well, leaving you two lovebirds aside, what about this glamorous guerrilla fellow? Is he in love with you?"

"Oh, yes. At least he was the last time I saw him. That's a long time ago, of course. He asked me to marry him."

"The swine," Sammy said.

"And you said no."

"Actually I said I'd think about it."

"Meaning no, of course."

"Well, no at the time. Everything's so different now."

"Right. That was before you met me."

"Oh, Sammy, shut up, that's enough. What's his name?"

"I'm really not supposed to say, but it's Brad. Brad Stone. Don't tell anyone, please."

"Is he handsome?"

"Handsomer than me?"

"Well, not *that* handsome, of course. But yes, he's very good-looking. And he's just the right height."

"Five foot six and a half?"

Judy laughed. "No, Sammy, a bit taller than that, I'm afraid."

"Nobody's perfect."

———

Judy had to wait forever before she got a second letter from Brad. Indeed, this mail system was not at all like the post office.

Amos's face looked rather peculiar when he handed her the folded sheet of paper, but his voice was cheerful enough. "Some more good news from our friend Coach," he said.

Why did Amos have that funny look on his face? "Does that mean you've already read it?"

"Well, I have to," he said.

She thought he looked embarrassed. As well he should. Reading other people's letters. "Why do you have to? If Brad wants to tell you something, he can write you himself."

"Oh, he did, he did. But—" Amos spread his hands and did not finish the sentence. He started over again. "I'm sorry, Judy, but I have to know everything that's going on."

Nosy old bird. No privacy in Santo Tomas, not even for smuggled letters. "Look," she said, "how would it be if I just *told* you what he writes me?"

"It's not the same."

"Or if I promise to *show* you? Don't I at least have the right to read it first?"

There was some sympathy in Amos's expression, but not much. "Nobody has any rights these days. I'm sorry, you just have to get used to it."

"I don't have to get used to anything."

"I admire your spirit. Aren't you going to read it?"

"I don't have to read it in front of you, do I?"

"No, no, of course not."

She walked all the way back to Room 6, holding the paper tightly in her hand. She wanted to be as alone as it was possible to be in Santo Tomas. This was the most exciting thing that had happened to her in weeks—since the first note, in fact. She supposed she should have thanked Amos, in spite of his being so nosy.

In the corridor four of her roommates were playing mahjongg, loudly slapping the tiles onto their flimsy bridge table. Half a dozen women were inside Room 6, reading and talking. Judy walked over to the big ground-floor windows looking out on the sunny campus. A small corner of privacy.

As soon as she began Brad's letter, her face grew hot. She thought of Amos Watson reading this. It was much more intimate than Brad's first brief note. This was a real love letter. He reminded her of the last night they had spent together, the night of the Simpson dance at the Polo Club. Although he did not actually mention their making love, it was easy to figure out what he was talking about. Easy for Amos to figure it out too. Brad said he had "carried the memory of that night" all these long months. He was sure from her letter that she did too.

Judy could not imagine what made him think that. Men were always reading into words meanings that were never intended. But she did remember that night very well. It rushed back to her right now, vivid and sweet and passionate. He said he wished "with all his heart" he could have that night again. So, in fact, did she. She could suddenly recall just how he had felt inside her, such a long time ago. Her face grew hot again, but this time with desire. The first time in a long time.

The rest of his letter was so deliberately careful that she could learn little from it. He was in good health and hoped she was too. He hoped things were not too bad "where you are." He said he had many new friends and that some people were being "very helpful." He wished he could see her now, but even though that was impossible, he knew they would see each other again. "Meantime, I send you back all your love." No signature, of course.

She closed her eyes. She felt the warm, loving sunshine on her face.

———

The heavy rain started in the middle of the night. No warning wind, no patter of preliminary drops. One moment the night was still and silent, the next moment the rain came thudding down. It rained all night. It was still raining relentlessly at dawn. Roll call was late and perfunctory. Breakfast had to be skipped because the rain was too heavy for the cooks to work and no one was willing to stand in the food line and drown. The rain kept on.

All the men who had slept in their shanties overnight came one by one, sloshing and sodden, into the buildings, jamming the already-crowded rooms and halls. Clothes that had been soaked when the water reached the floor level of the shanties were hung everywhere to dry, on the furniture and window ledges, on the pipes, on lines of string. Treasured objects like stoves and pots and straw hats floated out of the shanties and down the paths that had turned into rivers of mud and water. The vegetable gardens flooded. The STIC campus, which never drained well even in light rains, was underwater.

Hearing how much was being lost from the shanties, some people dared go out in the downpour to rescue what they could not bear to lose. They brought back whatever belongings they could salvage, piling them helter-skelter in the corridors and sleeping rooms. Three thousand people were crammed indoors with all their possessions and all their soggy, mud-smeared clothes. The Japanese, sensibly deciding to have nothing to do with this impossible situation, stayed away, leaving the internees to their own useless devices.

The merciless rain pounded down, hour after hour.

Judy sat on her wooden bed platform in Room 6, surrounded by damp, miserable, complaining women, and wrote her answer to Brad. She wondered if it was raining like this wherever he was.

Two other women in the room were writing, but

Judy knew these were diaries, not letters. A number of internees, both men and women, kept diaries. It was something to do, something to alleviate boredom. But since nothing much happened in STIC, Judy wondered what they found to write about.

The Japanese confiscated diaries whenever they came across them during an inspection. Whenever one of these random searches was in progress, the codeword "Tally-ho!" was passed from room to room. The papers or notebooks were hurried up a stairway to be hidden on a different floor until the search party had gone through. This mammoth rainstorm gave the diary writers something to record today. But in the entire camp, Judy bet she was the only one writing a real letter to a real person.

It was hard to do. She knew she could not be explicit. Nothing must indicate she was a prisoner in Santo Tomas, or that Brad was a guerrilla in the mountains. If the letter should be intercepted, Amos said, it must reveal nothing that might identify either the sender or the recipient.

Like Brad, she decided to write about the past, but with more discretion. She would not mention anything so intimate as a night of special memory for Amos Watson to snigger at. Instead, she wrote of parties and dancing and sunsets and swimming and long walks and tennis games with good friends. She told him she still wore the monkeywood bracelet he had bought for her that day in the Baguio market. They all came back to her, those wonderful days before the war. She had shared those days with many other men, to be sure, but all those men were now either dead or in prison, many of them here in Santo Tomas. They no longer counted. Only Brad was free. Only Brad was still himself, still his own man, as he had been then.

Writing furiously, her pencil moving across the paper in quick, jagged strokes, she invested their times together with the glow of remembrance. She re-created a world that was even better than it had been.

When she finished, she reread her letter. All around her in Room 6 were women leading lives of apathy and boredom, rumor and gossip, while outside the rain beat down. The drudgery of internment. But here, in this letter, was Judy's real life, a lost life she was determined to lead again.

She folded the sheets of paper. I'm in love with him, she thought. It's no longer just maybe. I'm in love with him. But of course she could not put that in the letter for Amos Watson to read.

———

She's in love with him, Amos thought, reading Judy's letter to make sure it was safe to send. Why doesn't she say so?

"Well, is it all right this time? I don't want to have to write that whole thing over again."

"It's fine," Amos said. He folded the sheets and put them in his pocket. "I know Coach will be very pleased to get it. I know I would be."

"Well. Well, thanks. And thanks for doing this for me. It makes a real difference."

"You're welcome. I'm doing it for both of you, of course."

"Yes, of course. But thank you."

"Judy? Wait a second."

"Yes?"

"I hope you won't mind an old man butting in, but why don't you just come out and tell him you love him? It would mean a lot to Coach, I'm sure. It's probably a very lonely life."

"I can't—it's none—" She stopped.

"Don't tell me again it's none of my business."

"But it really isn't."

Too much pride, Amos thought, shaking his head as she walked away. This is ridiculous. But if she couldn't bring herself, for whatever reason, to put it down in plain English, he would do it for her. He took out his pencil.

————

Moving from the death camp of O'Donnell to the new camp at Cabanatuan was not an instant improvement. Five hundred American prisoners died the first month. Eight hundred more died the second month, before the dysentery and malaria finally ran their fatal course. The younger enlisted men, with no money and no experience and no resources and no families back home relying on them, were the most frequent victims. Jack Humphrey hung on.

Dear Sara,

We all thought anything would be better than O'Donnell, but that's because we didn't know anything about Cabanatuan. We're in bamboo barracks out in this immense flat field five miles north of the town. From anywhere in camp you can look way over east and see the Sierra Madres. Every other direction there's nothing to see but flat open space, except for Mount Arayat poking up from the plain maybe twenty miles away. Seems like everywhere I go—Fort Stotsenburg. O'Donnell, Cabanatuan—I get a view of Arayat. Only the angle changes. Remember how we used to wake up in the morning and admire Arayat from our bedroom window? Frankly, I'm getting a little sick of it.

I had a pretty bad malaria attack soon after we got here. Fever was so high I thought for the first time, maybe I'm a goner like all the others. Maxsie managed to get me some quinine, and I pulled out of it. I don't know how he got it, and he said don't ask, so I didn't. The Japs have finally, finally brought in some quinine and other medicines, so Jerry Baron and the other docs have something to hand out besides kind words.

Several thousand prisoners came here from Corregidor. I can't believe how different they look. I guess they couldn't believe how we looked either. They're a hell of a lot healthier and heavier, and they even have spare clothes and toothbrushes. Toothbrushes, for God's sake! Well, you remember what Dad used to say. It always takes the infantry to go in there and win a battle, but if you lose, God help the infantry.

The commandant here is a lieutenant colonel named Mori. He's strict, even fussy. He's put out a whole lot of nitpicking rules and regulations, including the one that all of us, even officers, have to salute *every Jap soldier, even the privates. Sure does put you in your place, as Maxsie says. He makes fun of it by snapping to full attention and throwing these sensational highball salutes. The Japs don't know what to make of it.*

I started to say, Mori is plenty strict, but at least he's not a dope like Tsuneyoshi. His head is screwed on, and he's got things organized. The water supply's much better than when we got here or than it ever was at O'Donnell, and he's fixed it so that if you have any money—as we do, thanks to our outside friends—you can buy extra food. Mori organized that according to rank. A lieutenant colonel can buy a can of corned beef, a major can buy a can of milk, and so on down to an enlisted man, who can buy a piece of candy. Makes everybody pretty sore, except the lieutenant colonels. All the bird colonels and generals are in prison somewhere else, so lieutenant colonel is king of the hill at Cabanatuan.

Of course, if you don't have any money, all you get is the standard ration, rice soup for breakfast, rice with vegetables for the other meals. When I get home, you're going to have to change a few of our favorite dishes. No more rice with curry, no more rice with turkey, no more rice with anything. And I don't even want to be in the house while the boys are eating rice pudding.

Maxsie says tell you hello. Give Terry and Jeff a hug and tell them to behave themselves. Take care of yourself.

Love, Jack

Since that first morning outside Camp O'Donnell, Humphrey had never seen any of his "outside friends" who were sending in help. Corporal Santini, who had wangled the same supply detail he'd had at O'Donnell, was his closest contact.

"You know, Major," Santini said, while they were divvying up a smuggled shipment of pesos and medicines, "most of this stuff is coming all the way from Manila. You really got to hand it to them, whoever they are."

"That's right," Humphrey said. "A lot of men wouldn't be alive today. Including you and me."

"Oh, I'd be alive, sir," Santini said. "Maybe you wouldn't, but I'd be alive."

Humphrey thought that might be true. The skinny little corporal with the big mustache looked and sounded as sprightly as ever. Santini had so much energy that Humphrey didn't know how he managed to sit still on those plodding five-mile trips to and from the town of Cabanatuan aboard what they had christened the Carabao Clipper. The daily supply train of carabaos moved even more slowly than a man could walk.

"It's easy," Santini explained. "All the way into town I think about all the times I got laid, and all the way back I think about the times I'm going to get laid."

When they had finished dividing the loot hidden underneath the sacks of rice, Santini said, "Oh, there's one more thing, Major, I got a message for you. From Manila."

Because he had been writing so many imaginary

letters to his wife, for a few wild seconds Humphrey thought it might be an answer from Sara, but of course that was impossible. "Jesus Christ," he said, "why didn't you give it to me right away?"

Santini grinned. "Then you wouldn't have paid attention to the supplies. It's got no address, but the Filipino who slipped it to me said it was for a Major Humphrey. I figured that just might be you, sir." He pretended to pat his pockets. "Must be here somewhere. I couldn't have lost it, could I? Nope, here it is."

He produced a slip of paper and handed it over.

Humphrey opened it and read:

It's beginning to look like you were right about our lack of preparation. I just heard recently where you are and am very glad you are still among us. I've been sending a few gifts through friends without realizing it was you on the receiving end. I hope to continue. Sorry I can't send you a steak with sautéed mushrooms and lots of garlic, like that earlier time. Best wishes.

My God, Jack Humphrey thought, remembering that dinner, it's old Amos Watson. He wondered where Watson was and how he could have learned Humphrey's whereabouts.

"Good news, sir?"

"You going to tell me, Corporal, you didn't have time to read it on the way back?"

"Who, me, sir? Read an officer's mail? Mushrooms with lots of garlic . . . is he Italian?"

"The cook was Chinese. Many thanks, Santini."

———

"Hey, guess what? The Japs are going to let us write home."

"Oh, sure. And MacArthur just landed in Manila."

"No shit, it's true. Hawkins just got it straight from the commandant. Orders from Tokyo. Only one post-card and only fifty words, but just the same."

"Who needs fifty words? I can do it in five. 'Get me out of here.'"

"My old lady's probably married somebody else by now. This is going to be a shock to her."

It was also a shock to Jack Humphrey. Now he could write a real message instead of an imaginary one. He did not know what to say, or how to say it in fifty words. The rules were strict: no criticism of the Japanese command, no criticism of prison con-ditions, no complaints, no mention of where they were imprisoned, no speculation about the war. Any-thing too emotional would be censored.

When the cards were passed out and the men took turns using the few pencils, Humphrey tried to com-pose a message in his mind. Nothing would come.

"Listen, Hump," Maxsie said, "I got nobody dying to hear from me. How about I write Sara? Then she'll get two cards when everybody else gets just one. Okay? What's her address?"

Humphrey gave it to him.

While Humphrey was still trying to think what to write, Maxsie was back in ten minutes with his card. "Here, you better read it so we don't say the same thing. Fifty words exactly."

Dear Sara,

You don't know me but your old man and I are buddies. He talks about you and your kids so much it's like I know the family. I'm taking good care of him and will give him back to you in good shape so don't worry.

Sincerely, Maxsie

"I really appreciate that," Humphrey said. "Sara will too. I know it."

"I wanted to say I'd seen her picture about four hundred times, but I figured those Jap fuckers would confiscate it."

"Maxsie, I don't know what to write."

"Well, you'd better think of something before they come around to collect the cards."

Jack Humphrey got out Sara's crinkled picture and looked at it once again. The slim face with the straight blond hair and long straight nose and the big warm eyes smiled back at him. He had taken the picture three years ago at Fort Benning. It had always been his favorite because it caught both the affection and the humor in her smile.

No more time to waste. He began to write, counting and recounting words as he went along.

Dear Sara,

I think about you and Terry and Jeff every day. I hope you are fine. I'm well and getting enough to eat but miss you very much. Don't worry, I will come

*through this and see you again. A hug for the boys
and for yourself.*

Love, Jack

He wanted to make it a "big" hug but saw that
he had already used up his allotted fifty words. He
hoped Sara would know that was what he really
meant.

When his and Maxsie's cards were collected along
with all the others, he did not know they would have
to wait a year for an answer.

≡ 18 ≡

Tricks and Treats

Hitoshi Buto, admiral of the Imperial Japanese Navy and director of the occupied Port of Manila, told Papaya to massage his shaved head. In spite of herself, she always found this erotic. Beneath the taut, smooth scalp, her fingertips felt every ridge, knob and small depression in the hard, well-shaped skull. She had never before known a man with a shaved head, much less touched one. It was strangely exciting—and only partly because of anticipation. By now she knew what would happen next.

After her massage, Buto took the bottle of mineral oil from the bedside table and poured a few drops into the palm of his hand. He rubbed the oil on his head. Continuing to pour just a few drops at a time, careful not to spill, he meticulously oiled his bare head all over until it was slippery and gleaming in the lamplight.

Then he put his head between her full breasts and began to move it slowly back and forth. He did this for a long time, five or ten minutes, squeezing her breasts against his head with both hands and stroking her nipples with his oily fingers. He moaned with pleasure and kept muttering soft Japanese endearments that she did not understand. Beneath his strict public posture, he was extremely sentimental. She held still for him and kept silent, waiting.

Then he moved his oiled head between her legs and slowly rubbed his way up one thigh and down the other, up and down, up and down. In the center he paused for a moment and pressed a little harder each time he reached it. For Papaya this slithering movement of the hard, solid head was excruciating. She tried not to make noises. The slippery head slid up and down, pressing and pressing, until at last he stopped and put his tongue on her.

She was determined from the beginning that she would never take the slightest pleasure for herself. "It's just a job," as Enrique Sansone said with his cheerful, careless smile. She made up her mind never to have an orgasm, not even to want one. But Buto was too skillful and imaginative a lover. She could not help herself. Going to bed with him in his third-floor corner suite of the Manila Hotel became much more than a job. She had to remind herself constantly of her real purpose—her sole purpose.

While it was sometimes hard to remember in bed, it was easy when she had to walk through the spacious hotel lobby. She could see the looks on the faces of the Filipino doormen and bellboys and elevator operators. Here comes Buto's whore.

The first time the looks had been more surprised than disgusted. Since the Japs had taken over the hotel as military headquarters and living quarters for high-ranking officers, Filipina prostitutes entered and left during the evening hours—a common sight. Everybody understood that. These were hard times in Manila, and the girls had to get along somehow, even when it meant having to obtain a medical certificate every three months. But this was Papaya coming in on the arm of the bald admiral. Everybody recognized her, and everybody knew it was not necessary for such a successful singer and movie star to do anything like this. Bad enough that she was singing regularly at the Jap dinner club and being well paid for it. Having an affair with an enemy officer when, unlike the poor *putas*, she didn't need the money was an insult to the Filipino people. Why would she do such a terrible thing?

She could not tell them, or anyone else.

That first night the admiral dressed afterward and took her home, but that quickly stopped. He explained that he needed his rest. Now after the Mabalinga Club, she entered the hotel with him, but she always left alone, driven home in his Packard. The doorman could hardly bear to hold the car door open for her. The elevator operators never smiled at her and never spoke. If it had not been for Buto's exalted position, she might have had to endure the demeaning medical checkup for venereal disease and show her certificate to the Jap guard at the door. Her father refused to speak to her. Her mother pretended not to know what was going on.

While Papaya showered to get rid of the mineral oil and everything else, Buto sat on the edge of the tub and talked to her. She had always been good at

getting men to talk about themselves, from her first
teenage boyfriend right down to Amos Watson and
now Hitoshi Buto. Most men were full of themselves
anyway and eager to talk about their favorite subject,
especially after sex. Even the naturally reserved ones,
like Buto, could be seduced by sympathetic questions.
In fact, Papaya thought, the greater the reserve, the
fuller the response, once that reserve evaporated.

"He has a wife and four children," Peanut reported
to Zorro. "Not like Americans—he says his wife understands him. He is very proud of the two sons,
Shimayo and Taki. Shimayo is favorite because he is
navy, a gunnery officer on the *Kyishi*. That's a cruiser.
It is on patrol in the southern islands but comes back
to Manila every couple months, and they always have
dinner together at the hotel. Younger son, Taki, is a
bomber pilot. He was in the attack on Pearl Harbor.
Buto says he helped sink a big American battleship."

"Which one?"

"*Oklahoma*. Buto can't believe how lucky they
were. He thought it was suicide mission. He resigned
himself that Taki was going to die for the Emperor.
He says many more ships were sunk than the Americans admit."

"How many does he say?"

"I don't know. I can ask."

"Yes. It would be interesting to know what they
think they accomplished. Where did Buto learn his
English?"

"He studied in school. Then after naval academy
he spent two years in San Diego."

"The American navy base. What a charming co-incidence."

"He is a sad man. He— You really want to hear all this personal stuff, Enrique?"

"Yes, yes. Everything is useful. Why is he sad?"

"Well, partly because of this job in Manila."

"But it's a very important job. After Homma and Miyama, he may be the most important officer in the Philippines."

"He wants to be at sea. He says he could have his own ship, probably his own—how you call it?—task force to command. Instead he is stuck here in Manila in charge of a port. All his classmates and friends are fighting and winning medals and much honor. This big war and he is living in a hotel."

"If he had a task force, he wouldn't have you."

"I told you, I won't talk about that."

"Yes, sorry. Did he see the prime minister when he was here?"

"He had dinner with him in MacArthur's penthouse, where Tojo was staying. He doesn't like Tojo."

"Why not?"

"It's partly Tojo is army, but also he says Tojo has no kindness."

"Funny thing for a Jap admiral to say. So he is sad because he is stuck in Manila?"

"Yes, but more than that. I think he is sad deep down. He likes very sad songs. I know five Jap songs now, all sad. He says they make him want to cry, but of course he is an admiral and does not cry. But he sometimes cries when he is alone."

"How do you know that?"

"He told me. Also he is sad about this country."

"Who isn't? Sad how?"

"He thinks Japs and Filipinos should be friends. He asks me, why are they not friends?"

"What do you tell him?"

"I tell him his people are not nice to our people. That makes him sad, too. He says he tried to be nice to all the Filipinos who work for him at the port and docks and warehouses, but they just take advantage, so he has to get strict."

"Good. We are not looking for Japanese friends. Anything else?"

"He says the transfer of all our soldiers from Bataan to the prison camps was badly managed."

"Badly managed? I'll say!"

"Yes, but he says bad planning. He is disgusted with the Jap army commanders. He says good intelligence—no, his exact words, 'even minimum intelligence'—should report all our soldiers were starving and sick. Too weak to walk very far. And they guessed wrong on how many soldiers there would be—way too low—so there is not enough food and water. Also that many, many civilians were on Bataan, and they are coming out, too. And then, he says, besides all that, they put two different officers in charge of the south part and the north part, so neither one was really in charge. Big mess. He is embarrassed for his army."

"Indeed? How sweet. And what does he have to say about all the soldiers who were killed on the march?"

"He says victory troops—excuse me, 'victorious troops'—often behave badly, in any army. And they did. But he says only one big, deliberate bad thing happened. He says four hundred Filipinos executed on purpose, all together, all in one place. Swords and bayonets—very bad, very wicked. But he says everything else was bad intelligence, bad planning, and then sometimes bad behavior, too. Not on purpose. An accident."

"Some accident. Okay, very good, Peanut. Now find out all you can about what happens in the port. Especially ships coming and going."

"How am I supposed to do that? You want him to write me a schedule?"

Sansone laughed. "Certainly. That would be best. But any bits and pieces will do."

"Amos says to tell you Donato has found somebody in Voice of Juan de la Cruz. We are giving money. You know how they bought their radios?"

"How was that?"

Papaya could never be sure how much Sansone already knew, but she told him anyway. "They dug a tunnel under the Carnation Milk warehouse and stole the cans of milk. Then they sell them. The Japs didn't find out before nearly all the milk was gone."

"Very ingenious."

"Donato is helping sell the milk. Very high prices."

"Very high risk, too."

"Also we now help the prisoners at Cabanatuan."

"Yes, so are others. Peanut, you must concentrate on our good Admiral Buto. That's the most important."

"Amos says everything is important. Helping the guerrillas, too."

"Oh, dear. Well, yes, I suppose so, if you must. Just the same, don't forget about the ships."

She asked again, "What good is it if I find out? How can you tell anybody?"

He gave his usual answer. "There are ways."

———

Sandy Homobono was not used to anybody editing his copy, not even the Japs. In the old days as a columnist, and now as the star reporter of the *Tribune*, he knew all the rules and how to stay just within them as he wrote what he liked. If the Santo Tomas internees were classified by the Japs as "enemy aliens," that is what he dutifully called them. That sort of nonsense made no difference to him. What he cared about, what really mattered, was the story itself. Since he was a very good reporter and a better writer than any of his editors, he expected them to leave his copy alone and to print it the way he handed it in.

So he was furious when the *Tribune*'s token editor, Billy Bilisang, showed him "a few changes" in his feature story about the Voice of Juan de la Cruz. The financing of Juan de la Cruz fascinated him. How could these fiery young Filipinos, whoever they were, not only buy the elaborate equipment to transmit their long-wave broadcasts but also move their "station" all around Manila so that the Japs could never pin it down?

He set out to learn. He knew how to play it both

ways, as he had done ever since he took the *Tribune* job. While the Japs paid his salary and gave him assignments, he was careful to point out to a few discreetly selected patriots that his job enabled him to learn many useful things about Jap intentions. From time to time, he passed on such information. He did not, after all, want some misguided patriot to shoot him because he worked for the Japs and wrote what they wanted. He made sure that a very few key Filipinos knew he was really on their side, no matter what he wrote.

Now, confronted with the Juan de la Cruz puzzle, he told his selected Filipinos that even though the story had to be fiercely critical, it would be great publicity for Juan de la Cruz. More Filipinos would listen to the station, simply because the story called it such a wicked, illegal enterprise. Because he was indefatigable and had sources all through the city, he was able to piece together the basic outline. From hints and references and half-facts he discovered the Carnation Milk story.

The Japs knew about the elaborate theft from the warehouse, although it had never been mentioned in the *Tribune*. But Sandy was sure they hadn't found the direct connection between the theft and the financing of Juan de la Cruz. He made it a key part of his story. He wished he could be present to see General Miyama's face when he read it. Sandy never lost his zest for surprising his bosses.

Running his eyes over his edited story, he saw that the entire Carnation Milk passage had been deleted.

"What is this?" he asked Bilisang. He was very angry. "You took out the best part. I worked my ass off to get this."

"Well," Billy Bilisang said in a sheepish voice, "it isn't relevant."

"Not relevant! It's how Juan de la Cruz got started. It's how they've kept going. Don't give me this 'relevant' shit. What's the real excuse? Didn't I make it clear enough that this was a major criminal theft of government property? I said the theft alone was punishable by death. It makes the radio station an even worse offense. I said that too."

"Mr. Shugi says—"

"Yeah, I'm sure he does. I want to see him myself and get this straightened out."

"Now, Sandy, you know Mr. Shugi doesn't like to discuss these matters with the staff. He gives me advice, when I need it, and then it's up to me to pass it along."

"This is *my* story," Sandy snapped, "not yours. I'm going to see Shugi and get this stetted."

He did see Mr. Shugi, over Billy Bilisang's objection, but he did not get the passage restored.

Shugi was an owlish civilian with no newspaper experience. His background was government propaganda. Homobono had no respect for his journalistic judgment.

When Shugi said no to his arguments, Sandy asked, "Did General Miyama see my story?"

"I have no authority to discuss General Miyama."

"Well, I do, since I interviewed him, and his quotes are all through my story. Do I have to call him back?"

Shugi sighed. "That is not necessary, Mr. Homobono. He did read your story."

"All of it? Including the Carnation Milk?"

Mr. Shugi nodded.

Sandy was stunned. That meant Miyama himself
had deleted the passage. There was no further re-
course. He tried to figure out why Miyama would
have taken it out. Was it because the warehouse theft
made the Japs look foolish? Not as foolish as the
Voice of Juan de la Cruz was making them look every
day. Or was there some other reason?

———

Miranda was excited to be back in Carabangay. It
made her happy to bring presents and messages to all
the brave guerrillas. Well, presents to all the guerrillas. Messages only for Captain Stone. The beautiful
Captain Stone—such blue eyes.

Coach. She smiled to herself. She could tell how
much he appreciated the letter she had brought from
his girlfriend in Santo Tomas. It was sweet, it made
her feel good, but also sad, because her own Benny
was gone. She would never again get any letters from
Benny. She thought Coach also liked her, Miranda.
Maybe he even found her attractive. On her last visit,
he had hugged her twice. Second hug was longer. He
had very strong arms and was taller than most Filipinos. She never imagined she would be hugged by
an American army officer. And such a handsome one,
with that bright hair. The thought made her blush.
Almost all Filipinos had black hair—so boring.

This trip held extra excitement, because her young-

est brother, Hilario, was with her, about to join
Coach and Sergeant and Rosauro and the other brave
guerrillas. He was even more excited than she was.
In the concealed box under the cart, along with the
supplies and money for the guerrillas, was one of her
family's three shotguns, the oldest one. Rosauro had
told her Sergeant was more likely to accept a candidate if he brought a rifle. The Santos family had no
rifle, but surely a shotgun was almost as good.

"Turn down there," Miranda pointed, when they
reached the Carabangay market square.

"Do you think they will take me?" Hilario asked
for the twentieth time.

Normally he was not a nervous boy, but he had
been dreaming about this for weeks. He had said
goodby to all the family and his girlfriend. Miranda
had given him a haircut so he would look his best.
Now if he was rejected, he would return home in
shame. His eager young face showed his worry.

"Of course. It is the house where that pig is sleeping."

Hilario stopped the cart beside the pig. The pig
got up, moved a few steps away and flopped down
again in the sun.

A little boy, Rosauro's baby brother, came out of
the house to see who had arrived.

"Hello, Chico," Miranda said. "Where are your
mother and father? Are they home?"

Without answering, the boy went back inside, and
soon Rosauro's mother came out to greet them. She
was now a woman of importance in Carabangay because of her son's role with the guerrillas. She and

Miranda shook hands, and Miranda introduced Hilario.

"So we are back," Miranda said. "Will you send word to the camp?"

"No, he is here today." She turned to the boy. "Chico, go get Rosauro. He is at Maria's house. Run."

The little boy scooted off, giving the pig a friendly barefoot kick as he went past. The pig grunted acknowledgment but did not move.

"You brought supplies? Good. Any trouble with Japs?"

"No, they stop us, of course, mostly around the air base. We show them the vegetables we carry, and they let us through. Not even search."

"Good. You are hungry? Come inside. Rosauro will be here right away."

"No food, thanks, we ate on the way. How is Rosauro?"

The mother shook her head. "He and Maria should get married, but her parents say first he must give up guerrilla. So nothing will happen." She smiled. "Unless there is baby, then we see."

The house was clean but modest. The main room was everything all at once—living room, dining room, kitchen. Rosauro's parents had a small bedroom almost filled by their bed, while Rosauro and his brothers and sisters all slept in the other room on mats on the floor. Miranda slept there too on the nights when she stayed over. Very crowded.

Also very different from her own family's farmhouse outside San Fernando. She and her sister had their own joint bedroom with real beds, and so did her brothers. Even her grandmother had her own small room. The kitchen was a separate alcove set apart by a straw curtain, and, because the farm was successful, chicken or pork emerged from the alcove almost every evening. The floors were wood and linoleum rather than bamboo, and the roof was corrugated metal rather than nipa—noisy in a heavy rain, but it did not leak and did not have to be repaired and replaced all the time.

It was not a grand house, like the wealthy sugarcane haciendas, but it was spacious and comfortable. The difference, of course, was that Rosauro's father owned a tiny store in a small country town, while Miranda's family ran a large farm outside a big city. The farm had grown in size over the generations, because the Santos family always took pains to marry land. Miranda's own fiancé, Benny, came from a family with adjacent farmland. Miranda sometimes felt that her parents and brothers regretted Benny's death more because of the loss of the land than because of the loss of Benny himself.

The farm was everything to her family, and every member was expected to be devoted to it. Miranda had had the fight of her life to go to secretarial school and then to take the job with Mr. Watson in the wicked city of Manila. But her family was impressed by Mr. Watson's importance in spite of itself. She saved money to contribute to the family, and of course her engagement to Benny, or rather to Benny's farmland, made up for a lot.

Hilario had an easier time escaping because it was so patriotic to be a guerrilla, especially with Coach and Sergeant. Besides, the whole family knew he would return to the farm when this bad war was over. Miranda hoped Coach and Sergeant and Rosauro would accept him.

When Rosauro came in, all smiles and charm and happy greetings, Miranda introduced her brother. She had told Hilario how important Rosauro was and that he must make a strong impression. She told Rosauro what they had brought, including the family shotgun, and asked if they could go up the hill right away.

"In the morning," Rosauro said. "I must be here tonight."

The mother winked at Miranda.

"Right now your brother and I will talk."

"Can I listen?"

"Man talk," Rosauro said pleasantly. "You talk with Mama."

For well over an hour, while Miranda worried about how her brother's interview was going, she and Rosauro's mother traded news of San Fernando and Carabangay and Manila, where Miranda had paid another visit. The mother told the story of the capture and punishment of the Tatloc brothers. Miranda thought the punishment was just, but she was glad she had not been there to witness it, and glad that Captain Stone had not been the one to execute the two men. She did not like to see killing, not even farm animals. Mr. Watson and Papaya would be very in-

terested in that meeting with Major Quintano. She
would have to learn more details from Coach and
Sergeant.

When at last, late in the afternoon, the men's talk
was finished, she tried to determine from Hilario's
solemn face or from Rosauro's smiling one what decision had been made. She waited for one of them to
say something explicit. They said nothing. Men were
infuriating when they were like this.

Early next morning she finally asked if Hilario was
coming with them.

"No, he must stay here," Rosauro said, "until I
talk to Sergeant and Coach. We go now."

Two other guerrillas helped unload the box under
her cart. By request she had brought mostly clothes
and shoes this time, bought with Mr. Watson's money
that Papaya had given her. She was encouraged to
see Rosauro take the family shotgun. Surely he would
not do that unless he was ready to recommend Hilario. But of course Sergeant was the one to worry
about.

They set off into the hills, Rosauro leading, the
other two men carrying the new supplies, Miranda
following with the letters in her skirt pocket. A lovely
morning, not too hot.

Rosauro said they had returned to their old camp,
now that the Jap guerrilla hunt was over, so it would
not be as long a walk as last time. She did not care.
Soon she would see them all again, especially beautiful Captain Stone. She felt sure he would hug her
again with his strong arms. She would be disappointed if he did not.

Rosauro called out his "*Hoy! Hoy!*" greeting while they were still some distance from camp, so when they walked into the clearing, everybody was waiting for them. There he was, right in front, hat off so she could see his bright hair. He was smiling and waving. She waved back. He looked just the way she remembered.

The men gathered around to see what she had brought them from San Fernando. It was several moments before he could push his way through to her.

"Miranda. Did you bring any letters for me?"

"Oh, yes, Coach." She smiled up at him, into his very blue eyes. "And one is very long."

"Good girl!"

She moved into his arms even before they came completely around her. His arms and his trim, hard body felt so strong against her. She let herself go and melted all the way into him. Oh, yes, she thought, oh, yes, yes, he does find me attractive. A wonderful warm, deep, sinking feeling flooded over her. And yes, he wants me. I know it, I can feel it, he wants me. Oh, yes, I will do it with you, beautiful Captain Stone. I will be happy, happy, happy to do it with you. Whenever you ask.

She did not want to separate any more than he did, but at last they let each other go. His hands softly grazed her breasts as they stepped apart. She looked up at him. His eyes were brilliant blue. His face flushed dark beneath his tan. Perhaps her face was flushed too. He felt so good she did not want to wait. She was ready this very second. So was he.

However . . .

She managed a little laugh. "Here are your letters, Coach."

He cleared his throat. "Thanks. Thanks very much." Without glancing at them, he put the letters in his pocket.

She saw that Sergeant was looking at them, not quite smiling. "And how are you, Sergeant?" she asked.

"Okay," he said. "Maybe now we talk business?"

Her laugh was more natural this time. "Fine. I bring my brother Hilario. He is in the town, wanting to join you."

Sergeant nodded.

"Rosauro talked to him yesterday, a long time. That is his gun." She pointed to the shotgun Rosauro was holding.

"Rifle is better."

"My family does not own a rifle."

"Shotgun is only good up close."

"Hilario is a brave boy—man. He will get close, you will see."

"Coach and I talk it over with Rosauro. You bring what we ask for?"

"Yes, everything. Also more pesos. When will you talk about Hilario? He is waiting. How about right now?"

Sergeant grunted. "You sure you brought everything?"

"Yes, yes."

"Rosauro."

"Yes, Sergeant?"

"Come on, we talk. You, too, Coach. Unless," and

now he did smile, "you rather stay with Miranda."

She saw Coach blush again. Oh, yes, he would like very much to stay with me. But he followed Sergeant and Rosauro away from the group. The three men hunkered on their heels—Coach could do it just like a Filipino—and began to talk in low voices. Sergeant was asking, Rosauro was saying, Coach was mostly listening.

She hoped the discussion was coming out all right for her brother, but what she kept thinking about was Coach. She looked around. This camp was not such an easy place for them to be alone—all these other men, very hard to be private. She didn't care. Maybe they would just have to go off into the forest with the bugs and snakes. Everybody would laugh. Let them—she didn't care. Even if they laughed, they would be pleased for her and Coach. But she knew Coach would be embarrassed, because he was an American.

At last the three men finished talking. Sergeant beckoned her to join them.

She sat down on the ground beside them. She smoothed her skirt over her legs. Coach was watching her, so she smoothed it a little more. She was glad she had nice legs.

"I will talk to your brother," Sergeant said. "I go down and see him when you leave. Now. Business. What messages?"

Coach took the letters from his pocket. He selected the one from Mr. Watson and read it aloud. Mr. Watson was extremely glad to get all the news and the many details about "their friends"—meaning the

Japs. Nothing was more interesting these days than the latest news from the provinces, so he hoped they would send more.

Sergeant and Rosauro reported again on all the Jap activities the men had seen or heard about. Miranda forced herself to concentrate so that she could remember and pass everything on to Papaya. This was much more difficult than last time because she could feel Coach's distracting presence only a few inches away, and he kept watching her. But she knew this was important, very important, Papaya and Mr. Watson said so. She made herself take everything down in her mind, just as though she were taking shorthand dictation in Mr. Watson's office.

When they were finished with the Japs, she asked about Major Quintano and the story Rosauro's mother had told her. Coach took over. He described Quintano, making him sound glamorous, and Quintano's fancy U.S. Army tent and his dirty camp and his shabby men. She knew Coach used to be a teacher at the Simpson School. He was good at describing. She felt she could see all that he had seen and also knew what it meant. When he described Sergeant and Quintano negotiating over the tommy guns and the bullets, he made her laugh. Then he told about Quintano suggesting that they join forces.

"And is that possible?" she asked.

Sergeant snorted. "No."

"Mr. Watson will want to know, should we try to give them help? Supplies and money, like you?"

"No."

"I don't trust Quintano," Coach said.

"His men steal much food," Rosauro added. "The people say they are afraid of his men. It is not like here in Carabangay."

"Also women live in his camp," Sergeant said, with obvious disapproval. "He is not serious." Sergeant did not care how often his own men visited the girls in Carabangay or even if they lived with them or married them, but the girls could not stay in his camp.

"He was serious about the tommy guns, though," Coach said.

"Yes, that was serious. Guns are always serious."

When they finished all their "business," Miranda thought surely Coach would ask her to go off with him. She would go wherever he said.

Nothing happened.

He kept looking at her, sometimes directly, sometimes from the corner of his eye, so she knew, and she smiled at him to tell him all right. Still nothing happened. They had their noon meal, everybody altogether, rice and chicken cooked in a big iron *kawa* pot, everybody helping himself, most of them eating with fingers, although Rosauro found a fork for her.

After lunch the sky clouded over and the afternoon rain began. They took shelter under the nipa roofs of the huts and sheds. She was discouraged. It was a light rain, only a shower, but now the forest would be all wet. Soon she would have to start back. She wondered if she had done something wrong. Maybe something that would seem all right to a Filipino but not to an American. She could not imagine what that could be.

And then it occurred to her. The girlfriend, the

Judy in Santo Tomas. She knew he had not yet read
the Judy letter, he had not been out of Miranda's
sight, but he must be thinking about her. Maybe he
was thinking he must be faithful to her.

This made no sense to Miranda at all. The Judy
was in Santo Tomas, and Coach was way out here
in the mountains. They would not see each other until
the Americans returned, as General MacArthur promised they would. That might be a long time. But Miranda herself was right here—right here in the
mountains with him. There could be no harm to the
Judy or anybody else for Coach and Miranda to enjoy
each other. It didn't mean she hadn't loved Benny,
and in some ways still did and perhaps always would.
Or that Coach didn't love his Judy, if that was how
it was. All it meant was a chance for Coach and
Miranda to be happy together, no harm in that.

When the rain stopped, it was time for her to go.
Would he still hug her goodby? It would not be the
same.

She asked Sergeant, "You come with me now to
see my brother?"

He nodded.

"I know you will take him. He is a good boy—
man."

He shrugged. That remained for him to see.

"Paradiso, I'm coming too," Coach said. He put
on his straw hat.

"You don't need to. I take care of it."

"No, I want to. Let's get started." He turned to
her. His voice was eager and friendly. "Come on,

Miranda, I'll help you down. It'll be slippery after the rain."

She did not need his help, it was really easier to walk by yourself, but she took his hand and sometimes his arm as they walked down the hill to Carabangay. Sergeant, who had grown up in the mountains, kept his footing, but she and Coach fell down several times on the slick red earth. They helped each other up, laughing. She could feel the warmth of his touch. He certainly wasn't thinking about the girlfriend now. Their clothes and skin and even their faces collected red mud smears. He looked like an American Indian in war paint.

Before they reached the town it rained again. Their clothes soaked through. Her short black hair plastered against her head, and her wet skirt clung against her legs. She could not look so attractive now, but Coach did not seem to mind. She felt happy with him in the rain.

They went straight to the house of Rosauro's parents, where Hilario had been waiting all day long. He was standing on the porch when they walked up, looking as though he had been standing there forever.

He saluted Sergeant coming up the steps and then saluted Coach, who was right behind. Then he looked at Miranda and said, "What a mess!"

She laughed and pushed back her wet hair. "Sergeant, Coach, this is my brother, Hilario Santos."

Rosauro's parents came out onto the porch. The rain still dripped from the thatch of the roof, but the porch with its overhanging eaves was dry.

Sergeant was looking her brother over, studying him. He said to the parents, "We want to talk to him alone."

"Fine. Right here?" the father said. "We go inside and leave you here."

But Coach was looking at her, not at Hilario. She could not see his expression under the shadow of his hat.

"Paradiso, you talk to him," he said. "I want to talk to Miranda."

Oh, yes, Coach, she thought, and how much I want to talk to you too!

Sergeant grunted, not saying anything, not even acting surprised. The parents seemed a little puzzled. Hilario was puzzled too. They all knew Sergeant and Coach both had to approve a new recruit. Well, not this time. No, not this time.

The next step would normally be up to Coach, but he would not know the right thing to say. So she said to Rosauro's mother, "Captain Stone and I have to discuss messages to take back. Can we go in the bedroom so we don't bother you?"

Rosauro's mother smiled. She understood right away. "Of course," she said. "I get you a towel to dry off."

She led them into the house, where she handed Miranda a coarse cotton towel, bright orange. Coach put his wet straw hat on a table. She shooed them through the hanging curtain into the bedroom. "Have a nice talk," she said smiling. "Nobody disturb you here."

As soon as the curtain dropped back into place

behind them, they were holding each other as tight
and hard as this morning, only now he moved his
hands all over her. They felt wonderful on her breasts
and hips and up and down her back. How foolish to
have worried. Their bodies crushed together through
their wet, mud-smeared clothes. At last he kissed her.
Oh, yes, beautiful Captain Stone. Your tongue is so
warm and lovely.

Half smiling, half desperate, they helped each other
with their clothes, dropping them on the floor in wet
heaps. He was tan all over, deep tan, except for the
one startling white, white band of flesh, with curly
hair the same red-blond color as his head and chest.

She had never seen anything so beautiful; it made
her almost want to cry. She took the bright orange
towel to dry him and wipe away the red smears of
mud, but he would not wait. He tore the towel from
her hands and pulled her against him, nothing but
pure flesh.

She sank back onto the bed, pulling him down with
her and then straight, straight into her. She kept her
eyes open, staring up into his eyes. She had never seen
anything so blue—bluer than sky, bluer than anything, burning blue.

———

When she finally drove away from Carabangay, alone
in her horse cart, leaving her brother Hilario behind
as a new guerrilla, her beautiful Coach still had not
had time to read the letter from his girlfriend. She set
about trying to remember all the things Sergeant and
Rosauro had told her about the Japs.

⚌ 19 ⚌

The Killing Ground

The instant Amos Watson learned that his young driver, Donato, was selling Carnation Milk for the Voice of Juan de la Cruz, he sent an immediate order for him to stop. Donato must only supply anonymous funds, not get mixed up in trying to collect them.

The order came too late. Donato was arrested with the others. The Voice of Juan de la Cruz was dead.

Amos heard about it from Federico the shanty-builder on the morning of the arrests. For the first time since he had been interned, he was frustrated by lack of information. Extreme care had to be exercised. Papaya and Carlos must not risk messages that could make the situation even more dangerous, and yet Amos was desperate to know what was happening.

How had the Japs learned about the milk? How had they found the radio station? And above all, who was talking and what were they saying? The network Amos had built was in extreme jeopardy.

While Federico waited, pretending to make small improvements in the shanty, Amos tried to imagine the chain of consequences he now faced. How much would unravel? How much had Donato told the other members of Juan de la Cruz? Nothing, if Amos was very, very lucky. But that seemed almost too much to hope for. All those young men risking their lives together, bound together in unique comradeship, wouldn't they naturally tell each other their secrets?

Still, if Donato had told nothing, and if he managed to keep silent under Jap interrogation, the damage just might be contained. Then the only major threat would be to Carlos. General Miyama was no fool. If one of his own drivers turned out to be a member of Juan de la Cruz, then what about the rest of his Filipino household staff? Especially what about his head houseboy? Wouldn't Carlos have known what Donato was up to?

Amos tried to put himself in General Miyama's mind. If suspicion fell on Carlos, as it must, Carlos, with his wife and children right there under Miyama's hand, would be vulnerable to enormous pressure. And if Miyama could force Carlos to talk, there went Papaya. Also Miranda and Federico, and perhaps Enrique Sansone, and then maybe Brad Stone and even Jack Humphrey and that corporal in Cabanatuan. And, of course, Amos Watson himself. He had to be prepared for that. The only one who might be isolated from such general ruin was Felix Logan.

No point in pursuing that line of thought. If Carlos broke, nothing could be saved. Therefore Carlos must not break. Therefore Carlos must be protected at any cost. And Donato must not break, either. And if Donato had indeed talked to the other members of Juan de la Cruz, they, too, must not break. Christ, Amos

thought, what a brutal string of *ifs*—and about most
of them, he was helpless to act.

Amos could think of only one way to protect Carlos. And it must be done instantly. Less than an hour
after first hearing the terrible news, he sent his urgent
oral message back through Federico to Papaya. Speed,
he told Federico, was absolutely essential. Risk the
telephone.

———

General Miyama had every reason to be pleased with
himself. He would have been still more pleased if the
hunt had not taken so many months, a quite embarrassing length of time, but the final result was excellent.

According to the first reports he received, nine men
had been captured, and the Voice of Juan de la Cruz
would never be heard again. He was more interested
in the two radios than in his nine prisoners. One radio
had been concealed in a refrigerator and the other in
a car. Both could be moved from place to place
around Manila. No wonder it was so difficult to pin
them down.

The milk had been the key. When he read about
it in the draft of Homobono's *Tribune* article, he
realized the opportunity. He had been furious about
the warehouse theft, but such things happened in any
occupied city, and he had wasted little time regretting
it. Now it was different. He deleted the passage from
the article so that others would not know what he
knew. He assigned all his men to pursue the milk
lead, not only his own troops but every Filipino spy

in his service. Who was selling the milk? Find them and follow them.

Well, now he had them, but far more important, he had those radios. The acute embarrassment to his command was finally ended. Now only administrative details remained—and, of course, the executions. He would leave all that to his staff officer, Colonel Iseda, who was returning from Baguio this afternoon. Miyama could turn his attention to the many other matters he had had to put aside.

The houseboy, Carlos, entered his office with the tea tray. Miyama looked at his watch. Carlos was fifteen minutes early. He opened his mouth to reprimand him, then closed it. Carlos was an excellent servant, and this morning's achievement perhaps deserved the celebration of early tea.

"Pour tea, sir?"

Miyama nodded. Carlos's voice sounded shaky. The hand that poured the tea was less steady than usual. Carlos actually spilled a few drops, which he hastily wiped up with the linen napkin.

"What is the matter with you?" Miyama asked sharply. First fifteen minutes early and now this clumsiness.

"Oh, sir," Carlos said, "I am afraid there is a terrible thing." His face was working. He twisted his hands.

"Yes, what is it?"

"It is Donato, sir. I suspect him."

"Donato?" The charming and very reliable young driver. "Of what?"

"Oh, sir, I fear he may be a traitor. I hope I am wrong."

Miyama was astonished. "What makes you think so?"

"Many things. He is not at work this morning. It is not the first time."

Miyama did not tolerate tardiness in his employees, as Carlos well knew. However, that was hardly traitorous. But Carlos was continuing.

"He has been talking with bad young men. I see them sometimes in the back. They talk in whispers. I know they are planning bad things."

"Why have you not told me before?"

"Because I hope it is not true. I—I like Donato."

That was understandable. Miyama liked Donato himself. "What do they talk about?"

"I cannot hear much because of whispers. And sometimes Donato goes away with them. I ask him where he is going. He smiles and says, 'Big secret.' I think sometimes he is with them all night doing bad things. Once I hear them talking something about radio."

"Radio!"

"Yes, sir. I wonder if maybe they are listening to the San Francisco shortwave that is so illegal."

A worse possibility occurred to Miyama. "Would you recognize these men?"

"I don't know, sir. It is not many times, and it is different ones, I think. And now Donato is gone again, and he does not even send message he will be so late. Oh, sir, I am afraid. I had to tell you."

"Quite right."

"Sir, if I am wrong, if he is all innocent, please do not tell him I speak to you. I think it will make him very angry in his heart."

"Take this tray, I don't want it. Send my aide in."

"Yes, sir. Sir, you will not tell him if I am wrong?"

"That is all. Do as I told you."

When his aide appeared a few moments later, Miyama said, "I am going to Fort Santiago at once. Order the car."

The aide started to explain that the general's number-one driver was absent, but Miyama angrily cut him off and told him Alfonso would do.

All the way down Dewey Boulevard, past Rizal Park and the Luneta and the Manila Hotel, General Miyama sat in rigid silence. On the very day of triumph, he feared another embarrassment to his command, this time a personal one. But if he appeared unannounced at the prison and made the discovery himself, in front of all the officers and guards, it would be less dishonorable. In fact, they would wonder how their general had had such special insight. It might even add to the image of aloof mystery that he strove to create. He was fortunate that Carlos had spoken his suspicion.

The car was passing the ancient black stone walls of Intramuros and the foolish golf course the Americans had built around the base of the walls, filling in the ancient moat the Spanish had dug to protect themselves from insurgents. It would not be long now. Fort Santiago lay at the far end of Intramuros, guarding the entrance to the Pasig River. The Spanish had built that, too. They had a fortress mentality.

The car turned and pulled up at the barricaded gate. The insignia on his license plate brought a flurry of salutes and great scrambling to open the gate quickly. More salutes and bows as he drove through. Now, he knew, there would be a frantic phone call from the gate to the main office, announcing that General Miyama had suddenly appeared. Yes, yes, the general himself.

The car drove through the long plaza to the main entrance of the fort. Except for its strategic location, Fort Santiago did not impress Miyama. The low, thick walls built out of square blocks of dark gray stone had no grandeur. The fort was too low and squat, too spread out to be imposing. It needed height, concentration, perhaps a few lofty towers. He much preferred the ancient Japanese castles.

However, the Filipinos considered Santiago a national shrine, making pilgrimages to the cell where their hero José Rizal had spent the last fifty-six days of his life. Quite spacious for a cell, Miyama thought. A good four meters by eight meters, it now made a convenient office. The fort itself, for all its lack of grandeur, now served as an excellent prison. The many tiny cells were jammed with occupants.

His car drove through the main entrance into the oval-shaped Plaza de Armas with the flagpole in its center. Officers and soldiers stood at attention in ranks to greet him. Alfonso opened the door of the car, with less flourish than Donato, and Miyama got out.

He saluted the flag, then returned the commandant's salute. As he did so, the ranks bowed low with military precision. Proper training. On another occasion he might have expressed his satisfaction by shaking hands with the commandant, but not today.

"We will go to your office," he told the commandant. "Have the Juan de la Cruz prisoners brought there."

Ordinarily he would have waited in silence for the prisoners to appear, but now it was important to establish that he was not here out of curiosity. "I have a suspicion about one of these men," he said to the commandant. On the other hand, he must allow for the possibility of error. "We will see if I am right."

The commandant was flattered by such intimacy, but that could not be helped.

The prisoners entered in single file under guard by soldiers with bayonets. They were remarkably young. Several were mere teenagers. All looked defiant. Donato was the fourth man through the door.

"Ha!" Miyama said. "As I suspected. That one"—he pointed—"is my own driver."

The commandant hissed his astonishment. Everyone stared at Donato, who stared back without any sign of fear or apology.

"You were foolish," Miyama said in his coldest voice, "to think you could deceive me. I have kept my eyes on you. So has Carlos. Now you will pay like the rest." He turned to the commandant. "Take them back."

———

Papaya tried to comfort Carlos, but the little man was inconsolable.

"It was necessary," she said. "To save us all. You did not hurt Donato. He was lost the minute they arrested him."

"I loved him," Carlos said. His voice was miserable, close to tears. "He is like my son. I found him for Mr. Watson."

"You had to do it. Mr. Watson said so."

Carlos nodded. "Yes, Miss Papaya, I know. But this is very hard times. Donato would never say against me, I know that. Never. But I had to say against him. I am ashamed."

Papaya knew she must talk him out of this dangerous mood. As Amos's message said, Carlos must be strong. He must persuade General Miyama that he was totally loyal. "Carlos, you know what I think? I think Donato would be proud of you. He would say, 'Carlos fooled those Japs. Carlos saved Mr. Watson and Papaya and everybody. Carlos is a *hero*.' That is what Donato would say. He would be laughing and saying how smart you are."

Carlos shook his head. "Miyama says they will be killed."

She could not deny that. "Yes, it is the chance they all took. They are brave young men. They knew what would happen if they got caught. Just like us."

"Maybe Donato hears what I told General Miyama. He will think I betrayed him."

"Nonsense. He knows you wouldn't do that."

"Please, can we send a message to him? Tell him why I had to say against him?"

Papaya got up from the couch in her music room to put her hand on Carlos's shoulder. They were almost the same height. "Santiago is not like Santo Tomas, Carlos. No Package Line. The prisoners have to stay in their cells, not talk to anybody. Even in the same cell they only whisper. Very strict. We can't send a message. The Filipinos who work in the fort, they sometimes tell what things they see, but no way to reach the prisoners. Don't worry. Donato probably never hears what you said to Miyama. If he does, he will understand."

"I think they will beat Donato. Beat all those boys. Try to make them tell things."

"Maybe not," Papaya lied. "I tell you why it will not matter. You know why? Those boys are in the same place where José Rizal was a prisoner. They will want to be just like Rizal. Now you must go back home. Just remember. Mr. Watson counts on you. So do I." She patted his shoulder, then kissed him on the cheek.

Carlos finally began to cry.

"No," Papaya said. "No crying. Nobody is allowed to cry."

"It is for Donato."

"Listen, Donato isn't crying. He is telling all the Japs to go to hell."

———

Enrique Sansone so rarely told Papaya anything that she knew he was making a special exception.

"Peanut, you are not to try to find out anything. Fort Santiago is too dangerous. I will tell you whatever I know. It is said that none of them is telling the Japs anything."

"How do you know?"

As usual, he did not answer that. "They will all be court-martialed in Old Bilibid Prison. When they come out after the trial is over, some people will be watching. If they are wearing handcuffs, it is the worst. No handcuffs, then maybe they are free, but more likely they are going to prison for a while, perhaps a long time."

"I should be there. Maybe I could see Donato, catch his eye so he knows we are with him."

"You will definitely not be there. Why would Admiral Buto's girlfriend be hanging around the Bilibid gate? Don't be ridiculous."

"Amos would want somebody to be there."

"He would not."

"Yes, he would."

"Why don't we all go? We could have a picnic."

"I think it will be very lonesome to walk out of Bilibid with those handcuffs."

"It is not lonesome. There are nine of them."

"I think there will be many handcuffs, don't you?"

"Oh, yes. Nine. What does Admiral Buto say about the case?"

"He thinks it is very sad. He says if his country was ever defeated, he would want his own sons to fight back some way, like those young men. He thinks they were brave, but of course now they must be punished."

"Well, of course."

"You sound like you don't care."

Enrique twisted his head to get rid of the crick in

his neck. His neck made a little clicking sound. "I'll keep you informed," he said.

———

General Miyama ordered his head houseboy to testify at the court-martial. Not that such testimony was needed. There was ample evidence from the officers who had made the arrests. What Miyama wanted from Carlos was a public demonstration of loyalty from a Filipino servant to a Japanese general. That would impress the military court. It would also show how promptly Miyama reacted to treachery in his own household.

Carlos was unbelievably reluctant. "Oh, sir, I cannot do that. I will be too frightened of all those high officers."

"They won't hurt you. Besides, I will be there. I have higher rank than any of them."

"But, sir, I am never in court all my life. I will be too scared to speak."

"It is simple. You just tell the court what you told me. Then you point out Donato and any others you recognize. Then the chief officer says thank you and lets you go. Ten minutes."

"Oh, sir. Oh, sir."

The little man's lack of sophistication was appalling. These Filipinos. Still, if Carlos's testimony was to have any value to Miyama, he must be reassured. "I will order the chief officer to treat you with respect. After all, you are my personal servant."

"But, sir—"

"Enough! And remember to speak up so the court can hear you."

Carlos trembled at the anger in his voice.

"When it is over," Miyama said more kindly, "you will get a bonus."

Right up to the day of the court-martial, Miyama had to keep buttressing Carlos's courage. He decided that Carlos's testimony should be as brief as possible, just long enough to make the desired impression. Too many questions, too much examination in detail, and Carlos might fall apart. Miyama gave instructions to the chief officer.

Old Bilibid Prison was a depressing structure eight blocks from Santo Tomas. The Spanish had built it as their central prison seventy-five years ago, but Miyama thought it looked even older and uglier than that. Thick cement-and-stone walls, an open prison yard with a high guard tower in the center. In the old days three thousand Filipino criminals had lived in the long cellblocks. Now Miyama used it for American prisoners. Bilibid's very ugliness made it a suitable setting for a court-martial. The atmosphere could hardly seem more ominous.

Carlos, dressed in his white uniform, his head barely showing above the front seat of Miyama's car, looked from side to side as they drove through the steel gates. He had not spoken since leaving the house. Outside the gates, a crowd of Filipinos watched silently from across the street. It was well known that this important trial was taking place today, but Miyama was constantly surprised at the way Filipinos could find time to stand around doing nothing. His own people were too industrious to waste time in this fashion.

The court-martial sat in the largest office of Old Bilibid. Although Carlos was to appear at exactly eleven o'clock, Miyama sent Colonel Iseda inside to make certain. He did not want Carlos waiting in that courtroom a moment longer than necessary.

Iseda returned to the corridor. Yes, the court would hear Carlos at once.

"Now then, Carlos," Miyama said. He smiled to show that everything would be all right, as promised.

Carlos did not smile back. He was shaking. He closed his eyes.

When Miyama entered the courtroom, followed by Iseda and Carlos, the officers of the court rose from behind their long table and bowed. Miyama nodded in recognition and took the seat that had been placed for him. Iseda led Carlos to the witness box, then returned to sit behind Miyama.

The nine ragged prisoners sat in two rows between armed guards. Although they looked thinner and shabbier than on the morning of their arrest, Miyama could detect no sign of submission. Donato, at the end of the first row, recognized Carlos, but Carlos did not look at him.

The prosecutor took Carlos through his story. His questions in Japanese had to be translated by the interpreter, and then Carlos's answers had to be translated back into Japanese for the benefit of the court.

Carlos followed orders. Yes, he was the head house-boy of General Miyama. Yes, he had known General Miyama's driver Donato Sanchez for three years.

Yes, he had seen and heard Donato Sanchez conspiring with other young men. (The witness was instructed to repeat his answer in a louder voice and did so.) Yes, he had heard the conspirators use the word "radio" but had not known its significance. Yes, he had warned the general of his suspicions. Yes, General Miyama had immediately ordered his car to take him to Fort Santiago. Yes, the general had later told the witness that Donato Sanchez was one of the Juan de la Cruz prisoners.

Even with the translation, it went quickly. Miyama was satisfied.

"Does the witness recognize any of the conspirators who talked with Donato Sanchez?"

Carlos shook his head. "No, sir."

"The court requests that the witness look at the prisoners before answering the question."

Carlos turned his head to look at the two rows of young men. Then he repeated, "No, sir."

"Does the witness recognize Donato Sanchez?"

Carlos nodded. A very slight nod.

"The witness will please identify him."

"He is the one on the end."

"Which end? The witness will please point him out to the court."

Miyama could see the struggle on Carlos's face. He knew the old man had been fond of Donato before he turned traitor.

Without looking at the prisoners, Carlos said in a small voice, "First row, left end."

Miyama stood up, indicating to the court that Carlos was to be excused. The court thanked him and dismissed him.

As Carlos turned to leave, he took a last, quick glance at the prisoners. To Miyama's amazement, all were smiling. Donato actually *winked*. Such arrogance, such defiance, was astonishing. They all seemed to be saying, "The hell with you, old man. Who cares what you say?" Miyama was impressed in spite of himself.

Outside the courtroom, Miyama told Carlos. "You did well. I will not forget your bonus."

Now that the ordeal was over, Carlos seemed much more himself. He was almost cheerful with relief. "Thank you very much, sir."

———

"Nine handcuffs, Peanut. I'm sorry."

"I already know. Everybody in Manila was outside that gate except me."

"We couldn't expect any other verdict."

"I know. It is still cruel. One good thing, though. They forgave Carlos. Not just Donato but all of them. They were all smiling at the end to say it was okay, they understood."

"Yes."

"You already knew that?"

"Well, let's say I had an idea it might happen."

"Carlos feels so much better. What will happen now?"

"I'm afraid it's the killing ground."

"That field out between La Loma and the Chinese Cemetery? When?"

"Whenever they decide. And Peanut, you will not go there, either. Others will be behind that fence to observe, but not you."

"No, I know. But Carlos wants to be there. To say his goodby."

"That would be just as foolish."

"No, it wouldn't. He is going to ask Miyama special permission to watch the traitors die."

"Now that is a nice touch."

"Thank you."

"It was your idea?"

"You don't have all the ideas."

———

General Miyama took no pleasure in executions. He did not attend them if he could avoid it. However, this was such an important occasion and he had played such a central role in the affair that he must make an exception. He must be a public witness to the final silencing of the Voice of Juan de la Cruz.

The condemned men had remained in Fort Santiago, shackled in their handcuffs even while eating. They were handcuffed now as they climbed out of the truck stripped to their underwear. The soldiers roughly shoved them into a line.

The morning was pleasant, with no threat of rain. Off to his right Miyama could see the famous Chinese Cemetery, crammed with ornate monuments and crypts and urns—one of the major tourist sights of Manila. Some distance behind him stood a ramshackle fence, and he knew that behind the fence Filipinos were hidden, friends and families of the condemned. He could have them cleared out, but he was content to let them watch. A lesson in stern Japanese justice was worth teaching.

His houseboy, Carlos, was ten yards away, his hands behind his back. When he had asked to attend, Miyama realized he should have thought of it himself. Another visible demonstration of the houseboy's loyalty to his general. Miyama could not see Carlos's face, but his clean, starched white uniform shone starkly in the open field. The *Tribune* reporter Homobono, in a rumpled black suit, was also present to provide the official account for tomorrow's paper.

The condemned men had asked for a priest to be present. Request denied. Everyone must know these were the worst kind of criminals, not entitled to the solaces of their religion. No doubt there was a priest or two behind the fence, offering last prayers. Small comfort at that distance.

The nine men were kneeling now, their almost-naked brown bodies gleaming in the sunlight. Several stared at the ground, but most, including Donato, held their heads up, looking in the direction of Miyama and Carlos. Defiance would do them little good now.

All was finally ready. The commander of the execution party turned to Miyama and saluted with his saber, asking for permission to proceed. Miyama nodded.

The commander gave the order.

A soldier with two service revolvers walked behind

the line of men and shot each one in the back of the head. The appropriate style of death for traitors. The bodies toppled forward one by one.

When it was finished, the execution party picked up the bodies and swung them onto the bed of the truck.

Miyama turned away and walked back to his car. The driver held the door open, and Miyama climbed in. As he drove away, he saw that the two small figures, one in white, one in black, were still standing there.

Miyama had already given Carlos his bonus. He must tell Shugi at the newspaper to give a considerably larger bonus to Homobono. General Miyama was a fair man. Without the information about Carnation Milk provided by Homobono, the Voice of Juan de la Cruz might still be broadcasting its filth.

⚊ 20 ⚊

Santa

Eli Phipps was checking out the new message center at Port Moresby to make sure everything was functioning. Everything was—except for two of the little telephone-size coding machines that were misbehaving in the extreme New Guinea humidity. Port Moresby felt even hotter and wetter than the Philippines, but that might just be in contrast to the wonderful weather Phipps had enjoyed all these past months in Australia. The technician promised both machines would be cranking away before noon.

While Phipps was inspecting, one of the General's barefoot native servants appeared at the entrance clutching a piece of paper. MacArthur's servants were easy to identify. All wore a white wraparound skirt with red stripes and blue stars. The garment stood out splendidly and patriotically against the dark Papuan skin.

As senior officer present, Phipps took the note. In the General's familiar handwriting, it was a brief wire to his four-year-old son, Arthur, back in Brisbane:

"Terribly sorry but Santa Claus held up in New Guinea for a few days."

So MacArthur was not going to Brisbane for Christmas, and therefore neither was Phipps. No holiday celebration with his two favorite Aussie girls. He gave the message to one of the code clerks.

Christmas in Port Moresby. Eli was not surprised. The move to Moresby in early November had been exciting. Moresby, the former seat of Australia's colonial government, was only a few degrees south of the equator—and another fifteen hundred miles closer to the Philippines. At first MacArthur flew back and forth so often between Moresby and Brisbane that no one knew where he was going to have lunch on any given day. The table was set in both places.

But the battle against the Japs at the coastal point of Buna, only a hundred miles away across the fierce Owen Stanley Mountains, was going very badly. Even with Eichelberger in charge, the fighting was bitter and the situation hazardous. The veteran Japanese troops were dug in behind strong positions, and their ships brought them fresh supplies and ammunition at night. U.S. supplies had to be flown over the rugged, cloud-shrouded Owen Stanleys, which was frequently impossible because of weather. On the ground at Buna, American and Aussie casualties were high. No wonder Santa Claus thought he'd better stay close to the scene.

Eli Phipps had been standing there on the screened veranda of MacArthur's bungalow, along with other members of the Bataan Gang, the day Eichelberger arrived from Australia to take command. The palatial bungalow had once been Government House for the Aussies, but MacArthur renamed it Bataan.

While everyone else stood still, MacArthur paced back and forth across the veranda, laying out the dismal battle situation at Buna. Then he stopped right in front of Eichelberger.

"If you capture Buna," he said with passion, "I'll award you the Distinguished Service Cross, I'll recommend you for a high British decoration, and I'll release your name for newspaper publication."

This last was quite a promise, Phipps thought. He had written enough communiqués to know that the only officer supposed to be mentioned by name was Douglas MacArthur.

MacArthur paced again. The veranda was silent except for the sound of his footsteps, back and forth, back and forth. Then he turned on Eichelberger and said, "Bob, take Buna or don't come back alive."

Well, Eichelberger was doing his best, and he was still alive, but he had not yet taken Buna. Phipps wondered if he would take it before he ran out of men.

Phipps was glad not to be asked to write the Christmas communiqué about Buna. He didn't mind using flowery language—in fact, he enjoyed it—or exaggerating here and there for effect, or making it sound as though MacArthur were personally leading his troops in battle—after all, that was spiritually true, even though MacArthur had never gone near Buna. But Eli Phipps did balk at flat lies.

He shook his head as he read, "On Christmas Day our activities were limited to routine safety precautions. Divine services were held."

Eichelberger and all his men who were fighting for their lives on Christmas Day, without benefit of any religious service whatsoever, would be furious when they read that.

Sometimes Phipps really hated MacArthur. Christmas Day was one of those times.

———

Amos Watson was carving and sanding his third toy train engine. Not only was this one going much faster than the first two; it was also his best. His hands, which had not worked with small tools in many years, were beginning to recover their former skill. He could probably finish another four or even five before Christmas, provided he didn't snap off the smokestack, as had happened with his first engine. The soft wood was easy to shape but also easy to break.

He sat on his stool in the museum gallery of the Main Building, along with the hundred other men and women who constituted Santa's Workshop. On his left, Toby Compton had just finished his hobbyhorse and was screwing a pole into the base of the horse's head. Toby, an outstanding polo player in the old days at the Polo Club, was passionate about horses but inept as a craftsman. The horse looked more like a giraffe—and an abnormal giraffe at that. On his right, Millie Barnes was stuffing kapok taken from her own mattress into an ungainly but charming Raggedy Ann doll. Millie didn't have enough material to make clothes, so the doll had only a nude, multi-colored body formed out of scraps of cloth sewn together.

"I never did like dolls," Millie said, as she patted the kapok into the crude shape of a leg, "but I have to say I love this one." She held it up for inspection. "If no kid wants it, I think I'll keep it for myself."

"I wouldn't worry about that," Amos said. "They'll be fighting over it."

"You think so? They better not fight too hard or these stitches will pull apart. Half this left arm is mosquito netting."

All the cloth for dolls and stuffed animals was contributed to scrap boxes placed in the lobbies of the Main Building and the Annex. Any scrap was welcome: pillows, curtains, old clothes, handkerchiefs, socks, bedding. Color and material didn't matter. Everything was useful to Santa's Workshop. After all, more than four hundred children in Santo Tomas had to get presents.

Amos thought Christmas was the best thing to happen to Santo Tomas in the entire year of internment. For once, people climbed out of their apathy and listlessness. Petty grudges were forgotten for a while. Even Judy Ferguson, a paragon of determination but not of community spirit, was working hard on the Christmas-tree ornaments. When Amos teased her about it, she said defensively, "I like pretty things."

Once a day the Triumvirate paid a visit to the Workshop to check on progress and to encourage the toymakers. The Christmas spirit was so pervasive that

Boris Cutter actually spoke to Amos in what, for him, was an almost friendly tone.

"I see you've found something useful to do," Cutter said, looking at Amos's carved engine.

Amos put down his sandpaper. "Just one of Santa's elves," he said. "Is it true about the Red Cross packages?"

The rumor was all over camp. Amos knew from Felix Logan in the commandant's office that this particular rumor happened to be true. A huge shipment of Red Cross gift packages had arrived in Manila from South Africa and Canada. There were enough packages so that even after the Japanese siphoned off some for themselves, everybody in camp would get one. Felix said the commandant guaranteed it. Would Boris Cutter now confirm it?

Not on your life. "We're looking into it," Cutter said shortly, having exhausted his goodwill for today. He walked on to other benches.

"That man," Millie said when he was out of hearing, "thinks he's much too important."

"Yes. But unfortunately, he is."

Boris Cutter ran the finances for the entire camp. He handled the monthly allotment from the Japanese with which all supplies for the food line were bought. He set the shanty fees and the punishment fines and the prices charged in all the shops and boutiques. He decided what equipment had to be purchased and how much to pay for it. Whenever and wherever money was involved, Boris Cutter had final say. He was more powerful now than he had been as president of American City Bank. He used his power with great

skill and total absence of charm. It was Boris who
announced the slogan for all this Christmas activity:
"Money will be used modestly and personal effort
extravagantly." Amos Watson had never admired
him more, or liked him less.

Cutter had got hold of a stack of Christmas cards
from somewhere in Manila and put them on sale in
one of the shops to help pay for the holiday program.
Internees wrote messages and dropped their cards in
"mailboxes." Amos was surprised Cutter had not
thought of charging a postage fee.

Amos himself, who used to have a Christmas mail-
ing list of more than two hundred names, bought eight
cards. He dropped only three of them in the Santo
Tomas mailbox. One for Felix, who still had not
heard from his parents in Cebu, one for Judy Ferguson, who would not hear from her Coach again
before Christmas, and one for Millie and Sammy
Barnes, whom he had come to know because they
were Judy's good friends, and because both disliked
Boris Cutter as much as he did.

His other five cards, unsigned and unaddressed,
would slip out through Federico to his close colleagues: Papaya, Carlos, Miranda, Coach Stone and
Jack Humphrey. Alas, none for his driver, Donato.
Ordinarily, Amos sent only essential messages, but
real live Christmas cards were too good to miss. He
wished, briefly, that he could send cards to his wife
and family in California. He thought about them as
seldom as possible. It was easier for him to concentrate on this life right here.

The next time he saw Judy, she asked again, "Do

you think we'll hear from Brad before Christmas?"

Amos shook his head.

"It's been almost a month. Twenty-seven days."

"I'm afraid it's too soon."

Judy had received four letters from Coach, and she knew by now how long it took, although Amos had not told her how the system worked. Letters to and from the Zambales Mountains took forever, and sometimes might not arrive at all—just like the real post office, but with more justification.

"I hoped—maybe for Christmas."

Amos thought it would be nice to care for someone as much as Judy did, but he was too old for that. She still looked very pretty, although makeup and dressy clothes were seldom to be had. Her worn blue blouse and tan cotton skirt were clean but now too loose at waist and hips. Everybody's clothes were loose these days.

He liked the way she did not give in. Her head was up, the green eyes still flashed. Her figure, which she carried just short of a swagger, was still splendid, although his own preference had always been for big-breasted, fuller-bodied women. She might be selfish, as beautiful young women so often were, but he admired her refusal to be pushed around by anyone—not even by Amos himself.

"I'm sorry, Judy," he said. "Maybe on New Year's. You have to be patient."

"No, I don't."

———

Christmas in the Zambales camp was grim. Two days before, Jap guards at Clark Field had caught three of their men trying to sabotage construction equipment at the new auxiliary airstrip. They were beheaded next day, Christmas Eve, in the church square at Angeles, after first having their hands and feet cut off. Word of the execution reached camp on Christmas morning.

Paradiso had given most of the men permission to celebrate the holiday with friends and families in Carabangay and other nearby towns and barrios. Brad Stone knew there would be no celebration now. Only church services and tears and prayers.

Fewer than a dozen men were guarding the camp with Brad and Paradiso. They cursed the awful news, then fell silent, their faces solemn and angry.

Paradiso's own face was dark with fury. He had authorized the Clark Field expedition, in spite of the danger. That was not what made him furious. "Everybody knows, you get caught, they kill you. Okay. But this thing. Cutting up people. On a holy day. Sons of bitches."

"We have to talk," Brad said. "You and I."

Paradiso nodded. He looked at his men. "*Umalis kayo*," he said—go away.

When the men were out of earshot, Paradiso said, "Don't tell me I did wrong, Coach."

Brad had thought the expedition was too hazardous and said so, but he was not going to repeat that now. Paradiso felt terrible enough. "No," he said, "I won't. You did what you thought best. That's all anybody ever has to go on."

Paradiso was silent for a time. "Good men," he said at last. Their epitaph.

"Yes. Especially Despido."

"Despido."

They both thought about Despido, the man Paradiso had selected to kill the Jap guards on the famous night when they blew up the ammo dump at Bamban. The man who helped screen all guerrilla candidates because he was so tough and mean and suspicious. The sabotage attempt had been Despido's idea—and was now his fate.

"Goddamn, Coach. Sometimes I have to let them *do* something. Can't say no all the time."

Brad nodded. They had discussed this many times. All very well for Amos Watson down in Manila to say their most important guerrilla assignment was to collect accurate information about Japanese strength and movement and activity. God knows they did that and did it damn well. They always gave a full report to Miranda, and she got the information down to Manila, one way or another, to Papaya. Miranda had no idea, and Brad and Paradiso had no idea, where the information went from there—or what good it did.

If American troops had been fighting right here in the Philippines, the value would be obvious. But according to the shortwave-radio hearsay, the American army had only got as far as New Guinea—and only southern New Guinea at that. That must be at least a couple of thousand miles from Manila. Even if their reports somehow reached MacArthur, what good could it do him to know, at that distance, what the Japs were doing around Clark Field? The Philippines was way out of bombing range.

Brad and Paradiso talked this over endlessly but of course never told the men their doubts about the value of the information gathered at such risk. For the men, it was not enough. They wanted action. They wanted to hurt the Japs right here and now—kill them, blow up their trucks, steal their ammunition and supplies, cut their communications, make their lives as miserable as they were making the lives of Filipinos.

Brad and Paradiso wanted that, too, but they had to choose targets with care, not only to avoid heavy risk but also to avoid retaliation against civilians. The Japs didn't care who was responsible, just so long as somebody got punished.

"We have to skip Clark Field," Brad said now. "It's too important to the Japs."

"Then it's important to me."

"We can still get information about it, find out everything. All the Filipinos who work there, they'll tell us. But we have to stop trying to damage it. It's too big. Too many guards and soldiers."

"I know," Paradiso said. He scowled. "I would like to cut them up. Each one."

"Maybe someday."

"Yes, someday."

"When MacArthur comes back."

"Maybe I will be too old then."

"How old are you now?"

"I don't know."

Brad guessed Paradiso was over forty and might even be fifty. There was much more gray in his hair than a year ago, but he was still hard as a rock. "Don't worry," Brad said. "I know you'll still be here. After all, Napoleon was about forty-five at Waterloo."

"That's the one he lost?"

"Yeah, but it was a hell of a fight."

"I am not losing."

The rest of Christmas Day they did not speak of Despido and the other two men. They had planned to roast a pig for Christmas dinner, but nobody in camp was in the mood. Rice cakes and vegetables for anyone who was hungry. That afternoon the fog swirled down from the mountaintops, and through the fog came rain.

Brad Stone lay on his mat under the shelter of the nipa roof, watching the fog and the rain dripping from the thatch. He wished Miranda were here. And Judy. But not at the same time, of course. He felt confused. And guilty. On that first day with Miranda he had not even read Judy's long, wonderful letter until Miranda left and it was too late to send back an answer. A terrible thing to do, especially when Judy's letter was so intimate and so eloquent about their old days together in Manila. Whatever could he have been thinking of to behave like that? He knew the answer perfectly well.

Miranda. What a delightful, happy woman, and what a cheerful lover. On her next visit, they again went to bed in the home of Rosauro's parents. While they were resting, she asked, "Why were you so quiet?"

Brad whispered, "I don't want them to hear us."

"They don't mind. They give us this room."

"Just the same."

"If they don't hear us, they think we aren't having a good time. They think maybe I am no good for you."

"Oh, you're very good for me."

"I am glad. You are nice for me too, Coach."

"My name's Brad, you know."

"No, you are Coach to me. I never before make love with an American. Have you with a Filipina?"

"No."

"Am I different?"

"Yes."

Miranda giggled. "Tell me."

"Well, for one thing, an American girl never uses Philippine words in bed."

"Is that nice?"

"I don't know what they mean."

"I will teach you. But I think maybe they sound a little dirty in English. What else?"

"An American girl never says '*Ay, ay, ay, ay*!' when she is—you know, when—"

"What do they say?"

"I don't know, different things. But not that."

"Okay, what else?"

"Well, your skin's a different color, of course. And then there's your gold tooth."

"Isn't it nice? A present from Mr. Watson. What else?"

Brad thought about the way her body felt so soft in all the right places but very muscular underneath. Growing up on a farm and doing so much hard work as a girl must have given her that strength. When her legs wrapped tight around him, she almost squeezed the breath out of him.

"I think," he said, "we should practice some more."

She sat up quickly on the bed, eager to play. "Okay. Then will you tell me?"

"If you're good."

"I will be very good for you, Coach." She smiled her warm, gold-tooth smile. "And you can tell me so. Out loud. They won't mind hearing."

Now Brad stared out at the Christmas rain and fog. He wondered how soon Miranda would be back. Bringing, of course, another letter from Judy.

Judy. Her letters made him feel for the first time that she might be serious about him. But he would not ask her again to marry him until all this was over—if they both made it. He wondered what she looked like now. Any different? That was over a year ago, their last night in Manila just before the war. He wished he had a picture of her, but he hadn't imagined they would be separated like this for such a long time.

People changed, of course, but he wasn't sure how much they changed. This past year, fighting the Japs and living in the mountains with Filipinos, was as different as possible from being a history teacher and basketball coach in a small American school. He had learned many new things, but at heart he thought he was the same person. He believed in the same things.

Judy was used to being popular, to having many dates with many different men. She loved the good life, and still missed it, as her long letter made clear. It had always been hard to pin her down, to cut her away from the pack that was Manila society. Would she ever be willing to give that up? He wondered what her life was like in Santo Tomas. There would be lots of men in there, young and old. Quite a lot of rich ones, too. Lots of men with time on their hands and nothing to do. He hoped Judy wasn't screwing around.

Like I am, he added.

————

Everybody in Cabanatuan who could play an instrument or carry a tune took part in the Christmas Eve show. Everybody else not confined to hospital came to the outdoor "theater"—a wide-open space with no stage and no seats—to listen and applaud. Even the Japs watched.

Jack Humphrey and Maxsie had discovered that between them they knew most of fourteen verses to "Abdul A-bul-bul Amir," and they patched together the lines they couldn't quite remember. Humphrey played that "bold mamaluke" Abdul, and Maxsie was his savage opponent, "the cream of the Muscovite team," Count Ivan Skavinski Skavar. Maxsie tried to talk the Japs into letting them borrow two bayonets for the big duel, but the commandant's lenient Christmas spirit did not extend to putting weapons in the hands of prisoners. When he refused, they made do with sticks. Each wore an enormous black mustache drawn on with charcoal. The mustache together with the livid birthmark made Maxsie look especially sinister when he "put on his most truculent sneer."

They sang equally badly—and with enormous success. The clatter of their wooden sticks during the duel was accompanied by their howls of rage and defiance and pain. At the end, as they lay on the ground, both mortally wounded, Abdul breathing his last sigh to the Sultan and Ivan exchanging a last line with Tsar Petrovitch, laughter rolled through their audience.

"Next stop Broadway," Maxsie said as they rose to take their bows to whistles and applause.

The orchestra was made up of instruments smuggled into camp one by one during the last months. The Japs were strict about smuggling, but once an object had actually made its way into Cabanatuan, they seemed curiously indifferent as to how it got there.

The orchestra played almost as badly as Humphrey and Maxsie sang, but with equal success. When it got to "My Blue Heaven," a Jap soldier watching the show grew very excited, smiling and clapping his hands and waving his arms in time with the music. It was obvious he knew the song. When it was over, the clarinet player beckoned the soldier to join them and sing along. At first, the soldier shook his head, but when the tune started up again, he suddenly changed his mind and sang it all the way through—in Japanese. His applause was as generous as anyone else's.

Next morning, Christmas, brought everything they had been promised. A day of rest with no work details. A special breakfast of extra rice with raisins and cocoa. A church service. And, most wonderful of all, for every man in camp an eleven-pound Red Cross food package.

Dear Sara,

I can't believe it. All the fake rumors and disappointments, all the feeling that we're forgotten men, and here I am looking at this incredible Christmas package. It's from the Red Cross, but as far as I'm concerned, it's from you and Terry and Jeff.

It's the best present I ever had. Thank you for everything. I hardly know where to start. Yes, I do. Thank you for the cigarettes. Also for the pipe tobacco. I can trade it to a pipe smoker for more cigarettes, but I think if I wait a couple of weeks, I can probably get a better deal.

Thank you for all the wonderful food. I'd forgotten some of this stuff ever existed. What do I like best? The canned meat, I guess. The corned beef and the tuna fish and the sardines. It's hard to know which one to open first. They're pretty just to look at. Also the cookies and crackers and cheese, and especially the hard candy. But I shouldn't really say "especially" about anything because it's all so great. The soup, the evaporated milk, the instant coffee, the whole works. Remember how I wouldn't drink instant coffee? Not anymore. You didn't leave out anything except the steak-and-kidney pie. I guess that wouldn't travel so well. You and Terry and Jeff must be around the

Christmas tree at your mother's, with a big turkey dinner coming up. I hope you gave the boys something with my name on it. Next Christmas I plan to take care of all that in person. I'm going to get you the best ring you ever saw. With all my back pay, we can afford it. We'll pick it out together. I don't care what you pick, as long as it's big.

I hope you got the postcards Maxsie and I sent you. That was quite a while ago, and no answer yet. Maxsie says Merry Christmas, by the way. He and I were a great hit singing "Abdul A-bul-bul Amir" at the Christmas show. Wish you could have heard us. We'll give you a special repeat performance when we get back.

Thanks again for everything. I miss not spending Christmas with you, but the presents are the next best thing. Give the boys a holiday hug for me. Merry Christmas, and let's hope it's a Happy New Year for all of us.

Love, Jack

= 21 =

Love at a Distance

Brad Stone was mixed up. To make it worse, he wasn't used to it.

Whenever he faced a problem or had a decision to make, he thought over the pros and cons, sometimes listing them on paper, and then made up his mind on the basis of what he thought was right. Although results were not always what he hoped, he had the satisfaction of doing the right thing.

He had become a teacher because he believed in education and the value of the lessons of history. He had gone to Simpson because he thought he could have more impact as a teacher and coach at a small school, and because he knew that his own knowledge would be enriched by several years in the very different world of the Philippines. He had left Simpson to volunteer for the army because he thought his country needed him. And he had become a guerrilla because he knew somebody had to go on fighting. None of these had been a particularly difficult decision. They were all clear-cut.

But now this. Now Judy and Miranda. He didn't

know what he thought, or even what he ought to think. There were Judy's letters, longer and warmer each time, almost everything he could have hoped for in those last prewar days when he asked her to marry him. Her "love" was mentioned in every letter. True, it was only scribbled at the end, almost as an afterthought, but it was always there. And "love" was in every letter he sent back to her.

Neither of them mentioned the word "marriage." He knew he must save that subject until they met again—if that ever happened. But it was in his mind. Perhaps it was in hers, too. She used to say, lighthearted Judy, that she wasn't ready even to think about marriage, to him or to anybody else, because she was having too good a time just the way it was. But now, of course, all that was changed. Internment in Santo Tomas replaced the good times in Manila. Maybe Judy had changed, too. He wished he could talk to her, really sit down and talk and discuss and find out. But there were only the letters.

And all their letters were delivered by Miranda. He looked forward with fierce impatience to Miranda's visits and to the lovemaking they shared with more and more pleasure each time. Although he was not *in* love with her, or didn't think he was, he certainly loved her and had wonderful times with her.

And then, after each time, he would have to pull himself together to write a letter for Miranda to take back to Judy, with whom he *was* in love. This process became so awkward that now he wrote the bulk of his letter to Judy ahead of time, before Miranda's visit. Then all he had to do at the last minute was add a few appropriate lines of response after he read her letter. More efficient that way, although it made him feel guilty.

None of this seemed to bother Miranda. She took life simply, without complications. And it couldn't bother Judy, who didn't know about it. But it certainly bothered Brad.

———

Reading Brad's latest letter, Judy wondered how much he might have changed. He sounded as affectionate and as serious as ever, but surely guerrilla life must have changed him in some other ways. Perhaps important ways. Living out there in the mountains— a lonely, dangerous life, Amos Watson said—must make a great difference, but Judy couldn't tell by his letters what that difference might be. Maybe it didn't really matter. The main thing was that Brad, unlike all the men around her in Santo Tomas, was free. On his own. Not under the Japs. It was exhilarating to think about, even though it made her jealous. She would give anything to be out of STIC.

After poring over his letter several times, she went to visit Amos, who was reading in his shanty.

"Well," Amos said, putting down his book as she walked up the plank steps, "did you get a nice letter?"

"You're asking me?"

"Oh, *I* thought it was a nice letter. But did you?"

"Yes. Wonderful."

"I'm glad we agree."

"Amos, can I ask you something?"

"Of course. Here, take this chair."

"No, the stool is fine. Does Brad say anything in his letters to you? I mean, things I don't know?"

Amos took a while to answer, and then all he said was, "Like what?"

"About himself. What he's like today."

"You mean, is he well? Yes, he's fine. Very healthy, I understand. But surely from your own letters—"

"No, I don't mean health. I mean, does he say anything to you about what he's like inside? What he's thinking?"

Amos shook his head and smiled. "No, we just discuss business."

"Business! Brad never cared about business."

"Guerrilla business. In fact, I learn much more about Coach from his letters to you than I do from his letters to me." Amos smiled again. "Mine are much shorter."

"Could I read them?"

"No, I'm sorry. That's not possible."

"Why not? Especially if they're so short."

"It's just better that way. Take my word for it."

"You ask me to take your word for an awful lot of things."

"Yes, well. Just be glad he's alive and able to write to you."

"I am. I'm very grateful. It's the most exciting thing that happens around here. The only exciting thing."

"My pleasure. But Judy, I've been thinking. There is something you could do for me in return."

Judy was instantly on guard. Was Amos going to make a proposition after all?

It must have showed in her face, because Amos

threw back his head and laughed. "No, no, young
Judy. Your honor is safe with me, I assure you."

Judy was put out, both because she'd been caught
thinking that and then because of his much-too-quick
assurance. "What is it?" she asked stiffly.

"Well, as you know, I'm sort of out of things here.
Not on any of the committees. I kind of miss knowing
what's going on. Habit, I guess." He shook his head
in sadness, apparently remembering the way it used
to be before the war. "When I was in business, I liked
keeping track of everything. Now I can't." He shook
his head again, then looked at her. "I was wondering,
since you work in the records office, if you'd mind
filling me in on this and that. From time to time."

"What sort of this and that?"

Amos, who was never vague, looked rather vague.
"Oh, you know. Numbers. Camp statistics. For instance, how many people are in here this month? I
know it keeps changing all the time, as the Japs move
people in and out. Or food supplies—how much do
we have in that emergency reserve? Or medical reports. How much TB? How much beri-beri? How
many heart attacks?" He waved a hand. "That sort
of thing."

Judy knew men too well to be fooled by Amos's
guileless look. "You want to know all about camp
conditions. Why?"

"Just curiosity. An old man's curiosity. As you say,
there's not much excitement here. It would help me
pass the time. I thought since I was running a post
office for you and Coach, you wouldn't mind . . ."

Whyever he wants it and whatever he plans to do

with it, Judy thought, it seems like a fair trade. Besides, it was no problem for her, since she had to work on those files every day. "Okay," she said. "You ask me something and I'll try to find out. But I can't get you copies of anything. The paper shortage, you know."

"No, no, of course not." He considered this as though he had never thought of it before. "Maybe, though—say at the end of a day—you could bring out a record sheet and let me look at it, and then put it back the next morning. I've always found," he explained, "that I'm more comfortable seeing numbers for myself."

"I suppose so. But it would have to go back right away. The Triumvirate's very fussy about the records."

"I'm sure. Oh, and another thing, Judy. Just as we don't discuss our mail system with anybody, it might be a good idea to keep this strictly between us."

Judy couldn't help smiling. "You really love secrets, don't you?"

"Well, I've always believed in privacy. Even here, where there isn't much available."

"You don't have to worry. If the Triumvirate found out what you're asking me to do, I'd be the one in trouble. They're always saying that after the war the records will help them write an important history about Santo Tomas. I can't imagine who'd want to read it, but that's what they think."

"Yes," Amos said, "no doubt. Of course, you only get history after something's all over. I've always been more interested in here and now."

———

When they'd finished arguing about how many of the new pesos should be spent to redeem the farmers' food chits, Brad changed the subject.

"Paradiso, were you ever married?"

"Yes. One time. Long time ago. She died having baby. Baby died too." He shrugged. "Too much trouble. Why you ask, Coach? You ever married?"

"No. But I'm thinking about it."

"Miranda?"

"Well—uh—no, not exactly."

Paradiso grunted. "Right. Too much trouble, Coach. Have fun with a nice *dalaga*, Miranda is very nice. But men like us, it's no time to marry. Or Miranda either."

"Oh, not now, I agree. Actually I was thinking about after the war." Brad felt embarrassed by what he was about to say, but Paradiso was the only one to talk to. "Actually I was thinking—there's this girl in Santo Tomas."

"Sure. The one sends the letters."

"That's right. Judy. I knew her before the war. I liked her a lot."

"More than Miranda?"

"Well, in a different way."

Paradiso smiled. "There's only one way, Coach. Make *suksok*. Everything else, just trouble."

If only it were as simple as that, Brad thought. "I keep worrying I'm not being fair to Judy. Or to Miranda, either."

"I don't know this Judy, but very far away. Long

war. And Miranda, she is having good time with you, and later she will marry rich Filipino farmer and have many babies. Why worry?"

But Brad did worry, and not just about fairness. He had no idea what life was like in internment camp. He understood why neither Judy nor Amos could write any revealing details. But Judy had been so popular before the war that he couldn't believe she was any less popular in Santo Tomas. She never wrote anything about that, but then he never wrote about Miranda. He hoped the Japs who ran Santo Tomas were strict about sex.

An unworthy thought, but it must get pretty boring down there. And a popular, beautiful woman with all that time on her hands . . .

———

"What do you suppose a guerrilla does all day?" Millie Barnes asked.

"They're supposed to be busy bothering the Japs," Sammy said. "But from the evidence, I think what a guerrilla mostly does is write love letters."

All three laughed.

Judy felt comfortable talking with Millie and Sammy about Brad. Even though Sammy pretended to be hurt by what he called Judy's "infidelity," he was really as sympathetic as Millie. Brad was a different subject from all the standard Santo Tomas topics that everybody had already jabbered to death. Best of all, it was their secret that nobody else in STIC knew about. Except Amos, of course, but Judy had never told Sammy and Millie who her pipeline was, and they were careful never to ask.

"From his letters," Judy said, "it's what he calls 'a very quiet life.' I suppose he has to say that. I have to read between the lines, because we both have to be so careful. He says it's mostly 'keeping in touch with friends.' That means," she explained with authority, courtesy of Amos, "both our own people and the Japs."

"Well, I think it's just nifty," Millie said. "We all get messages from Manila friends, but that's nothing like hearing from a real live guerrilla. You've got to feel real proud, Judy."

She did feel proud. Nobody else in camp had what she had. It was very special. "I do," she said. "I just wish I knew where he was."

"You still can't figure it out?"

"No, never a hint. Just that he's in the mountains." She knew that Amos knew where Brad was, but to her extreme annoyance he wouldn't tell her.

"That could be almost anywhere," Sammy said. "Lots of mountains. I'll bet it's up around Baguio, since you say he taught school there. He'd probably go back to the place he knows best."

"That's what I'd guess, too," Millie said. "But he could be on Bataan. That's the nearest mountains."

"I keep trying to imagine him," Judy said. "How he looks, how he lives."

"You don't remember how he looks?"

"Oh, very well! He has these bright, bright blue eyes, and wavy hair, sort of reddish-blond. And he's a good athlete, very strong and light on his feet. Good shoulders. Oh, I remember all that. No, I mean, how does he look today? How is he dressed? Maybe he's grown a beard. Or a mustache."

"You must be quite a couple together," Millie said. "You going to marry him?"

"We don't talk about that."

"Why not?"

"It's—well, he's— I told you, Millie. Brad and I want different things."

"Hell, that's no problem," Sammy said. "Millie and I, we want different things, too. What I'd like is a really snappy young girl like—well, mentioning no names, but start with big green eyes and long pretty legs. And Millie, what she'd like is a glamorous guer-rilla about six feet tall. But here we are."

Millie slapped his shoulder, and they smiled at each other.

Yes, Judy thought, but they really want the same life. Brad and I don't. It has nothing to do with love. We want different things. Unless he's changed. Unless, of course, he's changed.

———

Judy was seeing much more of Amos Watson since she began bringing him reports from the internee rec-ord office. Amos's appetite for numbers was quite remarkable. He was always asking her for something.

Whenever possible, when she finished her day's work, she would slip the appropriate sheet of paper under her skirt or inside her blouse. Sometimes too many people were bustling around the office, but usu-

ally she had no trouble. Then she would deliver the
sheet to Amos at his shanty. She rather enjoyed it.
Amos was always grateful. He would scan the sheet
in intent silence for a few moments, then smile and
hand it back to her. The first few times she thought
he must be uninterested, because he did it so quickly.
But once when she began to speak while he was reading, he frowned, never taking his eyes from the paper,
and quickly held up his hand to stop her talking.

When he gave it back, she said, "You're memo-
rizing that stuff, aren't you? How can you do that so
fast?"

"Oh, if you're used to numbers," he said. "Now
how about some sardines and crackers?"

He always had a snack for her, brought in like
everyone else's goodies through the Package Line.
Judy thought money might be even more important
in Santo Tomas than it had been on the outside.

Once or twice the young man Felix Logan was at
the shanty when Judy came. She knew Amos was sort
of looking after Felix, making sure he got enough to
eat, because his parents were interned in Cebu. She
did not need Amos's slight shake-of-the-head warning
to tell her to keep her sheet of paper out of sight while
Felix was there.

"You're very nice to him," she said after Felix left.

"Well, he's a very nice boy. And pretty much alone
here."

"Alone! Nobody's alone in STIC."

"No, but his school friends are up in Baguio, and
his parents—old friends of mine—are way down in
Cebu. Besides, Felix works in the commandant's of-

fice. That doesn't make him too popular with other kids."

"There's a job I wouldn't do."

"No, I wouldn't either. I can't figure out why he does it, although I suppose somebody has to."

"As long as it isn't me."

"Or me."

But Judy didn't want to talk about Felix Logan. "Amos, I've been thinking a lot about Brad. Do you suppose he's changed at all?"

"Oh, I suppose so. It's quite an unusual experience he's having. That's bound to have some effect."

"That's what I think. I just wonder if he's any more practical."

"Now there's a romantic thought for a young woman in love."

"I never said I was in love."

"True. Anyway, if it will cheer you up, I suspect that guerrilla life is extremely practical."

"Oh, I don't at all. It must be so—so exciting. Compared to this."

"Well, but there's a certain amount of necessary drudgery in almost anything you do."

"How can you say that about Brad's life? He's out there free. He's fighting the Japs. Blowing up things."

"Yes, that part would be nice. But he must also have to pay a lot of attention to getting food and clothes for his men. And making sure he doesn't get caught by all the Japs who are looking for him. It's a hard life."

"I know, you always say that. But I think it must be a wonderful life."

"Well, Judy, what do you want? Do you want him to be carefree and gallant? Or do you want him to learn to be more 'practical'?"

She thought hard about it. "Both, I guess."

"And what about you? Has all this made you more practical?"

"Oh, I've always been practical. It's Brad I wonder about."

———

A warm, hazy, quiet afternoon. No breeze stirred the dusty streets of Carabangay.

Miranda smiled and waved, then clucked to her horse.

Brad and Rosauro and Rosauro's mother waved back from the front steps as the horsecart rolled away for the trip back to San Fernando. Just before the cart disappeared around the corner, Miranda leaned out to give them a final wave. She was carrying Brad's notes to Judy and Amos and, in her head, all the information collected by the guerrillas since her last visit.

It would be at the very least two weeks before they saw her again. More likely a month, and perhaps even longer, although she always promised to come back as soon as possible.

As Brad and Rosauro climbed up the mountain through the warm afternoon sunshine, Brad thought about Judy—or tried to. It was hard to think about Judy when he had just spent such a good time with Miranda.

It wasn't only the lovemaking, although that was

certainly wonderful. Miranda was also delightful
company, whether alone with him or talking with the
others. The whole camp liked her, even Paradiso, and
not just for the gifts she brought. Although she talked
about Brad and the guerrillas being "the brave ones"
and called herself "only a messenger," he considered
her as brave as any of them. She had to face the Jap
soldiers far more often than they did. Each time she
went through a checkpoint, she ran the risk that her
cart would be searched and the supplies discovered.
Brad was proud that she was very especially his.

But, he reminded himself, so was Judy. Judy. Sometimes when he took out all her letters and reread them,
he could convince himself that she was thinking solely
of him. That was how the letters sounded. But this
afternoon, for some reason, his thoughts went the
other way. She must surely have a liaison in Santo
Tomas. Maybe several.

Just the thought made him jealous.

———

Judy thought later that she might not have done it,
or not done it quite that way, except for the coincidence of timing.

After a month's wait another letter from Brad finally came through. She snatched it from Amos and
hurried away to her most private place beside the
corner window of Room 6. It was a short letter, just
both sides of a single small piece of paper, but it was
warm and loving. She glowed with pleasure. She read
it over three times. Then she folded it and tucked it

in her pocket to read again before going to bed that night.

When she left the Main Building and walked out into the plaza, Frank Otis was waiting for her, holding a small package.

"Hey, Judy," he said. "They told me you were here. Guess what I got through the Package Line today?"

She didn't really want to talk to him just now. "What?"

"Two perfect little steaks. Of course, I thought of you right away."

This was probably true. Frank did keep after her, ever hopeful, and shared many treats with her. She knew he considered her an adornment when she went with him to one of the little STIC "restaurants" or visited his shanty. He always had money. Even though she kept her physical distance, resisting his attempts at patting and pawing, she knew from what some women said that Frank spread the impression she was as generous to him as he was to her.

"We'll take them down to my shanty," Frank said now. "Just imagine how they'll taste over charcoal. I'll cook them for us."

But she had just put Brad's letter in her pocket. "No thanks, Frank."

He looked surprised. "What do you mean, no thanks? These are real steaks. Fresh. Come on."

"No, I'm not coming."

"What's the matter with you?"

Then she heard herself saying, "It's not me. It's you."

"What's that mean?"

"I don't like your hands."

"I don't get it." He held out his soft, plump hands and looked at them. "What's wrong with my hands?"

"Everything. And I don't really like you, either."

She turned away, leaving him standing in the plaza with his little package of steaks.

That's not like me, she thought. That's not like me at all. I just burned a bridge.

Just the same, she felt good about it.

═ 22 ═

Honorable Revenge

Eli Phipps could feel the boiling excitement as soon
as he walked into the big Quonset hut. A dozen men,
including General Sampson himself, were huddled
around the table where a radio operator with earphones was taking down a message.

"What's going on, sir?" Phipps asked.

Red Sampson looked up. "Eli," he said, as though
announcing the Second Coming, "we're talking to
Mindanao."

At last, Phipps thought, they were in touch with
the main southern island of the Philippines. They
weren't "talking" to Mindanao, of course. They were
receiving dots and dashes that made up coded five-
letter groups.

"Who is it, sir?" Phipps asked.

"Some guerrilla leader nobody ever heard of. The
navy monitor station picked him up in San Francisco.
They've checked him out and handed him over to
us."

The radio operator put down his pencil, tapped
out an acknowledgment and took off his earphones.

He gave that sheet of paper to General Sampson, whose hand was stretched out for it.

"How can he have any current codes?"

"He doesn't," Sampson said. "This is double transposition. San Francisco set up the key words with him. His family's names—wife, sister, daughter—hometown, birthplace, all that. Things only he would know. That's how they proved he wasn't a Jap station."

Double transposition was a simple but effective coding device, provided both sender and receiver knew the key words that set the pattern. Phipps had learned double transposition long ago in cryptography class. The clear message was transposed into a box of letters according to the dictates imposed by the key word, then transposed again according to the dictates of the second key word. The double-encoded message was sent in five-letter groups that gave enemy cryptanalysts no clue to the length of individual words.

"Wait till the Old Man reads this," Sampson said. He handed the message to a code clerk to decipher. "He's going to flip."

Although they had heard from transmitters in the central islands of Panay and Negros, this was the first message from Mindanao. Phipps knew, like everyone else, that Mindanao would be MacArthur's first Philippine landing place, once the New Guinea campaign was over.

That might be a long time, Phipps thought. When the Japanese stronghold of Buna finally fell, Eichelberger's troops had gone on to wipe out nearby Gona and Sanananda Point. MacArthur described it as "a mopping-up operation." Some mop-up. Altogether, MacArthur lost over three thousand dead and over five thousand wounded before that little eastern corner of New Guinea coast was secure. Far worse than Guadalcanal.

The message from Mindanao turned out to be disappointing. Instead of giving information, it asked for supplies and ammunition and weapons and medicine. That didn't matter. It was a first step. Information would surely come.

———

Papaya was nervous. Hitoshi Buto was bringing his navy son, Shimayo, to the Mabalinga Club for the first time. Papaya was told exactly how to behave.

"You will know who I am," Buto said, "because I have told Shimayo I come here often. I have also told him I think you sing our lovesongs very well. But you and I are not intimate. We are only acquaintances. You will come to our table, but only when I invite you. And you will sit down with us only if I ask you."

"So are you going to ask me?"

"That will depend on Shimayo."

"I thought he was only a gunnery officer. How come he decides?"

Buto looked at her coldly—what she called his admiral look. "I will decide," he said. "But it will depend on his reaction."

"Toshi, what makes you think he doesn't already know about us?"

"Of course he knows. Somebody has told him. But out of respect to his mother, it would be impolite for either of us to acknowledge it."

"So he knows we have an affair, but we all pretend we don't?"

"Exactly."

"And if he likes my singing, maybe he comes back to Mabalinga every night, and we go on pretending?"

"Yes."

"God! How long is he going to be here?"

"Six days. They sail first thing Sunday morning."

That meant Papaya would have six nights when she could go straight home from the club. Her mother would be pleased.

Buto sighed. "I wish I were going back to sea with him."

"I hope it is a long trip."

"That is a rude remark."

"I'm sorry, but I will need to rest up after all this pretending."

Buto smiled. He was never angry with her for more than a moment or two. "You will have plenty of time. It is the same old patrol cruise, out around Palawan and then down to Mindanao. Shimayo finds it boring."

Papaya saw them enter the Mabalinga just after she started a set. Shimayo, dressed in a white uniform like his father, was a little taller and slimmer. She had known from the picture Toshi kept on his dresser that Shimayo wore a pencil-thin black mustache, not a full bushy one like his father's. He had black hair cut short. He was rather handsome, for a Jap, but lacked

Hitoshi's big mournful eyes. As she sang, she watched them sit down at Buto's usual table and order drinks.

She ended her set with one of the lovesongs Buto had taught her. It was supposed to be a favorite of Shimayo's, so she put a little extra sentiment into it. Hard to do with the Japanese words. She was never going to like this language.

She hung around the bandstand for a few minutes, talking with her trio about the next set. When no summons came, she decided Shimayo must not have liked her singing and returned to her dressing room. As soon as she closed the door, a knock came.

Aurelio Lopez, the manager. "Surprise, surprise," he said. Aurelio never stopped taking little digs at her. But she was too valuable for him to say anything really nasty. "Admiral Buto wants you to come to his table."

"Thanks," she said, and closed the door on him to check her makeup.

Another knock. "Papaya? If you don't come right away, he will think I didn't give you the message."

She let Aurelio worry while she patted the perspiration from her face with a paper towel and put on fresh lipstick. Toshi could wait, too. He should not take her for granted.

When she approached the table, neither of them stood up to greet her, as Amos Watson and most Americans would have done.

"Good evening, Papaya," Buto said, in a formal but not unfriendly voice. Both men had glasses of beer in front of them. "We enjoyed your singing. This is my son, Shimayo."

"Good evening, lieutenant," she said, equally formal.

Shimayo looked her over, his father's mistress. Up close he was less handsome than in his photograph. Even sitting down, he held himself stiffly, as though on parade. Maybe because he was seated beside an important admiral, who was only incidentally his father. He was in his late twenties, a few years older than Papaya. He struck her as arrogant, like so many Jap naval officers. His first words confirmed the impression.

"You sing the 'Hyacinth' song quite nicely," he said. His voice was lighter than his father's deep bass. His English was clipped, learned in the schoolroom. "It is interesting to hear a Filipino pronounce Japanese words."

"Thank you." She bowed her head in false gratitude, then decided to correct him. "I am a Filipina, not a Filipino. We say it both ways, masculine and feminine."

Hitoshi Buto, who had been beaming proudly at his son, turned quickly to Papaya, having caught her tone, but she had a wide innocent smile all ready for him.

"Will you be in Manila long, lieutenant?"

He hesitated. "A few days."

"That's nice. I hope you have a pleasant time in our city."

"I am afraid it is not a time for pleasure."

So what was he doing here at the Mabalinga Club? And what about those fancy dinners with his father at the Manila Hotel? "Oh? Such a pity. Maybe on your next visit."

She was slightly disappointed that Buto did not invite her to sit down, because she had made up her mind to say she had to get ready for her next set.

When she returned to the bandstand fifteen minutes later, they had already left.

Next day she reported to Zorro.

"Two freighters and an oil tanker are arriving Wednesday. Buto is concerned because so much unloading comes all at one time."

"Good. What are their names?"

"He didn't say."

"Did you ask?"

She shrugged. "Sometimes it's easy to ask. Sometimes not. Anyway, I think all freighters and tankers are the same to him. He doesn't care, except about how the port handles them."

"Yes, but we care. It's interesting to know which ships are coming in, and how often they come here. You must try to get more facts."

She shrugged again. She had learned not to be hurt by Sansone's constant requests for more details than she was able to collect. "I met his son last night."

"Yes, I know."

"You know everything."

"No, no, Peanut, don't be testy. What did you think of him?"

"Not too nice. We only spent a few minutes. But Buto dotes on him."

"What did the son say about his cruiser?"

"Nothing."

Enrique Sansone was plainly disappointed, just as she intended him to be. But now she told him what she had been saving for last.

"You want to know about the *Kyishi*? It is sailing Sunday morning."

"How do you know that?"

"Because I am such a good spy."

"What time?"

"Thirteen minutes after six."

"Don't joke, Peanut."

"Then don't ask that kind of question. But it is first thing Sunday morning, I know that. So maybe six o'clock? Maybe seven o'clock?"

"Very good."

"That's not all. *Kyishi* is going all the way around Palawan on patrol and then down to Mindanao. After that, I don't know where it goes. Also, Buto's son finds it boring because nothing ever happens."

"Very good, Peanut. Now try to get more ships' names."

"I won't see Buto again until the son leaves."

"Why not?"

"It is out of respect for the wife and mother."

Zorro shook his head. "A curious people."

———

Two weeks later Papaya was getting ready to leave for the club when Buto's black Packard drove up to her house. His driver came to the front door and insisted on seeing her. Annoyed, she went to the door.

The driver handed her a sealed envelope with the crest of the Imperial Japanese Navy.

She opened it and read Buto's curt, handwritten message: "Cancel club. Come at once."

This was too much. He had never summoned her like this. Several times when he had not come to the club, he sent his driver to pick her up after the performance. That was all right, she didn't mind that. In fact, one of those times when she walked into his suite, he was lying on the living-room floor, completely naked, ready for her. He would not even let her take off her dress. It was very exciting.

This was different. A blunt order to skip her performance an hour before she was due to appear. And a second blunt order to report for duty in his suite. She knew what that meant. And without even a "please." She was not used to such discourtesy. She would teach him a lesson, teach him manners, and go to the club. It was flattering that he was so hungry for her, but his rudeness was not acceptable.

Then she reminded herself what Enrique Sansone always told her: *This is a job, think of it as a job.* Buto was not normally rude to her. If he wanted her as desperately as this, maybe she could use the occasion to get some of the information Zorro was always asking for. She would try to get the names of two freighters tonight but would settle for one. Besides, she thought with a certain curiosity, maybe he has some new game in mind. He was such an inventive lover.

She told the driver to wait while she phoned the

Mabalinga to say she had severe stomach cramps and could not appear tonight. Then she climbed into the backseat of the Packard and was driven to the Manila Hotel. The sun had already set over the bay. The sky was a darkening purple. She hummed "Deep Purple" to herself. She missed hearing the new American songs.

The stone-faced doorman took his time opening the car door for her. She was used to it now. She walked across the spacious white-and-green lobby, still beautiful even under military rule, and told the elevator operator third floor. He did not answer. She was used to that, too.

At the corner suite she knocked. "Come at once" was the message, and now she had to wait. She knocked again. Finally his deep voice said, "Who is it?"

"Me."

A long pause before the door opened.

She could barely see his figure in the dark foyer. The dim light from the corridor showed he was wearing a floor-length white kimono. The apartment was dark behind him. She could not see his face. She wondered if the darkness was somehow part of his new game, whatever it was.

"So here I am. What's the big hurry?"

"Come in," he said, stepping back from the door.

When she walked through, he closed it behind her. Now it was completely dark.

"What is this?"

"I'm sorry," he said. "Wait, I'll turn on some lights. I didn't realize it had gotten so dark."

While he was finding the light switch, she heard his voice say out of the darkness, "My son is dead. Shimayo has been killed."

"Oh, Toshi! How terrible!"

"Yes."

The lights came on in the living room, first the overhead light and then the two lamps beside the couch. The lamplight gleamed against the pale cowrie-shell shutters. He crossed the room to slide back the shutters, letting in the night air and the sight of a rising half-moon.

He turned to face her. His expression was calm, stoic. The big mournful eyes held no self-pity. He must have been talking to himself for hours to arrive at this level of acceptance.

"How did it happen?"

The answer came with the detached precision of a senior naval officer making a formal report. "An American submarine at Balabac Strait. *Kyishi* took two torpedoes, one forward, one amidships. There was severe damage. And heavy casualties. The ammunition blew up. The fires could not be controlled. The captain was able to run his ship aground on Balabac Island before it sank, so some of the crew survived. But *Kyishi* is almost a total loss, except for what can be salvaged. When the rescue operations were completed, the captain killed himself."

Buto turned away and stared out the window at the moon. "He was my classmate at the academy," he said in a different voice. "That was why I arranged Shimayo's assignment to his ship."

"What about Shimayo?"

"He was on the forward gun turret. No one survived."

"Are you sure? Maybe——"

He interrupted her. "One thing about being an admiral," he said, "is that everyone is careful to give you accurate information."

"How long have you been sitting here alone?"

Buto shrugged and turned away from the window. "All afternoon. I had to—think about Shimayo. I had to console myself that he died in the service of the Emperor, as he would have wished. And then I had to write my family to tell them. They will be very—upset. Particularly Taki, who admired his older brother extravagantly. Perhaps too much. Then finally I didn't want to be alone anymore, so I asked you to come."

"It is very sad," Papaya said. She felt sorry for him, truly sorry, but she could not help gloating that one whole Jap cruiser had been destroyed, along with many enemy sailors. All she wished was that his son could have been one of the survivors. "Where is this Balabac?" she asked. "I never heard of it."

Back to the official tone. "It is at the southern tip of Palawan. The strait connects the South China Sea and the Sulu Sea. *Kyishi* was on her way to Mindanao, and the submarine must have been lying in wait just outside the strait. It is a dangerous place. Obviously our antisubmarine defenses must be improved in that area. Immediately."

It was as though he were giving orders.

"Would you like a drink? Have you had anything to eat?"

"No, I'm not hungry."

"What about a beer? Or some saki?"

"Well, yes, perhaps some saki."

"I will heat it. Sit down and rest."

She went into the kitchenette, where she poured the saki into a pot and heated it to the temperature of tea. She had never been much good in kitchens, but she could manage saki, which Toshi often asked for after making love. She had grown to like it, and he had trained her never to let it boil. When it was warm enough, she poured it carefully into the small porcelain pitcher and placed it on a tray with two tiny porcelain cups. He had brought this saki serving set from his home in Japan.

When she returned to the living room, he was sitting on the couch with his hands clasped in front of him. She placed the tray on the coffee table and bent over to pour the saki. He had told her that Japanese women usually knelt to pour, but Papaya explained that she was not Japanese and that her figure was not designed for kneeling.

She placed the warm cup in his hand and took the other for herself.

He rose to his feet. He stood very straight in his white kimono with the wide, short sleeves and the broad black sash at the waist. "To the memory of my son," he said in a thick voice.

"To your son," she said. And to herself she added, *To that submarine*. Was it possible? Could it be possible?

They drained their cups. Then Hitoshi Buto burst into tears.

Papaya held his bald head against her breast and stroked it while he wept. He went on and on. When his tears finally stopped, she persuaded him to come to bed, where she was able to distract him with gentle and thorough attentions.

Afterward he was not at all sleepy. He wanted to talk, not only about Shimayo and his family, but also about the war and his work, and about his desire, now stronger than ever, to return to sea. They finished a second pitcher of saki and talked long, long into the night.

Papaya got her two freighters and much more besides.

———

"Peanut, that is very good. In fact, extraordinary."

Zorro had never used that word about any report she had ever given. She knew she had earned it.

"You're quite sure what he said about the cruiser?"

"Yes, yes. 'A total loss.' "

"What kind of antisubmarine defenses will they put in?"

"He didn't say."

"That's a pity."

"How come you never satisfied?"

"Oh, I'm very satisfied. But one always hopes for more. It gets to be a habit."

"Tell me something. Important. Did I sink the *Kyishi*?"

He looked at her. He twisted his head and she heard the little crick in his neck go *pop*. "Don't be silly, Peanut. That U.S. submarine sank the *Kyishi*."

"You know what I'm asking. Was it my information?"

He sighed. "I can't say."

"That's not fair. Not after I do all this."

"You misunderstand. I am not able to say. I don't know. I passed on what you told me, the departure time and the route. After that . . ." He shrugged. "Who can say?"

"You think it is just some crazy coincidence that the Americans know exactly where that cruiser is going and when, and then that submarine just happens to be sitting right there in that Balabac place?"

He smiled. "Perhaps a little farfetched. But I don't think we'll ever know. Maybe after the war. Maybe not even then."

"Good. Until you find out different, it is my ship."

"All right, agreed. Now, Peanut, you must encourage our admiral to return to sea."

"He doesn't need encouraging. It's what he wants all along."

"Yes, but now he has lost number-one son. He should have revenge." With his forefinger he slashed his Mark of Zorro in the air. He laughed. "Honorable revenge. Maybe his superiors will respect that wish."

"But why get rid of him? Then I won't get any more information and sink any more ships. Unless you think I am going to fuck the next admiral too."

Sansone laughed with delight. Her occasional vulgarities always amused him. "No, no, perhaps General Miyama next. Now seriously, Peanut. Buto is a very good port administrator. Very efficient. Also better than most Japs at handling Filipino workers.

Whoever replaces him can't possibly be as good. And of course will have to learn the job."

"If you know all that, the Japs must know it."

"All we can do is encourage him."

"Who is this 'we'?"

"All right. I encourage you, and you encourage him, is that better?"

"Yes."

"Now tell me again what he said about their difficulties in New Guinea and the Solomons."

"Why? Weren't you listening?"

"Let's go over it again. You might have left something out. Besides, I like it."

———

Papaya was at home the night her house and grounds were vandalized. They came at four in the morning.

She was sound asleep when the screams of her half sister, Karen, woke her. As she jumped out of bed, she heard the crash of window glass. She pulled on a robe as she ran out of her bedroom to find out what was happening. The house was dark.

She found all her household in the living room— Karen screaming, her mother whimpering, the terrified servants. A rock hurled from the yard shattered another window, spraying shards of glass across the floor.

"Get back!" she yelled. "Everybody get back! Don't turn on any lights. Karen, shut up. Shut up, goddamn it."

She grabbed the phone and called the metropolitan

police. Then the Jap security force. Then, just in case, she insisted that the Manila Hotel operator wake up Buto. When she finally got him to understand what was happening, he promised to send men at once.

By the time the large quantity of help arrived, the yard was silent and deserted. They turned on all the living-room lights, and she had to answer questions over and over again. Men with flashlights and pistols roamed back and forth through the yard, looking for evidence. There was plenty of it.

Her flower gardens were trampled and smashed. Horse dung and human excrement littered the walkways. Cardboard signs, painted in black, were planted in the lawn. They read: "Jap singer!" and "Jap whore!" and "Traitor!"

Karen was so hysterical that Papaya sent her off to bed with her mother and one of the servants to soothe her. While Papaya answered questions, two other servants swept up the broken glass.

When she had calmed down a little, Papaya realized there was actually very little damage aside from the broken windows. The yard was a mess but could be cleaned up. Even the flower gardens could be replanted in a few days. But when would they come again?

The Jap officer treated her with great respect. Through an interpreter he expressed his regret, deplored the vandalism in Manila and suggested that she hire a full-time guard.

"I thought you were supposed to protect loyal citizens."

When this was translated, the officer bowed and said that unfortunately his forces could not protect every private home against these evil elements.

Papaya saw no reason to spend her own money. She would ask Buto to provide protection. After all, much of this was his fault.

In the morning she had a difficult telephone interview with Sandy Homobono.

"Who were the men?"

"No idea. I didn't see them."

"Do you think it was because you sing at the Mabalinga Club?"

"Probably. One sign said 'Jap singer.' "

"What about the one that said 'Jap whore'?"

"You aren't going to print that, Sandy?"

"Well, it's part of what happened last night. Do you think it could be because of your relationship with Admiral Buto?"

No comment.

She warned Buto about the interview, and he must have taken care of it. The story that appeared was totally sympathetic to her and did not mention the "Jap whore" sign. It did say that from now on the singer's home would be heavily guarded.

When she told Sansone about the event, he did not seem disturbed. "No real damage," he said.

"What about my family and servants?"

"Well, they weren't hurt either, were they?"

"They were scared to death."

"They'll get over it. Especially with your new guards."

"It's not fair. I am doing all this dangerous stuff for our people, and they wreck my house."

"That proves you are doing a good job. Who is going to suspect you now?"

Something in his voice, some note of satisfaction, made her realize what must have happened. No serious damage, nobody hurt. Yes, and no one could suspect such a victim of being a spy.

"Enrique, you did this. You did it."

"I was home in bed."

"Your people did it. I know it. Goddamn you. You owe me for all those windows. And the flowers."

"I think somehow the Japs will pay for everything. Our admiral has a great deal of influence."

"Why the hell didn't you warn me? We wouldn't have been so scared."

"But Peanut, it was better for you to be scared and raise so much fuss. You were perfect."

"Somebody could have been hurt."

"Oh, I hardly think so. They were very good men. Very careful."

"Karen could have had a heart attack."

"At sixteen? Surely not."

"My mother, then."

"Peanut, you are grasping at straws. Your mother is a strong person."

"I could have had a heart attack. I could lose my voice from shock."

"My dear Peanut, that would be difficult to imagine."

The Great Wind

Amos was facing his first mutiny.

"Mr. Watson, I can't take that job any longer," Felix Logan said. "I'm really sick of it. I want to be one of the Terrible Ten."

"Who are they? Is that one of the baseball teams?"

"No, it's a bunch of guys and girls. They go around together, doing things. They have more fun than anybody else in camp."

Amos had never heard of the Terrible Ten, but that wasn't surprising. Santo Tomas was now so large—over four thousand people, counting the new internees brought in from the provinces and the outer islands—that many little groups could exist without his knowing about them. Especially teenage groups. Amos paid no attention to teenagers other than Felix.

"What sort of things do they do?"

"Just mess around. Like they sneak out after curfew and have secret picnics in the shanties. Two of the girls made a banana cake last night."

"Out of what?"

"Well, bananas. And then some cassava paste for

flour, and cold cream for shortening. They hooked some saccharine pills from one of their parents to sweeten it up."

"It sounds delicious."

"Yeah, I hear it wasn't very good. But it sounded like fun."

"What else do they do?"

"They get in some dancing during the music concerts."

Amos was surprised. Dancing, like any other physical contact between the sexes, was forbidden. "How do they get away with that?"

"You know how the stage is closed by sawali screens when it's not being used? They dance in there. They do lots of things they aren't supposed to do."

"And you want to join them?"

"I can't. They won't let me. Mr. Watson, they call me a Jap ass-kisser."

"I see."

"They all know I go in the commandant's office every day and bow a lot and clean up the place. They kid me about it. You know what they call me? I told them back at Simpson I was called Felix the Fixer because I was good at arranging things. You know, trying to impress them, I guess. So now they call me Felix the Flexer. But if I quit that job, I think I could get in. If I said I was really fed up and hated the Japs and maybe told some funny stories about the commandant. They're all Manila kids, but I think they'd take me."

"And then you'd be the Terrible Eleven?"

"Well, I guess they wouldn't change the name."

Amos had had trouble with Felix before, but this time sounded more serious. He was being specifically excluded from an elite little group he was longing to join. A lonely proposition. However, Felix must be made to stick with it.

"Felix, you know I count on you."

"But Jesus, Mr. Watson, it's been over a year."

Amos nodded. "I know. This is a long war. We can't let down."

Felix ran his fingers through his hair, his nervous gesture. "Maybe if I told them what I was really doing? You know, working for you? They'd be impressed. They're good kids—I know they can keep a secret."

This was truly alarming. Amos put his hand on Felix's shoulder. The boy was taller now and, like everyone else, thinner. "Felix, I've told you before. What you and I and a few others are doing is so important—and so dangerous—that no one must know. *No one.* And most certainly not a bunch of teenagers."

Felix looked miserable. His eyes, behind the big glasses, were sad. "Mr. Watson, *I'm* a teenager."

Poor Felix, Amos thought; but he must not let that show. "No, you're not," he said sternly. "You're a man. You're as much a man, and as much a soldier, as anyone in uniform. Only what you are doing is more important than carrying a rifle."

"It doesn't feel that way. I don't want to do it anymore."

What could Amos say? "Felix, I have two sons back in the States and four grandsons. Maybe more by now. But I am closer to you than I am to any of them." This was true, although slightly misleading, since he wasn't that close to his own family. "I can't let you make the mistake of quitting. When the Americans come back, you'll be proud you stayed. Everybody will be proud of you. I wouldn't be surprised if they gave you a medal. You can't give it up."

"Well—but I'd rather be in the Terrible Ten."

Amos said what he had learned to say long ago whenever confronted by an unattractive business proposition. "Let me think about it."

Through the Package Line, Amos ordered a proper banana cake from Carlos and gave it to Felix as a friendly contribution to the Terrible Ten. They took it and ate it, but told Felix they'd liked their awful homemade one better. Teenagers were perverse creatures.

But as Amos hoped would happen, within a few weeks Felix picked up something important from the commandant's office. Whenever Felix learned something early, particularly when he learned it before the Triumvirate was notified, he took a different view of his work. Most of the day-to-day activities in Santo Tomas were too boring to talk about, but this one was not. Felix was excited when he came to Amos's shanty after siesta.

"Mr. Watson," he whispered, "they're going to move us! They're going to move Santo Tomas!"

This had been a constant rumor because of the overcrowding, but nothing had ever come of it. Felix saw Amos's skepticism. "No, it's true. I heard them, the commandant and that army colonel. They've picked out the place. It's called Los Baños. There's some kind of college there. You know where it is?"

"Yes. It's on Laguna de Bay." This was the huge inland lake south of Manila.

"Well, that's where we're going."

"All of us? The whole four thousand?"

"Yes, sir. Only not all at once. They have to build up a camp first. Build a lot of barracks. They're going to start with eight hundred men to fix it up. Then when it's ready, they'll move everybody else."

Amos thought about it. First, unlike so many of the earlier rumors, it was plausible. Los Baños was only some thirty miles away, a manageable distance for a move by train or truck. And there was indeed a small agricultural college, which could serve as the basis for a new internment camp, although nothing like one the size of Santo Tomas.

But four thousand people? Amos didn't know the normal population of the resort town of Los Baños, but it couldn't be anywhere near the size of Santo Tomas's population. The Japs would be dumping the entire "city" of Santo Tomas onto a tiny town. From his early construction days, Amos had a good idea what abrupt expansion would mean in terms of water supply, sewage and all the other practical matters. It had taken all these months to make Santo Tomas more or less livable, even with the intense overcrowding, and now they would have to start all over again out in the provinces, where materials and equipment were far scarcer than in Manila. A grand mess.

But that was not his main concern. If he was way off in Los Baños, how would he keep in touch with

Papaya and Carlos and, through them, with all the others? A whole new organization, a whole new system, would have to be created. It could take months to get it working smoothly. He would have to put together a different set of messengers, a hazardous undertaking. The process of passing information back and forth would take even longer than it did now. Oh shit, he thought. Maybe it wouldn't happen.

"When are they going to announce this?" he asked Felix.

"Right away. They want to get going before the rainy season."

"They don't have much time."

"No, sir. That's what the colonel said."

When the commandant did announce the move to Los Baños, he said he would choose eight hundred able-bodied men from among all those who volunteered to help build the new camp. Even with this chance to have a new adventure, to break the monotony of their life in Santo Tomas, fewer than three hundred volunteered to go. At least life in Santo Tomas was predictable. Everybody knew what to expect. The lack of volunteers was not a promising start for the new camp.

The commandant and the Triumvirate put the names of all eligible men in a barrel and drew them out one by one, reading the names over the loudspeaker. Amos, who was too old to have his name in the barrel, stood in the plaza that night with everyone else to listen to the drawing.

Every name that was read aloud brought a wail or cry from some woman—and sometimes from several

at once. Amos sympathized with the young married
women who were losing their husbands for a minimum of four months, but he thought the histrionics
of women bemoaning the departure of their boyfriends were excessive. In some cases the histrionics
were not only excessive but unfounded. One young
woman standing not too far from him wept over the
names of five different men.

Next morning the hospital line was endless. All the
men drafted for Los Baños were trying to get exemp-
tions for bad health. One man was vomiting very
convincingly because he had just drunk soapy water.
Amos shook his head at the sight. If there had been
that many draft dodgers back in the States, there
would be no U.S. Army.

On the day of departure the loudspeaker blasted
out "Onward Christian Soldiers" and "The Battle
Hymn of the Republic" to raise everyone's spirits.
Three men who had been in jail for drinking were let
out to join the group. All the women who were losing
husbands or boyfriends were jealous of the twelve
nurses assigned to keep the Los Baños group healthy.

As the men and their baggage were loaded into the
trucks for the ride to the train station, Amos saw the
familiar figure of Sandy Homobono watching the process. He walked over to see what he could learn.

"Hello, Sandy. Covering this for the *Tribune*?"

"Oh, hello, Mr. Watson. How have you been? Yes.
I am told this is a very happy occasion. All these
spirited volunteers going off on their great adventure."

"Yes, one can tell by their merry faces. I'm sure it
will make a cheerful story."

"No doubt." Sandy lighted a cigarette.

"When do you think the rest of us will go?"

Sandy squinted against the smoke. "As soon as the camp is built, I'm told. Four months. Six months. Whatever it takes."

"It seems like a great deal of effort."

"Yes. Frankly, Mr. Watson, I don't think it will ever happen."

This was by far the best news Amos had heard this week. "Why not?"

"Water. Have you ever stayed in Los Baños?"

"I had lunch there once or twice with friends. A beautiful view."

"Yes, quite beautiful. Did you know that water there has to be rationed? And that at night they shut it off completely?"

"I certainly did not. Do our hosts know that?"

Sandy shrugged. "They hope to find more water."

"Are you going to put that in your story?"

"That would not be cheerful. By the way, Mr. Watson, I see your old friend Papaya from time to time. She seems very well. Very well indeed."

Amos knew Homobono was baiting him for a reaction, perhaps wondering how much Amos might have heard about Admiral Buto. Amos deliberately did not think about Buto at all, except as a source of information. It didn't do to think about some things.

Amos knew much more about Homobono's various meetings and activities than the reporter might have thought. Through Papaya and Federico, he had heard about Homobono's sizable cash contribution to one Dr. Ronualdez, the leader of a prewar patriot group now engaged in working for independence from the Japanese. Homobono had received a bonus for an important *Tribune* story that pleased the Japs and had turned it over to Ronualdez—although, knowing Sandy, Amos suspected it was less than 100 percent of the bonus. The bonus was said to have come straight from General Miyama himself, which made Sandy's contribution especially welcome. A strange but delightful business: Homobono writing propaganda for the Japs and then using the money to help the opposition.

However, the press was the press. As usual, Amos chose not to give the reporter anything. "That's nice," he said. "I'd almost forgotten Papaya. It was so long ago."

If he was disappointed by this reaction, Homobono did not reveal it. "That's true," he said. "Well, if you'll excuse me, Mr. Watson, I must interview some of these eager adventurers."

————

Sandy Homobono's *Tribune* story was enthusiastic about the journey and about the new camp. It was only later that the Santo Tomas internees learned about the long, miserable train trip in steaming metal boxcars, the heavy rains when the group finally reached Los Baños, and the fact that six hundred of the men were jammed into a college gymnasium with just four toilets. Their drinking water was polluted. The mosquitoes were bad, and the nurses soon had their hands full with malaria cases. As more and more adverse reports came drifting back to Santo Tomas, Amos stopped worrying about moving to Los Baños. Sandy Homobono was right. It was never going to happen.

That summer the commandant finally bowed to pressure on women's clothing. Because cloth was now so scarce and because it was getting more and more difficult to buy dresses from outside, he agreed that women could at last wear shorts.

"But," Felix reported, "they can't be more than four inches above the knees."

"Who's responsible for measuring?" Amos asked.

Next time he saw Judy she was wearing white-and-tan striped cotton shorts, which he estimated to be five inches above her very nice knees. She probably had the best legs in camp, and he told her so.

"Thanks," she said, not disagreeing with him. "Isn't this just like the Japs? They wait until most of the young men are off in Los Baños, and then they make shorts legal."

"Well, Judy, it's probably best for the public safety."

"Some of these women shouldn't be allowed to wear shorts at all. Have you seen Marlies Wilmerding?"

"In shorts? No, thank God, I haven't."

"She has boils all over her legs."

"War is certainly hell."

"She just makes it worse."

With the onset of the rainy season, the weather had already been bad for three weeks before the typhoon struck. The campus grounds, with their poor drainage, were already saturated from the rains. Water stood in shallow pools and lakes all over the campus. The ground could not absorb any more water, and the fitful sunshine wasn't strong enough to evaporate it.

Amos was asleep in his shanty the night the typhoon came. He awoke to the wind and the rain. One more damn storm, he thought with disgust. In the pitch darkness he got up and lowered the sawali flaps, tying them down with the rattan thongs, to keep his things from getting wet. Then he returned to bed.

Because of the recent bad weather, most of the men permitted to sleep in their shanties had moved back to the dormitory buildings, but Amos remained. The buildings were already terribly overcrowded, even before the extra population came in from the shanties, and Amos didn't mind a little rain. He was used to it after all these years in the Philippines. He pulled up his damp blanket and went back to sleep.

He did not know how long he slept before the shriek of the wind woke him again. He could see nothing, but there was no mistaking thathigh-pitched, roaring scream. *Bagyo*—the great wind. Typhoon.

He could feel his bed shaking as the whole shanty rocked in the wind. He knew the floor timbers and sturdy bamboo poles must be creaking and groaning under the strain, but it was impossible to hear anything else through the enormous sound of the wind. He did not consider trying to get back to the nearest building, which was several hundred yards away. The best thing to do in a typhoon was stay put in a safe place, but he wasn't sure how safe this place was. Perhaps he should open the flaps, just let everything get soaked, so the wind could blow through the shanty instead of powering against it. Where was the flashlight? It should be in the corner of the cupboard. He got up, but stumbled and fell because the floor was shaking so hard. His shoulder hit the corner of the bed.

He crawled to the cupboard across the heaving floor and found his flashlight. When he shone the light around the shanty, he saw the walls and roof were shaking like paper, and the five-inch center pole arced back and forth. The wind had blown open the door, and thick rain was sheeting almost horizontally into the shanty. The door itself was flapping like a loose sail. Yes, better get those flaps open. Everything was wet anyway.

He crawled back across the floor. Holding the flashlight in one hand, he undid the rattan ties with the other. Instantly the force of the wind yanked the flap from its fastenings. It sailed across the shanty to slap against the far wall.

He had just started to untie the second flap when a tremendous gust hit the shanty and tore it away from the ground. The whole floor rose under him like the deck of a foundering ship. He felt the boards breaking and coming apart under him, splintering and shattering, but all he could hear was the wind. He lost the flashlight as the shanty went over.

Then he was lying somewhere facedown on the ground. He had to lift his shoulders to raise his head above water. Something heavy and massive had landed across his hips and legs. The bed? The flooring? The whole damn shanty? Whatever it was, he couldn't wriggle out from under it. With both hands groping behind him he tried to move it. No luck. His shoulder was hurting. Then he put both hands down into the rising water until he felt the ground and pushed upward and backward with all his might, at the same time trying to lift with his back and legs. He could feel the weight shift a little, but it wasn't going anywhere.

He thought of trying to call for help, but that was pointless in this wind. The water must be a foot and a half deep now. He had to press up with both hands to keep his head above water. The strain on his sore shoulder and his back was exhausting. The rain fell heavily. The great wind screamed.

This is silly, he thought. This is ridiculous. I'm going to drown here. I'm going to hold my head up until I get too tired. And if I don't get tired, this water's going to come up and get me anyway.

Maybe the rising water would float whatever weight was pinning him down. He tried his lifting maneuver again, this time putting all his strength into it and sustaining it for what must have been a full minute, but it was no better. He should save his strength to keep his head up as long as he could. How long was that going to be? Well, goddamn it, as long as he could—and then maybe a while after that. He closed his mind to everything else and concentrated.

He heard nothing but the violent wind and did not see anything until the flashlights shone on him. Then a hand touched his shoulder. He looked up. He could see nothing except the beam of two lights in his face. The beams went away. He felt several hands on his shoulders trying to pull him loose. He tried to tell them what the trouble was, but he could not hear his own voice. They would have to figure it out for themselves.

They did. After a while he could feel the weight shift as they tugged at it. He concentrated on holding his head up and let them worry about the rest. The weight moved again, then dropped back down on him. His arms buckled. His face went down in the water, but he lifted it out again. Then he could feel the weight definitely lighten. Somebody got him under the arms and dragged him out.

At first he could not stand. When they tried to lift him, he fell. Hands felt along his legs. They must think something was broken, but it wasn't that. He was just weak. He tried to make them understand with his hands that he would be all right if he could rest for a few minutes, but it only confused them. The wind howled, driving the rain against him. It would have been hard to stand against the wind even if he weren't so tired.

Finally he felt a little better. He put his arms over their shoulders, and together they sloshed down the river that used to be the shantytown path. The flashlights barely showed anything through the rain. It was a long way to the nearest safety, the Education Building. It took so long that he wondered if they had lost their way in the darkness.

Only when his feet stumbled on the steps did he realize there were no lights in the building, not even the low-level one at the entrance that burned all night so the internee Ground Patrol could stop anyone from going in or out. Of course not. The power would be out all over the campus, maybe all over Manila. That usually happened in typhoons.

In the lee of the building the wind and rain diminished. He took his arms from their shoulders and walked up the steps by himself. One of his rescuers used his flashlight to find the door handle. They moved inside quickly. Then it took all of them pushing together to close the door against the force of the wind. They were safe in the darkness, but they could still hear the typhoon beating outside. Even indoors behind the thick stone walls the wind was too loud for anyone to speak.

Amos reached out and took one of the flashlights to see who had saved him. Funny, there were three of them. He thought it had been only two who helped walk him back. He shone the light from face to face.

Harry Widdoes, one of the Ground Patrol, was smiling in relief. Water streamed down his face and clothes. The second was another GP, a big hefty fellow Amos had seen around but didn't know by name. This man shook Amos's hand. And Felix Logan. His wet face showed deep concern as well as fear of the giant storm.

Amos handed the flashlight back to Widdoes so that he could put both arms around Felix. He knew who had persuaded the GPs to brave the typhoon and come looking for him.

———

During the week after the typhoon, while the camp was drying out and all the damaged shanties were being repaired or rebuilt, Amos thought hard about what he should do for Felix. When he made up his mind, he wrote two short letters, one to his wife, Marian, and one to his attorney in California. They were not the same as a proper codicil, couched in legal language and typed and witnessed and notarized, but he knew they would be binding because Marian would see to it.

He gave them to Felix the first afternoon they were able to meet in his shanty, completely rebuilt by Federico.

"Here," he said. "Keep these in a safe place."

Felix took the two sheets, looked at Amos through his thick glasses and then read the first one slowly. He looked up at Amos in surprise, then read the second one. They said the same thing.

"But Mr. Watson—"

"Don't lose them."

"No, sir, but this is—I mean, this is—"

"Felix, I was always going to do something for you after the war, but I figured there was no hurry. It could wait. Now, after the typhoon, I think that would be foolish. I could easily have died in that storm—would have if you hadn't come looking for me. This is just a precaution."

"But, Mr. Watson, a *whole* college education. That's an awful lot."

"Well," Amos said dryly, "you'll notice you actually have to go to college to collect it. No tickee, no washee. Also, in case you didn't notice, it doesn't say 'all college expenses.' It specifically says 'tuition, room and board and all educational supplies.' You can buy books and a typewriter with that, but you'll have to earn your own spending money."

"Yes, sir. I—I'm—I really can't thank you. I—"

Amos cut him off with a wave. "Felix, you've worked hard for me, and I'm grateful. Also you're a lot more interested in business than either of my sons were. I know you don't much *want* to go to college, but I think you should, so this," he said with a smile, "is nothing more than a nice little bribe."

"Gee, I wish I could tell my parents. They'd really be tickled."

"Yes. Well. Now you'll have a surprise for them when you finally see them."

But Felix did not get to tell his surprise. The next month, when a load of internees from Cebu was transferred to Santo Tomas, adding to the severe overcrowding, they told Felix that his mother and father had died of typhus, more than six months ago.

≡ 24 ≡

A Nice Little Business

The new source of POW income at Cabanatuan was Jack Humphrey's personal favorite. Much as he appreciated the gifts of money that were smuggled into camp by Amos Watson's people, and much as he approved of the fact that Japs were now paying prisoners for their work, this one was the best of all.

It began the afternoon that Jerry Baron, the doctor, returned to barracks from his day at the hospital. His long, thin face was creased by a broad smile. Baron never smiled at all during the awful days at Camp O'Donnell or the early months at Cabanatuan when so many men were dying from dysentery and malaria. Things were much better now in the fall of 1943. Those diseases had run their course, and thanks to better food and sanitation and more medical supplies, deaths were down to one a month. But that was not why Jerry Baron was smiling.

"Guess who I treated this afternoon," he said. "Lieutenant Kokado. And guess what I treated him for."

"Leprosy," Maxsie said hopefully. Kokado was one of the least popular Jap officers.

"Almost that good," Jerry said. "The lieutenant has a severe case of gonorrhea."

"Clap-clap," Maxsie said, clapping his hands in the old army joke.

"Why'd he come to you?" Jack Humphrey said. "He's got his own hospital."

"And better doctors, too," Maxsie said. "I bet they could cure my back."

"You want a second opinion on your stupid back?" Jerry Baron said. "Be my guest. I'll arrange a consultation. No, the reason the lieutenant came to me is that he'd get his ass in a sling if he went to his own doctors. That's why he waited so long to get treatment. They're very strict about venereal disease. I can't imagine why. What's the point of having an army if you don't have VD?"

"The punishment for gonorrhea," Maxsie said with authority, "is it burns when you piss."

Baron waved his long, delicate doctor's hands. "Not in the Imperial Japanese Army," he said. "They cut their pay and restrict them or even take away their rank."

"So what did you do for Kokado?"

"Oh, I gave him a couple of sulfa pills and told him to behave himself. He was very grateful."

"Huh," Maxsie said with disgust. "You should've let his cock burn. Tell him maybe it'll stop in a couple of months. Save the sulfa for us."

"Unfortunately," Baron said, "none of you seems

to contract gonorrhea. For some reason, only the Japs have it."

"I'd sure like a pass to one of their cathouses in town," Maxsie said. "Just a fifteen-minute pass. What did you charge him?"

"I didn't charge him anything. You think all doctors are sharks? Maybe he'll treat us better."

"Well, next time—" Maxsie stopped. An idea had come to him. He stood up, rubbing his back. "Listen," he said. "Listen, they've got a lot of clap?"

"So Kokado says. Apparently hygiene in the local brothels leaves something to be desired. Even in the officers' brothel. You can imagine what it's like in the enlisted men's."

"Well, sure, here's all the whores doing their best with their patriotic pussies, giving the Japs the clap. That's one way to fight a war. But we got to do our part, too. Jerry, you got to treat them all, the whole Jap army, and charge them for it. Charge a lot, just like you'd do back home. We just pass the word, if you got clap, go see Dr. Baron."

"Medical advertising is unethical," Jerry Baron said, smiling.

"Don't give me that. We got a war here. Anyway, you don't have to tell them personally. Hump and I will get the word around, and Santini can tell all their enlisted men. How much can you charge? Couple of pesos a pill? We'll leave that to you. Listen, we're going to have a nice little business."

"We don't have all that much sulfa," Baron said.

Maxsie gave his savage smile. "Who said anything

about sulfa? We don't want you to *cure* those fuckers. Undo all the good work the whores are doing? No, we just want their business."

"You mean," Baron said, plainly shocked, "give them a placebo?"

"What's that?"

"A neutral substance. The patient thinks he's getting medicine, but he isn't."

"You got it. A placebo."

"Maybe it wouldn't have to be completely neutral," Jack Humphrey said, getting into the spirit. "Maybe you could give them something to make them feel kind of sick?"

"What would look right?" Maxsie asked.

"I'd have to think about it. Sulfa pills are scored. They have those little grooves."

"Of course, they can't all be placebos," Humphrey said. "If nobody got cured, they'd stop coming to you. You're going to have to slip in enough sulfa to cure a few of them."

"Yeah, but not too many," Maxsie said.

"I'll think about it," Baron said again, but they could tell he was intrigued. "I'm not sure this fits in with my Hippocratic oath."

"Why not? You won't actually be killing anybody, like most doctors."

"Maxsie, you are incorrigible."

"We got to fight any way we can."

After thinking about it and going through his medical larder at the hospital, Jerry Baron announced that the closest he could come was bicarbonate of soda pills. They were the same color and almost the same size as the sulfa pills. If they only had grooves, no one would be able to tell the difference.

"Maybe they won't notice," Jack Humphrey said.

"Oh, somebody will notice. Somebody always notices. A placebo has to be indistinguishable from the real thing. We're going to have to carve the grooves ourselves."

It was meticulous work. It took a scalpel and a steady hand to cut a groove without making the soda pill crumble into little pieces. Even when they got used to it, they still lost one out of five. Several days of intensive labor were necessary before Baron decided they had a big enough supply of grooved soda pills to open shop.

He mixed them in with some sulfa pills so that even he didn't know which were which when he handed them out. That was the way, he explained, that placebos were supposed to be administered. He would get some random cures. That made him feel better about the treatment, because he never knew when he might accidentally be practicing good medicine.

The money started coming in nicely. It reminded Humphrey of a song—*My father makes synthetic gin, my sister makes love for five dollars, my God how the money rolls in*. They spent some of the money in town to buy black-market bandages for their hospital. That made Jerry Baron feel better, too. The rest they spent on essentials like food and cigarettes.

But when Corporal Santini got the word out among the Japanese enlisted men, a new problem arose. They were in danger of running out of bicarbonate of soda pills. Maxsie and Santini talked it over and decided they should try to make their own pills out of cornstarch. For a piece of the action, they enlisted a mechanic who used to work in a motor pool. He built a contraption resembling a bullet mold that would stamp out pills from damp cornstarch, which could then be dried in the sun. They still had to carve the grooves—a grooved pill-stamping machine was beyond the mechanic's ability—but since the cornstarch pills were softer than the soda pills, it was easier to carve the little grooves. The supply of cornstarch was ample.

The business flourished for several months before the head of the Japanese hospital learned that the American POW hospital was treating Japanese soldiers for venereal disease. He was furious. Through an interpreter, he read Baron the physician's riot act.

As Jerry reported it, Major Tikirama considered Baron's behavior an outrageous transgression against the ethics of medical practice. Did Dr. Baron realize that the Imperial Japanese Army considered venereal disease an infraction of discipline? Of course he did. Did Dr. Baron realize that such infractions were subject to proper punishment by the Japanese command? Of course he did. Then how dared Dr. Baron, a mere prisoner of war, subvert the authority of the Imperial Japanese Army?

"But major," Jerry Baron said, with all the innocence of which he was capable, "it is every physician's duty to heal the sick. Nationality can't matter to a doctor. They came to me with a medical problem, and I simply tried to help them. Like any good doctor."

When this was translated to Major Tikirama, he jumped on the last phrase and started waving his hands around. Good doctor! Good doctor! Baron was a very bad doctor. Baron was a terrible doctor. He should have his license taken away. He should be barred from their honorable profession. Not only had he interfered with Japanese regulations, but a number of men he treated had not even been cured. They had finally reported to their own hospital to be treated properly and to accept the necessary punishment. Baron was guilty of malpractice, as well as many other crimes.

"So I hung my head," Jerry Baron reported to his fellow conspirators, "and promised never to do it again. I don't think Tikirama knows anything about the money. The men must have been too ashamed to tell him they paid us. Or else Tikirama does know about it and was too ashamed to mention it."

"Well, shit," Maxsie said, "we done our best. Can't ask for more than that."

"And our only leftover capital investment," Humphrey said, "is a secondhand pill machine."

"You forget about my reputation," Jerry Baron said.

Dear Sara,

We're doing better on food. I've even gained back some weight, so you don't have to worry about me wasting away. The Japs have us all working on a big farm just outside the camp. Everybody hates it except the guys who used to be farmers before the war, but at least we're getting more fresh vegetables—corn, cabbage, squash, spinach. As you know, vegetables aren't at the top of my list, but I guess they're healthy, and it's good to have something to add to the steady rice diet. The Japs are so serious about the farm they've even got us majors and colonels out working in the fields. They're even paying us, if you can call it pay. Enlisted men get about a dime a day, while we big shots get about fifty cents. Still, it's something, and we can use the money to buy extra food at the commissary the Japs have set up.

We've lost our pill business, but we're still getting extra money from outside. It's quite a system, since the money comes all the way from Manila and then has to be smuggled into camp. Some of it comes on the carabao carts that make the round trip to town every day. Amos Watson is the only contributor I know by name, and I'm careful never to identify him, not even to Maxsie. It's better to keep all names secret—just in case. There are others who are helping us out, especially two women called Miss U and High Pockets. Nobody knows their real names, but they are a godsend.

It gets very complicated. A couple of Filipina women pretend to sell small packages of food—bags of peanuts and sugar-cane candy and coconut cookies and so forth—to the men sent out to work on the farm. The Japs don't object to this—they think it's just a straight cash deal. What they don't know is

*that the girls hide money inside the packages, so the
men actually get back more than they pay out, and
then they have more to spend at the commissary. I'm
not sure this is capitalism, but it works.*

*You remember way back last Christmas we put on
a camp show? That was the time Maxsie and I did
our big "Abdul" number. The show was so successful—even the Japs liked it—that it's become an institution. Now we're allowed to give shows once or
twice a week—music, plays and so on. Pretty amateur
stuff but good for morale. Maxsie and I get asked to
repeat "Abdul" whenever his back's in good enough
shape, which isn't too often. When his back hurts, he
can't throw himself into the duel, and then it's not
nearly so good. He says he's like an old baseball
pitcher—he has to pick his starting spots very carefully.*

*I realize next week is Jeff's birthday. Wish I could
be there for the party. I keep wondering if you ever
got the postcards we were allowed to write, or if
they're ever going to let you write back. They keep
saying they are, but nothing ever comes. Maybe for
Christmas? That would be the best present. Take care
of yourself, and give the boys a hug for me, especially
Jeff on his birthday.*

Love, Jack

The letters from home did not arrive until spring, but
then they came all at once. Thousands of them.

Word spread instantly through Camp Cabanatuan
the morning the mail arrived by truck from Manila.

The Americans who worked in the Japanese headquarters area told how they had unloaded the big
gray canvas sacks of mail and carried them into an
office. There were so many sacks they could not all
fit in the office. The Japs were just going to leave them
piled outside, but the American officer in charge appealed right up to the commandant, who agreed that
to protect the sacks from the possibility of rain, they
could be put in a second building.

Jack Humphrey couldn't believe it. After all the
months of waiting, the mail was here. Right in this
camp. He was going to hear from Sara this very day.
Well, maybe tomorrow. It might take a while to sort
all that mail.

Nobody in camp could talk about anything else.
Everybody was smiling at everybody else, even at the
Jap guards. Until the evening meal.

Colonel Meacham arrived late in the officers' chow
line. His face was grim. He had been arguing with
the commandant, without success. "They're going to
censor it," he said.

Everybody within earshot groaned.

"That'll take forever," somebody said. "What
for?"

"The usual reason," Meacham said. "Security.
They don't want us to learn anything they don't want
us to know. And that's not the worst. They've assigned just one interpreter to censor all the letters."

"Jesus Christ!"

"I asked for more help. Get some more people on
it, I said. Get them from Manila if you have to. I said

we've been waiting over two years to hear from home."

"What'd he say?"

"He said nobody could be spared. They'll do it as fast as they can."

"But Jesus, colonel—"

"I have his promise," Colonel Meacham said bitterly.

The mail trickled out of the censor's office, a hundred letters a day.

The lucky early ones shared their letters with the others, reading them aloud. It did not matter that the letters were from Susie or Jane or somebody else they had never heard of and didn't care about and would never meet. They were voices from home. The letters were read aloud over and over again.

On the seventeenth day Maxsie came into the barracks waving a single sheet of paper. "Hey, Hump, I got one! I got one from Sara!"

Jack Humphrey closed his eyes. She was alive. He had never permitted himself to doubt it, but now he knew. He opened his eyes and said, "Give it to me."

Maxsie pretended to hold it back. "This one's for me. You got to wait for your own."

"Goddamn you—"

"Can't you take a joke? Here."

Humphrey snatched the sheet of paper. His eyes burned as he recognized the familiar handwriting, the steep slant to the right and the little circles for dots over the *i* 's, that schoolgirl affectation that he had

never been able to kid her out of. He had to wipe his
eyes before he could read it.

Dear Maxsie,

*Your nice postcard arrived in the same wonderful
mail with the postcard from Jack. What a great day!
I'm so glad to hear you are taking care of my "old
man" and that you are both all right. It's been such
a long time without news that I couldn't help being
worried. Jack has always known how to look out for
himself, but when you don't hear for a long time, you
can't help wondering. Now I don't have to wonder
anymore.*

*I read your card to our two boys. They were tickled
to hear their dad has talked so much about us that
you feel as though you already know the whole family. Well, someday you will. Jack will bring you home
with him, and we'll have a great celebration. That's
a firm, definite promise. What do you like to eat?
What do you like to drink? That's what we'll have
the day you get here, so let's all look forward to it.
I certainly do.*

*Write me again. I loved hearing from you. And
while you're taking care of Jack, be sure to take care
of yourself too.*

As ever,
Sara

She had signed it "Sara Humphrey," with her enormous capital *S*, but then drawn a line through "Humphrey."

He read it again. Then he read it again. She

sounded fine, very much like herself. It was just like Sara to be planning a big dinner party while they were still in prison camp. He kept staring at the hand-writing. It was really Sara.

Finally he folded the sheet and tucked it in his shirt pocket.

"Hey," Maxsie said, "that's mine."

"I'll give it back when I get my own letter."

"Maybe you won't get one. I think Sara's already nuts about me."

Humphrey smiled. "That's just Sara being friendly."

"You go ahead and think that if you want. But you notice she asks what *I* like to eat and drink? She doesn't care about what you like. And that she 'loved' hearing from me? Listen, Hump, the old Maxsie magic is at work. One fifty-word postcard and she's already crazy about me. I bet she wrote me before she wrote you—that's why my letter came first."

The mail trickled out, day after day. Still no letter for Jack Humphrey. Maxsie tried to kid him out of his growing impatience.

"She's forgot all about you, Hump. I'm the one she cares about. She probably didn't even write you. She didn't want to have to send a Dear John letter to a POW."

"Shut up."

"Listen, you can still come to that dinner she's going to give for me. Shit, I don't mind. But you got to leave when it's over."

"Shut up, Maxsie."

He reread her letter to Maxsie many times. He

could have recited it, but he liked to look at her handwriting. It helped him imagine her seated at the fold-
ing-top desk they shared, her papers and bills and
letters in the right-hand cubbyholes, his on the left.
She always wrote sitting up straight, her back not
touching the chair. She had good straight shoulders.
Her off-blond hair was pulled back neatly and held
in place with a rubber band—or a white ribbon if it
was nighttime. Her head and shoulders were tilted a
little to the left, her left arm and hand flat on the
desk, holding the paper steady as her pen raced across
the page. She was a busy correspondent, keeping in
touch with all the friends they had known at other
army posts.

Even before the trickle of letters came to a stop,
Jack Humphrey went to Colonel Meacham. He and
Sara had been stationed with the Meachams at both
Benning and Meade. "There's something wrong,
Sam," he said. "There's no letter from Sara."

Sam Meacham was sympathetic. "They're still cen-
soring," he said. "They probably haven't got to it
yet." He spoke without conviction. They were almost
finished.

"I don't think that's it. For some reason they're
holding it up."

"Yes, maybe. Or maybe her letter got lost in the
shuffle. You know, it was a hell of a long trip, Jack.
From the U.S. to a neutral ship, all the way to that
neutral Portuguese port in India, and then up to
Tokyo and then back down here. Probably a lot of
letters got lost."

"Maxsie got one from Sara."

"Yes, I know. So his didn't get lost."

"Sam, it just wouldn't have happened. They're holding it. I want you to ask the commandant about it."

Meacham frowned. He did not like to press the commandant on anything but major matters.

"I don't care if they censor everything except 'Dear Jack.' I just want to hear from her."

"All right." Reluctantly. "I'll ask. But not until they've finished the pile."

Three more days before Meacham reported back.

"I'm sorry, Jack. The commandant says they've released all the letters. That's all there is."

"What about the ones they censored? The ones they didn't let through?"

"They didn't keep records, and they didn't keep those letters, either. All the ones that were 'unacceptable'—that's his word—were destroyed. I'm sorry, but that's it. At least you know she's all right."

"Yes, but could you—"

"Jack, I can't do anything more. You know I can't. Anyway, there's nothing more to do."

"Yes, okay, Sam. Thanks for trying."

"I'm sorry. It must have got lost."

"Yeah, maybe so."

But Jack Humphrey refused to accept this.

Dear Sara,

You must have written a red-hot letter. The Jap censor refused to let it through. I wish I knew what

you said, but I'll just have to guess. Next time you'd
better be more careful. I hope there is a next time.
Anyway, your letter to Maxsie came through, so I
know you and the boys are all right. That's the main
thing, I guess. I miss you all, and especially you. Try
to write soon.

Love, Jack

═ 25 ═

Miranda

Sometimes she thought the happiest moments of her life came while driving her horse cart along this final stretch of back road between Bamban and Caraban-gay. She had passed the last Japanese checkpoint on the main road, and now it was a gentle, quiet, un-interrupted ride the rest of the way.

Not that the checkpoints bothered her so much. Miranda was used to them. She always behaved the same way toward the soldiers—pleasant, shy, pre-tending to be a little nervous as she showed her forged pass. She tried to give the impression of being properly cowed in the presence of armed Japanese soldiers but not so nervous that they would have any reason to be suspicious. Every once in a while she thought she recognized some of the checkpoint guards around Clark Field, at Dau or Mabalacat, but to them she was just one more harmless Filipina on her way to visit her family. She carried a sack of vegetables or a stalk of bananas in the cart—a present to "her family." Her trips came so far apart that they paid her no attention.

Now, after Bamban, she no longer had to pretend. She could relax and really smile. She hummed tunes and talked cheerfully to her horse. Soon she would be seeing her wonderful Coach and her brother Hilario and all her friends in Carabangay and the guerrilla camp. And they would all be glad to see her because she was bringing presents and messages from Manila. Soon, also, she would be back in bed with her Coach. This part of the ride was always one of happy anticipation.

She wished she would get pregnant. It would present many complications in her work, of course, and climbing the hill to camp would certainly be more difficult. But it would be very nice to have his child. In her mid-twenties, she was getting rather old not to have had any children. Sometimes she wondered if anything was wrong with her, since she had never got pregnant with either Benny or Coach. She always reassured herself that in neither case had conditions been favorable. One had to make love regularly and frequently and at the right time of month to have babies. Still, she would feel better if it happened.

Her family would mind, but perhaps not too much. They all knew about Coach, and Hilario practically worshiped him. Many strange things happened these difficult days. The rules of life were so different. She knew Coach loved the Judy down in Santo Tomas and would probably marry her if this war ever ended. But he loved her, Miranda, too, and they had happy times together. Who could say? Maybe this war would never end, and they could go on like this forever.

"Maybe this visit," she told her horse, "I will get pregnant." She shook the reins and clucked him on. This visit would be her last for some time, because Mr. Watson and Papaya needed her to help the others working at Cabanatuan. Coach would be disappointed. "He better be," she told her horse.

At Carabangay that afternoon she learned bad news from Rosauro's mother, Lila. The guerrilla camp had received a letter, an order, from some American officer in the mountains up around Baguio. It placed them under the command of Major Quintano. "He will be the one for this area," Lila said. "The new boss. Rosauro says everybody is very unhappy. They hate it."

This made Miranda change her mind about spending the night in Lila's house. She knew what Coach and Sergeant thought about Quintano. "Lila, I must go up there tonight."

"It's too late. It will be dark before you get there."

"No, not if I hurry. This is such bad news for them. I have to go."

She put the messages and the packet of pesos in her straw bag, leaving Lila's people to unload the blankets and hemp rope and tools that Sergeant had requested on her last visit. She set off up the mountain, hurrying so that she would not get caught on the trail in the dark. As well as she knew the way, it was easy to get lost in the darkness of the mountain jungle. It was no wonder the Japs had so much trouble finding the guerrilla camps in the Zambales.

The sun dropped behind the high mountains to the west, but the sky still held enough light for her as she

climbed upward. The plain was darkening behind her.
She had never spent a night in the camp before. No
woman had—it was Sergeant's rule. She wondered if
she would be allowed to sleep in Coach's shed. She
smiled to herself. They would have to let her sleep
somewhere.

The light was a deep dusky brown when she
reached the place where she had to wade across the
mountain stream. She had better call here before
the sentry took a shot at her.

"*Hoy! Hoy!*" She did not know the current pass-
word, which Sergeant changed every three days.

No answer.

"*Hoy!* It's me, Miranda."

A voice out of the dusk told her to come ahead,
but very slowly. She did so.

It was too dark for them to recognize each other
except as shapes. Whoever it was was surprised to
find her coming up the trail so late in the day, but
when she said she was bringing her usual messages
and money from Manila, he let her through. In a few
more minutes she had the glow of the campfires to
guide her the rest of the way. She identified herself
to the second sentry at the outer edge of the camp,
and he called out, "It's Miranda!"

Black silhouettes were outlined against the cooking
fires. The tallest one came hurrying forward and
threw his arms around her and then kissed her. He
was not so shy anymore. He felt very strong against
her. Oh yes, she was certainly going to spend the night
in his shed. And maybe this time, up here in the mountains . . .

They gave her supper. While she was eating, her brother Hilario sat beside her in the circle and she told him all the family news. He looked older and harder than the young boy she had first brought here. She saw he was growing a mustache, so skimpy that it looked silly. She would catch him alone tomorrow and suggest he shave it off.

When she had eaten, Coach and Sergeant and Rosauro took her to the headquarters shack. They sat on straw mats on the bamboo floor around the kerosene lamp. She could feel Coach's knee against her leg while they talked.

"This Quintano business," Coach began.

"He is a fake," Sergeant said.

"Yes, but this colonel up in Baguio doesn't know that."

"How did you hear?"

"One of Quintano's men showed up yesterday with the order. It was typewritten with a lot of mistakes, but it looked real, and it was signed. It said it was time to set up organized guerrilla commands for all of Luzon north of Manila. It gives Quintano both Tarlac and Zambales provinces."

"He is a fake," Sergeant repeated. "He never does anything except steal from the people."

"And make rape," Rosauro said, reminding everyone of the Tatloc brothers.

"Just the same, it's an order," Coach said. He turned to Miranda. "We've been arguing about what to do."

"No argument," Sergeant said. "We don't work with Quintano. He tells big lies how hard he fights the Japs. He sits in his big tent all day and thinks up lies."

"You can get court-martialed for disobeying a direct order," Coach said. "Especially in wartime."

"Who is going to court-martial me?"

"The Americans, when they come back."

"Huh. When is that?"

"We want you to get word to Amos," Coach told Miranda. In the lamplight his face was intense, concentrated. "I'll give you a letter tomorrow. We really can't report to Quintano. He'd take all our weapons and equipment and even our money. We can't do it. He'd screw us up completely. I don't know what Amos can do, but he's got a lot of contacts. Maybe something. Get the order changed somehow. I don't want us to get in trouble with the U.S. Army."

"What U.S. Army?" Sergeant said. "I don't see them."

"Miranda, you get word to Amos," Coach said. "Ask him to see what he can do. Now what do you have for us?"

"I brought everything," she said proudly. "All except the nails, they are very scarce. And two of the blankets are old, with many holes. But it's all down in Rosauro's house, everything. Except for these."

She opened her straw bag. She gave the packet of pesos, held together by a rubber band, to Sergeant, who riffled the notes, nodded his pleasure and handed the packet to Rosauro.

"We should pay back some of the farmers," Coach said.

Sergeant grunted.

Miranda knew Sergeant thought the farmers would wait till the Americans returned; Coach thought it was wise to keep the farmers happy by paying something from time to time. Both were right, and they always compromised.

"And then," she said, "one fat letter for Coach."

He was always embarrassed when she gave him a letter from the Judy in Santo Tomas. He was glad to get it, but he felt guilty because Miranda was the one who brought it. She thought this was sweet—and so American. She watched him put it in his pocket to read later.

"Now," she said, "two new things. Mr. Watson was almost killed in that typhoon. Papaya say he almost drowned, but he is all right. A boy saved him, a boy from your Simpson School. You know him, Coach. Felix Logan."

"Felix? Of course I know him. He practically ran the school."

"Yes, that is the one. The other thing is, I cannot come back here for a while. Maybe quite a few weeks. I am sent to Cabanatuan."

"What for? We need you here."

"Oh, Coach, that sounds so nice. You will miss me. I will miss you, too. One of the girls who brings things to the prisoners is very sick. I am going to take her place for a while."

"How long?"

"I don't know. Until Feling gets better. Now," she said innocently, "it is late, and I am tired after my long journey." She looked at Sergeant. "Where am I supposed to sleep?"

They all looked at Sergeant. His dark face was stern in the kerosene lamplight.

After a silence Rosauro suddenly laughed. "She can sleep in my bed," he said. "I will sleep on the ground." He thought this was very funny. Then he had another funny idea. "Or she can sleep in her brother's bed. Hilario will keep her safe."

Coach was smiling too.

"Or maybe I should walk back to town," Miranda said, deciding it was safe to make her own joke. "Through all those snakes and bugs."

"There is a rule," Sergeant said. Then he shrugged and joined the circle of smiles. "Coach, you are the wise man. What is your advice?"

"I have the best bed," Coach said, "so she should sleep there." He paused for a few seconds. "And I will sleep with you, Paradiso."

"Huh." Sergeant got to his feet. "I am not your *binabae*. Think of something else."

The men had been damping down the fires while they talked. It was time for the camp to go to sleep.

With the lights gone, it was very dark under the high canopy of trees. The stars could not shine through. The night was warm. She and Coach lay on top of his blanket, under the mosquito netting, while they made love. The first time urgent, as always, because they had been apart so long, but then the second time for slow pleasure.

They could not see each other at all, not even shapes, but they knew each other so well it was not necessary. She gave him *sipsip buto*, a favorite pleasure for them both. It was especially exciting in the total darkness

as she felt him change in her mouth from soft and
silky to harder, and then very hard. But much as they
both loved the final moments, she would not let him
finish that way tonight. She did not want to waste a
single chance. At the last minute she stopped and
jumped on top of him and threw her hips violently
twice, three times, and felt the fierce leap inside her.

There, she thought, as she snuggled her face against
his chest to fall asleep beside him, to spend a whole
night with him for the first time. There.

———

In the morning she woke up early and dressed before
the camp was up so that the men would not see them
in bed together. It was still early light when they ate
a breakfast of bananas and papayas and coffee made
from burned rice. Real coffee scarcely existed anymore, but burned rice had some of the same harsh,
bitter flavor.

She wandered around camp talking to the men
while Coach read his letter from the Judy and then
wrote his own letters. It was midmorning before he
finished and gave them to her. She hid them in the
bottom of her straw basket.

"I want to talk to you," he said. His bright blue
eyes looked serious.

Miranda did not feel serious. She felt happy.
"Okay," she said, smiling up at him. "Here I am."

"I don't like your going to Cabanatuan. It's too
dangerous. You don't know those people."

"No, but they are all friends. They will take care
of me. I will be all right."

"I've written Amos to say you shouldn't go."

"It is up to Mr. Watson. And Papaya. I think they will want me to go. They need somebody they can trust. It is important to help all those poor prisoners."

"Let the others do it."

"Oh, Coach, I am sorry. I must do what they tell me. Just like here, everybody does what you and Sergeant say. It is the same. Besides, it is not dangerous. It is okay."

"You might be gone a long time."

"I don't think so."

"Where will you stay?"

"There is a house in town where our people live."

"Maybe I'll come visit you."

Miranda was shocked. "Oh, no!"

"Why not? I can get around the country. I do it all the time, and the Japs don't notice me. I look like any other farmer."

"Filipino farmers don't have blue eyes. Or blond hair."

"I wear my big hat and I keep on the back roads. Nobody pays any attention to me."

"It is too many miles."

"Not that far. Two days, maybe two and a half. Less if I get some rides."

"Coach, if you really like me, you don't do this."

He smiled. "Somebody has to look out for you."

She smiled back. "I look out for myself. Don't worry."

Before she left, she told Hilario his new mustache looked silly. He was very offended.

Cabanatuan was a big town, although not as big as her hometown of San Fernando. It had the dingy sadness of all Philippine towns where the Japanese had a strong military presence. The streets had none of the noisy bustle of daily life. The people seemed quiet, subdued. The only motor traffic was an occasional military vehicle.

She had come by train, the usual endless, stop-and-start trip that took hours to cover a few miles. Papaya had told her to bring only her clothes and the concealed packets of pesos and a few careful messages to be passed on to some of the prisoners. "You don't need anything else," Papaya said. "Terry has everything."

When she got off the train, she followed directions and walked to a dilapidated two-story house a few blocks from the station. She would recognize it, Papaya said, by the broken yellow Magnolia Ice Cream sign propped carelessly against the side of the house.

She knocked at the screen door. Instantly a woman's figure appeared behind the screen. She could not have been more than a step or two away, perhaps waiting for the knock.

"I am an old, dear school friend of Peanut," Miranda said, using the exact words.

"What do you want?" The woman's voice was flat, cold.

"I have come to visit my other school friend Terry."

"What is your name?" Same flat voice.

"Feling," Miranda said.

"Ah! Come in, come in." The voice was suddenly
warm and cheerful. The screen door opened, and Miranda entered.

"I am Terry," the woman said, shaking hands. She
was a buxom middle-aged woman, taller than Miranda, wearing a loose, floor-length housecoat that
was a faded, dusty red. She was very light-skinned—
obviously some Spanish blood. Her gray-black hair,
mostly gray, was pulled back into a severe bun.

"I am Miranda."

"Yes, of course. First things first," Terry said. "Did
you bring the money?"

"Yes. Quite a lot."

"Good! What we are doing here is so expensive.
Come on, I will show you where you sleep. Then you
can meet everybody."

Six women and an old man named Ortiz lived in
the house. Ortiz did all the cooking and sweeping.
The women were engaged, under Terry's direction,
in smuggling food, money, medicine and other supplies to the American prisoners. Some worked at the
town marketplace, others outside the prison camp
half a dozen miles north of town.

Each morning Miranda and another young Filipina
named Felicidad walked to the marketplace carrying
heavy sacks filled with small, individual packages of
food. The big square was like every other market in
the Philippines. An open shed with a battered tin roof
gave protection against sun and rain. The sellers,

many of them old women, had their specific locations under the shed, often handed down through the family.

What little meat was for sale, mostly pork and a few chunks of carabao, was expensive. The flies buzzed on the meat. Live chickens and ducks lay in small feathery heaps, their legs tied together. Chicken eggs and speckled duck eggs were spread out on flat trays, and sacks of rice were open at the neck for inspection. The rice women would pick up a handful of their grain and let it run slowly back into the sack to show its quality. Many of the old women, squatting on their heels, smoked ropy, misshapen cigars twisted out of native tobacco.

Miranda and Felicidad lugged their sacks to the stall of their confederate, Ramon. He was the largest vegetable-and-fruit dealer in the Cabanatuan market. He sold everything—*pechay*, camotes, squash, pumpkins, the round, dark-green watermelons, the huge *upo* gourds used for soup, coconuts, mangosteens, papayas, half a dozen varieties of bananas. A silent, thin-faced merchant, Ramon helped Miranda and Felicidad place their food packages where they could be reached easily when the time came. Then they waited for the shopping expedition to arrive from the prison camp.

It was always the same. They came in the hot middle of the day, five big, empty carabao carts driven by American prisoners and escorted by Jap guards in uniform. The dark gray animals plodded slowly into the market square, their heavy heads with the thick curved horns swinging from side to side with each ponderous step, their lazy tails swishing at the flies. The carts halted in a line outside the shed, and the prisoners climbed down to buy their daily supply of food for the camp.

They had only so much money to spend each day, so there was serious bargaining and negotiating at every stall—except at Ramon's. Here the argument over prices was strictly for appearance. As each purchase was made and then loaded onto the carabao carts, Miranda and Felicidad slipped their special packages into the pile. Each package contained a few tightly folded pesos tucked in with the food. When the prisoners returned to camp and opened them, they would have more pesos to spend on next day's shopping or at their own commissary. It was, as Terry said, an expensive operation.

Papaya had told Miranda to look for a thin, black-haired prisoner with a black mustache who drove one of the carabao carts. This would be Santini, the corporal who worked with Major Humphrey at bringing in and distributing supplies. She spotted him the first morning. He wore only shorts and sandals, and his bare chest was covered with the same curly black hair as his head. She did not find a chance to speak to him until the third morning, when he stood near her to inspect a stalk of *lakatan* bananas.

"You are Santini?" she whispered.

"Yeah," he whispered back, not looking at her, still looking at the little yellow *lakatans*.

"I have a message for Major Humphrey. You see him?"

"Every day."

"It is from his old friend in Manila. The message is—" She stopped as one of the guards came near, then strolled on. "The message is: 'Chin up. We're still with you.'"

"Okay, got it," Santini said.

"Also this pack of cigarettes." She slipped it to him below sight level and he quickly stuck it in the pocket of his shorts.

"Better than messages," he whispered.

Miranda worked in the market for a week before Terry transferred her to the farm outside the prison camp. "It's best to change around," Terry explained. "That way the Japs don't start wondering why the same woman is always doing the same thing."

Miranda was excited that she was going to see the famous prison camp where thousands of American soldiers were held. Her partner was a lively little Filipina named Vicki, whose American husband was a POW. They drove out together early that morning in a two-wheeled *calesa*, their straw bags of sugar-cane candy and peanuts and hidden pesos on the floor beneath their feet.

"It is not like the marketplace," Vicki said, "where everybody argues about the prices. Here we have to make our sales quick-quick, while the prisoners are walking out to work on the big farm. The guards don't mind, they think we are just trying to earn a few centavos. But the guards get angry if we make delay. So you walk along beside the line, hold up your little bags and say, 'Candy, Joe? Peanuts, Joe?' And if somebody hands you money, you take it, whatever

it is, and give him the bag. But be sure you don't make
the line stop."

"Do you ever see your husband?"

Vicki shook her head. "Not once. But he is in there.
He is sick but still alive—they tell me so. Maybe I
will see him someday. Anyway, he knows I am out
here working for him."

"I know one of the prisoners, too," Miranda said,
thinking of Major Jack Humphrey. "He's a good
friend of my old boss in Manila. Maybe I will see
him."

"Maybe. But there are so many prisoners. Many
many. Look, there is the camp."

Up ahead, off to the right of their dirt road, Miranda saw a vast flat plain dotted with long rows of
low buildings surrounded by barbed wire. Around
the rim, spaced every few hundred yards, stood tall
watchtowers. Beyond the prison camp and its towers,
the level fields of cogon grass stretched to the horizon.
Far, far to the east were the pale shapes of distant
mountains shimmering in the morning sun. Many
miles behind them, the way they had come, the solitary cone of Mount Arayat rose up from the plain.
Everything else was blank, flat, monotonously empty
land.

Miranda shivered at the emptiness. It looked so
lonely.

"We leave the cart at that farmhouse," Vicki said.
"They won't let us come near the gate and the wire."

They left the *calesa* tied under a mango tree in the
farmer's yard, where the horse would be out of the
sun, under the thick shade of the deep green oblong

leaves. They slung their straw baskets over their shoulders and set out across the fields.

Miranda was excited because in a few minutes she would be helping the poor American prisoners. And maybe, in spite of what Vicki said, she would see Mr. Watson's friend Major Humphrey. She wished Coach could see her now, even though he did not approve. She wondered if she really might be pregnant. It was too soon to tell.

"Here is the path," Vicki said, stopping at a wide dirt track through the cogon grass. "They will be here soon. First day we will work on the same side so you can see what I do. Tomorrow we take different sides of the line. Remember, everything quick-quick."

In a few more minutes Miranda could see a long line of men coming across the plain from the prison camp. They were walking in groups, like squads of soldiers.

"Always the same," Vicki said. "Four in a row and one hundred in each group. The Japs count them before they leave camp and count them again before they come home."

Miranda felt nervous, because now she could see the armed Jap guards walking along both sides of the Americans. They were in uniform, with those ugly short-peaked caps and pistols at their belts. She told herself she must not be afraid. She must do her job.

As the line came close, she could see how bedraggled the Americans looked. Old worn-out clothes, tattered shorts and sleeveless shirts with holes, some with caps or beat-up sun helmets, some with only handkerchiefs or pieces of cloth over their heads to

protect against the sun. They looked sad. She felt so
sorry for them. She wanted to cheer them up somehow. At least she and Vicki were bringing them little
gifts. Here they came.

Vicki, who was walking down the line ahead of
her, was saying, "Peanuts and candy. Candy and peanuts. Buy nice candy, Joe?"

Miranda made up her mind she would not look at
the nasty Jap guards walking along the outer edge of
the line. She would look only at the Americans and
give them all a great big smile to say how much she
liked them and wanted to help them. After all, if
things had been different, her own Coach could have
been one of these men.

"Peanuts, Joe? Very nice candy. Very cheap."

She held up her bags, one in each hand. As hands
came out of the line with coins or paper money, she
quickly gave out her packages and then took new
ones from her shoulder bag. She smiled warmly into
each face to say she was truly their friend.

She was halfway down the third cluster of prisoners when she felt a hand grab her arm and yank
her around. She found herself staring into the face of
a Jap guard. In surprise she dropped the bags she was
holding.

They were almost the same height. He was stocky,
with a broad, flat face. His eyes, black and shiny,
were only a few inches from her own. The hand that
gripped her arm dug into her flesh.

She was terrified. "What is it? What is it? Let me
go." She tried to squirm loose, but he held her hard.
Was he going to rape her? She had heard such things.

The line of prisoners kept shuffling past them. Up ahead she saw that Vicki had stopped and was looking back in concern.

The guard's other hand came up to her face. To her horror he stuck a thick thumb and finger into her mouth and drew her lips apart. He was staring at her gold tooth. He nodded to himself.

I should not have been smiling, she thought. Oh, I should not have been smiling.

He let go her arm, held her lips apart with one hand and with the other tried to pull out her tooth. Luckily it was cemented in place. He pulled again. She bit down on his finger and struggled free. He made an angry sound and hit her across the face so hard that it dizzied her.

He looked around and called to another guard. The first guard said something in Japanese. The second guard smiled and wrapped his arms tight around her, squashing her breasts, holding her so close against his chest that she could smell him. When she tried to kick at both of them, the first guard punched her in the stomach, knocking the wind out of her.

Then he spread her lips apart again and made another effort to pull out her tooth. She was too breathless to fight. She was numb with terror. The prisoners were looking at them as they moved past. Where was Vicki? Why didn't Vicki help her? Then she remembered the rule they had all been taught: if you get in trouble, you are on your own. Don't expect help.

The first guard drew his pistol. He was going to shoot her. No, he wasn't.

Aiming carefully, he smashed the barrel of the pis-

tol against her mouth. There was a terrible shock of
pain as she felt her teeth break. She could taste the
bitter blood of her crushed lips. She tried to scream.
The pistol barrel hit her again. She almost fainted
from the pain, but the arms held her erect.

The awful fingers reached into her mouth again,
twisting and pulling. The pain made her close her
eyes. Finally the guard grunted and then the fingers
left her mouth. She opened her eyes to see his bloody
hand holding her beautiful gold tooth, and one of the
teeth attached to it. The guard put his prize in his
pocket and wiped his hand on his trousers.

The arms let her go. Crying, she sank to the ground
and held her quivering hands to her mouth. The two
guards stood looking down at her with total indifference.

"Pigs!" she said. Her voice was thick with blood.
"Pigs! Pigs! Pigs!"

The second guard, the one who had held her, swore
something at her. He picked up the straw bag she had
dropped and emptied all her food packages on the
ground. Then he bent down and deliberately began
to tear them apart to punish her for insulting the
Imperial Japanese Army.

Oh Jesus, she thought. But maybe they won't notice. Maybe they won't notice. Jesus, don't let them
notice.

The first guard said something, and she saw his
bloodstained hand come down and pick up one of
the tightly folded peso notes. He unfolded it and
looked at it. Then both guards were crouching beside

her, poring through the scattered bits of candy and peanuts, picking out the notes.

Then they dragged her to her feet and said something angry that she did not understand.

Vicki was nowhere in sight. The long line of prisoners had passed, but she could still see some of the men in the last group turning their heads to look back. She was alone on the dusty road in the open field with the two furious guards.

They seized her arms and began to drag her back toward the prison camp. Her mouth hurt very much, but she tried to force that from her mind. Instead, she thought about all the dear names that she must not tell. Would not tell. Would never tell.

≡ 26 ≡

A Family Matter

"Peanut, it is not your fault. Or Amos Watson's. It isn't even God's fault. These things happen."

"Miranda was not 'these things.' "

"No, of course not. A very good girl."

"Better than that. Zorro, everybody loved her. We all loved her. I tell you, once before the war, when she was Amos's secretary, she organized my whole record collection, the whole thing. It was a big terrible mess. I kept buying new records all the time as soon as they came out and, you know, just adding them to the piles. You couldn't find anything. And Miranda took her own spare time and straightened out the whole mess. And then—and then—"

"Peanut, stop."

"No, I want to tell you because you never knew her. She wrote out labels, all very neat. Organized. Just like a library. She was so proud of what a good job she did. And then she wouldn't take any money, not one peso. Not even a gift. You know how often that happens in the Philippines?"

"Yes, not very often."

"And now—"

"You mustn't blame yourself."

"But we *sent* her there. Amos and I *sent* her there."

"Yes, to do a job that needed to be done."

"And a good job, too. Terry wanted to keep her there permanently. All the others liked her. Even the old man who keeps the house, Ortiz, Terry says he cried for two days. We should not have sent her. She would still be alive."

"Perhaps. Or perhaps something else might have happened. You can't be sure."

"I am sure."

"Well, Peanut, if you are so sure of things in this business, then you are smarter than anybody else."

"They have to stop now at Cabanatuan. Terry says they have to stop. The Japs are suspicious of everybody, looking everywhere, checking everything. None of the girls can do anything for the prisoners."

"No, obviously."

"Even though she never talked."

"No, she was a very good girl. Amos picks good people." He made a little bow of his head, including her.

"I was thinking maybe not to tell Amos. Just pretend nothing happened. Let him think Miranda is—is—still okay. But I can't do that."

"No. He should know. He has a right to know."

"So Federico will tell him next chance."

"Good. Now Peanut, you have to find somebody else to collect those reports from Coach and Sergeant. They are the best information we are getting from the Clark Field area."

"Yes, and somebody has to tell Coach about Miranda. She was crazy about him. I was thinking, maybe I make one trip there myself to tell him in person."

Enrique looked at her and shook his head. "Ridiculous."

"Okay, I know."

"Good. So who will you use in place of Miranda?"

"How can you say 'in place of Miranda'? Like it was just nothing?"

"Because we have to go on. Who?"

"I want her older brother, Timoteo, the one who sometimes brings messages to Manila with the vegetables. If he will do it. I think he will do it for Miranda."

"All right, good. Now I have that order for Captain Stone. It should take care of the Quintano problem."

"Whose order?"

As usual, when he did not choose to answer one of her questions, he ignored it. "It looks very official," he said with a smile, pleased with himself. "It is even on genuine U.S. Army stationery."

"How did you get that?"

"You will let me know what Miranda's brother says?"

———

Amos Watson listened carefully to Federico's story, told in a low voice as he worked on a new chair for Amos's shanty. Amos was surprised that his own voice was steady as he asked Federico a few questions. Were they sure Miranda had told nothing? Yes, there had been no other arrests. Were they sure the other girl got away? Yes, she had left Cabanatuan, so they wouldn't find her.

When he could think of nothing more he needed to ask, Amos thanked Federico for his information and went for a walk by himself.

He remembered the Christmas, now long ago, when he had given Miranda her gold tooth as a special present. She had been so pleased, smiling all the time to show it off. He remembered suggesting to her that a white false tooth, matching the others, would be less conspicuous, but she had said, no, no, that was not the point. "Gold is more charming." Charming—that was Miranda.

He had lost two now, two of the best. Donato and now Miranda. Neither had talked. Good people. Wonderful people, very brave.

He sought out Judy Ferguson.

"I have some bad news," he said. "There won't be any more letters, at least not for a while."

"Why not? Is Brad hurt? Has something happened to him?"

"No, he's all right. As far as I know."

"But it's already been over a month since the last one. What's the matter?"

"The girl who brought the letters. She's—" He wondered how much to tell Judy. He supposed it did not really matter. "She's dead."

"Can't you get somebody else?"

That made him angry. "Judy, this was a very special person. The Japs killed her."

That took her aback. "I'm sorry. I'm really sorry."

"Well, you didn't know her. But yes, you should be sorry."

———

Brad Stone looked at the sheet of U.S. Army stationery without seeing it. How different it would be if Miranda had brought it. She would be all smiles, pleased to be bringing him something so valuable. *Here, Coach, this is for you.* The paper made them a special, independent unit, reporting not to Major Quintano but only to "Central Command"—whatever that might be. He didn't care.

"Here," he said to Paradiso. "We're on our own."

"Coach—"

"Don't argue with me. I'm going. Me and Hilario."

"Coach, you tell me all the time, 'Think serious.' "

"What the hell do you think I'm being?"

Paradiso shook his head back and forth. "You are not serious. What is there to do in Cabanatuan?"

"I don't know."

"Then why go?"

"Because—because that's where she was. She can't just die someplace that I've never seen."

"I don't think that is good reason."

"I don't care what you think."

"Huh."

"That's right. Not this time."

"Okay. I give you advice anyway. Take somebody else. Hilario is still new boy."

"You don't understand. This is a family matter."

Paradiso was silent, staring at him. Finally he said, "You talk like Filipino, Coach." He stuck out his arms and they shook hands—firm, hard grip. "Watch out, Coach. No dumb things."

Even with one long ride in a carabao cart and a shorter one in a horse cart, it took two days traveling over back roads to reach Cabanatuan. Hilario carried a farmer's work bolo strapped to his belt. Brad had his service revolver tucked in the back of his waistband beneath his long loose shirt. As agreed, Hilario did what little talking was necessary. By now Brad knew enough Filipino words to get along, but there was no point in letting someone wonder about his accent. As Paradiso said, he would never sound like a native.

Cabanatuan was the biggest town Brad had seen since the war began, much larger than Carabangay or the other villages and small towns around their camp. It was late afternoon. They saw a number of Jap soldiers on the streets, for this was where all the guards from the prison camp came for their supplies and recreation. From under the shadow of his hat, Brad glanced at their faces, wondering if one of them had done those things to Miranda.

Miranda's brother Timoteo had told them how to find the house where she had lived. They went straight there and knocked on the door. They had to wait. Hilario knocked again.

An old man finally came to the door. He had deep wrinkles in his mournful face. He had white hair and a thick white mustache.

Hilario said, "Sir, we are looking for Terry."

The old man studied them, eyes shifting from one to the other. He did not say anything.

Hilario, thinking the old man might be deaf, said in a louder voice, "We come to see Terry." Still no answer. "Are you Ortiz? You must be Ortiz."

"Yes, I am Ortiz. This is my house. There is no Terry here."

Hilario looked at Brad for advice, but Brad said nothing.

"Look at me, sir," Hilario told the old man. "I am Miranda's brother. We know she stayed here."

At the name, Ortiz's eyes filled with tears. He studied Hilario's face for the resemblance. He was being extremely careful with strangers. "There is no Miranda here."

"We know," Hilario said. "The Japs killed her. We know all about it. That's why we are here. To talk to Terry."

"Who is this one?" Ortiz asked. He looked at Brad.

"He is a friend of Miranda's. His name is Coach."

Ortiz's eyes grew still more tearful. "Ah, you are Miranda's Coach?" He almost bowed as he held the door wide for them to enter.

He took them to the main room and asked them to sit in straight-backed rattan chairs while he went to get Terry.

This is where Miranda was, Brad thought, looking around him. Perhaps she sat in this very chair. This is probably where the woman called Terry gave the girls their instructions before sending them off to the marketplace or to the fields outside the prison camp. Miranda was probably right here in this room that last morning.

A tall woman in a loose housecoat came into the

room. Brad got to his feet, and then Hilario did, too. Ortiz followed behind her, wiping his eyes with his hand. She was an imposing woman with a strong face and straight gray hair. She looked at them and shook her head.

"Our poor Miranda," she said. It was more a statement than an expression of sympathy. She seated herself, waved Brad and Hilario to their chairs and told Ortiz to bring glasses and a pitcher of *basi*, the Philippine sugar wine.

When Ortiz had served them and pulled up his own chair to join their circle, she said, "Why have you come?"

Hilario looked at Brad, who said, "We came to learn about Miranda. We wanted to hear it from you."

The woman nodded. She sipped her *basi*. "This is not a time to make trouble," she said. "The Japs are very strict now. You should not have come."

"I am her brother."

She nodded again but made no comment.

"We aren't here to make trouble," Brad said.

"Good. We have enough trouble without your help."

"Was anyone with Miranda that morning?"

"Of course. Vicki. But that one is gone now. After Miranda, the Japs were looking for her. All the girls are gone. Maybe later we can start again, but it will have to be some other way."

She held out her glass, and Ortiz filled it.

"Do you know which of the guards did it?"

"What does it matter? No, we don't know."

Brad thought she was lying, but she was right. What difference did it make? He could not go out and hunt down those two guards, even if he knew who they were. He and Hilario would have to avenge Miranda some other way and in some other place. "The girl who was with her, this Vicki. She told you what happened?"

"Yes. But she had to run away when she saw what was happening, or they would have killed her, too. Many of the prisoners saw it also, and the ones who buy food for the camp managed to get word to us. It was very bad—I do not wish to talk about it. Then I sent all the girls away for safety."

"But you stayed. You and Ortiz."

"We are old people. The Japs don't know us. Besides, someone must stay to find out what is going on here."

"I would like to see the place where it happened."

Terry shrugged. "What good will that do?"

"I want to see it too," Hilario said.

"We have come a long way to pay our respects to her," Brad said. "Besides, nobody in our group has seen the prison camp. We have to see it, now that we're here."

Terry thought about it. "Perhaps it can be arranged. You cannot go too close to the camp. I don't think you should stay here very long."

"We won't," Brad said, "but we want to see that camp. And the place where it happened. You see, we both loved her."

This was too much for Ortiz, who began to weep again. "She talked about you both," he said. He looked at Terry for permission to continue. "In the evening, all the girls talked about their other lives. Miranda was proud of her younger brother the guerrilla. And very proud of Coach and Sergeant. Especially Coach."

Brad was glad she had talked about him. "Thanks for telling me. I'm very grateful."

Terry's face softened a little. She finished her *basi* and held out her glass. "She was very fond of you, Coach. It was her great hope that she might be pregnant."

"What?"

"Oh, yes."

"My God. She never said anything. But then—that could mean—"

"Who knows? But that was her hope. She was very happy about it."

Brad could not say anything. He did not know what to say. He held out his glass to Ortiz.

"Yes," Ortiz said, pouring Brad's glass full. "All the other girls teased her, but you know what I think? I think they were jealous. She was a happy girl."

The *basi* was so mild that they were able to drink two more full pitchers before everybody became quite drunk, and Hilario and Ortiz put their arms around each other and wept together for Miranda.

Brad wept alone, and only inside.

Next day Terry refused to let Ortiz show them the way. "They should not see you together," she said. She gave Brad and Hilario detailed instructions about the road they should take northeast of town and told them how to recognize the farmhouse where Miranda and Vicki had left their *calesa*. From there it would be only a few hundred paces out to the wide dirt track that led to the prison farm. That was where it had happened.

"You can see the prison camp from there," Terry said. "Don't go any closer. They shoot from the watchtowers if you come too close."

Brad started to thank her, but she stopped him. "You must leave Cabanatuan today," she said. "Go home."

On her advice they timed their trip to reach the spot in the late afternoon when the prisoners and their guards had returned to camp from the day's work on the farm. They walked one behind the other under a cloudy sky, Hilario leading the way. They kept to the side of the road. It was strange to be retracing Miranda's last journey. Brad wondered how she had felt that sunny morning, and what she and the girl Vicki had said to each other.

There was the farmhouse with the white door and the big mango tree in the front yard. They turned off the road into the fields. These were the same steps Miranda had taken, with her straw bag of food packages and the hidden pesos slung over her shoulder. She had strong legs and a vigorous walk. She would have strode across this cogon-grass field with high hopes for helping the prisoners.

Brad could see the huge prison camp and the watchtowers, desolate under the gray clouds. He tried to count the buildings and to figure out how they were arranged, but they were too far away. In spite of what Terry had said, they would have to get closer if he wanted to learn anything useful.

Hilario came to a stop in front of him. They had reached the wide dirt track.

They stood together on the track and stared down at it. The dusty earth bore the scuffled footprints of many men walking past, the American prisoners and their Japanese guards. Brad looked across the field to the bleak prison camp and beyond it the dim far mountains, their tops hidden under rain clouds. This was where Miranda had stood. This was what she had seen, just before . . .

Brad and Hilario looked at each other. Hilario's face, reminiscent of his sister's, was as remote as the mountains. There was nothing for them to say. The sun came through for a few moments while they were standing there, then disappeared again behind the clouds.

"Come on," Brad said. "I want to get a better look at that camp before it gets dark."

"But she said—"

"We'll keep a safe distance. They'll think we're farmers going home from work. I'm not going to get this close and not even see what it's like."

"Yes, sir, Coach."

It took them an hour to walk a wide circle around the camp. They could not risk stopping. They did not come close enough to the watchtowers to attract a warning or a shot. Brad wished he had his binoculars. He could see little figures moving inside the camp. He studied carefully as they walked, and he told Hilario, who had even keener eyesight, to try to remember everything exactly so that later they would be able to draw an accurate map of the camp layout and the various buildings. He could see there were two camps—a smaller, neater one for the Japanese guard force, and the sprawling, ramshackle rows of barracks for the prisoners. Amos's friend Jack Humphrey was somewhere in there. So were those two guards.

By the time they had completed the circle and again struck the main road above the camp, it was nearly dark. Even in this poor light it would have been dangerous to walk the road past the main gate. They had to slog through the rice paddies on the far side of the road, but from the fields Brad could see the big gate and the guardposts. They found a broad ditch opposite the gate and hid there to study the entrance. Only when they were well past the camp did they dare return to the road. Rain began to fall, light but steady. It was going to be a long wet night, but living in the mountain camp, they were used to being wet.

If they kept going, Brad thought that, before they stopped to sleep in the fields, they should be able to get around the town of Cabanatuan and onto one of the back roads that would lead them toward Carabangay. Too many Japs for them to feel safe in Cabanatuan.

On the outskirts of Cabanatuan they came upon something quite unusual in these times, a brightly lighted building. From the open windows on the second story poured the tinkling sound of Oriental music. A cheap victrola, Brad guessed. Behind the building he could make out the shapes of several army vehicles.

"Whorehouse, sir," Hilario said.

"Right. We better go way around behind it."

They moved into the darkness behind the parked vehicles. As they did so, a door opened, throwing an added rectangle of bright light into the parking area. They ducked down into the shadows, safely out of sight.

Two Japanese officers came through the door. One of them stumbled on the steps, and the other caught his arm and said something. Both men laughed. From the way they walked they must be more than a little drunk.

"Sir," Hilario whispered, "we take them."

He had his bolo in his hand. Brad felt the hard shape of his own revolver against his back. It would be easy.

"For Miranda," Hilario whispered.

Brad was deeply tempted. The two officers would be unsuspecting, and they were obviously in no shape to fight back. It could be done. For Miranda. Then Brad thought about Terry's admonition that Cabanatuan was in enough trouble already. The reprisals for the murder of two officers would be severe. Both the townspeople and the prisoners would suffer. The price for personal satisfaction would be too high.

"No," he whispered.

"But—"

Brad put his hand over Hilario's mouth. "No."

They watched the two officers stumble into their truck. After a few moments the motor started and the headlights came on. The truck backed around and drove up the road in the direction of the prison camp.

When it was gone, they stood up. The light rain was still falling.

"We have a long way to go," Brad said. "Let's get started."

Hilario sighed. "We could have taken their teeth," he said, the disappointment heavy in his young voice. "All of them."

BOOK THREE

RETURN

⸗ 27 ⸗

Changing Times

From his pyramidal tent in the lowlands that he shared with two other officers, Eli Phipps could look way up the mountain and see the General's spectacular new home. You could hardly miss it from anywhere in Hollandia. Bad enough that it consisted of three big adjoining prefabs set on a flattened mountaintop, but the engineers had had the appalling bad taste to paint it a dazzling white. Dugout Doug's White House, the troops and war correspondents called it, in anger and contempt.

Phipps would probably be an old man before he made up his mind about MacArthur. But the "White House" was not MacArthur's fault, even though he got all the blame. His own misguided staff officers had built it for him while he was off in Australia, and he practically never stayed in it. Still, there it stood, an unfair but perfect symbol of the General's grandeur.

A fairer symbol was the amazing fact that the U.S. Army was here in Hollandia at all. Everybody "knew" MacArthur would have to slog his way west-

ward along the endless New Guinea coast, knocking
out the Japanese strongholds one by one with heavy
casualties, just like Buna. Everybody knew it but
MacArthur himself.

Eli Phipps remembered the day Red Sampson told
the message center that MacArthur wanted to hear
about every single Japanese radio mention of Hollandia. They were not to miss a single one, or "the
Old Man will have your ass." When the radio traffic
showed that Hollandia was only a rear-area headquarters and that all the Jap infantry and artillery had
been sent down the coast to await MacArthur's obvious next attack, the General bypassed the whole lot
and leaped four hundred miles westward to capture
Hollandia. He took it with only a handful of casualties, and here they were. And then in late July, the
General leaped again, this time all the way to Sansapor, right smack on the equator at the very western
tip of New Guinea.

The attack went so smoothly and the place was so
lightly defended that noncombat GIs were confidently
walking around on the open beaches only a couple
of days after the invasion. The great thing about Sansapor was that it was the last stop on New Guinea.
From Sansapor, you could practically smell the Philippines, some six hundred miles away across the Mo-
lucca Sea.

Already the submarines were sneaking in to deposit
"the New Guinea boys" on the various Philippine
islands, all the way up to Luzon. They were Filipinos
recruited in America and trained in Australia to operate radios and handle codes, and now they were

being shipped in from New Guinea to work with the guerrillas.

The guerrillas were now a hot subject in Mac-Arthur's headquarters. Eli Phipps managed to keep close track of the increased activity, not only through the message center traffic but, more important, through his membership in the General's Bataan Gang. If you were in the Gang, even as a junior member, you were certified worthy to share the most closely held secrets. General Sampson, who now encouraged Phipps to call him Red, at least when they were alone, was his best source.

Sampson told Eli the story of the Japanese cruiser *Kyishi*, which had been sunk by a navy sub at Balabac Strait off the southern end of Palawan. "We knew just when that ship was coming through," Sampson said, rubbing his hands with pleasure. "You know how? One of our people in Manila, fellow named Zorro, found out the ship's schedule from a Jap admiral and passed the word."

"Zorro?" Eli asked. "Like *Mark of Zorro*?" A vision of Tyrone Power in black hat, black mask and long black cape sprang to mind.

"Yeah. Apparently he's old-family Spanish in Manila, but he must have a sense of humor. He runs a hell of a little group. Actually, the one who found out about *Kyishi* was a singer who's having an affair with the Jap admiral. You probably heard of her, she was big stuff before the war. Called herself Papaya."

"Heard of her? I even heard her sing. She was terrific."

"Well, Whitney acts as though he invented her.

And Zorro too. Claims he knew him in Manila before the war."

At the mention of Whitney, the familiar note of sarcasm returned to Red Sampson's voice. General Courtney Whitney, in charge of guerrilla activities, was not a member of the Bataan Gang. Once a successful Manila lawyer, he had been in the States when war started and was assigned to MacArthur's staff because of his knowledge of the Philippines. Both Sampson and Phipps considered him unbearably stuffy.

"Personally," Sampson said, "I doubt that old courtly Courtney associated with anyone who was merely Spanish. And of course Papaya's even worse— she's only a mestiza. I bet Whitney had a real deep struggle before he could let himself be proud of them."

Grudgingly, Red Sampson admitted that on the other hand, Whitney certainly knew another member of the information network, a wealthy American named Amos Watson, who was now a prisoner in Santo Tomas. Watson had, after all, been a leading member of Manila's prewar high society. "But maybe Watson didn't like him," Sampson said hopefully.

Eli thought this Amos Watson must be a strange person, as well as a very ingenious one. He remembered hearing that before the war Watson had gone around predicting military disaster and had even dared say this to the General himself. And now, somehow, Watson was getting valuable information into and out of Santo Tomas Internment Camp and even, according to Zorro, supplying funds to an armed guerrilla group in Zambales. Eli wondered how he did it. He wondered how all of them did it. It had to be extremely dangerous. Soon, surely fairly soon now, Eli might have a chance to find out for himself, because clearly they were on their way back.

You could practically smell it.

So could MacArthur. He told one of the officers, "They are waiting for me up there. It has been a long time."

———

Life at Santo Tomas was unraveling so fast that Amos Watson could watch it happen almost day by day. Ever since the hated Kempeitai, the Japanese military police, took over the camp last February, it was plain they were deliberately making life miserable for the internees. Almost every day Felix Logan reported some painful new regulation or deprivation that would isolate STIC more and more from the outside world.

The worst, from Amos's point of view, was the closing of the Package Line. From the beginning it had been his main conduit to the outside for food, laundry, shanty supplies and, most critical of all, his precious notes and information. Now he had to take greater risks with his messages, trusting Filipinos he did not really know but who were recommended by Papaya and Federico. Each time he encountered Judy Ferguson, she asked him why there were no letters from Brad Stone.

Even the way the Kempeitai shut down the Package Line was malicious. When they announced that the

line would close forever on Tuesday, every Manila
friend and servant brought a final gift of food or
clothes or bedding on Sunday morning. They came
from all over the city, most of them on foot because
transportation was now so scarce. The street outside
the main gate was crammed with people holding baskets and bags and sacks filled with last presents.

Hearing about the mass outside the gate, the commandant decided to declare that the Package Line was
already closed.

The people waited in the street. The internees
waited behind the sawali fence near the gate, hoping
for a last glimpse of their friends. Amos thought there
might well be rioting outside. If there was, it would
surely be followed by shooting.

The situation was saved by the Japanese sergeant
in charge at the gate. He turned to the internees,
waved his arms and said, "I will let them come in.
My gift to the camp!"

The gate opened, and the people poured in, dragging their bundles. Amos wondered what would happen to the generous sergeant.

With the end of the Package Line, the food in camp
deteriorated rapidly. Manila prices were high and
supplies short, and the Japs were taking everything
for themselves. The Kempeitai brought in less and
less food for the internees. Almost never any meat.
Fried fish three times a week, but the fish were so tiny
that it was difficult to clean them of guts and bones.
Often the fish were rotten; always they stank. One
small banana at breakfast and another at night. Hard
mongo beans and shoddy rice. One spoon of sugar

every other day. The hours for the camp's fruit and
vegetable market were cut to two a day, the lines
were endless, and there was never enough to go
around, even for those like Amos who still had
money. Everyone had lost weight in camp, but now
the weight losses grew serious.

Like others, Amos developed edema from the inadequate diet. The collection of fluid in his tissues
swelled his feet and his hands. The swelling itself was
not painful, but some days the extra weight of the
fluid made it very difficult to walk and hard to keep
his balance. On bad days his feet were so swollen and
heavy that he could wear only large, loose slippers
and get around only with the help of a sturdy bamboo
cane. For the first time, he began to feel old. Others
began to die.

Roll call had always been conducted by room monitors and shanty-area supervisors without fuss. Now
the Kempeitai demanded that everyone line up in the
halls twice a day for an interminable inspection by
Jap officers. Each internee had to bow when his name
was called. Lieutenant Abiko, the most hated officer,
conducted long classes in the art of bowing properly.

The Kempeitai made everyone in camp sign a new
oath: "I hereby solemnly pledge that I will not under
any circumstances attempt to escape or conspire directly or indirectly against the Japanese Military Authorities." Although the camp was in an uproar over
the oath, Amos signed cheerfully. It meant nothing
to him. He wasn't interested in escape, and he had
been conspiring for so long that he wouldn't know
how to stop. Signing a false promise appealed to him.

In June the Kempeitai stopped the city truck from collecting the camp's garbage, saying no more alcohol fuel could be spared. The camp went back to burying its own garbage. It was brutal work for underfed men.

In August the Kempeitai made the internees turn in all their money except fifty pesos apiece "for deposit in the Bank of Taiwan." Warned by Felix, Amos spent two days carefully hiding packets of pesos around the campus but then handed in the rest. He hated to do it.

"But why didn't you hide all of it?" Felix asked, when Amos told him where the caches were, just in case.

"Well, when you go into business, one of the things you must learn to do is accept your losses. Cut your losses."

"But they'll never give that money back, will they?"

"Of course not. But if I didn't hand in a respectable amount, they'd be very suspicious. Listen, Felix, in business you have to recognize when you're in a losing situation. You wish it were different, but it isn't, so cut your losses. Save whatever you can. But if you're stuck, you're stuck."

In spite of the steadily worsening diet, the Kempeitai increased everyone's compulsory work hours because there was too much "idleness" in camp. Amos's toilet duty went up to three hours a day, which he did not mind. The good part was that the time Felix spent sweeping and cleaning and taking care of the commandant's office went up to five hours a day—more time to listen to more talk between the Japs.

That talk was the only hopeful thing to come out of these terrible Kempeitai months. Felix reported the Japs were sure Manila would soon be bombed by the Americans. Amos could hardly wait. It had been close to three years.

———

Brad Stone could not believe the vision that had appeared.

The two Filipino-American soldiers—born in California, they said—spoke colloquial, unaccented English. They wore green combat fatigues, with no holes or patches, and sturdy jungle boots and camouflage helmets. Sergeant Dagopino and Corporal Perez, fresh from New Guinea, courtesy of a U.S. Navy submarine.

"We landed off Botolan Point four nights ago," Sergeant Dagopino explained. He and Perez both seemed very cheerful. "It took us a while to unload and hide everything, but here we are, sir."

Brad shook his head, not understanding. "I don't even know where Botolan Point is."

"West coast, sir. South of that old radar station at Iba. Then we came over the mountains as soon as we could to find you. The rest of our stuff will take a couple of days to catch up, but then we'll be in business."

"What stuff?" Paradiso asked. "What business?"

"Mostly radio equipment," Dagopino said. "Our

transmitters. But the sub brought some other things that ought to come in handy. Greaseguns, carbines, ammo, atabrine."

"Ha!" Paradiso said. "For the attack."

"Not yet. For later."

"What's atabrine?" Brad asked.

"Malaria pills. Here, sir." From his knapsack he took a bottle of little yellow pills and handed them to Brad. "One a day, sir, and then no malaria."

"What business?" Paradiso repeated.

"When we get our radio set up, we'll be sending out your reports. In code. That's what Perez and I and the other guys have all been learning for the last year."

"How did you hear about us?" Brad asked.

"No idea, sir. Our orders were to find the Coach and Sergeant guerrillas and team up with you. They told us right where to find you." He smiled. "You're supposed to be the best there is in this area."

"That's right," Paradiso agreed. "When do we get the guns?"

"Soon as they get lugged over that mountain road."

"You need help? We send helpers to carry."

"All taken care of," Dagopino said. "The Botolan people are supplying the porters. In the meantime . . ." He turned to Corporal Perez. "Sammy, hand out the presents."

Perez opened his bulging knapsack. All the guerrillas crowded around to see what wonders would appear. Perez began to hand them out, first to Brad and Paradiso, then to the other men.

Brad felt the saliva gather in his mouth as he looked down at his hand holding a real, live, genuine, unmistakable, all-American chocolate bar. The men were tearing away the wrappers, smiling as they bit off chunks of the rich chocolate. The first chocolate candy in forever.

The other present was an ordinary yellow packet of paper matches. Ordinary, except that against the yellow background was a black-and-white picture of MacArthur saluting, above the words "I Shall Return—Douglas MacArthur."

He looked up from the matches and his chocolate bar and said to Dagopino, "When are they coming? How soon are they coming?"

"Don't know, sir. Not for a while, I guess, or they wouldn't ship us in here to send them reports. But they're coming all right, or *he* wouldn't have sent the matches." There was a confidence, almost a reverence in his voice when he spoke of MacArthur. "We got some magazines in the baggage, too. A couple of copies of *Life* with pictures of General MacArthur."

During the next few days the New Guinea boys' baggage came trickling through the mountain pass, carried on the backs of porters. The heavier pieces of radio equipment were dragged in two-wheeled carts. The greatest cause of excitement was the new carbine—lightweight, fast-action, far better for jungle fighting than any weapon the guerrillas had ever seen. There were only six, but the men were as thrilled as if there had been cases of them. Dagopino gave one to Brad and one to Paradiso and said it was up to Captain Stone to distribute the others.

"I take care of that," Paradiso announced.

Dagopino and Perez assembled their radio transmitter and receiver high up the mountain above the camp.

"Better signal." Dagopino explained to Brad and Paradiso. "Besides, any Japs come up, you'll be in between to protect us."

"We protect ourselves," Paradiso said. He was not about to turn over his command to the New Guinea boys.

The first message received in code from New Guinea was an explicit order. Offensive action against the enemy was strictly forbidden. What headquarters wanted was information about Japanese troop movements, supplies and military installations. A list of specific questions followed.

"Huh," Paradiso said when Brad read him the message. "If that's all they want, why send carbines?"

Paradiso wore his new carbine over his right shoulder all day long, his dark brown hand constantly caressing the webbing of the sling. Brad had offered to give up his own carbine so that one more guerrilla could have the extreme pleasure and honor of carrying one. "No, Coach," Paradiso said. "This is like general's star. You can't give away."

What headquarters was asking for was basically the same kind of information Brad and Paradiso and their men had been reporting all along, first through Miranda and more recently through her brother Timoteo. But Miranda never knew what happened to the reports after she delivered them. Brad had always wondered if they were actually useful. He even won-

dered if their main purpose hadn't been to keep old
Amos entertained during his long dreary months of
internment. If so, Brad had been willing to provide
entertainment in exchange for the pesos and supplies.

Now he knew better. Somehow, in some way that
he suspected he would never learn, the reports had
been passed on and appreciated. Otherwise Brad and
Paradiso's relatively small band would never have
been selected for Dagopino and Perez to work with.
"The best in this area," Dagopino said. If their reports
had not got through, and if they had not been valued,
Dagopino and Perez might well have been assigned
to Quintano's Marauders. Quintano's was, after all,
a much larger group. Brad explained all this to Paradiso, who nodded agreement.

"They know Quintano is fake," Paradiso said.

"Not necessarily. What they do know is that we're
very good."

"We know that all the time, Coach."

Brad wished Miranda could share their success.
She would have been proud of them and proud of
her own contribution. He could not get over her loss.
Sometimes he dreamed of making love to her. Or he
would catch himself idly thinking it was almost time
for her to pay another visit to Carabangay, and then
always he felt the reminding jolt that she was not
coming back. He never discussed Miranda now with
anyone, not even Paradiso or Hilario or the older
brother, Timoteo. She was his private memory, sad
and lovely.

He wondered if he would ever tell Judy about Miranda. Well, yes, he would have to if things worked

out between them. He was much less sure of that now
than before Miranda. He had got over feeling guilty
about Miranda, but she was still very much with him,
and Judy was far away. No letters from her for a long
time. Or from Amos, either. As Timoteo said, Santo
Tomas was very strict now, and messages were extremely difficult. Brad wondered if Judy was still all
right. Sometimes he got out her few old letters and
reread them. They were more than he had of Miranda,
but then he didn't need letters from Miranda to remind him.

The biggest difference the radio made was that now
everything seemed immediate. And urgent. Headquarters wanted to know everything and wanted to
know it right away. In the second week Brad received
a long query about Cabanatuan. Incredibly, headquarters had the map of the prison camp that he and
Hilario had drawn after their visit and sent off with
Timoteo. How many yards from the road to the main
gate? How accurate was the number and placement
of buildings shown? What was their best estimate of
the size of the buildings and the distances between
them? What was their precise, repeat precise, estimate
of the distance between the prisoners' barracks and
the barracks of the Japanese guard force?

Brad sat down with Hilario and their copy of the
map. They went over the questions one by one. Brad
often had to jog his memory by staring and staring
at the map, trying to remember just how something
had looked, but Hilario seemed to have the prison
camp engraved somewhere in his mind. Brad would

read a question, and Hilario would close his eyes in silence, sometimes for a minute or more, and then out would come his recollection. Together they were able to answer almost everything, give or take a few distances that were pretty much guesswork. Brad composed a long message for Dagopino and Perez to encode and transmit. Headquarters would know as much about Cabanatuan as anyone who had not been imprisoned there.

———

"These fuckers," Maxsie said, peering into the canteen cup of thin rice soup Jack Humphrey had brought to his cot, "they forget a man's supposed to eat. At least now and then."

Jack Humphrey was worried about his friend. Maxsie's back was in spasms again, severe enough so that he could not go out on work detail. No work detail, no rice and corn, only the thin *lugao* soup. He was losing weight. Hell, they were all losing weight. Even the "full" ration didn't amount to much. They had not been so hungry since the early days at Camp O'Donnell.

Everything was falling apart. The farm where they all worked so hard was producing vegetables, but the Japs took away most of the crops to feed their own troops. The camp commissary was almost empty. Prices were high. The loss of smuggled pesos, ever since that poor girl had been caught by the guards, made it almost impossible to get extra food. Nothing had come through from Amos Watson in a long time.

Corporal Santini would come back from town on the
Carabao Clipper and shake his head at Humphrey:
nothing doing, no extras.

Dear Sara,

Yesterday a barrio dog strayed into camp and we
were on him in a flash. He was pretty skinny, like all
these village dogs, but we boiled him up, and Maxsie
and I and a bunch of others all got a little chunk of
meat. I've eaten lizard, too, but dog is better. So is
cat. So is rat. You get used to almost everything. So
far I've been able to hold out against what some of
the men are doing. They're catching the frogs that
fall in the latrines and can't hop out again. They wash
them off, but even so.

A few of the younger men have slipped out of camp
through the barbed-wire fence, found some food, then
slipped back in again. They come back because they
know that ten other men would be shot if they escaped
for good. Maxsie and I talked about trying it before
his back got so bad again, but then we saw what
happened to one of the men they caught. He was on
his way in through the wire, but they said he was
trying to escape. They tied him to a post right by that
spot in the fence and beat him for two days. Then
they turned out the whole camp to watch him dig his
own grave.

I keep telling myself—we keep telling each other—
that the only reason it's turned so bad it that the Japs
must be losing, and they're taking it out on us.
They've moved a lot of the POWs out of the Philippines—off to Formosa or even Japan, they say, but

*of course nobody really knows. Tough as it is here,
I don't want to be moved. I'd be worried it's even
worse somewhere else.*

*We hear a U.S. sub sank a Jap ship filled with
American prisoners. What a way to get killed. Maybe
it's not true. But most of us go along with what
Maxsie calls Maxsie's Law: if it sounds awful, it's
true, but if it sounds good, it's a lie. That way you
don't get your hopes up and don't get disappointed.*

*Wish I could be more cheerful, but anyway I'm
alive. And I'm going to stay alive, goddamn it. Give
the boys a hug.*

Love, Jack

September 21, 1944. Judy Ferguson was sure she
would remember the date as well as she remembered
her own birthday.

An ordinary-looking morning—cool, the sky covered with high clouds. Breakfast was the usual horror,
corn mush and weak tea, and this was the alternate
day when there was no sugar. She ate alone in the
dining shed.

In Santo Tomas, "alone" never meant you were
by yourself. With the intense overcrowding and the
endless lines, that was impossible. It only meant that
during breakfast Judy spoke to no one, and no one
spoke to her. More and more people withdrew into
themselves, trying to hang on. Even Millie Barnes and
Judy spent less time together. They were still friends
and they still lived together in Room 6, but Millie

was preoccupied with her husband, Sammy, now in hospital with severe beri-beri, his nerves and stomach and heart inflamed by lack of decent food. Judy was sorry for Sammy and sorry for Millie, but it took all one's strength and concentration just to hold one's own. Millie was holding hers, and Judy was holding hers. Sammy didn't seem to be holding at all.

When Judy left the dining shed, she heard the drone of planes in the gray sky. A familiar sound these days. The Japs were running practice drills, day and night. During the recent total Manila blackouts, their searchlights pierced the skies, and in daylight hours the Jap planes served as tracking targets for the anti-aircraft crews. This morning they were at it again.

Suddenly, as Judy watched the sky, she saw the puffs of exploding antiaircraft shells. Others saw them too.

"Hey," somebody said, "they're practicing on their own planes. Maybe they'll make a mistake and hit one."

Everybody was looking up now, because this was something new. Live target practice. The black shapes of many planes were outlined against the gray clouds.

Out over the bay the planes began to dive down on the great harbor. Judy could hear thudding sounds deeper and louder than the antiaircraft shells.

"Jesus Christ! They're ours!"

"Those are *our* planes!"

"Our planes! Our planes! They're ours!"

Judy closed her eyes. She felt sudden, exultant tears running down her face. Dear God, those were *American* bombers. At last, at last, at last.

She opened her eyes. All around her people were crying with happiness, hugging each other. Somebody hugged Judy. She hugged back. Our planes, our planes. Such beautiful, beautiful planes.

The sky was filled with planes, diving and swooping and dropping bombs. She didn't even care if the bombs hit anything. They were American bombs. American bombs falling on Manila. After all this time, after all this time, they were here at last.

———

Watching the havoc of the bombing, the ships exploding and burning in the harbor, the columns of smoke rising from the nearby airfields, Sandy Homobono decided it was time for him to make certain adjustments.

He had kept his options open these last three years. He had worked for the Japs—what the hell, they were running the country, and many Filipinos worked for them. But he had used the information he collected as a reporter not only to write Jap propaganda but to warn and advise the independence movement. Dr. Diosdado Ronualdez, the liver specialist, was Sandy's main contact with the freedom fighters. Several times his warnings to Ronualdez had actually saved lives. Sometimes Sandy gave Ronualdez money as well as information. He felt sure Ronualdez would tell his secret friends about Sandy's contributions to the cause.

All Sandy Homobono wanted was his own country. Not an American country, not a Japanese country. Once the Philippines was run by Filipinos, Sandy would be on top of the world. He knew all the right politicians and businessmen, and he knew all the right buttons to push. He had done well under the Americans, and he had done well under the Japs, but just wait until it was under the Filipinos. That would be his time.

Independence. The Japs had officially proclaimed Philippine independence on October 14, 1943, but that was a massive joke, because the Japs owned and ran the country. And the Americans had promised to grant Philippine independence on July 4, 1946, now less than two years away. That would be a joke, too, because Sandy couldn't imagine the Americans really turning over the country—in military or political or especially business terms. All the Americans he had ever known wanted to cash in on the Philippines. It was all a joke.

But watching the sky full of American planes, and hearing the sound of American bombs falling, and seeing the feeble Jap response in planes and antiaircraft fire, Sandy Homobono decided it was time to commit himself to the American joke. He knew what to do.

≡ 28 ≡

"I Have Returned"

From his place in the middle of the landing barge, chugging toward the shores of Leyte, Eli Phipps could see the General standing toward the bow. MacArthur was dressed to the hilt for his return to the Philippines. He wore his giant black sunglasses and his famous floppy hat, its black visor festooned with swirls of gold. No tie, of course. The only time in months Eli had seen the General in a tie was on the cover of the propaganda matchbooks they had shipped to the Philippines. The General's khaki uniform was sparkling clean and sharply pressed. The first Filipinos to see him would catch him looking his gallant best.

Eli was scared. The first troops had gone in only four hours ago, and plenty of ugly battle sounds were coming from the land ahead. Eli wished the General had been willing to wait a day or two before exposing himself—and Phipps—but MacArthur was in a hurry. He had left Corregidor in March 1942, and now, almost a thousand days later, on October 20, 1944, he was finally coming back.

The original plan called for a November 15 landing

on the big southern island of Mindanao. But Admiral
Halsey, the only admiral MacArthur seemed to like
and respect, said that Leyte, in the middle of the Philippines, was lightly defended. Why not save both time
and casualties by going in there and going in quickly?
This obviously fitted in with the General's strategy of
bypassing enemy strongholds.

To Eli, Leyte didn't sound lightly defended. The
barge was now close enough for him to hear the rattle
of rifle fire along with the big bangs of mortar and
artillery shells. And there was still some naval bom-
bardment going on away from the landing zone. It
would be ludicrous to get killed now, this late in the
game, just because MacArthur was in such a hurry.

They were less than a hundred yards from shore
when, with a solid, grinding crunch, the damn barge
ran aground. They were supposed to be headed for
some dock where they could step ashore like con-
quering heroes, but here they were, stuck out in the
open.

Eli could see the General was furious. He wasn't
close enough to hear what MacArthur was saying
above the roar of the barge engine and those ugly
banging noises from the beach, but he could see the
wide, mobile mouth twisting as it always did when
the General was angry. MacArthur gestured imperi-
ously, pointing to the ramp. He pointed again, signaling them to lower the ramp.

Oh shit, Eli thought, we're going to wade in. He
would have to walk around all day in squishy wet
boots—unless, of course, he got shot before reaching
the beach.

The ramp cranked down and slapped into the water.

MacArthur led the way, stepping off into the knee-deep bay. There went the General's snappy, well-pressed uniform. Instead of being crisp and dignified, the long-promised return was going to be wet and sloppy. Eli slogged along in the General's rear through the warm water. One of the photographers waded quickly ahead to snap a picture.

Once ashore, MacArthur walked along the beach, collecting information and checking damage. The Signal Corps truck was not yet ready to broadcast the speech he had written last night, so MacArthur, to Eli's horror, walked inland to get a close look at the fighting. Eli didn't have to go along, so he didn't. The General might bear a charmed life, which was how he always acted under fire, but Eli had no reason to think that his own body was impervious to harm. Jap snipers would be all through that jungle.

At last the Signal Corps officer announced that they were ready for the radio broadcast, and a soldier was sent to fetch MacArthur. He came back to the beach as though returning from a pleasant stroll. He walked up to the Signal Corps officer, who handed him a microphone.

"All ready?"

"All ready, sir."

MacArthur took a sheet of paper from his pocket and unfolded it. Holding the paper in one hand and the microphone in the other, he read with great emotion in his firm, resonant voice:

"People of the Philippines, I have returned. . . .

Rally to me. Let the indomitable spirit of Bataan and Corregidor lead on. As the lines of battle roll forward to bring you within the zone of operations, rise and strike. Strike at every favorable opportunity. For your homes and hearths, strike! For future generations of your sons and daughters, strike! In the name of your sacred dead, strike! Let no heart be faint. Let every arm be steeled. The guidance of Divine God points the way. Follow in His name to the Holy Grail of righteous victory."

Great stuff, Eli thought. Pretty purple, to be sure, but the Filipinos would love it. They should; it had been written just for them.

————

Two days after the Leyte landings, Papaya reported to Enrique Sansone. She had important news.

"He's leaving," she said. "They finally give him a ship."

"Good news everywhere, it seems. I'm surprised they let him go after all these bombings. The harbor's a mess."

"It's because of the landings, he says. He says it is very serious. His navy has to attack them. Attacking a landing force and their support ships, it is his specialty."

"Who takes his place?"

"A civilian named Saiti. He ran the harbor in Yokohama. Sorry, but Buto says he is a genius. They fly him down from Japan."

"No matter how good he is, he'll need time to adjust. When does our good admiral leave?"

"As soon as the other one gets here. Maybe day after tomorrow, he thinks."

"He must be happy to return to sea."

Papaya shook her head. "To go back to sea, yes. But he says it is too late."

"Well, well. We always knew he was very intelligent."

"It makes him sad."

"Very strange if it didn't."

"Everything makes him sad now."

"Good. It's their turn to be sad. What is his ship?" Then, after a pause, he repeated, "What is his ship?"

"I don't know."

"Peanut."

"That's right, I don't know."

"Don't shrug like that. Of course you know. He trusts you. Why are you lying to me?"

"I'm not."

"You are being silly. Everybody will know in a couple of days anyway."

"Listen, if he gets killed, okay. But I am not going to be the one. Not this time."

"You are being sentimental."

"He is—a nice man."

"I don't think they will think so down in Leyte. He is the enemy."

"I know that. Better than you. Just the same, find out from somebody else."

Enrique sighed, then smiled. "All right, Peanut. It doesn't really make any difference. Now listen. There is a meeting this afternoon you must go to. Five people. I think you may know some, but nobody will use real names. They will recognize you, of course, but you will just be Peanut, understand?"

"What meeting?"

"It is our people who have had some special dealings with Santo Tomas. It is time to put our information and ideas together, just in case."

"In case what?"

"In case our hosts decide to do something with all those prisoners."

"You will be there?"

"Unfortunately I have to be somewhere else. The man in charge is called Tin-Tin."

"Where do you have to be?"

"Now let me tell you how to get there."

The meeting took place in the dining room of a private home in Pasay. They sat around the table on straight-backed wooden chairs, nothing to eat or drink. She was the only woman. Tin-Tin was an elderly Swiss national named Hauptlessen or Hauptlesser, she couldn't remember which. She knew he had something to do with the Red Cross. There was a tall, thin Spanish Jesuit priest in black cassock who was addressed as Wafer. The other two were Filipinos. The distinguished-looking one called Rollo, who apparently was a doctor, she didn't know.

The other was the shanty-builder Federico. She had used him all these months as a messenger to and from Amos Watson without ever knowing that he also worked for Enrique Sansone. Now he was introduced, to her astonishment, as Simon. He was equally astonished to meet Peanut.

"We have two main problems to discuss," Tin-Tin said, after everyone had been introduced by code name. "The most obvious one is the health of internees. The food situation is very serious. Wafer?"

"I am still able to enter the camp several times a week," the priest said. "To visit the other fathers," he explained to the rest of the group. The Dominican fathers who had run Santo Tomas as a university before the war still lived on campus in their own seminary building, screened off from the internees and all the other buildings by a high wire fence. "The fathers say the Japanese are supplying less and less food, so the internees have been forced to draw on their own emergency reserves to supplement what the Kempeitai allow them. Even so, rations remain scarce. Sometimes only two scant meals a day. Internees are stealing meal tickets, even counterfeiting them, to get extra food. Firewood is also scarce, so cooking has become difficult. A little bit of extra food comes in now and then by secret deliveries, some even in the trunk of the commandant's car, but the amounts are too small to make any real difference. The result of all this is that the internees are seriously undernourished. One of the fathers says a camp doctor expects a dozen deaths this month and even more in the months ahead." He looked around the little group. "I see no solution."

"I treat a few Santo Tomas patients at our hospital," Rollo said, "at least those with liver problems. Some of the deaths Wafer mentions are from heart attacks or beri-beri or even old age, but the underlying cause is starvation. Starvation is especially hard on the old people. As near as I can determine, they are getting only about a thousand calories a day. I see no solution, either."

When nobody else said anything, Papaya asked, "Is there any chance the Package Line will open again?"

The priest shook his head. "None. The Kempeitai never liked it to begin with. They thought it showed too much friendship between the internees and the people of Manila. Now, of course, with all the American bombing going on, they have become nervous—and even more strict. They have already canceled the November third visiting day, when families were to be allowed in camp to see relatives. And they are making the internees dig trenches and build fences."

"How long will the camp reserves last?" Tin-Tin asked.

Wafer spread his long, thin hands. "Everything depends on how much regular food the Japanese supply. Another month or two? Difficult to say."

"Red Cross packages?" Rollo asked.

"Unlikely," Tin-Tin said. "We know of nothing on the way, except possibly money. Money would help buy more supplies, but there will be no food packages. Not even for Christmas."

Papaya wondered how Amos was. She had not heard for some time. Amos was a strong, healthy man, but he was getting on.

"The other problem," Tin-Tin said, "is, in a way, even more immediate. The Japanese have begun to fortify the camp. Four truckloads of soldiers came in two weeks ago and set up tents on the grounds. Military stores, too. Sandbags. Obviously they think Santo Tomas is a safe place for them. They—"

"Excuse me," Wafer interrupted. "I am told the Triumvirate has already protested to the commandant. They are afraid all the soldiers and stores will make the camp a military target for the American planes."

"They are still bringing in army stores," Federico said. "I see them go through the gates."

"There is something worse to worry about," Tin-Tin said. "All those soldiers and weapons. Even machine guns. When the Americans get closer, what will the Japanese do with their prisoners?"

A long silence while they all thought about that.

"I know a man in camp, an old friend," Papaya said. She nodded at Federico to include him. "Simon and I, we have an old friend. He used to send us messages. He has a way of hearing what the Japs talk about between themselves in the commandant's office. A young man who understands Japanese. My friend can find out what they may be planning. But now it is hard for us to get his information."

"I also have a friend who could be useful," Rollo said. "Not in the camp but outside. He has very close contact with the Japs. You all know him. The reporter Sandy Homobono."

"I didn't know Homobono had friends," the priest said.

"That's because you don't know him," Rollo said. "He is many things, some of them not nice, but he is smart, and he knows how to find out things. And he is a patriot."

"Is that why he works for the *Tribune*?" Wafer asked. "Writing all that Japanese propaganda?"

"He has his reasons," Rollo said. "Besides, he says everybody knows they are lies, so it doesn't matter. From time to time he has told me things that were very useful to know. I know some other people he has helped with important information. One man was about to be arrested and taken to Fort Santiago, but Sandy warned him in time. It is not unlike our friend Peanut here. She entertains the Japs, but she is one of us."

"The difference is," Papaya said, "I trust me. I don't trust Sandy."

Rollo shrugged. "He doesn't like the Japs, and he doesn't like the Americans. And if you will forgive me, father, he would not have liked the Spanish, either, when they ruled our country. He is strictly for the Philippines. And now he wants to help us actively against the Japs. He has told me so."

"I think," Wafer said, "that Homobono always knows which way the wind is blowing. Somehow it always blows for him."

"I still say he can help us."

Tin-Tin said mildly, "I see no reason why we should not accept his information if offered."

"Are lies information?" Wafer asked. "He has written nothing but lies."

"They tell him what to write," Rollo said. "But he learns many things that could help us. As a reporter for the Japs, he can go anywhere. I think he can still get into Santo Tomas. Maybe, Peanut, he could talk to your 'old friend' and tell us what the Japs are planning."

"We want all the facts we can get," Tin-Tin said, "especially about the Santo Tomas people. It would be tragic if anything happened to them now, just when there is hope. I will, of course, discuss it with Zorro, but personally I think Rollo should encourage Homobono. We don't have to trust him."

"What's your old friend's name, Peanut?"

"I think I rather not say."

———

Her last night with Hitoshi Buto.

He was all packed—his clothes, his uniforms, his family photographs. Everything had gone aboard except for a single overnight bag. He was taking command of his ship tomorrow. Because of the bombings and the curfew and the blackout, the Mabalinga Club was closed, so they would have the whole evening together.

The dark shades were drawn for the blackout. The living room glowed pleasantly from the lamps beside the couch and the candles on the small dining table where their sushi supper was laid out. He wore a long kimono with bold vertical black-and-white stripes. The black sash at his waist and his black mustache were the only horizontal lines. His bare feet were in straw sandals with thick black thongs. Papaya had chosen her pleated white dress, no jewelry, only the white orchid tucked in her black hair. He liked simplicity, and she would please him this last time.

Her feelings were all mixed up tonight. Over their long time together she had learned many, many useful bits of information from him, things that Zorro said were invaluable. "A *very* profitable relationship," Zorro said. Yes, she had made it pay.

As for Buto himself, he was not generous to her the way Amos had been, but he was always courteous, and he was an exciting lover, a benefit she had not at first expected—or even wanted.

And Buto was protective. There was nothing he could do about the way the Filipinos on the staff of the Manila Hotel looked at her, but when her home was vandalized, as carefully arranged by Zorro, he had been angry and concerned. He had posted guards for her and kept them there long after she said they were no longer necessary. He had given her a pretty little pearl-handled pistol and taught her how to use it, just in case. He was, as she told Zorro, a nice man.

And tonight was the end. The end of the information, but also the end of her enthrallment. With the closing of the Mabalinga and the departure of Buto, she no longer had to work for the Japs, as either singer or lover. The indignity was over—along with the profit. After tomorrow morning, she would not have to endure the looks of the Manila Hotel staff or the snide comments about being a Jap entertainer. She could start to be herself. She knew her reputation would not change, not right away. Not until the Americans won, and she and Zorro and Amos could tell everybody what she had *really* been doing all these years. Then at last she would be Papaya again, not "the Jap whore."

While they ate their sushi supper, he with chopsticks, she with a fork, she tried to make him talk about the war, but he was reluctant.

"This is our last night together," he said. "It will be just for us."

"But what will happen to me after you go? No one will protect me."

He poured tea for them both. "Nonsense," he said. "All our people know you have been my friend. You will be safe."

"Yes, but what if the Americans come here? They will be angry with me."

"If the Americans come—" He stopped. Then he said in his deep, quiet voice, "If the Americans come, it will be very bad for everybody. Everybody. You must try to get away from Manila."

"Where will I go?"

He looked at her with his big mournful eyes. "Where will anyone go? To the mountains, that's where the army will go. Let's not talk about that tonight. Our last night must be beautiful and memorable, for both of us to treasure."

"But if we don't talk tonight, then—"

He held up his hand, the palm toward her. "No. Tonight there is no war, only a man and his woman."

"But, Toshi—"

"Come," he said, rising from the table and taking her hand. "Tonight is to remember."

In the bedroom she let him undress her, as he liked to do. He did it slowly, taking his time, touching her and stroking her and kissing her bare shoulders as he slipped down her dress. He was never in a hurry, that was one of the things about him that made her eager in spite of herself. For him, lovemaking was not a release but a complete ceremony. He left the white flower in her hair.

She lay down on the bed and watched him untie the sash of his kimono. He was very ready for her, as she knew he would be, but still in no hurry. He took the bottle of mineral oil from the bedside table and unscrewed the cap. She knew what that meant and could not help being excited: he was going to oil his head and then rub it against her until she could not stand it.

He sank down on the bed beside her and stroked her. Now she wanted him to hurry, to really begin.

"Turn over," he said.

"Why? I want you to—"

"Do as I say. Turn over."

She obediently rolled over on her face so that she could no longer see him. This was different, his not wanting her to watch him prepare himself. She considered that part of the excitement and did not understand why this time he wanted her to miss it.

Then she felt his hand with the oil. For a moment she did not realize what he was thinking. Then she did.

"No, Toshi."

She started to turn over, but he pushed her down firmly and went on with his hand.

"Toshi, no! I don't want that."

"Yes," his deep voice said behind her, "you do want it. We both want it."

"No! Let me up. Let me up!'

Then she felt a sudden stab of pain. It hurt so much she gasped. She could not believe such a hurt.

The pain grew worse, deeper.

Her face pressed into the pillow, her body pressed into the bed by his full weight, she began to cry from the hurt and the deep humiliation. She went on crying and crying and crying until it was over.

Afterward, he was all tenderness and sentiment. He soothed her and gently rubbed her shoulders. "I'm sorry," he said. "I'm sorry if I hurt you. But that was very special. Just for you and me."

———

"It is a carrier," she said, "The *Matusaka.*"

"Well, that's better," Enrique said. "I'm glad you told me. What made you change your mind?"

"It has forty-two planes," she said, ignoring his question. "Dive bombers. And there is this new plan they are going to try. Suicide bombers. They will fly the planes right into our ships. So they don't miss."

"This is Buto's idea?"

"No, no, somebody else. Some admiral named Onishi. But Buto thinks it just might work if the pilots are very, very brave."

≡ 29 ≡

Every Man for Himself

Sandy Homobono took his seat in the tiny consulting office of the liver specialist, Dr. Diosdado Ronualdez. He lighted a cigarette. The nurse gathered up the papers of the previous patient and put them back in a file folder.

"You shouldn't smoke so much," Ronualdez said.

"It won't hurt my liver."

The nurse left the office, closing the door behind her. This was the safest place to meet. Nothing was wrong with Sandy's liver, but as Ronualdez said, anyone can visit a specialist to discuss a liver complaint. The liver is always mysterious.

"So, Dado?" Sandy said. Ronualdez had told him to come in for an appointment but had not said why. Sandy was hopeful that he was about to be brought into some inner circle, a circle that would find favor for him with the Americans.

Ronualdez studied him through steel-rimmed glasses that gave his slim face a detached, intellectual look. Actually, Ronualdez was not at all detached. He believed passionately in two things: the high calling of medicine and the complete independence of the Philippines. Ronualdez was not practical about either one, certainly not as practical as Sandy, but the strength of his two great convictions made him easy to deal with. One had only to play along.

"I have reported your willingness to help us," Ronualdez said. With a precise forefinger he carefully pressed the bridge of his glasses against his nose. "I must say, some suspicions about you were expressed."

Sandy shrugged. That was inevitable.

Ronualdez paused for an answer. When none came, he said, "There is great concern about what will happen to the Santo Tomas prisoners."

"Why? They aren't our people."

"No, but when the Americans come back, we will get much credit if we have managed to help the internees. Besides, many of us have good American friends in Santo Tomas."

"Why do we need American friends?"

"Oh yes, I know how you feel. But remember, it is still up to the Americans to give us independence."

Sandy gave his short bark of a laugh. "We have already been given independence," he said wryly, reminding Ronualdez of the Japanese proclamation of more than a year ago. Another joke. Nothing had changed.

"Listen, we can argue this some other time. The question is, what can you find out about Japanese intentions? About Santo Tomas?"

"Very difficult," Sandy said. If he could learn anything, as he was sure he could, he did not want Ronualdez and his friends to think it was easy. "The Kempeitai are too strict these days."

"Can you get inside?"

"Inside the camp?" Now he had to underline his special advantages as a trusted reporter. "Probably. I can go most places to look for stories."

Ronualdez thought about this. Sandy stubbed out his bitter cigarette and lighted another. When the American army came back, at least the quality of tobacco would improve.

"We have," Ronualdez said, "certain—uh—contacts inside the camp."

Sandy waited.

"There is a priest." Ronualdez paused. "A priest who visits the Dominican fathers. He is able to tell us a number of things, but unfortunately, he has no direct dealings with the prisoners. Or with the Kempeitai."

"Anyone else? Anyone I can talk to?"

"Well, there is a singer." Ronualdez stopped to measure his words. Again he pressed his glasses, which had not moved, firmly against his nose. "She works for the Japanese, much as you do. She knows someone in camp she calls 'an old friend.' He apparently has access to all kinds of information. He is even said to have a young spy in the office of the commandant."

"Who's this old friend? Who's the young spy?"

"I'm sorry to say she doesn't want to tell us."

"That's not much of a contact," Sandy said. But his mind was already clicking away at the possibilities. There were not many variables.

"No, I realize that."

"What does this singer hear from her friend?"

"Very little recently. As you say, the Kempei-tai . . ."

"Dado, you are not giving me much to work on."

Actually, Ronualdez had furnished him quite a lot to work on. The doctor might be a keen analyst of the slightest clues concerning the mysteries of the human liver, but he was naive about other matters.

Ronualdez looked at his watch. "I have a patient coming now. Do the best you can."

Sandy stood up. "When will I be able to meet with your people? As I've told you, I'm in a good position to help them."

Ronualdez stood too. "Perhaps it will depend on what you can find out."

Perhaps, Sandy thought, but Ronualdez sounded evasive. He would have to bring off something significant before he would really be accepted. No time to waste, either, the way the war news from Leyte seemed to be going. Well, he was used to this sort of challenge. And he already had some promising ideas.

———

Sandy Homobono knew four Filipina singers who could be said to work for the Japanese—at least until recently, when the curfew and blackout shut down all the night spots. He could eliminate two of them at once. Fernanda Lopez, who had performed at a succession of beer joints that were virtual brothels, was so sick—supposedly with syphilis—that she had gone home to her family in Tarlac Province. Tippi, who sang at the Jap officers' club, the former Army-Navy Club, was at least as stupid as she was pretty—far too stupid to be an effective source of information. That left Papaya and Miguela Santan.

His instinct, which he trusted almost as much as he trusted solid facts, leaped at Papaya. She had both the temperament and the imagination. That big sunny smile masked a shrewd mind and an intense ambition. He liked the facts, too, when he thought about them.

She was an actress as well as a singer, and this role required excellent acting. The Mabalinga Club was a superb spot to collect all kinds of tidbits. And she had been Admiral Hitoshi Buto's longtime *kabit*, not only another splendid source but the best possible cover. Everybody in Manila, including Sandy himself, considered her a total collaborator. Her house had even been vandalized by patriots, at least once that he knew of, and maybe more often than that. What could be better?

The more he thought about it, the better he liked Papaya. Quite a remarkable performance. He had never even been suspicious of her, which meant the Japs wouldn't have suspected her, either. And, maybe most persuasive of all, Papaya had a very dear "old friend" in Santo Tomas. Yes, indeed. Her former lover, Amos Watson. And Amos Watson, a tough old loner, a man who never talked to reporters, a man who went his own way, doing exactly what suited him, never tipping his hand, fitted perfectly. Now if Sandy could get into Santo Tomas, and then get to Amos Watson, and then have something valuable to report back to Ronualdez . . .

He thought he saw how this might be done. There would be some risk, because he could not clear it ahead of time with the Japs, but he felt sure he could handle it. They trusted him. Besides, there was a greater risk if the Americans came back and found no one to say a good word for his loyalty. The Americans took loyalty seriously.

Next morning Sandy Homobono, who never bothered with a notebook, presented himself, his Japanese press card and a conspicuously displayed notebook at the main gate of Santo Tomas on Calle España. The guards showed no interest in letting him through.

"Call the commandant's office." he demanded. "I'm doing a story."

"No visitors."

"Ask the commandant. I work for General Miyama." This was quite a stretch, but it was almost true, because Miyama was, ultimately, in charge of almost everything in Manila. Years of reporting had taught Sandy that the main problem was getting his foot in the door, by whatever means. Everything else followed from that.

It was twenty minutes and two more mentions of Miyama before he was allowed through the gate. A uniformed guard accompanied him up the driveway to the commandant's office in the shadow of the Main Building. Santo Tomas had really changed since his last visit—and so had the prisoners he saw digging a trench along one wall of the camp. They were ragged men, scrawny, their clothes in tatters. They worked very slowly. Many more Jap soldiers seemed to be inside the camp. Tall stacks of cartons—probably military supplies—were piled in clumps on the open ground, protected from rain by gray rubberized tarpaulins and surrounded by swirling spools of barbed wire. The place looked more like a military stronghold than a civilian internment camp.

The guard delivered him to the door of the commandant's office. Half a dozen Japs, all in neat military dress, were seated at tables, working on papers. A young American man, sweeping the floor with a worn broom, glanced briefly at Sandy, then went on with his work.

The commandant, a suspicious-looking officer seated at the one large desk, studied Sandy, then nodded to the soldier standing beside him.

"The commandant has no orders on you," the soldier said in slow but clear English. "He does not want any stories on this enemy camp."

"This is a special story," Sandy answered, also speaking slowly. "I am here to interview one of his prisoners." He flourished his notebook.

Some back-and-forth in Japanese between the soldier and the commandant.

"The commandant knows nothing about interviews. There are no orders on any interviews."

"No, naturally." Sandy took his Japanese press card from his pocket and placed it on the desk where the commandant could read it. "I do many stories. As the commandant will see, I am permitted to go anywhere in Manila. Except, of course, military installations."

Lengthy jabbering.

"The commandant observes that the Kempeitai is

a military organization. Therefore you are not permitted."

"We," Sandy said, deliberately not specifying who "we" might be, "are not interested in any military aspects. This camp is for enemy aliens," he pointed out, using the standard term he had written so many times. "All of them are civilians. I only want to interview a civilian."

"The commandant asks, who is this civilian?"

Sandy had given this point careful thought. "The commandant, I believe, was not stationed in Manila before the war. But of course he had heard that the Americans were very confident in those days. General MacArthur promised that if the Imperial Japanese Army and Navy attacked the Philippines, he would defeat them. Everybody believed him."

He waited through the translation and saw the commandant nod in agreement.

"But one leader of the American business community saw the truth. He predicted the Americans would be defeated. I wrote several stories about him. Here, I brought one with me."

Sandy, who kept a complete file of every story he had ever published, opened his notebook, extracted the three-year-old clipping he had dug out last night and handed it to the interpreter. The interpreter read it through, moving his lips silently, then spoke at length to the commandant. Sandy waited. Apparently the commandant wanted to hear a complete translation of the article. This took even longer. Sandy looked around the office. The other Japs kept busy at their papers. The young American, having finished sweeping, began to empty wastebaskets, taking his time. Mr. Watson's "young spy" perhaps?

"The commandant asks if this—Watson—is the prisoner you wish to see?"

"Yes, sir." This was the tricky part. "We think it might be interesting to hear what he has to say about the current situation. Since he is such a great admirer of the Imperial Japanese Army—as the record shows." He shrugged carelessly. "It is, of course, only a possibility. I won't know until I talk to him." He tried to enlist the commandant on his side. "By the way, he's quite old. Do you know if he is still alive?"

When this had been translated, the commandant spoke to one of his other men, who went to a file drawer and pulled out a thick sheaf of papers held together by paper clips. He leafed through the pages, running a finger down the lines. The finger stopped. He spoke respectfully to the commandant.

"Yes, he is here," the interpreter said. "The commandant asks, suppose this—Watson—does not give nice comments?"

"Then there will be no story."

"How does the commandant know your story will reflect favorably on the administration of this camp?"

Sandy disliked being censored, but now it was useful. "Tell him General Miyama reviews important stories before they are published. Obviously my story will speak highly of the Kempeitai administration."

The commandant had a great deal to say about this, but it boiled down to a simple statement.

"You will be permitted to talk to the prisoner in the commandant's presence."

Halfway there. Sandy shook his head. "I know this Watson. He will not talk in front of other people. I must see him alone."

The commandant had some firm opinions about this, too.

"Impossible."

Sandy revealed his grave disappointment. "Those are not my instructions. That is not what we want." He leaned forward and put his notebook on the commandant's desk. "Look," he said, being utterly reasonable. "After I have talked with Watson, I will show the commandant all my notes. He will see for himself exactly what is said. If he finds anything objectionable, I will take it out. And please remind the commandant that General Miyama himself will review the story—if there is a story." He spread his hands in total innocence. "There is no danger of anything going wrong."

When this was translated, the commandant spoke sharply, pointing his finger and jabbing to emphasize his words.

"The commandant says *he* will not permit anything to go wrong and therefore does not require your promises. In any case, as an officer of the Kempeitai, he does not fear danger."

Sandy bowed his head in respect, acknowledging the commandant's supreme lack of fear. Pompous bastard.

"You will wait outside."

Sandy collected his notebook and press card from the commandant's desk, bowed again and walked out the door into the hot sunshine. He lighted a cigarette. It was going to work out.

The plaza area was empty except for a few Jap vehicles in the parking space and little clusters of internees crossing the broad space. Sandy could not get over how shabby the prisoners looked.

No seats or benches anywhere in sight. He was not surprised. Firewood for cooking was scarce all over Manila, so it was bound to be scarcer still in Santo Tomas. He did not want to sit on the stone steps of the Main Building, because people would be coming in and out. No privacy. He decided on a low stone parapet at the edge of the parking area as the best site for the interview. There he and Mr. Watson would be in plain sight if the Japs were watching, as they were sure to be.

A long wait, all the way through a third cigarette, and then came a shock at the end of it. At first he did not recognize the figure shuffling across the plaza, trying to keep up with the uniformed guard. Only when they turned in the direction of the stone parapet where he was sitting did he realize it was Amos Watson.

The white bristly hair and shaggy white eyebrows were the same, but the tall figure was now stooped over, leaning on a bamboo stick that served as a cane. His face was thin. His hands and lower arms were swollen and puffy. So were his feet, tucked into loose slippers.

Sandy put out his cigarette and stood up. "Good morning, Mr. Watson. It's nice to see you again."

Watson didn't answer until he had settled himself on the parapet. He shifted his weight with some care

before he said, "Good morning, Sandy. To what do
I owe this honor?" The voice was still deep but
sounded hoarse and cracked. His blue eyes seemed
faded.

The guard moved away to the front of the Main
Building, from where he could keep them in sight.

Sandy sat down, opened his notebook and took a
pencil from his shirt pocket.

"Mr. Watson," he said, "we have to be very quick.
I don't know how much time they will give us. I'm
supposed to be interviewing you for your views on
the war situation. The strength of the Jap army, the
defense of Manila against the bombings—that sort
of thing. So you must keep talking to me. But I'm
really here on behalf of your friends."

Amos Watson looked him over, shifting his weight
again as he tried to make himself comfortable.
"Really? What friends are those?"

Sandy scribbled a few words in his notebook.
"Your good friends on the outside. Dr. Ronualdez.
And, of course, Papaya."

Amos Watson seemed mildly amused. A small
smile. "I don't know any Ronualdez. As for Papaya,
I haven't seen her in three years. Whatever happened
to her?"

Sandy wrote some more, making up quotes about
the impressive quality of the Japanese defense of the
Philippines. "They want to know what the Japs plan
to do with you prisoners. I understand you have a good
source in the commandant's office." He raised his eyes.
"Perhaps that young man I just saw sweeping up?"

After a long moment Amos Watson smiled—broadly enough to reveal that he had lost a front tooth—and shook his head. "Now, Sandy, some things never change. You know I never talk to the press. Especially the Japanese press."

"Mr. Watson, listen. Listen to me. I am on your side. I am working with your friends. I've taken a real chance coming in here and asking to see you. You have to help."

"Oh? Well, then, let me see. You can say I've been observing your antiaircraft defense with great interest. I think it's piss-poor."

"Mr. Watson!"

"Aren't you going to write down my comment?"

For the watching guard's benefit, Sandy jotted down "antiaircraft defense." He didn't know what to do. "Mr. Watson, this is vital. This is your one chance to—"

But Amos Watson was leaning on his bamboo stick, hauling himself to his feet. "You'll have to excuse me. It's time for me to get in the food line."

"But Mr. Watson—"

"Will you stay for lunch? Mongo beans, I believe. Or else camote greens. Nice talking to you, Sandy. As always."

He hobbled away, an unforgivably stubborn old man.

Sandy closed his notebook. Now he would have to go through the charade of showing his few lines of scribbling to the commandant and explaining that there was no story. What could he report to Dado Ronualdez? Only that he had managed to see Watson. After all this, nothing. He had taken the risk for nothing.

———

Standing in the dreary line for the dreary food, Amos tried to sort out his degrees of alarm. He was appalled that Homobono knew about him, and apparently even about Felix. No one in camp knew those secrets. Even Judy Ferguson, who had once benefited from his mail system, knew nothing of Felix. All anybody knew about Felix was that Amos was looking after him because he had lost his parents.

And yet here was Homobono marching into camp, armed with notebook and pencil and the most dangerous kind of information. Not only about Amos and Felix but even about Papaya. He was sure Homobono had not learned anything from her. She didn't trust him any more than Amos did. They had agreed he was unscrupulous. She would never have changed her mind, certainly not with Sandy working for the Japs' propaganda newspaper. So how had he learned? If not from Papaya, from his old houseboy, Carlos? From Federico the shanty-builder? Amos thought not. Then where?

Sandy now claimed to be on Amos's side—the side of Amos and his "friends," whoever they were supposed to be. Well, that was possible. Sandy was always out for himself, whatever agility that entailed. With the Japs in serious trouble in the Philippines, he could easily be switching sides. But even if one believed that, even if it was actually *true*, what fool could have sent Sandy Homobono into Santo Tomas to talk to Amos? The irony was that Amos had nothing to tell him. According to Felix, the Japs themselves didn't know what to do about the prisoners. They spoke of moving them, but the process of moving over three thousand internees from Santo Tomas to some other location while the Philippines were under American assault was impractical, perhaps impossible. And yet Sandy had been sent here to interrogate him.

It meant that Amos had been singled out to the Kempeitai, at a time when the Japs were suspicious of everything and everybody. Arrests and imprisonment and torture in Fort Santiago had become commonplace, on virtually no evidence. Executions, too. Three internees had been sent to Santiago on the merest suspicion of communicating with the outside. They had not yet returned. Many people never returned from Fort Santiago.

And Felix. Sandy was plainly guessing about Felix, but he had guessed right. It might be a good idea not to be seen with Felix for a while, just in case. But first he would have to find out what Felix had overheard this morning.

Even with most of his weight on the bamboo cane, Amos had trouble keeping his balance on his swollen feet as he stood in line. He knew he could plead medical hardship and have his scant meals delivered to him, but he had no intention of giving in. Giving in was the first step toward giving up.

———

"General Miyama wants to see you. Now."

Sandy Homobono had made contingency plans months ago. If the request had come by telephone, this might have been the moment to act. But the black car and the Filipino driver and the Jap soldier with the pistol at his waist were waiting.

There was no conversation during the drive to Amos Watson's old home on Dewey Boulevard. Sandy sat in the backseat, smoking furiously and thinking. The boulevard, which ran along the edge of the bay, had been damaged by the harbor bombings, so the driver took the back streets and drove in through the rear delivery entrance.

The soldier got out. Sandy got out. They did not speak to each other. The soldier's hand rested on the butt of his pistol as they entered the back door, held open for them by Watson's little old houseboy, who evidently was still in good grace with his master. Sandy wished he could say the same. He had bad feelings about this meeting.

The soldier and the houseboy followed him all the way to General Miyama's office. The general was sitting at his desk, upright, his slim shoulders square, reading a report. At the old houseboy's light knock, he looked up and put the report aside. The sharp black eyes bored into Sandy. Yes, Sandy thought, serious trouble. He wished he could smoke.

General Miyama kept him standing in front of his desk and continued to stare at him. His austere face and thin mouth were set hard. His hands lay folded on the desk. It was difficult for Sandy not to start babbling, but he knew he must wait for the general to speak. The silence went on.

"Santo Tomas," the general finally said.

Sandy waited for the questions. What had the commandant reported? What would he have to answer?

"Santo Tomas," Miyama repeated after a moment, in the same hard, even voice.

"Yes, sir. I went there to look into a story."

"What story? You had no assignment."

Sandy desperately wanted to smoke. He put his hands in his jacket pocket where he could at least feel the pack and the matches.

"No, sir. No, sir. I had an idea I wanted to look into. I often do that. It didn't work out." When Miyama said nothing, he went on. "I remembered that Amos Watson—the old man who used to live here in this house—was still a prisoner. I thought he might have some interesting views on the progress of the war. You remember he was once very critical of—"

An abrupt wave of the hand cut him off. "The views of American prisoners are of no interest. You knew that."

"Yes, sir. Ordinarily. But I thought that in this case—"

"You had a private conversation with an American prisoner. You took great pains to arrange that. Your notes of that conversation were brief and"—Miyama still occasionally groped for an English word—"inadequate."

"Yes, sir. He's sick. He didn't have anything to say."

"I don't believe you."

"It's true!"

"I don't believe you. You used my name several times, without authority, to get access to the prisoner. Why was it so important—if he had nothing to say?"

This was getting to be far too much. Sandy pulled out his pack of cigarettes.

"Don't smoke!"

Sandy quickly put them back. This was going badly. Miyama looked implacable. If Amos Watson had cooperated, as he should have, Sandy could have at least produced a plausible interview, whether or not it was published. Watson had betrayed him. Yes, betrayed him.

"Why was it so important?"

"Sir, it wasn't. It wasn't at all. It was just an idea that didn't work out. A bad idea, I guess."

"Yes. A bad idea."

The silence hung between them.

"Is that all you have to say?"

"Sir, there isn't anything to say. What do you want me to say?"

"I have no more time for this." Miyama pressed the buzzer on his desk.

The houseboy—Carlos, that was his name— quickly appeared in the doorway.

"Ask Colonel Iseda to come in."

"Yes, sir."

Miyama's head swung back. "I think this conversation will continue better at Fort Santiago."

Sandy could not control his gasp. Terrible, awful things happened to people at Santiago. He had heard about them. Flogging with iron rods. A hose down the throat until the belly was brutally extended with water, then pounded into vomiting it out, repeated and repeated. Horrible torture to the genitals—always the genitals, everybody said so. He knew he could not stand it.

"Sir, wait. Just a minute. I—I do have something more to say."

As the general's chief of staff came to the door, Miyama held up his hand. "Well? Be quick."

No Filipinos, Sandy thought. I won't give them any Filipinos.

"Sir, I lied. Yes, I lied to you. That wasn't my real purpose in wanting to see Watson."

"Of course not."

"No, sir. I was hoping—I was hoping to get proof." Yes, that was it: proof. "There have been rumors, a few rumors here and there, that Watson was spying for the Americans. Sending messages. I thought—I thought if I could see him and trick him into admitting it—you know, by pretending I was a messenger myself—then I might get a—a big reward. If I did it all myself. A bonus. Like when I found out about Carnation Milk, remember? The Voice of Juan de la Cruz? I was hoping for another reward."

"Why didn't you say this when I asked you?"

"I couldn't get the proof. I was hoping maybe I could still find out some other way to prove it. I don't know how, but I was going to try. But I'm sure it's true." Then he had a brilliant afterthought. "Could I—would you consider a reward anyway? For this valuable information?"

A look of contempt crossed Miyama's hitherto impassive face. "I will consider it," he said coldly.

Quick, throw him another bone. "I think Watson has a spy in the commandant's office. A young American."

"On what basis?"

"Just rumor. You know how it is. Sir, you'll think about a reward? A bonus?"

"That will be all," Miyama said.

———

When the Homobono creature, bowing in relief, left his office, Miyama thought briefly and distastefully about the effectiveness of fear. Fear of Fort Santiago had forced the truth out of Homobono without the necessity of torture. His last thought of the Filipino reporter was not to reward him.

Then he turned to the far more important matter. Traffic with the enemy must be stamped out—quickly, instantly—before it became endemic. No chances could be taken. The whole country was rising against the Japanese army. In this perilous situation, with Leyte already lost and the invasion of Luzon certain to come, swift action was imperative.

Miyama thought it might already be too late, but he must not allow that to make any difference.

When Iseda returned, Miyama told him to get War Prisoner Headquarters on the phone.

Something Different

Through the high-powered binoculars brought by the New Guinea boys, Brad and Paradiso took turns watching the Kamikaze ceremony at the little Mabalacat fighter field. They had seen it before, all during the air-and-sea battle for Leyte, because Mabalacat, not far from their own town of Carabangay, was the birthplace of Kamikaze.

On their hillside, hidden by tall cogon grass, they were too far away to read facial expressions, but they could see all the familiar farewell gestures.

"They're about to tie on the headbands," Brad said, handing over the binoculars.

Paradiso grunted and took the glasses. He thought the headbands were the most interesting part. The first time he saw them, Paradiso said they reminded him of the headbands Igorot women wore in the mountains to carry heavy loads to market. Only those were brightly woven and these were white. Also, these served no useful purpose.

"It's what the ancient samurai warriors used to wear into battle," Brad had explained. "White is for courage. Also it's their color of purity and death."

There were only three this morning. At the height of the Leyte battle there had been as many as a dozen at a time. They're running low here, Brad thought. But there were now Kamikaze fields all over the Philippines, so Mabalacat by itself meant little. He knew other guerrilla units were reporting over their new radios about their own areas. He assumed that somewhere all this information was being put together by somebody.

At the end of the short runway the young volunteer suicides stood bareheaded near their battered old Zero fighters. Each plane was already loaded with a single 550-pound bomb. Close friends chosen for the honor stood behind the pilots to tie on the white bands.

Paradiso watched until the bands were tied. Then he handed back the glasses. "Saki time," he said.

The commander walked down the short line, pouring the ritual cup of saki for each pilot. They bowed to each other and the pilots drank.

Then the commander gave an order Brad and Paradiso could not hear, and the pilots turned and climbed into their planes. They carried small flags and family photographs. They had already written their last letters home, enclosing poems, salutations to the Emperor, locks of hair, fingernail clippings.

These obsolete, banged-up Zeros were required to make only this one last flight. The better Zeros were kept for the more experienced escort pilots who would drive off American planes so the Kamikazes could complete their final run.

The engines started and revved. All the men left standing on the field began waving, both arms held high in the air. As the planes slowly rumbled into their takeoff, a mechanic ran beside each one, keeping a reverent hand on the wing as long as possible until the speed became too great. The three planes wobbled into the air and headed south toward their targets.

Brad shook his head in disbelief. Somewhere American ships would soon come under crazed attack, but these young Kamikaze pilots were the only Japanese in this long war who aroused his sympathy and pity and grudging admiration.

"We better go report," he said.

————

Standing on the deck of MacArthur's flagship, the cruiser *Boise*, Eli Phipps saw a lone Kamikaze come diving toward him out of the sky. The target was the ship, but every time he saw one of these insane attacks, Eli felt the target was himself. Like everybody else on deck, he jumped for cover—this time a gun turret—but his eyes froze on the screaming plane. Jesus, right toward him!

The antiaircraft guns were pop-pop-popping all over the ship, but the plane kept diving. If the guns didn't get it right now, right away, Eli knew he was finished. At what seemed like the last second the death-Zero spun off toward another ship in the armada, and then the gunfire from both ships caught it, and it blew up, bomb and all. The midair explosion rocked the deck.

Shaking, Eli got up to look. Shattered bits of

wreckage were falling into the sea. That could be me, he thought. That could be little pieces of me dropping into the ocean.

Kamikaze had been going on close to three months, ever since Leyte began. Eli was not embarrassed by his fear. He hadn't talked to one man, army or navy, who wasn't terrified by the attacks. A few more Kamikaze successes, on the right ships at the right time, might have cost the great Battle of Leyte Gulf. We were lucky, Eli thought. Instead, the Japanese navy had been knocked out of the war—four carriers, three battleships and God knows how many ships.

If there were any justice in war, this long-awaited invasion of Luzon should now be easy sailing, at least until they landed at Lingayen. Eli always felt safer on land than at sea or in the air. But it was not easy sailing. Here were all these damn Kamikazes harassing the thousand-ship armada all the way north. The invasion force was losing ships and men.

In the afternoon MacArthur came on deck to see the landmarks they were passing far to the east. Eli watched him standing alone, hands gripping the rail as he stared out at the old shapes, the rock of Corregidor and, to the left, the much larger lump of Bataan. Almost three years since they had left them behind.

The tall figure did not move. The head did not turn, the hands continued to grip the rail. Eli wondered what the General was thinking as he stared at those "hallowed" battlefields that he had sworn to "redeem." Not even a member of the Bataan Gang would dare ask him.

There were a hell of a lot of Japs waiting for them on Luzon under the command of Yamashita, the famous Tiger of Malaya. But thank God the latest guerrilla intelligence reported that Yamashita was moving his own headquarters, along with the puppet government, up to the steep mountains around Baguio. He was pulling many troops up behind him. That would mean bitter fighting for somebody, but not for those close to MacArthur. MacArthur wanted those places he was staring at—Corregidor and Bataan and, behind them, his beloved city of Manila.

The General had another profound concern, the fate of the American prisoners, both the civilians in Santo Tomas and the military POWs at Cabanatuan. Reports from that Spanish fellow Zorro and from others in Manila said the Japanese were bringing weapons and ammunition into Santo Tomas. No one knew whether they intended to fight there, which would cause the death of many Americans, or whether they might even be planning to execute the three thousand prisoners en masse. This prospect was unthinkable, especially after three long years of survival.

At Cabanatuan, according to guerrilla reports, there were now only a few hundred POWs. But these were MacArthur's very own, the soldiers who had fought for him on Bataan and Corregidor. They were sacred. The General was determined to rescue them. Eli had actually seen a detail map of the Cabanatuan prison camp, drawn by a guerrilla leader known as Coach, apparently an American army officer. The

General would be picking somebody to go in there, but at least it wouldn't be Phipps.

MacArthur had his fifth star, all the stars there were, and he was returning in glory to the scene of his only defeat. Eli Phipps was glad he was no longer writing the occasional communiqué for the General, who now had a full-time professional public relations staff to deal with the regiment of war correspondents and photographers. They turned out embarrassing stuff, but it was obviously just what the General wanted.

Only two weeks ago, on the day after Christmas, MacArthur's communiqué proclaimed that the battle for Leyte "can now be regarded as closed except for minor mopping up." This was even more outrageous than his Christmas communiqué about Buna two years ago.

There was something about Christmas, some sentimental Santa Claus need to give the American people a Christmas present straight from Douglas MacArthur himself, that brought out the worst in the General. He would stoop to any lie. Phipps knew the "minor mopping up" on Leyte was expected to take at least three more months and would cost thousands of casualties.

The silent figure at last turned away from the rail.

Tomorrow MacArthur would be wading ashore at Lingayen Gulf. Phipps was dead certain of that. MacArthur had collected so much favorable worldwide publicity when he had been forced, against his plans and wishes, to wade ashore at Leyte that he was damned sure to wade again at Lingayen. Think of all the wonderful pictures and all the proud headlines: MACARTHUR RETURNS TO LUZON!

Once this war was over, Eli Phipps hoped he would never again have anything to do with any general—and most certainly not with this one. But right now, if he had to follow somebody ashore to begin the battle for Luzon, as he knew he must, better MacArthur than anybody else.

———

Jack Humphrey and the other prisoners could not believe what they were seeing. The Jap guards were packing up to leave Cabanatuan.

Jack wondered if the remaining POWs would be shot first. Or would the Japs take them along? If the POWs had to walk, he didn't see how Maxsie could make it. Maxsie had lost too much weight, and his bad back now kept him in constant pain. He got up from his bamboo platform only to go to the latrine, and even then he had to lean on Humphrey's shoulder. He was slipping away.

The camp was much smaller now. All through the late fall the Japs had been shipping out large groups of prisoners, sending boatloads to Formosa and Japan, where, according to the commandant, they would be "safe" and would have more to eat. Nobody believed him. Rumor had it that some of the POW ships were being sunk by American planes and submarines. The commandant would not say whether or not this was true. He claimed no knowledge of such matters. He just kept shipping out his prisoners whenever he was told to. By New Year's Day the camp was down to fewer than six hundred men.

Maxsie and many others were too weak or too sick to be shipped out. So far Jack Humphrey, now the senior officer for a cluster of three barracks, had managed to stay at Cabanatuan, but he knew that sooner or later he would be forced to go.

But instead it was the Japs who were going. And the solution for the POWs was the most surprising twist of all. The commandant summoned Humphrey and three other senior officers to tell them.

"The Imperial Japanese Government," he announced, quite formally, through his interpreter, "has decided for its own convenience that you are no longer considered prisoners of war."

Jack Humphrey and the other three American officers looked at each other. If they weren't POWs, what were they?

"My men and I leave today to join the Imperial defenders of Luzon. You will remain in this camp. You will not leave this area. You are responsible for seeing that your men do not leave this area. If they do, they will be considered enemy soldiers and will be shot. You understand? I have been instructed to leave you thirty days' supply of rations."

Thirty more days of near starvation on these miserable rations, Jack Humphrey thought. And after that, total starvation. But maybe with the Japs gone, the Filipinos might bring them extra food. Or maybe the American army was finally coming. It had been four months since they had seen the first American warplanes fly overhead.

"You are forbidden to enter the Japanese section of the camp. Other Japanese forces will be moving through this area, and they will use our barracks. You will therefore remain in your own prison area."

Dear Sara,

They're gone! For the first time since Bataan, the Japs have left us on our own. We don't know what the hell's going on, but we can't help hoping MacArthur has landed. At night we can sometimes see what look like artillery flashes up north of here. Today was the best day ever. We made an inspection tour to see what the Japs had left us. The food's been so skimpy for so long, we didn't believe the Japs' promise that they were leaving us thirty days' worth of food. But guess what? Down in the Jap storage sheds, where we were told not to go, we found the pot of gold. So many big fat bags of rice we couldn't even count them. And hundreds of cans of milk and even some canned fish. Everybody's so weak we thought we didn't have any strength or energy left, but I tell you when we found all that stuff, we suddenly turned into a bunch of rhinoceroses. We got some carts, and everybody who could stand up was loading the carts and dragging and pushing them back to our own area. Everybody was laughing and some men were even singing. It was crazy. Halfway through, a lot of the men wanted to stop and have a feast, but we figured we better move as much of it as possible before the Japs come back.

It took most of the day, and everybody was pretty bushed, but then we really laid into it. We tore down part of an empty barracks for firewood and cooked up big pots of rice. We threw in some fish, and then we poured milk over it. Sounds like a mess, doesn't it? I never tasted anything so good. Some of the men ate so much they got sick.

I got a couple of bowls of rice and milk into Maxsie, and he seems a little better. At least when I was feeding him the second bowl, he said, "Hump, you remember that mango we ate on the Death March? This is damn near as good." His voice is real weak, but at least he's talking for a change. I don't know. Now that we have food, maybe he'll get better. Hope so. We've been together a long time.

Tonight I feel better than I have in months. It's not just the food, it's the feeling that something different is finally happening or going to happen. Maybe—well, I better not say it.

Give Terry and Jeff a big strong hug for me. And one for you, too.

Love, Jack

———

"I've told you, you shouldn't phone me these days. It may not be safe."

"Never mind, I had to. That prick Homobono. He told them about Amos."

Papaya waited through a long stretch of silence before Enrique answered her. Usually he was so quick, but now she could tell he was thinking it over, weighing things.

"When? How do you know?"

"Right now, an hour ago. Carlos heard him."

Enrique's normally casual voice was sharp with concern. "You mean he told Miyama himself?"

"Yes. Yes, right there, right in Amos's own house."

"Peanut, stop crying. I can't think if you're crying. What did Homobono actually say?"

"I told everybody I didn't trust him. And Amos never trusted him, either. And now—and now—"

"*Stop it*. Tell me quick."

Papaya took two deep breaths. "He went into Santo Tomas and talked to Amos. It's all your goddamn friend Rollo's fault, I know it. He's the one who said Homobono could be useful. I don't know what they said in Santo Tomas. Anyway, the Japs got suspicious, and Miyama said he was going to send Homobono to Santiago, where they would make him tell the truth. Then Homobono said he was trying to get proof that Amos was spying for the Americans. And he asked Miyama for *money*."

There was another long stretch of silence. Then: "Peanut, I'm afraid that . . ."

"I know, I know."

"We must see that it stops there. You may be in danger yourself. All of us. I have to think about it."

"Carlos says Homobono also told Miyama that Amos might have a young spy in the commandant's office."

She heard Enrique's sigh over the telephone. "Just when everything seemed—" He stopped abruptly. "I have to think. Meet me in an hour, usual place. No more calls."

———

The Luzon invasion was only a few days old when Dagopino, the New Guinea boy, came running down from his hilltop radio transmitter, waving a message.

"Hey, Coach! Special orders!"

At first Dagopino and Perez had addressed Brad as "sir" and "captain," but now, like the others, they called him Coach.

Brad read the long decoded message. All the men in camp gathered around, standing as close as they could get.

"About time," Paradiso said. They had all been waiting for action orders, ever since MacArthur's army came ashore at Lingayen. Paradiso carried his carbine everywhere, ready to leave the moment they got orders. "What they want?"

"Cabanatuan," Brad said. "They want to rescue the prison camp."

"Good," Paradiso said. "Let's go."

Several men cheered. They all smiled at each other.

Brad hated to disappoint them. He shook his head. "We have to split up," he said. He looked at Paradiso. "Only twenty of us can go."

"Twenty!"

The happy group turned silent.

"We can't do it with twenty," Paradiso said.

"It's not our show," Brad said. "We're to join up with the Rangers."

"Okay, but we take everybody."

"No. The order says twenty."

"We did fine three years without orders."

"Well, it's different now. They want just enough men to get across country through the Japs. The rest stay here and keep reporting."

"Okay, Coach. You stay here and run camp. I pick the others."

"They want Hilario and me because we've been there and seen the layout and sent in the maps. The rest are to make sure we get there."

Paradiso grunted. "Where is 'there'?"

Brad looked at the message. "A place called Balangkare."

"Rosauro?"

"Yes, Sergeant."

"You run the camp."

"But, Sergeant—"

Paradiso paid no attention to Rosauro's objections. He was busy selecting the other men he would take to Balangkare.

They reached the village by hard night marches along the same back roads Brad and Hilario had used when they went to see where Miranda died. When they came to a main road, they often had to lie hidden, waiting for an opening, because the Japs were moving too. All the Jap units, some with tanks and trucks, appeared to be headed north. To fight MacArthur on the Luzon Plain? Or to join forces with Yamashita in the Baguio mountains? No way for Brad to tell. But there was no traffic going south toward Manila. Out of long habit, they tried to keep track of the passing tanks and vehicles. Paradiso gave strict orders not to fire on the easy targets. Their job was to get through.

Brad and Paradiso found the colonel where he was supposed to be, in a tiny church. Two other Ranger officers, dressed like the colonel in camouflage combat fatigues, were with him. They were the first Americans Brad and Paradiso had met.

Brad saluted. He felt clumsy, because he hadn't done this in a long time. "Captain Stone reporting, sir, as ordered."

The colonel casually returned the salute. "On time," he said. "Good work." But then he added, in a harder voice, "Records say you're a second lieutenant."

"Yes, sir." Brad kicked himself for not using his proper prewar rank.

"Who promoted you?"

Brad didn't know how to begin to explain.

In the silence Paradiso said, "I did."

"Who are you?"

"I am Sergeant. Sir."

The colonel laughed. "Most of the guerrilla leaders we've met are majors or better. Even a couple of generals. You're very modest, captain. Where's the other fellow who was with you at Cabanatuan?"

"Right outside, sir."

"Bring him in. Let's get to work."

Brad and Paradiso and Hilario learned they were to be only a small part of an elaborate operation. There was a full company and a platoon from the Rangers and a special reconnaissance team. There were local Filipino guerrillas, more than two hundred of them, who knew the area. There were bazookas and grenades and tommy guns and red flares for signaling. There were rations for the prisoners, if they ever reached them. And there was a plan.

"Sir," Brad said, when he had heard all this, "excuse me, but why do you need us?"

"Because," the colonel said, "I asked for one American officer who had actually seen this fucking place. You're what they came up with, so you stick with us. This other one too," he added, nodding at Hilario, who was looking very proud of himself.

"Yes, sir."

"We come too," Paradiso said.

The colonel was plainly not accustomed to hearing pronouncements from a sergeant—and only a guerrilla sergeant at that. He looked as though he were about to blow up, but then thought better of it. "No, sergeant, you sure as hell are not coming. You and your men will help the other guerrillas keep the Japs out of our hair. At least you have weapons. Half of them don't."

"Coach and me always—"

"Okay, sir," Brad interrupted quickly, before Paradiso got in real trouble. "We'll get our men ready."

He hustled Paradiso and Hilario outside. "Listen," he said, "that's a Ranger colonel. Don't argue with him."

"I like it better when we decide what we do."

"It's different now."

"I rather go in the camp."

"Well, you can't."

"Maybe no Japs try to get to the camp. Maybe we just sit there doing nothing."

"How many Japs did we see getting here? They're all over the place. You heard what the colonel said. The minute we hit the camp, they'll try to send re-inforcements. They mustn't get there."

"Huh," Paradiso said. "I still think camp part is better. Maybe you talk him into it?"

"You don't talk colonels into things. Unless you're a general. You heard him. As far as he's concerned, I'm still a second lieutenant. Now come on, we better explain things to the men."

But they had to wait through the whole next day, staying out of sight in small groups. The colonel postponed the attack until he could get more accurate information from his reconnaissance team and from the local guerrillas. Many Jap soldiers were seen moving up the road near the camp. Others were stationed at the Cabu Bridge only a few miles away. And once again, the scouts reported, there were Jap soldiers inside the camp itself—several hundred at least. Brad thought it all sounded extremely busy.

"I don't like this waiting," Hilario said. He and Brad and Paradiso were killing the day in the steamy shade of a banana grove. "Waiting makes me scared."

Hilario had grown up a lot in his months as a guerrilla, Brad realized. In the early days he would never have dared admit he was frightened of anything. Now he had the confidence to say so.

"You scared, Sergeant?" Hilario asked.

Brad and Paradiso had never talked much about fear, but then they had never had to wait all day like this for someone else to decide what they would do.

Paradiso grunted. Without answering Hilario's question, he said, "I tell you my most scare time. *Manunuli*."

"Ooh, *manunuli*," Hilario said with a grin. "Very bad."

"What is it?" Brad asked.

"He is man who cuts off your prick," Paradiso said. He was smiling too.

"What?"

"Circumcise," Hilario explained.

"But they do that when you're a baby."

"No, no," Hilario said. "When you are a boy. Sergeant is right: very scary."

"*Manunuli* is always old man," Paradiso said. "In my village he was old barber named Kak-Kak. He cut all the pricks. Everybody says he is a nice old man, but all the little boys were scared of Kak-Kak."

"I would be too," Brad said. "What a job. He must have made a lot of money."

"No, always free," Hilario said.

"He makes boys into men," Paradiso said. "Big honor to be *manunuli*. All the big boys who already have their pricks cut, they tell us how much it will hurt." He shook his head, smiling. "Very great pain, they tell you." He rolled his eyes. "They tell us all week how bad it will be. Then the day comes and we all go off together, five-six boys, to private place. All serious, all scared. Kak-Kak is there with sharp razor and flat stone and piece of wood. He gives each boy guava leaves to chew. 'Chew up,' he says, 'make plenty juice.' Then we take turns, bravest boy first, and kneel down and Kak-Kak stretches skin way out on stone and takes razor and piece of wood and goes *tap-tap-tap* with wood on razor. Important not to cry. Not really so bad after all. Very quick. And then you spit guava juice on the cut so no infection. Then we are all men."

"Proud," Hilario said.

Paradiso nodded. "Ever since *manunuli*, I always think no reason to be scared. It won't be so bad."

Hilario was nodding and smiling.

Brad wondered what Napoleon told his troops when they were frightened. He couldn't remember reading anything about that. Probably something a lot less effective.

Paradiso stretched his arms and yawned. "Long wait," he said. "Coach, what you do after the war? You go back to Simpson?"

"I don't think so. That seems like a long time ago. I don't know what I'm going to do. We'll have a whole lot of back pay, so I'll have some time to think about it. Maybe go back to the States. A lot depends on that girl in Santo Tomas, Judy. How about you? You going back to Simpson?"

Paradiso shook his head. "No more houseboy. I think I stay in Carabangay."

"And do what?"

"Maybe be the mayor."

Brad laughed. "You can't just decide that. You have to be elected."

"I think I be elected."

Brad thought he probably could be, at that. "What would you do for a living? You're not a farmer, and they don't pay mayors much."

"Oh, Coach! In the Philippines, mayors do all right."

"That's right," Hilario said. "No poor mayors. Me, I'll go back to the farm, help my father and brothers. But," he added shyly, "I will miss this."

One of their men, Bobby Gong, found them under their banana tree. He saluted. Now that they were back with the American army, all their men had taken up saluting again, although the Rangers themselves didn't bother.

"Coach, the colonel wants to see you," Bobby Gong said.

Brad got up. "I'll see you later," he told Paradiso.

"We be here," Paradiso said. He was not happy.

The meeting was a small one, officers only, including the two Filipino guerrilla officers. The colonel, using an aerial photograph of the camp, went over the final plan. Brad found it hard to translate the picture into what he and Hilario had seen at ground level, but the Ranger officers read it easily.

"The scouts say this is some kind of back gate," the colonel said, pointing. He looked at Brad.

"Yes, sir. That's where they took prisoners out to work on the farm." And where they caught Miranda.

"How long will it take a force to circle around and get to it? Starting from right about there, when it gets dark. And not being seen."

Brad thought back. "About twenty minutes."

"Sure of that?"

"About that, sir. Hilario and I did it."

"Well, you'll get to do it again and see if you're

right. You two will go with that platoon. Now here in front of the main gate, this dark area across the road. Scouts didn't get close enough to be sure, but they say it looks like a ditch that could provide cover."

"Yes, sir. That's where we hid to study the gate. But to reach it, you'd have to cross some open rice fields."

The colonel looked around at his officers. "Crawling time," he said with a smile.

There would be two assaults. In the early-evening darkness the main Ranger force would take up position opposite the main gate and wait there. The other, smaller force would circle to the back gate, kill any guards and go in. Firing from the back gate would be the signal for the main force to attack. Total surprise at both gates was critical, the colonel said. Once inside, they must cut telephone wires instantly so the Japs could not call for help.

The two guerrilla groups, one north and one south of the camp, would delay any reinforcements until the Rangers got the prisoners clear. The northern force, which Paradiso and his men would be joining, had the more important role, because a Jap battalion was stationed near the Cabu Bridge. They must be kept away from the camp.

When and if the prisoners were safe, one red flare would signal all Rangers to pull out and head back to the Pampanga River, where native carts were waiting to carry sick or wounded POWs back to the American lines. Between the camp and the river, the Rangers would probably have to carry the weaker prisoners on their backs. A second red flare would signal the guerrilla forces that all was clear and they could withdraw.

"The *second* flare," the colonel repeated, glaring at the two guerrilla officers. Both nodded.

To Brad it sounded neat and clear, the way operations always sounded beforehand. Everybody in each group knew exactly what to do. The Ranger officers seemed confident and professional, but Brad could imagine a number of things going wrong. And if the Japs got any inkling that they were coming, things could go very wrong.

But to his astonishment, everything went right. Everything worked the way it was supposed to. Even the colonel could not believe their luck.

Brad did not time how long it took the Ranger platoon to reach the back gate, but it felt longer than twenty minutes. No one spoke. Brad sensed that Hilario, walking beside him, was more excited than scared, now that action was near.

They had good moonlight to help them. They crept to within a few yards of the gate. It was only lightly guarded, just as they had hoped. After all, Cabanatuan was many miles from any place the American army was supposed to be.

When they opened fire and saw the guards fall, they could hear instant gunfire from the direction of the other gate. Rangers quickly cut the barbed wire, and they rushed inside. The POW barracks were in the far part of the camp. The job of this platoon was to keep all Japs away from there. Their main target was a building the scouts had said was occupied by off-duty soldiers.

The Rangers tossed grenades and then burst in. The surprise of the attack was so complete and the Rangers so efficient that they wiped out the building without losing a man.

"They are very hot shit," Hilario said. "I think I will be a Ranger."

Above their own gunfire, Brad could hear the powerful *whoosh* of bazookas at the main gate, knocking out tanks and trucks.

After the building, the lieutenant spread his men to control the area, but there was little to control. The Japanese were so disorganized that they put up no real fight.

The sound of firing at the main gate began to diminish. Now, at a greater distance, Brad could hear the battle between the guerrillas and the Jap battalion at the bridge, mostly rifle fire but now and then an explosion. He hoped Paradiso and his men were holding out.

When the first red flare streaked into the night sky, the lieutenant blew his whistle. "Nothing left to do, I guess. Let's go home."

In the safety of the next morning, when the groups were finally back together, Brad and Hilario found that Paradiso and all his men were not only alive but unhurt. The Japs at the bridge had been caught by surprise as completely as the Japs at the camp. Paradiso was no longer sullen.

"Big night!" he said, as Brad shook his hand. "We

sit there and shoot up all the Japs across the river. *Bang-bang-bang*. Many hundred. And that bazooka! I think we steal one to take back with us."

"So you weren't bored after all," Brad said. He could not get over how glad he was to see Paradiso. Big night, as Paradiso said.

But it was not until the colonel called his officers together that Brad learned how truly incredible their success had been. The Rangers had lost only two men. The Filipino guerrillas lost not a single man. And every prisoner but one, who died of a heart attack, was safe.

"MacArthur is very pleased with us," the colonel said. "So am I. Let's hope First Cav is as lucky at Santo Tomas."

"That wasn't luck, sir," one of the officers said.

The colonel grinned. "Well, some luck. But not all luck. The whole unit's going to be decorated. Tell your men well done. Damn well done."

Brad stayed behind to ask a favor.

"Sir, what's this about Santo Tomas?"

"None of your business, captain."

"But, sir, I have a lot of friends in there. If the First Cavalry is headed there, I'd sure like to go along."

"Don't push your luck, captain. Cabanatuan was a miracle."

"My girlfriend's in Santo Tomas."

"Oh? Serious?"

"Yes, sir, very serious. And I haven't seen her for three years."

"A lot of us haven't seen our girls or wives for three years."

"Yes, sir, but mine is right there in Manila."

"She'll still be there. Listen, Stone, this isn't going to be a division parade. MacArthur's afraid they might kill all those folks before he gets there. He's sending one flying column to try to get there first. Sixty miles through the Japs. Anyway, I do not command First Cav."

"No, sir. But after Cabanatuan, maybe they'd listen to a suggestion from you. I spent a lot of time in Manila. I could help out there the same way I did here."

"You mean I'm supposed to suggest you."

"Yes, sir. If you wouldn't mind."

————

The instant he heard the racket of gunfire in the darkness, Jack Humphrey thought, Oh Christ, they're shooting us. All the prisoners had talked about this possibility for weeks.

"They're killing us," somebody said. The voice held despair rather than fright. "They're going to kill us all."

"Let's get out of here," somebody else said.

"We can't get away."

"It's better than just waiting for them."

Maybe there's a chance, Humphrey thought. Maybe we can get away in the dark. Then he wondered how far he could get carrying Maxsie, who lay in the next bunk. Not very far.

Then he heard the *thump* of grenades and an enormous *whoosh* followed by an explosion. He heard screams. No, they're not shooting us. They're blowing the place up. Or probably both.

That it would come down to this. After Bataan, after the Death March, after O'Donnell, and after all these endless months in Cabanatuan. Well, Sara, we hung on as long as we could.

The firing and the explosions continued. A hell of a lot of noise. That's funny, he thought. It sounds more like fighting.

They waited in the darkness for whatever was coming. The noise began to die down.

Two figures came through the barracks entrance— huge, tall figures outlined against the moonlight.

"Hey, everybody. It's okay, we're Americans."

The barracks was silent in disbelief.

"Hey, come on, we're Rangers. We got to get you all out of here. Let's go."

More figures came through the entrance.

"Maxsie. Did you hear? They're Americans. They're here!"

"High time," Maxsie said.

Now there were flashlights shining around the barracks.

"Come on, everybody. We got to be moving. Who needs help? Sing out, but let's go."

In the flashlight beams Jack Humphrey could see bewildered men climbing to their feet. He gave Maxsie a hand, knowing by now the best way to lift him to a standing position without hurting him.

The Rangers moved quickly around the barracks, helping those who could not manage alone. They were amazingly gentle.

Jack Humphrey got Maxsie's left arm over his shoulder. For some reason they could never figure out, this was more comfortable than his right arm. Together they walked out of the barracks into the open moonlight. A long, straggling line of prisoners, helped and encouraged by the Rangers, was moving down the central street to the main gate, which was wide, wide, wide open.

As they came near the gate, a big Ranger said, "Here, sir, let me give you a hand."

He untangled Maxsie from Humphrey and, with compassionate ease, slung both of Maxsie's arms over his shoulders and lifted him onto his broad back. He did not seem to feel the weight. Of course, it wasn't a great deal of weight.

"Put me down, you fucker," Maxsie said. "I can walk."

"Take it easy, sir. We got a long ways to go."

"Don't 'sir' me, soldier. I'm a master sergeant."

"Oh? Oh. Okay, sarge. Are you sure?"

"Goddamn you, I'm walking out of here."

Gently the Ranger let him down.

Maxsie flung his left arm over Jack's shoulder. "Come on, Hump. Race you to the gate."

Dear Sara,

We made it. Maxsie and I, we both made it. Home soon.

Love, Jack

High Prices

Amos was resting on his cot when the announcement came over the loudspeaker system:

"Amos Watson, Felix Logan. Report to the commandant's office."

So it had finally happened.

He could stay here and force them to come get him, but that would only make them angry. Not much difference one way or the other, he supposed, but he didn't want to leave Felix waiting alone with the Kempeitai. Poor Felix. If he had let Felix quit his job and join the other teenagers, those Terrible Ten, this wouldn't be happening. No point in thinking about that now. Goddamn Homobono—it had to be Homobono. But how could he have known about Felix?

Amos slid his swollen feet into his slippers, took up his bamboo cane and set off for the office. A bright, warm day, perfect weather for bombing. He hoped the American planes would come again today.

Five minutes to think. Of course, Sandy hadn't really known about Felix. Amos remembered his words exactly: "Perhaps that young man I just saw sweeping up?" He had been guessing. But still, there was Felix's name over the loudspeaker. Could that also be a "perhaps"? Could they just be fishing around for Felix? Slim chance. But that was what he had to work with.

Amos hurried his step as best he could. He hoped Felix would keep his mouth shut until Amos got there. And that he remembered his lessons.

A Japanese army car with a driver at the wheel and a soldier in the front seat stood outside the commandant's office, its rear door open. Could it have brought Homobono to accuse them in person? If so, Amos would enjoy saying a few last words right into Sandy's face.

Sandy was not there, but a lot of others were. Big excitement, everybody was standing. Eight or nine Kempeitai, including the commandant and his interpreter. There was also a short, squat lieutenant Amos had never seen before, who presumably had arrived in the army car.

And Felix, standing straight against one wall, taller and thinner these days. His eyes behind his thick glasses were huge. While all the Japs were watching Amos hobble into the room, Felix took the moment to shake his head slightly, telling Amos that nothing had happened, nothing had been said.

The squat lieutenant held a sheet of paper in his hand. He looked at it. "You are the enemy alien Amos Watson?" he asked in English. His voice was shrill but formal.

"That's right," Amos said. "What's this all about?"

682   RALPH GRAVES

In a low voice the interpreter began translating for
the commandant.

The squat lieutenant read from his paper: "War
Prisoner Headquarters has determined that you,
Amos Watson, have conspired to communicate with
the American enemy. You have been convicted and
sentenced to die."

"When was my trial?" Amos said. "I missed it."

The lieutenant looked up briefly at Amos, his eyes
hard and icy. Then he looked down at his paper again.
"And Felix Logan." His head turned toward Felix.
"War Prisoner Head—"

"You little shit!" Amos cried out at Felix. "You
dirty little Jap spy!"

Amos lunged forward on his swollen feet and
struck Felix hard on the arm with his cane. Without
the support of his cane Amos staggered and almost
fell, but he caught his balance and swung again, this
time hitting Felix on the chest. Shock and amazement
spread across Felix's face.

Amos was getting ready for a third swing when
the Japs came to life. Two of the Kempeitai grabbed
him and held him tight. He struggled with them.

"You bastard!" he said to Felix. "Sucking up to
these stinking Japs all the time. You told them, you
told them about me."

The interpreter was having a hard time keeping
up, but Amos was making sure they all heard him.
Come on, Felix, he begged, get in the game.

"How did you find out, you little prick? And to
think I even gave you *food*." Amos was very bitter.
"Fucking spy! Fucking Jap spy!"

And then Felix apparently remembered: sometimes you just have to cut your losses and save what you can. He took a deep breath.

"You didn't fool me," Felix said, rubbing his arm where the cane had struck him. "You never fooled me." There was a suitable measure of contempt in his voice, very good for such a young pupil. "I guessed what you were doing. You're the spy, not me."

The commandant and the War Prisoner Headquarters officer were talking hard at each other in Japanese. There seemed to be substantial confusion. Felix wore that blank, slightly stupid look on his face, mouth half open, pretending not to listen or understand. Amos wished he knew what the commandant and the lieutenant were saying. His feet hurt; he wished they would let him sit down. He gave them a minute or so to argue before he lashed out again.

"The Americans will get you," he threatened Felix. "They're coming back and they'll shoot every Jap spy. I hope you're the first."

Then Felix produced a splendid remark. "Not before the Imperial Japanese Army gets *you*," he said. His voice was a little shaky, but Amos was impressed.

The commandant and the squat lieutenant were still jabbering. The lieutenant pointed again to his official sheet of paper, but his voice was not quite so shrill now. The Kempeitai commandant in turn pointed to Felix and nodded his head in what looked like vigorous approval. What was the commandant praising? Felix's job performance?—Look at this spic-and-span office. Or his denunciation of the

American spy? Whatever it was, the commandant was plainly pulling rank.

Felix could not have been convicted and sentenced, or there would be nothing to argue about. The orders of War Prisoner Headquarters would have been absolute in such a matter. Maybe there was nothing more than vague suspicion, unfounded rumor. If so, the commandant seemed to be saying he would take care of it. No spies in his office. This was his camp, his responsibility.

At last the lieutenant bowed. The commandant replied with a nod of his head. The lieutenant turned back to Amos, and now his voice recovered its shrillness. "You will come with me."

Amos and Felix exchanged one brief look.

I owed you one for the typhoon, Amos thought. Make good use of it, Felix.

He followed the lieutenant out the door. The soldier hopped out of the front seat and held the door open for his superior.

"Backseat," the lieutenant barked at Amos.

Amos climbed in. The soldier took the place beside him. The doors closed. The car drove through the campus down to the main gate on Calle España.

Amos had arrived by special car in January 1942, and now, three years later, he was leaving by special car. Always in style, he thought.

The streets of his Manila were full of rubble. Almost no traffic of any kind. All the people they passed were shabby. A sad-looking city, he thought, but soon, surely soon, it would be joyful. He was sorry he wouldn't see that.

The driver seemed to know which streets were clear. The car took many turns. It had been so long since Amos had seen these streets that he could not always recognize where they were. Most of the street signs were gone.

He expected to be taken to Fort Santiago, but this was not the right direction. He knew they were headed south when the car drove along wide Mabini Avenue for several blocks before turning off again. A few more turns and they stopped in front of a dilapidated police station. Half a dozen armed soldiers stood around a dirty open-bed truck with slatted sides.

"Out," the lieutenant said, in the shrill voice that was beginning to grate on Amos's ears. "Get in the truck."

End of style, Amos thought as, with the help of his cane, he pulled himself out of the car. The tailgate of the truck was down. A rickety wooden packing crate served as a step. With one hand on the truck bed and one hand on his cane Amos climbed onto the crate, which wobbled beneath his weight, and then into the truck. He wanted to sit down and rest, but he made himself stand. He leaned back against the slats. The truck bed was filthy, covered with caked mud and twigs and bits of straw. Over the years, the tumbril hadn't improved much.

The lieutenant gave an order in Japanese. Two of the soldiers went into the police station. For five minutes nothing happened.

Then, through the door, flanked by armed soldiers on either side, came a string of prisoners. Their hands were wired, and then they were wired to each other in groups of three or four. There were eleven prisoners, all Filipinos. The last three, wired together, were nuns. Amos wondered what these particular eleven people had done, if anything.

Getting them into the truck was an awkward business because of the wires. The soldiers prodded and shouted at them. Two groups were already in the truck when the lieutenant realized that Amos was not properly restrained like the others.

"Come here," he told Amos, pointing to the street.

Amos did not intend to climb down and then climb back up again. "No," he said.

"Here! Here!" The lieutenant pointed furiously.

"No."

The lieutenant glared. Then he shouted a command. A soldier jumped up onto the truck bed. He grabbed Amos's cane and threw it over the side. The bamboo stick bounced and clattered on the pavement. Then he wrapped wire around Amos's swollen wrists with hard, tight turns. Amos closed his eyes in order not to wince. When he opened them, the soldier was attaching the end of the wire to one of the Filipino groups.

The nuns were the hardest to load because of their long black skirts. The soldiers had to shove them from behind. When at last it was done, four soldiers climbed into the truck with the prisoners. Another soldier slammed the tailgate. The lieutenant got in the cab beside the driver. With grinding gears the truck lurched off. That clutch is worn out, Amos thought, and they probably don't have any spare parts.

No one spoke during the short drive except the nuns, who were praying quietly. Two of the men were praying too, their eyes closed, lips moving silently. One man was sobbing aloud. The man next to Amos had a terrible red welt on his face. It could be a broken cheekbone. He kept raising his hands to touch the welt, and when he did so, all the other hands in his group were forced to rise too.

The truck slowed, then turned and bumped over the broken sidewalk into a vacant lot. The usual vacant lot in Manila where everybody threw trash and garbage into the scraggly grass. Three more soldiers were waiting for them.

Nobody had remembered to bring the packing-crate step. The soldiers had to drag the groups out of the truck bed. Each group stumbled and fell to the ground and had to be helped to their feet. They were lined up, then pushed to their knees. Amos saw one of the soldiers who had been waiting for them draw a long curved sword out of a scabbard. It made a slithering metallic sound.

Another soldier started down behind the line of prisoners, slipping black masks over their eyes. Amos was fifth in line.

This was intolerable. He refused to accept this.

What was that Japanese insult Felix had taught him? He could not remember. But it must not end like this.

"We're going to get you," Amos said loudly. He could hear the croak in his voice. "They're going to get you. They're going to get all of you bastards. Fuck you. Fuck all of you."

Something hard crashed into his back, knocking him facedown into the dirt. A rifle butt. Somebody yanked him up on his knees again, and the mask was slipped over his eyes, shutting out all sight. His shoulder blade must be broken. He had felt it crack. It hurt like hell.

And then, a wonderful thing. Somewhere down the line to his right, he heard a feeble voice say, "Fuck you."

Good man, Amos thought. Good man, but not loud enough. Not nearly loud enough.

He reached down, way down inside, and somewhere found his old deep voice.

"Fuck you!" he shouted into the darkness. "Fuck you! Fuck you! Fuck—"

———

Since meetings were illegal, they came to Rollo's house separately, ten minutes apart. Enrique liked her idea, but he reminded her, "This is my meeting, Peanut."

She asked if she could be the last to arrive. "I don't want to have to sit around and look at him."

Enrique refused. "You can be next to last," he said. "I come last. Anyway, he is to wait in another room until the meeting starts."

Papaya sat on the sofa, twisting her purse in her hands, until Enrique, dressed in an informal light-blue *barong* and slacks, walked through the living-room doorway. Then they were all there. The tall Jesuit priest, Wafer, in his worn black cassock. The elderly Swiss, Tin-Tin, in a red-and-white-striped sport shirt that ill became his years. The builder Federico—Simon at this meeting—in his khaki-colored work clothes. And their host for this afternoon, the doctor, Rollo, with his steel-rimmed glasses and a dark shirt and jacket.

"Well, everybody present," Enrique said cheerfully. He rubbed his hands together and took the vacant easy chair at the head of their little circle, next to Papaya. He looked at the doctor. "He is here?"

"Yes, Zorro. Waiting in the den, as you asked."

"I want to say," the priest said, "that I think this is a terrible idea." His expression bordered on anger. "I thought very seriously of not coming. I consider this an extremely dangerous decision."

Papaya saw Rollo flush, and his mouth opened to protest, but Enrique held up his hand. "Oh, come now," he said. "It's not as bad as that. After all, he did get into Santo Tomas. I think we should all hear him."

"He's worked for the Japanese."

"Oh, well, who hasn't?" Enrique spread his hands. "We have all had to play our little roles. In any case, it's my decision. Bring him in, Rollo, if you please."

The doctor got up and walked quickly out of the room. He could not have been gone more than a minute. Papaya gripped her purse tightly.

Rollo came back, with Sandy Homobono walking beside him. The familiar gnomelike figure wore his customary black suit and tie. He was smiling with satisfaction when he entered the living room, but Papaya saw his eyes dart from face to face, taking them in, filing each one in his keen reporter's mind. Papaya kept her face straight when he looked at her.

"Come," Enrique said, "sit here next to me. Pull up that chair."

When he saw where Homobono was going to sit, Wafer got up and moved away to the far end of the couch.

Homobono placed the straight-backed chair where Enrique indicated, right opposite Papaya, and sat down. Then he rose at once and picked up an ashtray from the end table next to Papaya. He was close enough to touch. She managed not to shrink back.

He sat down again and took out a pack of cigarettes. "Is it all right to smoke?"

"Of course," Enrique said. He was being most hospitable.

Homobono offered the pack, but nobody took one. He lighted his own cigarette.

"Now then," Enrique said. "We understand that you were able to get into Santo Tomas. Congratulations."

"Yes, as I told Dado—"

"Please, we don't use each other's real names. Tell us how you did it."

"Sorry. I thought up a story that the Japs might let me go inside the camp to do."

"That was ingenious. What was it?"

"An interview with one of the internees."

"Which one?"

Homobono hesitated. "You mean his name?"

"Yes, yes, that doesn't matter."

"Well, Amos Watson." He looked around the circle. His eyes crossed Papaya's briefly. "Some of you know him." He looked at Papaya again. "He was an important American businessman before the war."

"Yes, we all know who Amos Watson is. Why did you pick him?"

Homobono flicked ashes into his ashtray. Papaya saw that his hands were not completely steady.

"Well, you see, Watson was very critical of American preparations for the war. Back in 1941. He went around saying that the Japs might be able to take the Philippines. I wrote several stories about him at that time. I was able to persuade the Japs that his comments today might be equally favorable to them."

"Marvelous," Enrique said, caught up in admiration. "But what did you really hope to get from talking to Watson?"

"I knew from—" Homobono caught himself before saying the name. "I was told that your group wanted information on conditions inside the camp. I assumed that Watson, as one of the leaders in the business community, would be a good person to talk to." He stubbed out his cigarette. "Unfortunately, I was mistaken."

"That's a pity, after all your good planning."

A pronounced snort came from the far end of the couch where Wafer was sitting. Enrique ignored it.

"Yes, sometimes things don't work out the way you hope. Watson turned out to be quite old and out of touch. He seemed to know very little about what was going on. I'd say he's in very poor health." He shook his head sadly, but then brightened. "However, the visit was not a total waste."

"You learned something?" Enrique asked.

"I got a good look inside the camp. Would you like to hear?"

"Yes, of course."

Sandy Homobono lighted another cigarette, thought in silence for a moment and then launched into a lengthy, precise report. He was very good. He made them all see the look of the campus grounds, the state and placement of the military supplies and preparations, the activity in the commandant's office, the appearance and behavior of both the Kempeitai and the internees.

Glancing down the couch as the vivid details poured out, Papaya could see that even Wafer, who had been inside Santo Tomas, was impressed.

When Homobono finished, Rollo looked around the circle and then stared specifically at Wafer. "I told you he would be useful."

"Useful?" Enrique echoed. "No, brilliant. We could have used him much earlier."

"Thank you." Sandy Homobono was pleased with himself. His hands were steady now.

"But haven't you left out something?"

The reporter was puzzled by the question. "I don't think so. How do you mean?"

Enrique's smile was encouraging. "Won't you tell us about your talk with General Miyama?"

Homobono froze.

In the sudden silence, Tin-Tin said, "Miyama?"

"Yes, our good General Miyama," Enrique said. His voice sounded so happy.

Homobono said, "I—don't know what you mean."

"Oh, yes, come now," Enrique said. He beamed at Homobono. "A man with your extraordinary memory? You're among friends here. Please tell us."

They all waited. Homobono said nothing. He was staring at Enrique.

"No? What a pity. I'm sure we would all have enjoyed hearing it from you. But fortunately, I think someone else can fill us in. Not as well as you, to be sure. Peanut?"

"Yes," Papaya said, "I can."

Homobono swiveled his head to look at her. They were less than six feet apart.

"He told Miyama that Amos Watson was a spy for the Americans."

Someone gasped. Papaya did not look to see who it was.

"I don't believe it," Rollo said in a shaken voice.

"It's not true! I *never* said that."

"They were suspicious of his visit to Santo Tomas," Papaya said. She had written it all out this morning and memorized it, just like a movie script, so that she would make no mistake at this moment. "They did not believe his story about wanting to interview Amos. Miyama threatened to send him to Santiago. So then he told Miyama that he had been trying to get proof that Amos was spying. He knew it was true, he said, but he was trying to get proof. All this was overheard and repeated to me an hour after it happened." She took a deep breath. "Then he asked Miyama for money for this information."

"Ah!" the priest said. "Ah, dear God!"

"I'm surprised you couldn't remember that," Enrique said. "Frankly, very surprised indeed."

Homobono seemed locked in his chair.

"What's happened to Mr. Watson?" Federico asked.

"What would you guess?" Enrique said. He looked around his little circle. "Amos Watson, for those of you who don't know, has been extremely helpful to us for a long time. Helpful and most generous. At considerable risk he supplied his personal funds and a great deal of valuable information to our people and to one of the best guerrilla units. An excellent man." Enrique twisted his head to get rid of the crick in his neck. Now he smiled again. "Well, we mustn't dally over the past. I suppose," he said to Homobono, "that Miyama hasn't got around to paying you yet. We wouldn't want you to be discommoded."

He reached in the pocket of his *barong* and brought out some folded paper money. He spread it out, three bills. "What would you say? Does thirty pesos sound about right?"

"Yes," Wafer said savagely. "Thirty pesos. Exactly right."

Homobono looked at the money with alarm. He made no move to take it. Enrique refolded the bills and tucked them in the breast pocket of Homobono's black jacket.

Enrique rubbed his hands together, palm to palm. "Well, now that you are one of us, there is something you should know. We all use handy little code names, some of them rather silly. This is Peanut. I am Zorro. Your friend is called Rollo. That is Tin-Tin, and Simon, and Wafer." Enrique waved a hand at each of them as he made his introductions. "Now we must have a name for you, too. What would be suitable? I wonder. Something distinguished, to celebrate your fine work. Yes, I think you will be called Taksil."

The Tagalog word for traitor.

Sandy Homobono finally found his voice. "These are nothing but lies. I will not stay here for insults."

"Oh, yes," Enrique said, "you will stay here. Peanut?"

Papaya opened her purse and took out the pretty little revolver Hitoshi Buto had given her to protect herself.

When they had talked about this, Enrique said, "You don't have to do this. There's no reason. One of the men can do it." "He was *my* friend," Papaya said. "So was Simon," Enrique said. "Not the same way." "Well, I should hope not!" "Also, Amos and I worked the closest together." "But my dear Peanut, you don't know anything about guns." "Yes, I do. Buto gave me one and taught me how to use it. Appropriate, no? To use a Jap gun? I even practiced firing it." "Well. Well. All right, we'll put you close together. But don't try to aim for the head. It's too easy to miss."

So Papaya shot him in the chest. The revolver made a huge *bang* in the quiet living room. He did not fall at once. She shot him again, and now he toppled over sideways, his chair falling over with him. The smell of smoke was strong. He lay a few feet away, still moving. She did not even have to get up. She leaned forward from the sofa, stretched out her arm and shot him in the head. The result of this was very ugly and quite final.

She put the revolver on safety, as Buto had taught her, tucked it away in her purse and closed the flap.

After a few seconds Enrique put his hands on the arms of his easy chair and pushed himself to his feet. "I think that concludes our business," he said. "Unless, Wafer, you feel the need to say a short prayer?"

"No."

"Good. We will leave in reverse order then. Ten minutes apart, of course."

He turned to go, but Papaya knew he was not finished. There was one more thing. One public slap in the face.

Enrique stopped, then turned back to speak to the doctor. He was no longer smiling. "This mess was all your fault, Rollo. So you clean it up."

He glanced down at Homobono's body. Blood and other things were spreading over the woven straw rug, soaking into it. "Whatever you do with this, be sure to leave the money in his pocket. It must be found in his pocket."

Then Enrique smiled at Papaya. "Okay, Peanut?"

"Very okay," she said.

≡ 32 ≡

Roll Out the Barrel

Judy Ferguson and Millie Barnes spent the afternoon of February 3, Millie's fifty-second birthday, talking about death. Millie said she'd thought of selling her shanty after Sammy died, but "it was our last home together, so I decided to keep it."

There was nothing left in the shanty with which to celebrate the birthday, but Sammy had been saving two rice cakes for the occasion. Millie invited Judy to share them. "He'd have wanted you to. He said you always made him feel like a young buck." She sighed. "Sweet old Sammy. He was never a young buck even when he was young."

The rice cakes were stale, but they were the first food other than the skimpy mush of soybeans or corn or cassava that either had had for a week.

"Sorry I don't have a birthday present for you," Judy said.

"Me, too," Millie said. She licked the crumbs from her fingers. "Did you hear Annette Switzer died? She was number thirty-two for January."

"I heard, but I didn't know her."

"Oh, well, you still don't know most of the women, do you? She was a nice enough lady. Just ran out of gas."

"You heard they put Dr. Stevenson in jail?"

"Yes, over those death certificates."

Everybody in Santo Tomas was proud of Dr. Stevenson. He had signed eight internee death certificates listing cause of death as "malnutrition" or "starvation." The Japs were furious. They said it made them look bad and ordered Stevenson to change the cause of death. Stevenson told them the average adult male in Santo Tomas had lost fifty-three pounds, a lot of it recently, and if that wasn't malnutrition, he didn't know what was. Now he was in the camp jail for disobedience.

"How much weight you lost, Judy?"

"I don't know. More than twenty, though. I know I'm under a hundred." She would not weigh herself on the hospital scale because it could only be discouraging.

"The first ten or fifteen pounds I lost, I liked it. Slim at last. After that, not so great. But you know what I don't like? I catch myself looking at people now. People I know—friends. Or even just acquaintances. I look at them and I find myself thinking, You're going to die. It's creepy."

"And are you right?"

"Sometimes. There's a look."

"How do I look?"

"Oh, you." Millie laughed. "You're a survivor. Pretty gaunt in the cheeks. And Sammy would have said—" She had to pause. "Sammy would have said

Judy's legs are getting skinny. But you're not going to die."

"That's right," Judy said. "I'm not. Neither are you."

"No, I'm not. I've waited this long for our boys to come back, and I don't intend to miss it."

The sound of a large explosion somewhere far out in the city interrupted them. The Japs had been blowing up supplies and bridges and buildings for many days. Clouds of smoke constantly rose and hung in the air. All this demolition made the internees feel sure the Americans were coming soon. But they were afraid the Japs would blow up Santo Tomas first—with all of them inside.

"I wish they'd stop doing that," Millie said. "When we get out of here, I'd like to see something left of Manila. Of course, it won't be the same without Sammy." She was silent for a moment. "What about your fellow, Brad? You think he's alive?"

"I don't know. Sometimes when I get out his letters and read them, I'm sure he's alive. They sound—he sounds so— But it's been a long time. I just don't know."

"You never said how the letters got to you."

"No, I wasn't supposed to. I guess it doesn't matter now, since he's dead. It was Amos Watson."

"Sammy and I thought it might be. You used to talk to him more than you talked to most of the old geezers. That was a terrible thing about Amos. But I guess he really was some kind of spy."

"I guess so. He got me to bring him stuff from the records office. I never knew what he did with it. All

I know is, he fixed it so Brad and I could write to each other. And then the letters stopped, and now Amos is gone, and I don't know if Brad's alive or dead."

They heard another familiar noise, the roar of planes. This time the roar was unusually close. Looking up, they saw half a dozen American fighter planes swooping in low over the campus.

"Go get 'em!" Millie called out, and waved her hand.

When they had passed overhead, she said, "Jesus, those were low."

"They dropped something," Judy said. She stood up.

"I didn't see anything."

"I saw it. Over by the camp garden. Come on, let's go see."

They were not the first ones to get there. When they came in sight of the garden, Millie said, "I guess you're right. Something's sure up."

A small crowd of internees clustered in a camote patch. They were laughing and crying, and two men were slapping each other on the back.

As they hurried up, Judy said, "What is it? What is it?"

An old man with tears in his eyes said, "A message! A message for us!"

My God, Judy thought, a message. The first direct, official word from the U.S. Army in three whole years. Since Manila fell.

"He wrapped his goggles around the piece of paper," somebody said.

"But what's it say? What's it say? Does it say when they're coming?"

"No. It just says, 'Roll out the barrel.' "

A woman began to sing, in a cracked voice:

> *"Roll out the barrel,*
> *We'll have a barrel of fun . . ."*

Millie flung her thin arms around Judy's neck and kissed her. "*There's* my birthday present!"

More curious people came hurrying up to join the little crowd and find out what was happening.

"Come on," Millie said. "Let's go tell Sammy's brother. If I can't tell Sammy, at least I can tell George."

"But he's still in the Education Building," Judy said.

The Japs had taken over the first two floors of this building as offices and living quarters for the commandant and his staff. The internees, men and boys, had either been crowded onto the top floor or moved to other buildings.

"So what?" Millie said. "You're not scared of a few Japs now, are you? Not today. We'll walk right past those monkeys and look them dead in the eye. Come on, Judy, let's you and me roll out the barrel. I'll tell George, and you can tell all the other men. You'll get kissed fifty times."

———

The First Cavalry column was tearing through enemy territory, far ahead of the rest of the army.

At every river or stream, it found the bridge destroyed. The Sherman tanks had no trouble crossing, once a fording place had been picked out, but the soldiers had to climb down from the trucks and weapons carriers to lighten them. They waded across, holding their rifles and carbines overhead to keep them dry. Even so, the vehicles sometimes had trouble and, with gears grinding and clashing, had to be pushed from behind or pulled through the water by chains.

Brad Stone's new combat fatigues were soaked and mud-smeared. But when, just before takeoff, he had said goodby to Paradiso and the men, he had looked quite snappy—all clean and green, and with no holes.

Paradiso looked him over. "What you doing, Coach? You think you some kind of soldier?"

The men laughed with Paradiso.

"They said if I went with them, I had to be in uniform," Brad said, a little embarrassed by his finery. He did feel strange in an army uniform. "You guys be careful getting back to Carabangay."

Paradiso had orders to take his men back, assemble the main group and then harass the retreating Japanese throughout their area.

"Don't worry, Coach," Paradiso said. "You come back, we be there."

Brad had to wonder now if he would be coming back. The closer the column came to Manila, the more often they ran into enemy fire. At the first sound of ambush, the troops leaped from their vehicles and returned fire. The tanks fired their heavy 75mm cannons, and all the machine guns opened up from the weapons carriers. Brad would not have thought seven hundred men and a few tanks could make such an unholy racket.

As soon as the enemy fire stopped or softened to a patter of scattered shots, they all jumped back into their vehicles and raced on. The medics moved from one truck or weapons carrier to another, slapping bandages on the wounded.

All day Marine fighter planes had been providing cover for the column. Now they reported great news: the Novaliches Bridge a few miles north of Manila was still standing. If the column could get there before the Japs blew it, they'd have clear sailing into the city. The commanding officer gave orders to pour it on.

But when they reached the bridge, they were met with fire. Once more everybody jumped out of the vehicles, and the tanks and machine guns fired back.

"The bridge! It's mined!"

Flat on his stomach on the ground near the bridge, firing back with his carbine, Brad could see the fuses burning. Bullets streamed back and forth across the river. Suddenly he saw the navy bomb-disposal officer, James Sutton, go running out onto the bridge, bent over to avoid the firing. He knelt down to kill the fuses. Miraculously, he came running back.

Brad was glad somebody had thought to bring Sutton along.

After five more minutes of heavy fire, they all jumped back into the vehicles, and the whole column rumbled across the bridge, a tank leading the way. It was just beginning to turn dark.

For Brad Stone, riding in a truck a third of the way

back in the column, the last few miles were total
confusion. He knew they must be in Manila, but as
the night grew darker, he could not recognize a single
landmark. Firing was frequent and sporadic, but he
could not always tell who was firing at what. Occasionally he fired at something moving in the darkness
without being sure what he was aiming at. The night
air was heavy with the smell of smoke.

The front of the column must have picked up the
waiting Filipino guerrillas who had offered to guide
them through the land mines and tank traps and
around Japanese strongpoints, because now the column began to take strange twists and turns through
the dark streets. Each vehicle blindly followed the one
in front of it. The pace was slow, with many stops
and starts. The tank treads made a horrendous clatter
on the broken pavements. Brad wondered where the
hell they were.

He still did not know where they were when the
column stopped once again. Off to the right he could
barely make out what seemed to be a long stone wall.
It did not look familiar, but then nothing did.

Up ahead, a searchlight went on, revealing a tall
metal gate set in the wall. Seconds later the lead
tank rumbled forward and crashed right through the
gate.

More lights came on—searchlights, headlights—
and other vehicles followed the tank through the shattered gate. From inside the wall he could hear small-
arms fire and the sound of grenades.

We're here, Brad realized. We're here at Santo
Tomas.

When Brad's truck, headlights blazing, followed its leader through the gate, he saw a few dead bodies lying silent on the ground. The sound of firing was much less than it had been at least a dozen times during their race to Manila. Bright flares burst overhead to light the campus so that the soldiers could see to clean up what opposition there was.

The trucks and weapons carriers rolled up a wide driveway until they came in sight of large stone buildings and a broad open plaza. There they were forced to halt because the plaza was filling rapidly with a swarm of ragged figures. The prisoners. The column had reached them in time. Somewhere, somewhere in that mass, he would find Judy.

He jumped down from the truck. Instantly he and the other soldiers were surrounded by hysterical people, many of them weeping, all of them trying to get close enough to touch the soldiers. Brad felt hands grabbing at him and patting him. The hands were like claws. People tried to kiss him, men and women alike. They looked thin and frail.

It was lucky the opposition had been so slight. Some were killed, some surrendered. It would have been impossible to conduct a serious fight in this maelstrom of happiness.

Then the crazy prisoners began to sing "God Bless America," which they all seemed to know, and then a badly butchered version of "The Star-Spangled Banner." How would he ever find Judy? If she was here. There was no point in trying to look for her. Several thousand people must be out there, all crying and singing and laughing and touching the soldiers over

and over again, as though to prove to themselves that
the soldiers were real.

Officers tried to clear the plaza so they could root
out any remaining Japs, but it was hopeless. Nothing
was going to stop this night of celebration.

———

As soon as he realized they were American tanks and
soldiers, Felix Logan hurried into the plaza. After
three years of pretending he didn't understand Japanese, he was sure he could now be useful to the
American officers. The plaza was crowded with soldiers and internees.

Felix made his way toward the lead tank. That was
where the officers should be. Sure enough, an American major and several other officers and soldiers
stood grouped in the glare of a searchlight.

Before Felix could get the major's attention and
make his offer to help, he heard shouts from internees.
"Kill them! Kill them! Kill them!"

Four Japs, two civilians and two officers, were walking nervously through the plaza toward the tank, obviously coming to negotiate some kind of surrender.

Then Felix saw that behind them was a fifth Jap.
It was Lieutenant Abiko. Of all the Kempeitai, Abiko
was the most hated and despised. These last months
he had been responsible for the harsh work details,
the bowing classes, the endless roll calls with everyone
forced to stand at attention.

The American soldiers disarmed the four Japs, taking away their swords and pistols.

Then Abiko came up to the group. He was ordered

to put his hands up like the others. Instead he reached for the little sack over his shoulder, where, Felix knew, the Japs carried small suicide grenades.

"Look out!" Felix shouted.

But the American major needed no warning. As soon as Abiko's hand went toward his shoulder, the major shot him in the stomach. Abiko fell to the ground, twisting and groaning.

A hoarse, vicious cry of delight rose from the internees close enough to see what had happened. Two men grabbed Abiko by the ankles and began to drag him across the plaza toward the Main Building, forcing a path between the internees.

As they recognized who it was, men and women who had had to endure Abiko's outrages took their revenge.

Felix, following the gauntlet, saw people kicking and spitting as Abiko was dragged along the ground. The kicking was hard and relentless. A woman bent down and carefully stubbed out her cigarette on his forehead. A man with a knife almost managed to cut off Abiko's ear as the body went past him. Felix could see the blood and the dangling ear. Another knife cut an enormous gash in Abiko's cheek. More and more cigarette burns.

When what was left of him was finally deposited on the table in the Main Building clinic, the doctor shook his head. Abiko might have survived the gunshot wound, but not the rest of it.

Felix did not stay to watch. On this night of liberation, he could not bear to think about Abiko. He returned to the crowded plaza.

———

Brad took off his fatigue cap and stood where his face could be seen in the headlights. Maybe Judy would find him. He tried to think what he would say if she appeared. How would she look? He might not even recognize her. And how would he feel? Did he even really know her? It had been so long ago. All he had was a few letters and some ancient memories.

He had no idea how long he had been standing there—quite a long time—when a young man came up to him.

"Coach? Mr. Stone?"

Brad stared at a tall, skinny figure with thick glasses.

"It's me, Felix. Felix Logan, from Simpson."

"My God!" Brad said. "Felix!" He was three years older and several inches taller and much thinner, but now Brad recognized him.

They shook hands with great pleasure. Felix's hand felt as thin as all the others'.

"I heard you were in here," Brad said.

"You look great, Mr. Stone. You all look so great."

"How are you? Are you all right?"

Felix smiled. "Sure. One of the soldiers just gave me a chocolate bar. Best thing I ever tasted."

Brad almost did not dare to ask. "Felix, I'm hoping to find somebody. You remember that girl I brought to the Simpson dance? That last dance at the Polo Club? Judy Ferguson. Do you know her? Is she—is she still here?"

"Judy Ferguson? Oh, sure. I saw her sometime, a week ago, two weeks. She's around."

"Is she all right?"

"Yes, sir. I guess so. Of course, everybody's sort of . . ." His voice trailed off.

"How can I find her?"

"Tonight?" Felix gazed around at the swirling crowd that jammed the plaza. "I don't know."

But at least she was alive. "And how about Amos Watson? Do you remember him? He was—" Brad stopped at the stricken look on Felix's face.

"He's—dead. The Japs killed him."

Brad was very sorry. He and Paradiso and their men owed a lot to Amos. Amos and Miranda. And without them, he would never have been able to keep in touch with Judy. "I'm sorry. That's really too bad."

"Yes," Felix said. His voice was unaccountably sad. "That's too bad. He was—very good to me. A good friend."

"Mine, too. I've been in the guerrillas since the beginning of the war. He sent us a lot of help, when we really needed it. I wanted to thank him. We never knew how he did it."

After a long pause Felix said, "I'll tell you sometime."

Brad could see that for some reason Felix didn't want to talk about Amos Watson, at least not now. "You think you can help me find Judy Ferguson?"

"Well—"

A long burst of machine-gun fire came from somewhere way off to the right of the plaza.

Brad turned his head, trying to see over the crowd. He had thought all resistance was over. "What's that?" he wondered aloud.

"Oh, that's the Japs—Commandant Hayashi and his troops," Felix said. He did not sound terribly concerned. "When you all came in, some of them holed up in the Education Building, just like they planned. I tried to tell a couple of American officers, but they were too busy to listen. They've got a bunch of hostages. Your guys must be trying to get them out."

———

When the searchlights came on and the American machine guns began to rake the second floor, Judy and Millie and the two hundred other internees trapped on the third floor dove under the beds.

When the firing stopped, they got to their feet and crowded back to the windows. Looking down, they could see the American tanks ringing the building. Over in the plaza were more American vehicles and swarms of people.

Judy and Millie and the others had tried to leave the Education Building, but the Japs had piled chairs and tables and benches in the stairways so that none of the internees could escape.

Through the open windows they could hear shouting back and forth in Japanese between the ground and the second floor.

"Why don't they surrender?" a man said in an angry voice. "They're surrounded."

"Because they've got us," somebody answered.

Judy was furious. If they hadn't come here to spread the good news, they would both be out there in the plaza, welcoming the American soldiers. Now they could get killed, just when everybody else was free. They could even get killed by American bullets.

Suddenly word was being passed quietly from person to person, the way they always did it at Santo Tomas. Jap soldiers were moving up to join the hostages on the third floor, where the Americans couldn't afford to shoot at them. Everybody should be on best behavior—no remarks, no insults, and especially no jokes—because the Japs were very jumpy. Get under the beds and keep quiet.

Judy Ferguson slept on the floor, just as she had done on her first night at Santo Tomas thirty-seven months ago. She remembered that on that first night squawling infants had kept her awake. Tonight it was young boys who were so excited they couldn't stop talking.

But that first night had been the beginning, and this, one way or another, was surely the end.

———

All next day, while top officers were negotiating with Lieutenant Colonel Toshio Hayashi and the remaining Japanese in the Education Building, Brad Stone was assigned to help prepare for the defense of Santo Tomas. Another contingent of troops arrived behind the first column, but they were still an island of only thirteen hundred men in a city held by the Japanese.

Yamashita had declared Manila an open city, but Yamashita was far away in the Baguio mountains, and the local Japanese navy commander had ordered his troops to defend Manila to the last man.

Brad was busy. Trenches to be dug. Machine guns and mortars to be emplaced. Tents to be set up on areas of the campus where they would not interfere with fields of fire. More and more vehicles with supplies and weapons to be unloaded and then parked somewhere out of the way. Mess equipment and food stores to be set up so they could feed not only their own troops but the horde of internees.

American planes flew over the city, dive-bombing and strafing, trying to keep the Japanese forces fully occupied. And all day long, no matter what had to be accomplished in this tiny window of time, there were always the internees, euphoric with liberation, wanting to talk to the soldiers, interfering with whatever the troops were trying to do. Through all these years, Brad had never stopped thinking of himself as a civilian at heart, but now the true civilians were driving him nuts. People he had known in Manila before the war—the Thurstons, the Whitelaws, the Bradys—heard from Felix Logan that Brad Stone was here. They all wanted to talk to him.

And he still could not find the one civilian he was searching for. Felix Logan found out where Judy lived in the Main Building but reported that none of her roommates had seen her. As Brad worked deep into the afternoon on the defense preparations, he began to wonder if she could have been wounded, or even killed, during last night's break-in. But after checking both the hospital and the army medics, Felix, who seemed to be even more of a fixer than he was back in the Simpson days, guaranteed that Judy was not among the dead or wounded.

"You know something, Mr. Stone? There's a few women in the Education Building, along with all those men and boys. I think maybe she's in there with the hostages."

After the long race to Manila and then this day of hard work, Brad was almost too tired to think. "Can you find out?"

Felix shook his head. "No messages. They won't even let wives and mothers send in a message. They're still negotiating back and forth, and it's real tense. Hayashi wants to trade the hostages for being allowed to walk out of here. With an escort through our lines."

"What lines? We don't have any lines."

"They don't know that. And Colonel Hayashi says his men must be allowed to keep their weapons."

"We'll never agree to that."

"I think maybe so."

In spite of his weariness, Brad was curious. "How come you know so much?" He remembered that Felix had never shown a great deal of knowledge on his history tests, but he always knew everything that was going on in school.

"Oh, you know," Felix said vaguely. "Just ask around, listen a little bit. Well, and also I understand Japanese."

"You do? That must be useful."

Felix's head went up. A proud look. "Yes," he said. "Sometimes."

"So what can we do?"

Felix looked sympathetic. "Just wait, I guess. I don't see where else she could be."

———

The second night was much better. They did not have to sleep on the floor. The men doubled up to give beds to Judy and Millie and the few other women. The Japs allowed the Americans to send food into the building, and even after they took all they wanted, there was still plenty left over for the hostages. And it was not the usual STIC garbage. It was a real stew of corned beef and beans.

But the most important thing was that the Japs were apparently getting ready to leave in the morning. They must have struck some kind of deal with the Americans. Word was passed that the Japs were out in the corridors, polishing their boots and cleaning their weapons. Everybody must be careful not to disturb or provoke them.

Judy and Millie were up at dawn. So was everybody else. When the women were offered first chance at the bathroom, Judy borrowed a broken-toothed comb from one of the men. She stood in front of the cracked mirror, doing the best she could for her tangled brown hair. Her gray-green eyes looked enormous in her gaunt face.

Millie was amazed. "Judy, how in the world can you think about your hair at a time like this?"

Judy continued to pull through the tangles. "I'm not going to meet the American army looking any worse than I have to."

When she finished combing and patting, she washed her face and hands as best she could without soap and dried them with her shirt. She could do nothing about her dirty, wrinkled clothes.

"I don't care how I look," Millie said. "Just so we get out of here."

"Well, I do."

The hostages were looking down from their third-floor windows when, just before seven o'clock, Lieutenant Colonel Hayashi, the camp commandant, marched out of the building, followed by his men in orderly procession. Hayashi's high boots gleamed in the still-early light. He wore his long, curved saber and two holstered pistols at his belt. He was immaculate. His men carried their rifles and pistols. They quickly formed ranks and stood at attention.

The scene was tense and very quiet.

To Judy, the Japs looked far more military than the large, rather sloppy-looking band of American soldiers who stood waiting in front of the building. The Americans wore helmets and held rifles and submachine guns in their hands. Judy could sense that every one of them was ready to shoot at the first sign of trouble, the first show of treachery. There were many more Americans than Japs, but if she hadn't known better, Judy would have thought it was the Japs who were accepting a surrender.

Millie seemed to think so, too, for she said in a whisper, "I hate to admit it, but sometimes those damn monkeys have class."

An American officer with a star on his helmet looked at the third-floor windows and stretched up

his arm, palm toward the hostages. He pushed his
open hand at them three times: *Stay where you are.
Be quiet. Don't move.*

Hayashi gave some kind of order in Japanese, and
his men quickly formed into a column of three behind
their commandant. American soldiers, rifles at the
ready and hands on triggers, took their places along
both flanks of the column, covering the Japs, who
pretended not to notice.

For a long moment the scene was frozen in silence.
Not a sound came from either group. The hostages
held their breath.

Hayashi barked, and in parade-ground unison the
Japanese column stepped out and began its march
toward the distant gate. The Americans followed on
either side, watching carefully. As the Japanese
marched across the campus they had ruled for so long,
they counted cadence out loud.

Judy could hear the sound diminishing as they
marched away, out of her life.

"Okay!" the American officer shouted and waved
both arms at the hostages.

Everybody cheered and then made a wild rush for
the stairways. Judy and Millie managed to keep together in spite of being pushed and bumped and jos-
tled by the eager men.

"Hey, whatever happened to women and children
first?" Millie said. She was laughing.

It took fifteen minutes to fight their way down the
crowded flights of stairs and then at last into the open
air. Both American soldiers and internees, mostly

wives and mothers of hostages, were waiting for them in front of the building. Judy saw many couples kissing and hugging in their relief.

"Well, Judy," Millie said in triumph, "by God, we made it."

"There she is!" a young man's voice shouted.

Judy saw that it was Felix Logan. And he was pointing straight at her. He acted excited. Well, it was an exciting moment, true enough, but she couldn't imagine why Felix Logan would care.

Beside Felix stood—

"What's the matter?" Millie asked. "What's the matter? Are you all right, Judy?"

I don't believe this, Judy thought.

"Judy, what is it?"

"It's—Brad."

"Brad? Your Brad? Where?"

"Right there."

He was walking toward her. He moved with the same light athlete's grace that she remembered. Same red-blond hair, but longer now and shaggy. Same very bright blue eyes. Same strong, thin nose.

This isn't fair, she thought. I've tried all these years not to let down. And now, right now, I'm such a total mess, while he looks so wonderful.

He stopped a few feet away and looked down at her. Just the right height for dancing, she remembered. If there were still such things as dances. Up close she could see that his face was harder, older. The boyish look she had both liked and deplored was gone completely. She must look incredibly different to him, too. Skinny, dirty, three years older—three years that felt like ten.

"Judy?"

It was a question. He wasn't quite sure he recognized her. She had her own question. She stretched out her hand and felt his strong arm through the green cloth. Yes, he was real. He was real.

He looked down at her hand. "That's my bracelet."

Almost as though she had not written him that she still wore the carved circle of monkeywood he had bought for her at the Baguio market. Maybe he had forgotten. Maybe he had not believed her. She had not bothered to tell him it was all the Japs had left her. She guessed she would not tell him now.

"Yes," she said. "It's yours."

He smiled for the first time. Not a big smile, just the touch of one. "Then that proves it," he said. "You must be the real Judy Ferguson."

She pulled herself up straight, just as tall and straight as she could stand.

"Yes," she said. "Yes, I am. You bet I am."

Acknowledgments

I have taken some small factual liberties. Fort Stotsenburg was primarily a cavalry post; I have added a battalion of Scouts infantry. Tom's Dixie Kitchen closed in mid-1941; I have given this quintessential Manila restaurant another half year of life. The Santo Tomas Triumvirate is an invention, replacing the elaborate and revolving Executive Committees and Internee Committees. The Philippine Islands are a jungle of different dialects; for simplicity, I have used the dominant language, Tagalog, and I have omitted the confusing accents. My unnamed colonel in charge of the Ranger raid on Cabanatuan is an imaginary character; the actual commander of this brilliant operation was Lieutenant Colonel Henry Mucci.

I am grateful for all the help I received on this book, from both old friends and total strangers. Historian James J. Halsema and bibliographer Morton "Jock" Netzorg, both old Philippine hands, recommended sources, tracked down out-of-print books and told me where to find such rarities as World War II maps and terrain handbooks. Elizabeth McCreary, a prewar schoolmate and an internee at Santo Tomas, provided her fine collection of Santo Tomas memorabilia, right down to her camp meal ticket, and gave me valuable interviews, photographs, letters and the names and addresses of other internees.

In the Philippines, Gordon and Charing Westly answered endless questions, in addition to serving as generous host and hostess. Joan Orendain, who seems to know everyone in Manila, arranged important interviews with World War II survivors and chauffeured me all over the city. James Black took me on a long, expert tour of Bataan, the entire route of the Death March and the prison-camp site at Cabanatuan. *Time* stringer Nelly Sindayen helped make arrangements for my visit. Enrique Zobel, Gertrude Stewart, Senator Manuel Manahan and Tom Carter provided vivid recollections about the period of the novel. The U.S. Embassy Library gave me unlimited access to its fine collection of wartime publications under the Japanese occupation.

In the United States, *Life* correspondents Carl and Shelley Mydans told me at length about their experiences as Santo Tomas internees during the early part of the war. After being freed in a prisoner exchange, Carl Mydans returned to the Philippines with MacArthur and photographed the liberation of Santo Tomas. He gave me all his pictures and caption material. Margaret Hoffman Tileston and Lolita Rifkind Swiryn let me read their unpublished teenage diaries of wartime Manila. Dr. Jeremiah Barondess advised me on many medical details. My brother William Graves, who as a fifteen-year-old boy was on Corregidor with MacArthur and who later lived in Japan and learned the language, helped me extensively with both subjects. George Peabody and Minerosa Monserrat of the Philippine Association gave useful advice and information. Elizabeth Advincula, Cultural Officer, let me use the Philippine Consulate's library and answered many questions about Philippine language and customs. Tracy Bernstein at Henry Holt did a meticulous and sensitive job of line editing and cutting. I thank all these people and institutions who so generously helped me. Any errors, of course, are my own, not theirs. Finally, I thank my friend William Brinkley, who first suggested that I write a novel about the Philippines.

A historical novel is not the place for an extended bibliography. However, of the forty books and many articles read for research, two were so outstandingly helpful that I want to acknowledge them. William Manchester's biography of MacArthur, *American Caesar*, is not only a superb portrait of the man but a rich account of wartime events and conditions in the Philippines, Australia and New Guinea. I drew on it constantly. E. Bartlett Kerr's *Surrender and Survival* is a detailed and compassionate account of what American POWs in the Pacific endured. It contributed much to my picture of the Death March and the prison camps of O'Donnell and Cabanatuan. I suppose I could have written this novel without the help of these two books, but I'm glad I didn't have to.

My wife, Eleanor, contributed the title—and much else besides.

R.G.

About the Author

Ralph Graves began his lifelong career in journalism as a reporter for *Life* in 1948, eventually becoming editorial director of Time Inc. The stepson of the U.S. High Commissioner, he lived in the Philippines as a teenager. He later became a U.S. Army Air Force sergeant, taking part in the liberation of the Philippines. Ralph Graves lives in New York City.

You have just finished reading
one of the first books published
by Harper Paperbacks!

Please continue to look for
the sign of the 'H', below.

It will appear on many fiction
and non-fiction books, from
literary classics to dazzling
international bestsellers.

And it will always stand for a
great reading experience and a
well-made book.

Harper Paperbacks
10 East 53rd St.
New York, NY 10022